The GOLDEN EAGLE

The
GOLDEN EAGLE

A Novel of the American Revolution

M.S. WEISSBACH

Alchemyst Press

Alchemyst Press

PO Box 293, Port Washington, NY 11050

ISBN-13: 978-0-9905368-0-2
LCCN: 2014921966

Cover Design by Alan Pranke
Typeset by B. Cook

Printed in the United States of America

For Margaret

and

Olivia, Eva, Isabella, Zachary,
Asher, and Dahlia

I

Jonathan Wolfe awoke to the realization that he was in love. Prior encounters were not like this. He had never dreamed of a woman in the way he just had. His body still felt warm and aroused. The fact that Jonathan barely knew her was immaterial. He was certain she would continue to occupy his dreams. Wolfe lay there, thinking about why he was intrigued by this particular woman, and his desire to be emotionally and physically involved with her. Then, tossing aside the covers, he climbed from the bed.

His room was situated in the eaves of the house, small but comfortable. It was in the Philadelphia home of Doctor Benjamin Rush to whom he had been apprenticed for the past three years.

The early morning sun shone through the single tiny window. It was six o'clock. Despite a still present nighttime chill, Jonathan removed his nightgown. Crossing the room to where a pitcher and basin stood, he proceeded to wash and shave.

The doctor's features were not unhandsome, though his face showed several depressed pockmarks characteristic of a brush with smallpox. It had, in fact, been more than a brush. He had been just twelve years old at the time, and hung between life and death for several weeks. The pox had taken his mother and younger brother. His father was away, fighting Indians marauding near their Mohawk Valley home.

He and his sister had been saved by the care and forceful will of their mother's sister, Isabel. She was a spinster, quiet, gentle, and not a great beauty, but with a determination that confronted the challenge and overcame it. Isabel nursed Jonathan and Rose through their ordeal. When their father, Samuel, returned he asked her to stay on, and a year later they married.

Samuel Wolfe was a blacksmith, and not educated beyond a few years at school.

"I liked school but left when I was ten," he would say. "We could not afford it. There were too many mouths to feed and not enough coins to feed them. Poverty and education do not mix."

Their mother, Faith, and Isabel had spent a few more years in school than Samuel. Isabel read well and loved books. "Husband," she said, "You should allow the children to remain in school till they are older. Education will help them advance in life."

Giving it thought, Samuel kissed her, saying, "You are truly a good wife and mother, Isabel. It will be done."

Still, his aunt had further hopes for the boy. He seemed to devour knowledge. She saw in him a fire that deserved to be fed to a white heat. Even as a child, insects, animals, and birds enchanted him. He spent hours observing how they crawled, jumped, or flew. He trained his dog to follow him, fetch objects, and hunt. One winter, Jonathan found an injured robin, repaired a broken wing with a tiny splint and nursed it back to health. That spring, he released the bird. The entire family wished it Godspeed as it flew into the morning sun.

At thirteen years, he began working the forge and learned to shoe horses. At seventeen, he stood five feet and eleven inches. His face had his mother's high cheekbones and his father's strong chin.

He possessed a tall brow, and dark brown hair worn down to his shoulders. His blue-green eyes looked straight at those to whom he spoke. His smile revealed white even teeth, marred only by a chip off a lower one where a horse had kicked him as he was shoeing it. A neck of good length came into a broad chest. Hours spent at the forge had developed muscled shoulders and arms. A flat stomach and lean hips completed the torso. He presented as a handsome, if not a dramatic figure.

As Wolfe shaved and dressed, he remained bemused, thinking of the preceding night's events.

It was a Saturday, April Fools Day, 1775. Doctor Rush, always espousing the cause of colonial freedom, had been urging him to join the Sons of Liberty. Its membership secret, the organization was known to have originated in Boston, reputedly under the aegis of Samuel Adams. From there, it had spread throughout New England and to the other colonies, most prominently Virginia and the Carolinas. Communication between the groups was frequent. Dedicated to preserving the colonists rights as Englishmen, the members organized protests against taxes imposed from England and in maintaining militia units in case of conflict.

"Jonathan," Rush said, "The organization is not involved with medicine, but a man must expand his social and political horizons. You know how concerned I am about the dispute between the colonies and England. It is important you educate yourself. Everyone will be required to make choices. There is a meeting tonight. I will provide you with a note of introduction. If you wish, take a friend."

Wolfe decided to attend and ask Simon Hunt, a fellow physician apprentice, to accompany him. They had met early on, at a hospital training session. Jonathan had entered the hallway leading to the lecture hall. Leaning against the wall was a tall, thin young man with a freckled face and the reddest hair Jonathan had ever seen. He was dressed in a well-cut suit of excellent black fabric. A white shirt, showing lace cuffs, and an elegant ruffled scarf at his neck, gave him an almost foppish appearance. But the intelligence in his eyes and a pleasant smile belied that conclusion.

"Hello," said the redhead, "I'm Simon Hunt. You look like a fellow toiler in the world of physician apprentices."

"I fall into that category," he answered. "Jonathan Wolfe, sir, at your service," and extended his hand.

Hunt clasped it and both laughed. They spoke for a few minutes, then entered the lecture hall and sat together. As they continued to see one another, converse, and exchange ideas, a close friendship rapidly developed.

They came from totally different backgrounds. Hunt's father was a prosperous Philadelphia attorney. In middle age, he had married a socially prominent widow. Simon had been born two years later. His stepbrother, Alfred, eight years older, had entered the law and was considered an up and coming star. Though Simon had been urged to follow the same path, a combination of true interest and rebellious spirit led him into medicine.

Speaking of his feelings on the subject, Hunt said, "Alfred is quite the successful young lawyer. He is fast becoming recognized in his profession. I was urged by my father to also become an attorney, but I have chosen my own way. I observed Doctor Townsend who attended my uncle through his illness. He was kind and considerate, but could do little beyond prescribe laudanum for the poor fellow's pain. I would like to do more than that. Medicine's horizons will expand, and I wish to participate in the changes that lie ahead."

At times, Wolfe felt somewhat overwhelmed by his friend's easy manner with money, his fine clothing, and especially his sharp mind. Hunt, however, regarded Jonathan as equal in intellect and deeply enjoyed their discussions. Occasionally, he would say, "Wolfe, you have had life experiences that my sheltered upbringing has denied me. In many respects, I can learn more from you than you can from me."

Failing to find Simon at the hospital, Jonathan left a note telling him where and when to meet. They had recently been discussing the rapidly changing political climate. Without mentioning the Sons of Liberty, he noted they would be attending a political gathering and thought his friend might find it interesting.

The meeting was to be held in a nearby tavern, The Golden Eagle. Wolfe arrived at six. Although it was already crowded, he found a seat at a long table. The tavern's huge fireplace burned brightly, providing pleasant warmth from the chilly night. Candles and lanterns glowed. A feeling of camaraderie pervaded the atmosphere, spurred by the anticipated event.

Seeing the tall thin figure of Simon enter the room, Wolfe motioned to him. Hunt waved back.

"Here I am," he said, coming to the table and shaking Wolfe's hand.

"Glad you were free to come," Jonathan replied.

He moved to permit Hunt to squeeze in, as the men alongside made room. Simon, contrary to his usual well-dressed appearance, was modestly clothed. A plain white shirt open at the neck, an ordinary dark green waistcoat, brown knee breeches, pale green stockings, and well-worn black shoes adorned with a simple buckle, gave him the appearance of a clerk. Despite his attire, Hunt's bright red hair attracted immediate attention. Several men looked with amazement at such unfamiliar coloring. Almost before Simon was seated the others at the table, having already consumed quantities of ale, began to gently banter with him.

"You must be Irish for sure," said one.

"Of course you are not Irish," another insisted. "You are from the North, from Scandinavia. I know for a certainty you must be a descendent of Eric the Red."

Hunt took up the challenge. "Friends," he said. "You are both mistaken. My hair color is the consequence of an unfortunate event. My mother, in the early stage of bearing me, was employed at an establishment making vegetable dyes. One day, she somehow toppled into a vat of fresh carrot juice to which had been added a very red beet juice. That accident obviously resulted in my present situation."

The men at the table laughed on hearing Simon's tall tale. He was instantly accepted as a comrade, able to take a ribbing and give one back.

Jonathan put an arm around his friend's shoulder. "Well said, Simon. You were ever the master of the quick riposte. It has been over a week since we last met. I am delighted you received my message and were able to come."

"Good to see you, Jonathan. Sorry we missed one another at the hospital. I've been very busy doing anatomic dissections. Doctor Moore is quite insistent that we have a sound knowledge of anatomy. Your turn will be coming. They are now requiring all medical trainees to study anatomy on real corpses."

"And where are they getting the bodies?"

"It's haphazard. Most are dead prisoners and poor souls who died without relatives." He winked, saying, "I do not think they're robbing graves as yet, although one never knows. But enough of medicine, politics is the subject for tonight. I am looking forward to this meeting. Right now, however, I have an urgent need for food and drink. The day has been long and I am both parched and famished."

So saying, he signaled to the girl moving between the tables. She approached them and asked, "What fare would you like, gentlemen?"

"Boiled beef and potatoes," said Simon.

"The same for me," echoed Wolfe.

"Do your lordships prefer ale or something stronger," she said in a teasing tone.

"Ale will do for the two of us," Hunt answered. Then, as she turned to leave, he patted her buttock, and said, "You're a saucy lass."

The girl seemed not to notice. She continued on her way, shortly returning with their orders. First serving Jonathan, the waitress next placed Hunt's food before him. Then, starting to set down Simon's ale, she appeared to trip. The stein's contents spilled directly onto his lap. Startled, he snatched at his napkin, turned red and was about to remonstrate with her.

She stood her ground, and said, "I'm so sorry, sir, but I tripped. I will get more linen to soak up the spillage. It's fortunate the color of the ale is similar to your trousers'. It will not stain. Let me refill your mug." She took it, turned, and started to leave.

Simon became even more upset. As he began to rise in indignation, Wolfe grasped his arm and kept him in place. "That girl has spirit. She is not one to be trifled with," he whispered.

"My trousers are soaked through," sputtered his friend.

"The price of a lesson," responded Jonathan.

The other men at the table were smiling, obviously enjoying Simon's embarrassment. Their remarks, however, was carried out in a humorous vein.

"Do not feel you are alone in the treatment you received from Grace," said a gray-bearded fellow across from him. "Many of your present company have similarly suffered such punishment when stepping over her line. She does her waitressing well, has no favorites, and demands respect."

Grace returned and, with a straight face and steady hand, placed the replenished ale before Simon. "I told the barman I spilled your drink, sir. There will be no charge for this refill, and I also brought more napkins to help clean up," she said.

Jonathan almost burst into laughter, but restrained himself from adding to Hunt's discomfort. He instantly decided he liked this girl and turned so as to observe her more closely. She appeared to be about eighteen and was tall for a woman, standing about five feet five or six inches. She was quite pretty, with short curly amber hair, a high forehead, a thin nose, and wide full lips. What struck him most of all were her large brown eyes which sparkled with intelligence. Her breasts were full. A white collar served to set off a lovely neck. However, while most waitresses and barmaids showed distinct cleavage, the gray dress and blue apron she wore covered her entire front.

She returned his obvious stare with a slight smile, but showed no other interest and left to wait on other diners.

"I would like to know that young lady," Wolfe thought.

Simon wiped and patted himself until he felt reasonably dry. His mood improved. "Jonathan," he laughed, "I have learned my lesson. I will become the shy bumpkin."

"You may adopt that pose, but I well know you are neither shy nor a bumpkin," Wolfe replied. "You are truly quite extroverted and highly intelligent. I hold you in great regard, as both a colleague and friend. But your mishap with our waitress must not be permitted to spoil the evening."

As they finished their meal, the room became quieter. Men began to ascend a corner staircase. The two friends rose and started for the stairs. A tall burly figure barred their way. "A private gathering, gentlemen," he said.

"Excuse us," said Jonathan. "I have a message for you." He handed the note over, and the blocker read it.

Stepping aside, he said, "Welcome, glad to have you attend." Beckoning to another man, he added, "My assistant will show the way."

"I'm John," said the man, "Come with me."

Forming a threesome they climbed the stairway, reached a hallway and came to a large room into which several rows of chairs had been placed. It was crowded and the air hung heavy with tobacco smoke. Conversation buzzed about them. As they entered, heads turned and those already present examined the unknown arrivals. They seated themselves and John whispered, "The fellow who stopped you serves as our unofficial guard. The British have become more interested in the Sons of Liberty. We are concerned about spies revealing our meeting places and obtaining our names. John is not my true name. Names will not be used tonight."

The crowd continued to murmur among themselves and mill

about. A thin spectacled man with balding sandy hair called them to order. Briefly summarizing the last meeting, he leaned forward and spoke in an intense manner. "As you know, England's Parliament repealed the Stamp Tax, but then enacted the Trade and Tea Tax. The last has been somewhat splashed by the party they held in Boston Harbor."

Laughter and cheers erupted, but raising his hand the room quieted. He spoke again, saying, "Laughter and cheers are fine but, as a result, the Crown ordered the port closed. Shipping may not enter or leave Boston Harbor."

"My friends, the taxes, the reprisals for our protests, and the requirement that we quarter their troops on demand, are the result of our not having representation in Parliament. We have attempted to secure redress of our grievances and sent representatives to our own Continental Congress. It appealed to the Crown for assistance. We were rebuffed. Now, George III regards our activists as traitors and insurrectionists. The King and his Council are treating us as less than serfs. We are required not only to serve them, but also pay for the privilege. We must continue to protest and a second Continental Congress has been called."

A murmur of approval ran through the room. Some clapped and others stamped their feet in approval. "I agree in general," someone spoke. "Taxes without our representation are wrong. However, we must acknowledge that large sums have been spent to maintain British troops on the western borders. They protect us from Indian raiders. Vast amounts were also spent by England during the recent wars with the French and Indians."

Momentarily, Jonathan was distracted, thinking about the war that had been fought. It was only a portion of what the Europeans called The Seven Years' War and had raged from 1754 to 1763. Although a child at the time, he had felt the fear that spread among the adults when the French and their Indian allies had assaulted the Mohawk Valley. His father and others had fought alongside English regulars. Still, towns had been burned and many killed.

Wolfe was brought back to the current discussion when, from the back of the room, a voice joined in. "The taxes are for monies expended to not only fight the French and Indians here but also France, Spain, and Holland overseas. They are taxing us for many wars. Remember this well. The ability to tax is the ability to destroy!"

"The English complain about their financial expenditures, which they insist are upon our behalf. However, they do not mention we have already paid with our blood and our money. Further, they receive great benefit from our trade. There are goods we can only sell to them. They take our tobacco and rice at low prices, reselling the tobacco in Europe and the rice in the Caribbean at high prices. In return, they provide us cloth and inferior manufactured goods at inflated ones. We are forbidden to make finished goods, so as not to offer competition to English industries. Pretty much the only thing we can build is our ships, so we can carry on trade with the mother country."

"It's absolutely right to emphasize that the colonies paid with both blood and money for the French and Indian Wars," another seconded. "Funds were provided by the colonies to pay our militias. Our militiamen fought well here and provided some of the troops for Britain's victory at Quebec. It was not just their regulars, and it gave them all of Canada."

Others now began calling out, "Correct, right, or that's so."

John now rose from his seat and spoke, "We are achieving nothing with the government of George III and his Minister, Lord North. Ben Franklin is trying to negotiate a compromise in London. However, he must first work with Lord Dartmouth who is in charge of American affairs and has largely ignored him. I doubt he will get to see George III's Minister, and certainly not the King. I fear Franklin's efforts will prove in vain."

Again, the crowd expressed its assent, with people shouting out and stamping their feet.

"The situation is fast approaching the boiling point," said the first speaker. "We will continue to negotiate, but events require us to support and train our militia. Munitions and arms are required. We should hope for the best, but must prepare for the worst. Those of you who are militia members will be contacted as to the time and date of your next gathering. The various working committees must now conduct their business. Our general meeting is over. Notice of the next meeting will be sent in the usual manner."

With the mention of militia training and gathering arms, Wolfe felt a chill. Once more, he recalled the terror and battles along the Mohawk. Reconciliation was required, not armed conflict.

As he sat thinking, those assembled dissolved into small groups. John indicated the two friends should again follow him. Returning to the main floor, he turned to them, saying, "I hope your first meeting proved worthwhile. Notice of the next will be sent to the person recommending you. We hope you return and become more involved. Good night, gentlemen, I have further duties to attend to," and he again ascended the stairs.

The main room was quiet. The two friends went to a vacant table, sat down and spoke. "I am concerned about the present course of events," Hunt said, in a low but firm voice. "It seems the consensus here is that the King and Parliament are deliberately moving to deprive the colonies of their just rights. They spoke tonight of wanting redress of their grievances and representation in Parliament. However, they mentioned training militia and acquiring arms and munitions. I sensed an undercurrent of insurrection. I am a colonist, but still of English blood and loyal to my King. I am opposed to insurrection, and distraught as to what may become the need to choose between the Crown and a rebellious America. Jonathan, despite my foibles, you know I am a serious person. I must study both sides of this argument with care, and draw my own conclusions. You also know, I am not the type to report people to the authorities. I detest talebearers. The Sons of Liberty meeting and the words spoken are safe with me. I will bid you goodnight, my friend. It is always my great pleasure to see and converse with you." He shook Wolfe's hand and quietly left.

Jonathan remained at the table. The meeting, and his and Hunt's reaction to it, had made him better able to understand his mentor's statement "sides will have to be chosen."

From the corner of his eye he saw Grace putting on her hat and cloak. The thought came to him that, when it came to choices, he would certainly choose her. Though often shy with women, Wolfe gathered his courage and came toward her.

"I would like to apologize for my friend's behavior at dinner," he said.

"I do not know to what you refer," replied the girl, startled by his approach.

"I mean, when he did something inappropriate," Jonathan

stammered.

She quickly recovered her bearings. "I noticed nothing inappropriate, sir. He seemed upset when I tripped and the ale spilled. But that was to be expected."

Wolfe noticed her subtle smile and sparkling eyes. Recovering her poise, she was now toying with him, refusing to acknowledge that spilling the ale was her response to Simon's pat.

"Yes, of course, you are correct," he mumbled. Then, somewhat diffidently he added, "I am sure you are correct in all things."

"Not all things," she smiled. "But it's very nice of you to apologize, even if it was for something that did not occur. However, the hour is late. I must be on my way."

Grace started to step past him.

"May I walk you to your home?" Wolfe asked.

She offered no response, continuing to exit the tavern.

"My name is Jonathan Wolfe," he called out, frustrated in his failed efforts to engage her interest.

About to follow, Wolfe stopped in mid-stride. "No point in acting like a schoolboy," he thought. "To pursue her would only have Grace believe I am Hunt's twin. However, I am determined to meet and speak with her again, and will attend every meeting of the Sons of Liberty to ensure it."

Leaving the tavern, Wolfe felt like a chastised teenager. But, as he inhaled the night air, a sense of contentment came over him. Evaluating the evening further, Jonathan concluded that the outing had definitely proven worthwhile.

II

Rush spent his weekends engaged in politics. On Saturday, after seeing patients, he departed at noon. On Monday, his mentor was at breakfast when Wolfe came downstairs. "Good morning, Jonathan," he said. "How was the meeting? Did it prove instructive?"

"Good morning, sir. It was both interesting and instructive." A vision of Grace entered his mind and he added, "I shall certainly wish to attend more of them."

The Doctor continued, "I am delighted you are ready to become involved. But our own profession also demands attention. I will be giving a chemistry lecture this morning. You are welcome to come and improve your knowledge. Today's discussion will deal with the elements and how they combine to make molecules. Next week, I will present practical applications of today's material. Attending both would benefit you. After this morning's discussion, there will still be time to visit our homebound patients."

"Thank you, sir. I appreciate your invitation," said Jonathan. "I can definitely gain from further understanding of chemistry."

They rode in the Doctor's carriage and, arriving at the school, went to the lecture hall. Rush went to the podium and, as the room quieted, began to speak. "The list of known elements is almost certainly incomplete. Undoubtedly, more are yet to be found, and more information will be acquired about those of which we are currently aware."

He then moved into his presentation. As Jonathan sat through the two-hour lecture taking notes, he marveled at his mentor's knowledge of the subject. "I must study harder and continue to broaden my capabilities," Wolfe said to himself.

Ending amidst general applause, the Doctor took questions. Finally, he added, "Please remember that my text, *Chemistry*, is available at the nearby bookseller."

Again, there was applause as the attendees began leaving.

Rejoining his mentor, Wolfe said, "Sir, that proved a most interesting lecture. I realize there is still much to learn."

"Jonathan, you have the ability and desire for knowledge. Time is fleeting, but I have confidence you shall use it well. You have a long afternoon ahead of you. Let us take lunch together before you depart."

Their meal over, Wolfe began his rounds and gradually moved through the day's assignment. After the last visit, he found himself near a T-shaped intersection where he knew a carriage could be found to bring him home. Walking toward it, Jonathan saw there was heavy horse-drawn traffic. People stood together, waiting to cross the thoroughfare marking the head of the T. Among them was a woman wearing a black coat and bonnet, accompanied by a small boy. She held the child by the hand. In his other, he was fiddling with a large green hoop favored as a portable toy.

Wolfe was almost upon them when several things happened simultaneously. From behind, he became aware of the sound of hoof beats and a wagon moving rapidly forward. At the same time, he saw that the child had lost control of his hoop. As it rolled into the street, the boy pulled his hand away from the woman and dashed after it. The oncoming wagon would enter the intersection and turn either right or left. Jonathan feared the worst.

"Stay," he yelled to the woman in black, as she started toward the child. Discarding his medical bag, Wolfe raced into the street. He saw the little boy before him, kneeling to pick up the hoop. From behind, he heard the horses plunging into the intersection. They were slightly slowed by their driver as he started a left turn. Suddenly aware of the two figures in the street, he grasped hard at the reins and pulled back with all his might. It appeared too late. The horses continued ahead. But, as the driver maintained his pull, they reared up with forelegs raised high. Before their hoofs descended, Jonathan sprinted forward, stooped down, and snatched the boy. As he did, Wolfe lost his footing and, still clutching the child, rolled in the dust to the opposite side of the roadway.

The driver steadied the horses and jumped to the road. Running to Jonathan, he helped him stand and hugged him. He then picked up the boy, lifted him high, kissed his cheek and carefully put him down.

He was a big man with a ruddy face and a large mustache. Obviously shaken, he began to brush the dust from Jonathan's clothing and said, "You saved the boy and you saved me." Thankfully and almost in tears, he added, "I have two of my own and my wife is again with child. I could not live with your deaths on my head."

He patted and embraced Wolfe again. Slowly returning to his wagon, the driver climbed aboard and sat for a time, looking about to reassure himself that all was indeed well. Then, he twitched the reins to restart the horses and moved off at a slow pace.

People started to gather around. The little boy began to cry. The black-cloaked woman came running across the street. She held her purse in one hand and in the other was the medical bag. She handed the bag to Jonathan and picked up the child. Amber hair poked out from beneath her bonnet. It was Grace.

For a few moments she continued to comfort the child. Then, turning to Jonathan, began, "I wish to thank you for…." She stopped in mid-sentence at the sudden realization that he had been with that obnoxious fellow on Saturday night. The fact Wolfe had apologized also came to mind.

"I believe we have met before, doctor," she began anew. "Joshua and I are most grateful for your daring rescue." Her face, which had been ashen, was returning to its normal color. To the child she said, "Joshua, you must thank the doctor."

At first he buried his face in her bosom. Then, lifting his head, looked at Wolfe. "Thank you, doctor," he said in a very low child's voice.

"You're welcome, Joshua. Is the green hoop your favorite toy?"

"Yes," the boy murmured.

"Take good care of it," Jonathan said. "But you must also remember not to run into the road. Do you think you can do that?"

Joshua nodded his head.

Wolfe smiled at him. Grace, seeing the boy appeared unharmed, had put him down. The doctor quickly checked the child for signs of injury and said, "Please jump up and down." Joshua jumped several times. "Does it hurt any place?"

"No, I don't hurt."

"You're a brave lad," Wolfe replied. To Grace he said," On brief examination, the boy seems intact."

"Thanks to you," she said, and then added, "You know, doctor, we live just down this road. The least I can do is offer you some refreshment and properly brush the dust from your clothes. Unless, of course, you are presently occupied."

For a moment, Jonathan hesitated. He assumed Joshua was hers and noticed she wore no ring.

"Auntie Grace makes very good butter cookies," Joshua chimed in.

Jonathan laughed, "Those are my favorite cookies, Joshua." To Grace he said, "I have completed my visits and accept your invitation."

The small crowd had drifted away. They started to walk and Grace said, "It's rather peculiar. I've invited you to our home and do not know your name."

"Jonathan Wolfe, apprentice physician. I called it to you the other night."

"I am happy to meet you, Doctor Wolfe. At that time, I failed to properly gather it."

Jonathan recalled the lilt to her voice, as she continued, "My name is Grace Lockhart and my nephew is Joshua Goode."

"Delighted to know you both," he smiled.

They moved on. Joshua walked between them, holding onto both his aunt and the hoop. Shortly afterward, they came to an alleyway. "Right turn," she said. The alley was barely wide enough for a narrow cart. Walking together, they almost filled its width.

"Just a bit farther," she said to Jonathan.

The late afternoon sun came from behind a cloud and flooded the scene. Almost immediately, they came upon a small two-story house painted a soft blue gray. Darker blue shutters framed small windows. A single central chimney was showing smoke, and the smell of burning wood drifted toward them.

On either side the house, yellow-gold forsythia were coming into bloom and served to delineate the property. Their bright color, enhanced by the sunshine, added an additional glow to the already pleasant view.

Grace opened the front door, led them past a small parlor, then a dining room, and into a large kitchen. An older woman was preparing the evening meal.

"Aunt Evelyn, this gentleman is Doctor Jonathan Wolfe," Grace said, as she introduced him. "This is my Aunt, Evelyn McKenzie."

"I am happy to make your acquaintance, Doctor," said the aunt. She was obviously taken aback by Wolfe's and Joshua's dust covered clothing and smudged faces, but said nothing.

"They need some dusting and cleaning up," said Grace, opening a narrow broom closet and removing a whiskbroom. "I will tell you about our adventure later, aunt. You two, please come outside with me," she commanded.

Exiting the house through a side door, Grace used the broom to brush the dust off.

"Much better," she said. "But you must still wash," and brought a bucket of water, soap, and several towels. Following one another, they cleansed hands and faces. Satisfied, she smiled, "You both look quite presentable. Now it's time for refreshments."

Reentering the house, they passed to the parlor. Aunt Evelyn brought coffee, milk, and a large tray of butter cookies. Joshua had two cookies and a cup of milk, announced he was tired and, accompanied by Evelyn, trundled off to bed. Jonathan had three butter cookies and several cups of coffee before he felt it would be impolite to gorge further.

"I hope you have been somewhat restored," Grace smiled.

"I have been most royally treated," he answered, admiring her anew. "Your cookies are spectacular. I can still taste my mother and aunt's butter cookies. They learned how from a Dutch friend and she called them *koekje*. These are about the best I have ever eaten. You and your aunt have been very gracious." Looking about he said, "This is a wonderful home."

"Thank you," she responded. "The house is owned by my uncle. He is the proprietor of The Golden Eagle. I serve as a waitress, when he expects a large gathering such as the Sons of Liberty. It helps provide me with pin money. Otherwise, I teach at the school for poor children recently founded by Benjamin Franklin. The salary is not large, but I come newly to the field and thoroughly enjoy my work. Tell me about yourself."

"I'm sure you are a very good teacher," Wolfe responded. "As for me, I am apprenticed to another Benjamin, Doctor Benjamin Rush, an excellent teacher. I have been with him for three years and nearing the end of my training. I was on patient visits and had just completed them, when I came upon the scene."

"It was very fortunate for Joshua and me," she said.

"Fortunate for me, also. Otherwise, I would not be here enjoying your hospitality."

Grace blushed at the compliment. Just then, the front door

opened and another young woman entered the house, glanced into the parlor and came forward. Her features were similar to Grace's, but she appeared two or three years older and had long black hair.

Jonathan rose, as Grace said, "Jonathan, this is my sister, Martha Goode. Martha, meet Doctor Jonathan Wolfe."

"My pleasure," Wolfe said, taking her hand.

"Mine also," said Martha. Then, seeing his bag, she looked at her sister. "Is everything all right?"

"Oh, yes," Grace answered. "Doctor Wolfe and I met this past Saturday evening. We happened upon one another today and are renewing our friendship. By the way, doctor, would you like to stay for supper?"

Taking his cue, Wolfe answered, "I must excuse myself. I am really expected home. It was nice meeting you, Martha. Please say goodbye to your aunt and Joshua for me, Grace. I look forward to seeing you again, if that were possible."

Grace thought for a moment. "If you are free one week from this Sunday, you would be very welcome to have dinner with us. It will be with the family, those you have met and my uncle Elias. Two o'clock would be a good time to arrive."

"Agreed," Wolfe responded. He took his bag and Grace escorted him to the door. It was already twilight, but he made his way out the alley without difficulty. On reaching the road, Jonathan hailed a free carriage. and arrived at the Rush home in time for the nightly meal.

Meanwhile, Martha looked at her sister, "The doctor is quite handsome."

"Yes," Grace blushed. "He is also very nice and can act quickly in an emergency."

Martha picked up the "emergency" portion of her sister's statement. An anxious look appeared. Grace immediately spoke, "As I said, everything is fine. Joshua is perfectly all right. But Doctor Wolfe actually saved him. Truth be told, it was rather close."

Martha's anxiety increased. Her face became pale, her breathing rapid, and tears welled up. She sat down, saying, "Tell me what happened."

Aunt Evelyn had come downstairs from Joshua's room. She entered the parlor and also sat. Grace related the events of the day. "I don't know exactly how Joshua slipped from my grasp. It happened so suddenly. Usually, he is very good about staying with me. I tried to stop him but, when the hoop rolled away, he ran into the road like a rabbit. A large wagon came bearing down on him. It was a miracle Doctor Wolfe was there. He was so daring, risking his own life to save Joshua. We are indebted to him."

"Yes, indeed we are," said Martha, breathing easier. She knotted her brow, "As you said, he seems very nice. I can tell you like him, and he likes you. I sensed that as soon as I came into the room." She continued on, "Grace, please believe me, I am not upset with you. These things happen with small children. What matters is that Joshua is unharmed. But I must go upstairs, to see for myself he is truly all right."

"I have just been with him," said their aunt. "He is fast asleep. Sit for a moment and have some coffee, Martha. You've had a full day's work and look exhausted."

"I am tired," she replied. "Coffee would be good." Sitting down and turning to Grace, Martha said, "You mentioned originally meeting Doctor Wolfe this past Saturday evening. That is when you were working at uncle's tavern. Tell us how you actually met."

As they drank their coffee, Grace related the incident with Simon Hunt, her reprisal, and Jonathan's attempted apology.

"That's so like you, Grace. You rise to defend your honor. I am so proud of you," said her aunt.

"I, also," added Martha warmly, and kissed her sister's cheek. "But now, I have had my refreshment and wish to see my son. He may be asleep, but his mother needs to be further reassured by seeing him herself. Please excuse me."

"Of course," the others responded.

"Supper in an hour," Evelyn said. "I expect your uncle will be home then. Tonight the tavern will be slow. One of the barmaids will close it."

Starting to walk from the room, Martha turned to her sister. "Grace," she said, "I believe you have a new beau."

III

On Monday, April 10th, Rush was finishing breakfast when Jonathan entered the room. Looking up, he said, "I realize that you are on time, Jonathan, but please eat quickly. Before lecturing to several apprentices, I must discuss some political business with a gentleman meeting me at the school. We can review the patients on the way."

They were in the carriage and moving rapidly when Rush pulled out his list. "You know all these people," he said, handing Jonathan a paper with the names and addresses. "Also, I received a message to see a new patient. His name is Stiles. I put his name and address at the bottom of the list. Meet me there at two o'clock. You will need to take a carriage from your last call. The home is a distance away."

At an appropriate place, Rush halted the carriage. Jonathan descended and began his visits. Completing them shortly after noon, he took lunch at a small tavern and traveled to meet his mentor.

Wolfe arrived several minutes before the appointed time. It was a pleasantly sunny day. A slight breeze ruffled the surrounding trees. He examined the home they would shortly enter. It was nicely set back from the roadway, a five-over-five classic brick colonial. In addition to two stories, a dormer was set above each of the upper windows, providing additional space for servants' quarters. A central chimney, and an additional chimney at one end, added to its impression as the home of a very prosperous individual.

As Wolfe continued to look about, Doctor Rush rode up in his carriage. "How did your visits go?" he asked.

"Everything is fine. All the patients are doing reasonably well," Jonathan answered.

"Excellent," Rush replied. "Now let us attend to Mr. Abraham Stiles."

They approached the front door and knocked. After a moment, a young black servant girl admitted them, and the lady of the house came forward.

"Good afternoon, gentlemen," she said in a low tremulous voice and, looking at the older man, added, "You are Doctor Rush, I assume. I am Mrs. Stiles."

"I am indeed Doctor Rush," he said, taking her hand. "And this is my assistant, Doctor Jonathan Wolfe."

The lady glanced at Jonathan but did not smile or extend her hand. He saw she was about twenty-one, of medium height, and good frame. She was obviously distressed. Her narrow attractive face was pale and her eyes reddened from recent weeping. Blonde hair hung down in disarray. She wore a dark blue dress of good quality cloth and well fashioned. Holding a yellow kerchief in one hand, she kept twisting it with the other, as though the motion would somehow soothe the anxiety gripping her.

"Please excuse me, gentlemen," she said. "I must attend to my children. Adelaide will show you to my husband's bedchamber."

A middle-aged black servant had appeared. She led the way up the staircase. Following her along a hallway, they entered the patient's bedroom. It was commodious and well furnished, but had the heavy atmosphere and feel of illness. Despite the sunny day, it was darkened by thick drapes drawn over the windows.

They moved forward, as the servant said, "Sir, the doctors are here."

Stiles stirred and Rush came to the bedside.

"Mister Stiles, I am Doctor Benjamin Rush. I have been asked by your wife to visit you. I assume it is with your consent."

The man on the bed raised his head from the pillow. "Yes," he answered. "I asked her to send for you. Your name had been mentioned to me recently as a very competent physician. Being of good health, I never thought I might need your services."

Stiles sank back on the pillow, clearly exhausted by the effort of rising to speak. He was patently ill, with a flushed face, sweating profusely and breathing shallowly and rapidly. His black dank hair hung over his forehead and he had grown a stubbly beard.

"Sir, Doctor Wolfe and I are here to help you recover," said Rush. "We will examine you and determine the nature of your illness. Please begin, Jonathan," he continued, and moving to the drapes drew them open.

"Permit me to ask when and how you first became ill, sir."

"I believe it began some ten days ago," murmured Stiles. "I had business to the west, travelling by horse, and was caught in heavy weather. I finally reached shelter in a tavern, soaked through and chilled to the bone." His breath failed him and he paused. Then, breathing heavily, Stiles continued. "Well, I have been fevered these past several days, coughing and raising green, foul spittle." He again stopped, but recovering his breath said, "It hurts as I breathe." Suddenly, he shivered and his teeth chattered.

Jonathan listened attentively, at the same time observing the man's flushed, perspiring face. He felt the fevered brow. On request, Stiles opened his mouth. Jonathan checked the tongue and throat, and gently examined Stiles' neck. He tapped and sounded the front and back of the chest. Placing an ear, he listened to the heart and lungs and, feeling the abdomen, discerned no enlargement of the liver or spleen.

Sitting back, he said, "I fear Mr. Stiles suffers from both pneumonia and pleurisy."

"Indeed," responded Rush. "I am certain you are correct. Permit me to confirm your findings." He did a careful exam and then said, "You are quite correct. I had already concluded pneumonia, on learning the history from the servant who sought me out. Still, it is always best to find our suspicions confirmed by additional history and examination."

Looking at the exhausted man, he said, "We must bleed you, Mr. Stiles. Fortunately, I have come with the necessary equipment." So saying, he turned toward Mrs. Stiles. She now stood in the shadowed doorway, appearing diffident and with downcast eyes.

"Madam, I require a large bowl and a towel," he said. The wife nodded and disappeared. In a few minutes the items were brought in by Adelaide. Mrs. Stiles also returned.

Rush thanked her and said to both women, "I suggest you leave us for the while."

The wife looked at him, covered her face which now showed streams of tears, and reluctantly withdrew from the room.

The Doctor placed the bowl, the towel beneath it, adjacent to the patient's left side. Laying Stiles' wrist over it, he glanced at Wolfe and said, "Bleeding is the only sure method to combat this malady. Bloodletting removes malignant entities. It relieves stress on the heart, easing its work. The heart, lungs, and body can then purify themselves."

Rush reached for his medical bag, opened it and withdrew a linen-wrapped scalpel. Then, taking it in his right hand, he quickly made a small incision in Stiles' wrist. A vein was opened and blood came forth, rapidly filling the bowl.

"We shall remove about a half pint at this time, Jonathan," he said

As the bowl filled with blood, Stiles roused himself. He raised his head and glanced at his arm. Seeing the blood, he turned ashen. "My God," he groaned and fainted.

"A not unexpected response," Rush said in a serious voice. "Sometimes it is better when they faint. It is easier on their mind, and gives us less to contend with."

Once satisfied the appropriate quantity had been taken, Rush withdrew the bowl and placed it on the bedside table, wrapped the towel about Stiles' wrist and pressed firmly. After ten minutes the Doctor removed the towel and checked the incision. No bleeding was present. Rush covered the wound with a bit of cotton and bandaged it. Obviously proud of his skill, he smiled, saying, "That, my dear Jonathan, is how it is done. Quick and neat."

Wolfe saw that Stiles' face was still flushed. He felt the right wrist. The pulse remained rapid and thin.

However, the patient was breathing easier. He had recovered from his faint, opened his eyes and spoke weakly. "Is it over? I am still having difficulty breathing."

"We have completed the procedure, sir," the Doctor replied. "Rest easy, you are breathing more normally and will continue to improve. We will remain for several minutes to ensure you are satisfactory, and return on the morrow to check your progress."

Adelaide had reappeared. Rush handed her the bloody bowl and instructed her to bathe Stiles' forehead with cool compresses, but keep him well covered. Leaving, they descended the stairs to the central hall.

Mrs. Stiles stood there. Two small children, a boy and a girl, clung to her dress. The young servant girl was alongside them.

Benjamin Rush smiled and tried to reassure them. In a quiet, empathetic voice he spoke to Mrs. Stiles. "We have performed bloodletting and your husband is breathing easier. With your permission, we shall return tomorrow."

"Yes, of course," she said.

He patted her shoulder to further comfort her. The servant brought their coats and opened the door. Rush beckoned to Wolfe and they exited.

Once outside, the two doctors went to their carriage, climbed in and started for home. On the way, Wolfe thought about the experience. This was not the first time he had seen a bloodletting. It had, indeed, been expertly performed. Jonathan's regard for his mentor's ability gained another notch.

The following morning, Rush gave the second chemistry lecture.

His mentor began by saying, "Today, I will demonstrate practical applications of my prior presentation." Rush showed different reagents, and how they changed color when alterations in acidity occurred. He discussed combinations of different elements and molecules. Best of all, he revealed how to make and mix nitrates to form gunpowder. At the conclusion of the lecture, there was applause, and the Doctor appeared very satisfied at the response it had elicited.

Following a light lunch, they traveled to the Stiles. The day was gloomy and it rained heavily. The same young servant girl opened the door. Mrs. Stiles came forward and appeared under great stress.

"He does not seem better, Doctor," she said, her voice sounding both fearful and agitated.

"We shall see, my dear," he replied in a tone designed to soothe her.

Within the master's bedroom, the curtains had been drawn aside to permit the day's light to enter. Abraham Stiles lay covered by quilts and shivered beneath them. When questioned, he did not respond clearly.

Rush examined him extensively but did not ask Jonathan to do the same. "I must again request the bowl and towel," he said to the maidservant.

After their receipt, he followed the same routine and again removed half a pint of Stiles' blood. Rush then grunted in satisfaction. "I will examine him once more," he stated. After doing so, the Doctor said, "I believe the lungs are clearer."

Jonathan looked but could see no improvement. Their patient appeared to be less alert than on the previous visit. He was pale with bluish lips, still sweating heavily, occasionally shivering, and breathing shallowly and rapidly. His cough came frequently, and his spittle now showed streaks of blood.

Rush also seemed more concerned as to whether Stiles had actually improved. His statement that the lungs appeared clearer was not put forth with great enthusiasm. The previously confident Doctor had begun to withdraw within himself.

They left Stiles in Adelaide's care. Exiting the bedroom, they descended the stairs.

Mrs. Stiles approached them. "My husband is not improving," she said, again showing her previous anxiety.

"It takes time," Rush replied. "With care and prayers he will recover." He reached out to her, but was now more tentative in his assertion.

Distraught, Stiles' wife started to cry. Her shoulders slumped and her face lost all color. She appeared about to faint. Wolfe moved to support her. The young servant had come into the room and together they helped Mrs. Stiles to a chair.

"Is there any brandy?" Jonathan asked the servant.

"I will get some," she nodded, left and quickly returned with brandy and a small glass.

Wolfe poured the brandy, gave it to Mrs. Stiles, and supported her hand as she raised the glass and drank. She appeared to respond to its effect. Color returned to her face and she started to rise.

"Please remain seated," Jonathan urged. "You must rest."

He looked at the servant and said firmly, "Help me assist your mistress to a sofa." At first Mrs. Stiles resisted, but realized how weak she felt and settled on the cushions.

"Thank you," she murmured, "I will take your advice."

Doctor Rush had followed them. He was disconcerted, but said, "I am happy to see you are recovering your faculties. Doctor Wolfe has advised you well. Your servant should remain with you. We will let ourselves out and return tomorrow."

Saying this, he and Jonathan left and walked to the carriage.

On the morrow, a young man in his mid-twenties opened the front door. "Good afternoon, doctors. I am Mrs. Stiles' brother, Stephen Wainwright. My sister is very distressed. Despite your efforts, my brother-in-law continues to fail."

As he spoke, Mrs. Stiles ran down the staircase. She was sobbing and her blonde hair hung loosely about her flushed face. Tears flowed freely, but behind them there was fire. In a loud and strident voice she yelled, "Well, Doctor Rush, neither your bloodletting nor God has saved my husband. He lies lifeless in our bed. Now, you and Doctor Wolfe can bleed him no further." With that she turned and fled.

Rush sputtered. Rarely at a loss for words, he stood openmouthed and speechless.

Wainwright looked embarrassed. Apologizing, he said, "Please excuse my sister's outburst. She is understandably distraught."

Jonathan reached out and shook the brother's hand. "Sir," he said, "We fully comprehend the dreadful extent of your sister's loss and the loss to the family. But please permit us to check that Mr. Stiles has truly expired."

Wainwright thought momentarily, nodded his assent and accompanied them to Stiles' bedroom. The master of the house lay on his bed in the half-light of the closed curtains. There was a blue cast to Stiles' features. His eyes were still open and stared at the ceiling. His mouth had expelled a bubbly, yellowish-green, blood-tinged fluid.

Rush and Jonathan listened carefully, but there were neither breath sounds nor heartbeat. Mr. Stiles had indeed passed to his Maker. The Doctor closed Stiles' eyes and drew the quilt over his face. Examining him had restored his composure.

"Mister Wainwright," he said, "We have done our best. Your brother-in-law's illness was beyond the help of medicine. God was the final arbiter." So saying, his demeanor took on the sadness of failure.

"I am sure you have tried," replied Wainwright and silently bowed his head at the feet of Stiles' corpse.

They left the room. At the house door, Doctor Rush took the lead. He shook hands with Wainwright and spoke with sincerity, saying, "I have heard from several of Mr. Stiles' friends and business acquaintances. They all stated he was a fine, honorable person. Doctor Wolfe and I are both truly sorry we were not able to cure him. Please inform us if we can be of any assistance in the future."

Wainwright nodded, opened the door and they departed. Homeward bound, his mentor said, half under his breath, "Mrs. Stiles' brother is a gentleman. No doubt she is upset, but that woman is an ungrateful and hysterical harpy."

Wolfe remained silent, considering the bloodletting. The first treatment appeared to help. After the second, Stiles appeared weaker and definitely less alert. Perhaps, there was a point beyond which the body no longer responded positively to the taking of blood. Certainly, extracts from various plants proved beneficial in small quantities, but caused harm if given in larger ones.

Jonathan started to verbalize his thoughts. But, on reflection, he felt it unwise. Doctor Rush was in no mood to discuss his practice of bloodletting.

The evening meal was subdued. Wolfe had seen how Rush withdrew into himself when they had previously lost a patient. Tonight he was even more melancholy. Later, they sat silently, reading by candlelight in the study.

Jonathan was engrossed in a medical text when he heard his mentor suddenly exclaim, "Some may question it, but I stand by bloodletting as a vital tool in our armamentarium. Stiles' case was an aberration. Our failure should not be ignored but, given my almost universally good results, I remain a believer in the method."

Rush glanced at his disciple, rose from his chair and went off to bed without another word. Wolfe stared after him. It was obvious that a response was neither indicated nor desired.

IV

April 14-16, 1775

After breakfasting with Doctor Rush, Jonathan made rounds at the hospital. Finishing early, he stopped at the medical school. He had not seen Simon Hunt since the Sons of Liberty meeting.

Wolfe felt it best to be discreet and not mention Simon's interchange with Grace Lockhart. He was also uncertain as to what Hunt's response might be, if he revealed that he had met her again and was invited for dinner. About to enter the school, he almost collided with his friend who was just exiting.

Hunt spoke first, "Jonathan, what marvelous luck to find you here. I have been thinking about you. What business do you have here?"

"My business is with you, my friend. I have come searching for you. I need to refresh myself at your fountain of good spirits and erudition."

Simon laughed. "You are in good humor today. I am going to lunch, please join me."

"I accept the invitation with relish," Wolfe answered, attempting a pun.

Hunt laughed in response. They locked arms and marched along like two cavaliers. Coming to The Brave Pirate, a tavern favored by denizens of the school, they entered and found seats at an empty table.

"Only apple cider for me," Hunt said. "I must remain alert and on guard. Pater and mater have requested my presence for dinner and also for the entire weekend. A young lady and I are to be introduced. Our parents are friends but we have never met. I suspect that our families wish to lead us to the altar, as lambs to the slaughter house."

It was Wolfe's turn to laugh. "Simon, the time has come to meet your true love. Relax and enjoy the approaching encounter. You will duel with one another admirably. She will overcome you with wit, grace, and beauty. Consider yourself the most fortunate of men. At last you will secure happiness in the arms and bosom of a loving female."

"Most probably an ugly shrew they are attempting to shed on an unsuspecting young hero," Simon answered. "I will not permit my parents to coerce me into marriage. I have too many things to learn, to see, and to do, before settling into the fireside life."

"Simon, stay calm. You presume what may not be reality. Truthfully, I have never seen my good comrade so unnerved."

"Oh, Jonathan, dare to imagine what determined parents can do to a loving son. In particular, one who may at times be rebellious but is basically anxious to please them. I really have a caring family. My parents have been very good to me. Even my stepbrother, Alfred, has been quite decent."

"Simon, stay calm. Your parents are not ogres. Cease dwelling in such darkness. Frankly, apple cider is inadequate for your current state. I am ordering a glass of port for us both. You have succeeded in unsettling my nerves as well as your own."

Hunt laughed, and his better spirits returned. "Jonathan, you have buoyed me in an hour of need. You are my best and most loyal friend."

They ordered lunch. As they ate and sipped the wine, Simon asked, "Any interesting cases this past week?"

Jonathan knotted his brow. "On Wednesday we lost a patient. The case proved very instructive, but ended rather unpleasantly. Doctor Rush and I had been caring for a gentleman with extensive pneumonia. He passed away, shortly before we arrived for our third visit in as many days. The new widow was terribly upset. She railed at the two of us, bemoaning our failure to save her husband and singling out Doctor Rush in particular. The lady was in a fury, fuming and storming at him. He had performed bloodletting on our two prior visits and she challenged him about its use. I don't believe anything short of a miracle could have helped the man. He was gravely ill when we first saw him."

"Sorry to hear how it ended," Hunt responded. "I understand her shock and terror, but eventually she will come to realize that Doctor Rush did the very best any physician could. Surely, the circumstances were unfavorable. She should be grateful he agreed to treat him. Your mentor is highly sought after and is regarded as one of the best practitioners. It sounds like an interesting case. Tell me everything."

Wolfe related the facts of the illness, Doctor Rush's decision to carry out bloodletting, and the technique used.

"The treatment certainly sounds appropriate," his friend responded.

Jonathan frowned. "Actually, I have some doubts. The first letting seemed to help. I am uncertain about the second."

"Simon, let me tell you about an accident I just recently recalled. It happened years ago, one of those dreadful situations where you know the people involved. I went to school with Johnny Bolton, the younger brother of the injured fellow. His name was William Bolton. While hunting, he had been accidentally shot in the groin. I assume it damaged the artery. Somehow, his comrades had brought him back to town and he collapsed on a grassy area. The local physician was found and quickly arrived. A crowd formed about the doctor and poor Bolton. I had a good view and could see the blood spreading out from the groin. As it flowed, he became progressively weaker."

"I remember how that physician tried to stem the hemorrhage. He was sweating and swearing while he stuffed packing into the wound and applied pressure. Despite his best efforts, he did not succeed and Bolton died. The doctor was known to be competent and dedicated. When it was over, his hands and arms were covered with blood and his shirt soaked with it. I can still see the scene and, above all, hear the words he uttered, 'I tried, but I could not staunch the bleeding.' Simon, they will last in my memory forever."

"William Bolton bled to death," Wolfe concluded. "Tell me, if one attempts to stop bleeding in one instance, how do we gain by producing it in another?"

Hunt shook his head. "I don't truly know, Jonathan. We are both novices in our study of the medical arts. At this time, it's best we bow to our more knowledgeable elders. Let us hope that, as we continue to acquire learning and experience, we will find the answers. The questions you raise are most pertinent. However, it is getting late and I must scurry home. Let me again thank you for uplifting my mood and regret we meet so infrequently. I will be busy during the next ten days, but we can meet for lunch here on Friday, the twenty-eighth? Would one o'clock be convenient?"

"An excellent idea," said Jonathan. "The date and time are agreeable."

After paying their bill, they left the tavern.

Sunday morning, Wolfe had a quick breakfast and was on his way. He walked the short distance from the Rush home to the waterfront. It was early and the Lord's Day. Save for the calls of gulls circling overhead, the wharves were quiet. Usually, they were alive with activity. Tall ships from England, France, Spain, and Holland predominated, but other countries also showed their flags. Stevedores would be at work, straining to load and unload cargo. Despite the absence of the usual hustle and bustle, Wolfe knew he would find a carriage there and quickly did so.

Jonathan completed his rounds shortly after one o'clock, checked his watch and, since it was a pleasant spring day, decided to walk to Grace's home.

On reaching the lane leading to the house, he had some misgivings. "I was the hero rescuer of Joshua two weeks ago," Wolfe thought. "I wonder if the glow still persists." His pace slowed but, on seeing the house, he felt cheered and said almost aloud, "It is exactly as I remember it."

Chimney smoke rose into a blue sky, and the spring air carried the welcoming aroma of burning wood. A breeze swayed the golden forsythia. The afternoon sun smiled brightly and his spirits rose. He used the door's knocker to signal his arrival. In his hand were a dozen early-blooming yellow daffodils. Grace opened the door. She smiled and her eyes shone as she said, "You are right on time, doctor. It's so nice you were able to come."

"I have been looking forward to seeing you and joining your family for dinner," Wolfe said. "I brought these flowers. They match the forsythia, and I hope will add a festive mood. But please call me Jonathan."

"Hello, Doctor Jonathan," Joshua called out, running up from behind his aunt and hearing the last part of the conversation.

"Hello, Joshua. It's nice to see you again. How are you feeling? And how is your green hoop?"

"I am well," said the boy. "My hoop is well too, and I am holding on to everyone's hand very tightly." He said the last staring straight at Jonathan and in a most serious tone. He had obviously learned his lesson.

Jonathan and Grace both started to laugh. "Joshua," she said, "please bring these flowers to your mother in the kitchen. She will know what to do with them."

Grace turned to Jonathan, saying, "They are really lovely. I am sure Martha will use them well, probably as a centerpiece for the table. Now, please follow me to the parlor. My uncle, Elias, is there and is eager to meet you."

As they entered the parlor, a middle-aged man rose from a high backed rocking chair and came forward to greet Jonathan. He was about Wolfe's height, with broad shoulders. A shock of gray locks stood in sharp contrast to a preponderance of deep black hair. His face had a long slightly bent nose, a ruddy complexion, and the same brown intelligent eyes as Grace. Elias was dressed in a long-sleeved white shirt closed at the neck. Cuffs showed below the wrists of a well-worn black frock coat. He wore gray breeches, black stockings, and polished black boots.

Smiling broadly, he said. "Welcome to our home, doctor. I recognize you from your visit to The Golden Eagle." He shook Wolfe's hand and said, "I am Elias McKenzie, and must add my thanks for your brave rescue of Joshua."

Jonathan felt the power in McKenzie's grip and the sincerity in his voice. He blushed and answered, "Thank you, sir. It is my pleasure to make your acquaintance. I am sure many people would have done the same."

"Unfortunately, not too many," McKenzie answered.

Aunt Evelyn came in, wearing a blue apron over her Sunday finery. She put her hand out to Jonathan and said, "It's nice to see you again, Doctor Wolfe. We are all delighted you could come today. I believe dinner is ready."

She led the way to the dining room. It housed a solidly built oak table covered by a blue tablecloth, and surrounded by eight chairs and a sideboard. Jonathan's daffodils stood in a stoneware jar at the center. Places for six had been set with pewter plates, utensils, and yellow linen napkins. The setting added to the feeling of familial warmth.

At the head of the table, where McKenzie would sit, two still-steaming pullets lay on a large platter. Loaves of bread, churned butter, green beans, yams, roasted potatoes and a pitcher of milk had been placed.

Martha and Joshua joined them. They all sat about the table. Elias bowed his head, and said, "Thank you, Lord, for providing this food. We ask you to bless our house, those who sit here, and all good people."

The company responded with, "Amen."

McKenzie sharpened his carving knife with several strokes, held a chicken with a large fork, and proceeded to carve.

"Doctor Wolfe," he said. "You are our guest of honor. What is your pleasure?"

"I favor both the white and dark meat," answered Jonathan. "I find both to my liking."

"Well answered," smiled McKenzie, and placed meat from both the breast and thigh on a plate. He passed it to Jonathan and did the same with each of the others. But when it came to Joshua he paused. "How say you, lad? What portion would you like?"

Joshua looked at his great uncle and murmured, "A leg please, uncle. If that is all right."

"That is certainly all right, my boy," answered Elias, pleased with the child's response. He placed the remaining thigh on a plate and handed it to Joshua who smiled happily on its receipt. The food was passed around the table. They ate and conversed about the weather, crops, and the continuing growth of Philadelphia. Every now and then, Jonathan would glance at Grace. He would smile and realize she had been looking at him, smiling in return. Each time he felt his heart beat harder and faster. It was difficult for him to sit quietly and not reach out to clasp her hand.

Martha and Grace cleared the table. Aunt Evelyn brought in a warm quince pie and coffee.

"No tea is served in this house, to protest the manner by which the Crown has dealt with us. We drink coffee which, I believe, will become the colonial tea," said McKenzie.

"Coffee is certainly agreeable to me," said Wolfe. "Doctor Rush has also requested his sister to use it more frequently, although it has not yet fully replaced our tea."

"You are still serving tea at The Golden Eagle, uncle," Grace interjected.

"Commerce makes certain demands on one that are unavoidable," McKenzie said. "What one does at home is secure from prying eyes. It would not be wise to draw attention by not serving tea in the tavern. I am exposed quite enough, providing a harbor for the Sons of Liberty."

"Enough of the English and their tea," said Aunt Evelyn. "Martha, please cut the pie. I will pour coffee and I have a bit of sugar to share. Joshua, I will weaken your coffee to a suitable degree. If you wish, add a pinch of sugar. Please, just a pinch. Otherwise your sweet tooth will become even larger than it already is."

They all savored the home-cooked dessert and coffee. Jonathan addressed Aunt Evelyn. "Mrs. McKenzie, this has been a most excellent meal." Turning to the rest, he added, "You have all given me a wonderful reception."

"We have not yet finished with the reception, Doctor Wolfe," Elias McKenzie said. "Let you and I repair to the parlor and speak together for a few moments, whilst the ladies and Joshua handle the cleanup duties."

Jonathan saw Grace give her uncle an imploring look, but he only nodded quickly and continued on. Taking Wolfe by the arm he led him to the parlor.

Elias signaled his guest to take a seat and sat so as to face Jonathan. Then, taking his pipe, he filled it with fresh tobacco, lit it and took a deep draw. McKenzie appeared to be concentrating, collecting his thoughts. He began to speak slowly and in a serious manner.

"Actions such as you performed for Joshua speak not just of a man's bravery but of his innate character. Indeed, I have taken the liberty of asking about you and heard nothing but good reports. I must tell you that my duty to my nieces and to Joshua has changed the manner whereby I think and behave. Grace is a very independent young lady. She is bright, an excellent teacher I am told, and interested in the world about her. She appears to be quite taken with you and I can understand that."

"My nieces' father was my younger brother. He and their mother were slain in an Indian raid on their settlement ten years ago. Fortunately, the girls were at the schoolhouse in the center of the village and were saved. My wife and I assumed responsibility for them since that time, and have come to love both Martha and Grace very deeply." Elias paused for a moment, then continued. "I am aware you have only seen Grace a few times, but I must ask what your feelings are for her."

The topic caused Jonathan to feel uncomfortable, but he decided to push forward. "As you said, sir, I have seen Grace several times, but this is merely the second in which a conversation of substance took place. It is quite early to be discussing my feelings regarding her. However, since you have sought to question me, I will give you the courtesy of a reply."

"I first met Grace the night of the Sons of Liberty meeting. My friend behaved in a manner most contrary to his usual civility. Grace responded in a way I thought brought her great credit. Frankly, I was intrigued and, each time I meet her, find myself more amazed at her perception and appropriate responses. If you are asking if I intend to behave honorably, I can assure you I will."

"I trust your word," the uncle answered. "And may I inquire as to the response you had to the meeting of the Sons of Liberty?"

"You are surely aware that I am apprenticed to Doctor Rush who is an active supporter. He has been urging me to become politically involved, but I am not political. I fear any attempt to separate from England will provoke a terrible conflict, almost certainly worse then the French and Indian wars. I am not afraid for myself. I am fearful for the people at large, for the hardships, the terror, and the deaths."

McKenzie leaned forward so as to bring his face close to Jonathan's. His voice was angry but controlled. "What about present hardships, rape, false witness, false imprisonment, unreasonable search and seizure, billeting of troops in private homes, and the laws passed without our ability to even say a by your leave, sir? We already live with terror, Jonathan."

Sitting back he said, "I have confidence in your integrity, Doctor, so I will tell you about Martha and her husband."

"Harold is a surveyor. The frontier offers good opportunity for that work and they settled in Western Pennsylvania. The area was quiet, no Indian troubles. Nevertheless, a British troop was stationed there. A Captain Winston was billeted in a home adjacent to theirs. Joshua was asleep and Harold out surveying. While he was away, the captain entered their house. He was drunk and attempted to force himself on Martha. In fact, he tore her bodice open. Harold had finished early and arrived home at that moment. He pulled Winston away and struck him. The captain moved to draw his pistol, but being filled with liquor could only fumble for it. Harold was able to grasp a fireplace poker, smash Winston's arm and thereby disarm him. The captain left the house in a drunken rage. He kept muttering, "It's not over. You've struck His Majesty's officer. I'll be back with charges for you and your whore."

"Good Lord," Wolfe gasped. "Is he a prisoner?"

"Fortunately, no," answered McKenzie. "Dusk had fallen. Harold had befriended a young lieutenant named Conrad. He came to them and warned that they had to flee. He said everyone knew the captain to be a drunkard and abuser of women, but at a trial the jury of officers were sure to side with him. Winston was already claiming Martha had exposed herself to him, and he had paid for her favors."

"You're for a whipping with the cat, Harold," he said, "and years in prison will follow. They will make it a military trial, even though you are a civilian. Winston is a bully and he may seek revenge on Martha as well. They may also charge her. Do as you see fit, but my advice is to save yourselves by fleeing tonight."

"Well, they fled, leaving everything they owned. Joshua was all they cared about. Traveling light and fast, they reached us safely. Harold would not stay. He felt he was the one the British would seek and refused to jeopardize us. We really do not know where he is. He has not written or sent any message by word-of-mouth. I trust he is safe. At least we are confident they have not captured him. Save for brave Lieutenant Conrad, I have come to hate the British. He alone proved a true friend and a man of honor. Unfortunately, there are not enough men of honor, not enough in these colonies and certainly not enough in England."

The older man took several draws on his pipe and said, "I believe you are one of the honorable men, Doctor Wolfe. It is my great pleasure to have you in my home. I also believe that, with time, you will lean toward my politics. And what of your friend, who was also at the meeting, what were his feelings?"

"I do not think it is my place to discuss my friend's beliefs with you," Jonathan responded. "I can only say he is truly a thoughtful person and will consider all matters. My friend wishes to search out for himself the means appropriate for resolving our dispute with England. Whatever the decision, you can be certain he will never speak of the meeting or the place where it was held. His behavior toward Grace that evening was totally out of character. I have never before seen him perform any objectionable action."

McKenzie smiled. "People do step out of character, but rarely for the better. Let us hope the rarely will become the more frequent. But enough talk of politics and philosophy. I suggest we request the ladies and Joshua join us."

"Certainly," Jonathan replied.

The remainder of the family rejoined them. Grace sat next to Wolfe on a cushioned high-backed bench. He detected a scent of violets and a thrill went through him at her closeness. They spoke of common things. A local horse sale had ended tragically when the barn housing several animals had caught fire and two had to be destroyed. Jonathan mentioned that he had spent his teens shoeing horses and working a forge. They all listened, enchanted, and urged him on as he told of his experiences at the smithy.

Finally, Wolfe said, "I have been speaking too much about myself. Shall we ask someone else? Why not have Grace tell us about her work as a teacher?"

He felt Grace's body stiffen and saw a blush on her face. Then she relaxed and spoke. "It is really quite wonderful. Every day, I see the children's faces brighten and their eyes widen as they absorb knowledge. My class consists of twenty-six students and their age range from eight to ten years. It is hard work, but I love it. Benjamin Franklin, together with several other generous men, established our school to educate poor children. We also provide lunch for them, and it is often their only decent meal of the day."

"What subjects do you teach?" asked Wolfe.

"I teach grammar, speech, reading, writing, and arithmetic. I am also trying to teach them about money. That is, how to count and use it wisely. It is only on a very elementary level. I am amazed how they embrace it all and want to learn more."

"Joshua is one of the students, but in a younger class. They permitted his entry because of me. Uncle Elias offered to pay for a private school, but Martha wanted him to be at Ben Franklin's. In that way, he is under my watch while Martha works."

"I must say you are a very busy person," Jonathan smiled.

Getting up from his seat, he bowed to the company. "I must thank you all for an extremely enjoyable afternoon and evening. Time has flown quickly because of the pleasantries you provided. I would stay on, but you have things to do, and I must rise early. I am obliged to bid you farewell."

"I will show you out," said Grace, as the others murmured their goodbyes.

At the front door, Wolfe took her hand in his. "When may I see you again?" he asked.

She smiled and answered, "At the next meeting of the Sons of Liberty."

"When is that?"

"You will be informed," Grace answered teasingly.

"You are an unfair waitress," he shot back.

"I know," Grace said, gently kissing his cheek and easing him out the door.

Jonathan started back but stopped, touched his cheek carefully and smiled. He had never felt as lighthearted or as happy.

V

The shadowy figures slipped through the darkness, cautiously approaching the wharf at the water's edge. Peering through the fine fog, they sought to discover any nearby British patrol. Nothing was seen. The three figures remained still and listened carefully. Hearing only the lapping of the river on the wharf's pilings, they quickly moved to a moored rowboat. Untying it, they pushed off. Two rowed and, with muffled oars, slowly moved into deeper water, stealthily passing the anchored British warship HMS Somerset. Then, the boat was propelled across the remainder of the Charles River to the opposite shore.

Charlestown had been reached. Friendly faces from the Sons of Liberty were waiting. They helped the men ashore and led them to a nearby stable. A horse had been borrowed and already saddled. Hastily swallowing a cup of coffee, the third man mounted it. Brown Beauty snorted impatiently. The signal from North Church had been given. Two lanterns had been hung. The British were coming by sea!

The reins were flicked. Horse and rider moved slowly at first, avoiding sleepy patrols of George III's troops. Once on the open road, the rider urged his steed forward. Two British cavalry officers suddenly appeared and attempted to cut them off, but Brown Beauty outran them. Horse and rider felt the wind on their faces. Speed was a necessity. Warnings must be given. As they approached each scattered home, Brown Beauty was momentarily slowed, "The regulars are coming!" shouted the rider, "The regulars are coming!" It was an hour before midnight, April 18, 1775. Paul Revere was sounding the alarm.

Once in Lexington, Revere pounded on the door of the house occupied by John Hancock and Samuel Adams. "Wake up! Wake up!" he shouted. A lantern showed and Hancock opened the door. "I assume there is a problem, Paul," he said in a calm voice.

"Yes, a problem," Revere answered. "General Gage has learned that you and Adams have been hiding in Lexington and wishes to take you prisoner. You must hide in the woods. Our information indicates they are sending a large force. The consensus is that they will also strike Concord. They must know we have stored munitions there and wish to seize them."

"An obvious conclusion," Sam Adams interjected from behind his friend. "Fortunately, precautions have been taken. Most of the gunpowder and stores were moved to other towns and villages."

Dawes, another express rider, had ridden up. They welcomed him and Hancock said, "Your advice will be followed, Paul. Certainly, discretion necessitates we take to the woods. Adams and I are due in Philadelphia to attend the Continental Convention. We will leave from here. You and Mister Dawes must ride on and alert Concord."

"We are on our way," Revere responded, again mounting his horse. He flicked the reins and sent Brown Beauty racing ahead with Dawes at his side.

Earlier that night, Lieutenant Colonel Francis Smith stood on a Boston wharf. At his side was Major John Pitcairn. A blowing wind carried cold air and the grenadiers and light infantry serving under them were still waiting to board boats. It was already ten o'clock. Loading and transporting the troops was far behind schedule.

"Dammit, Pitcairn," growled the colonel. "As usual, His Majesty's Navy is late."

"Yes, sir," answered the major, "but that is only part of the problem. Apparently the navy arranged for only half the boats you requested."

Colonel Smith turned red, and his neck veins became distended. "General Gage specified speed and surprise in his orders. Delay could mean the colonials will have a chance to muster their militia."

"Yes, but a weak ineffective group of rowdies, sir," Pitcairn replied.

"I trust you are correct, major. Still, rowdies with guns can at times prove difficult."

The night wore on. Pitcairn was in charge of the first body of troops to be transported across the Charles River to Cambridge. The colonel revised his prior orders. "Pitcairn, surprise and audacity are required. It is unwise to wait till all our men are across. Yours have already done so. Proceed to Lexington. Search out Adams and Hancock. Arrest them and any other troublemakers you find. I will follow with the remainder of the regiment. Wait for me at Lexington."

"Very good, sir." Pitcairn saluted, turned, and descended into a waiting boat. On reaching the opposite shore, he strode to a white charger. The major swung aboard the animal and brought it to the head of his troops. Facing his command, he drew a sword. "Forward, Ho," he cried. Pivoting his horse about, he began the march toward Lexington.

Colonel Smith continued to fume. "Damn the Navy for botching our orders," he muttered. Removing a snuffbox from his coat pocket, the colonel took a pinch of the contents, inhaled deeply and sneezed. It appeared to calm him. Inwardly, however, he seethed and continued to rage and curse. It was two hours past midnight before his troops finally crossed the river. They were far behind schedule. Smith's anger did not abate, but he was finally headed toward his objective.

Major Pitcairn had long served in His Majesty's Army. Genuine concern for his men, and ability as their commander, created a bond with the two hundred and thirty troops who followed him. Arriving in Lexington, he sat astride his white steed proudly erect, an imposing figure with true military bearing.

It was four-thirty in the morning, and Lexington was not fully awakened. John Parker, the militia's leader, had been up for hours, attempting to assemble his men. He well understood the challenge posed by the coming regulars. But Parker had only been able to gather seventy militiamen. They stood with him on the village green, silent in the predawn stillness.

Pitcairn surveyed the scene. "This is laughable," he thought. Behind him, his men were drawn up, weapons at the ready and bayonets fixed. The Major rode directly towards the militia leader. He stopped several feet before him and looked down. Tension charged the air.

"Lay down your arms," ordered Pitcairn. "Disband at once, you rabble."

Parker evaluated the situation and noted the odds of more than three to one against his militia. "Step aside, men," he ordered.

The minutemen began to move aside, still retaining their weapons.

Suddenly, from somewhere, a shot rang out! It exploded the tension and screamed death.

Both sides started to fire. The colonials fell back, broke ranks and ran.

"Forward, men!" shouted Pitcairn.

The regulars surged forward, continued to fire and began bayoneting wounded militiamen. The pungent odor of gunpowder and smoke permeated the air. Eight of Parker's men lay dead from shot and bayonet, their blood staining the ground beneath and about them.

The search for Adams, and Hancock began. Their tempers aroused, flush with the feel of combat and victory, the English troops ran amok. They entered homes, ransacked closets, overturned chests, and took souvenirs. Major Pitcairn had seen similar behavior before, but he was in charge here. "Stop this madness," he ordered his officers, and they slowly restored order. Finding that the sought culprits were nowhere to be found, the search was called off.

Colonel Smith arrived with the remaining infantry and grenadiers. He consulted with his officers. Some advised terminating the mission. Finally, the colonel spoke. "Gentlemen, I am aware their riders have almost certainly alerted Concord and the surrounding hamlets. Viewing the opposition offered here, I doubt Concord will prove much of a challenge. Our orders are to seize and destroy the munitions stored there. We have well over seven hundred men. We move now!"

The British marched the six miles to Concord. Lexington had been a lark. They were in good spirits. The sun was up, birds were singing, and spring was upon them.

Concord was entered without firing a shot. Smith breathed easier. "Break into companies and search for weapons and powder," the colonel ordered. He was unaware that on the drilling field beyond town another colonel, James Barrett, local miller and militia leader, was organizing his colonials.

When young, Barrett had fought in the French and Indian war. There was no bluster in his manner. He was tough. He knew how to command and how to fight. He had received reports on the strength and composition of Smith's forces. Looking at his own gathering troops, he thought, "There are still not enough minutemen at hand to confront the British. But more are pouring in." Then, watching the men milling about, he called out, "Stay calm. Form into your squads and companies."

He turned his weathered face toward town, surmising what the British were doing. "They hunt for weapons and powder," he whispered. "They have been removed, except for a small amount of powder left to convince the enemy they found it all."

Captain Felton of the King's Own stood outside the town's arsenal. "Break in, men," he ordered. The doors were smashed and the arsenal entered.

"There are artillery caissons here," Sergeant Williams called out.

"Are there any cannon?" Felton asked.

"No cannon, sir."

"Drag the caissons forward and burn them," the captain responded.

They were set afire and smoke rose above the roofs of the village.

The militia had continued to gather on the drill field. "Look at the smoke," Private Sutherland shouted, pointing toward town. Men turned to see. "The regulars are firing the town," yelled Corporal Townsend.

The minutemen stirred expectantly. Their ranks had continued to swell, now numbering over four hundred and fifty. More were hurrying in from other villages.

"We wait no longer," Barrett cried out. "To the North Bridge and Concord! Stay in formation, maintain order, maintain discipline!"

Captain Fuller had been posted at the bridge and sighted the approaching colonials. "Form up, men," he called. He had one hundred and twenty light infantry under his command. Their mission was to hold the bridge and prevent any colonials from crossing to oppose those in Concord. The troops formed up as ordered.

"My God, there are hundreds of them," exclaimed Private Damon.

"Order in the ranks," growled Sergeant Overton.

Wide eyed, the British stared at the advancing minutemen. "Sergeant Overton, take your men and tear up the floor of that bridge," ordered Captain Fuller. "We must stop those rebels from crossing."

Hastily, the regulars started to rip at the bridge's platform. The colonials had not yet fired. They were coming forward rapidly, marching in ordered ranks.

Captain Fuller's armpits felt sweaty and his collar tight about his neck. The enemy was closing. One regular fired and several others joined in. Fuller could no longer stand the strain. "Open fire!" he shouted.

As several of his men went down, Barrett swore under his breath. He shouldered his rifle and yelled, "Return fire! Fire at will, men!" A sheet of flame erupted from the minutemen's ranks. Twelve regulars fell, three dead where they had stood. Fear overcame the remainder. They broke and ran. It was Lexington in reverse.

Colonel Smith sat astride his horse, Tally Ho. It was jet black, a stallion bred for speed and stamina. The day had turned warm and the colonel's forehead was moist with perspiration. He paid no notice. Steel blue eyes surveyed the scene. In his mind he retained an overall picture of his dispersed men. On hearing the repeated volleys echoing into Concord, he feared the worst. His troops were scattered about and it would take time to reorganize them.

An exhausted runner raced up to him. "Colonel, Captain Fuller wishes to report that he is under heavy attack from a large force of colonials," he gasped.

"Very well," replied Smith. He turned his horse and spoke to an adjutant. "We have done what was required here. Their gunpowder has been thrown into the river, and their stores and supplies burned. It is time to move out." His officers received their orders, "Return to Boston in an orderly manner. March in column."

But it was not to be an orderly return. The colonial hive had been broken into and the bees came storming out. From surrounding towns and villages, men arrived prepared to fight. For Colonel Smith and his men it was a retreat through hell. As the day became warmer, the fighting became hotter. The colonials were firing from behind hedges, walls, trees, barns, and every type of available cover.

Uniforms soaked with sweat, backpacks feeling ever heavier, the English shed their equipment. Anything and everything was cast aside to lighten their load. They were under almost continuous fire. Bands of colonials would discharge their weapons, retreat and hide. Then, when the search for them ceased, they would return and fire afresh as the next group of regulars came by. Exhaustion combined with fear. The retreating redcoats were no longer the men who had sallied forth from Boston.

Lexington's John Parker finally had mustered his full complement of militia. "We're out to even the score. Back to the fight, men," he ordered. Taking up positions alongside the battle road, their muskets and rifles wreaked havoc on the retreating infantry. "Revenge! Revenge!" was the cry, and revenge for their fallen brothers was exacted.

Sergeant Overton, his throat parched, filled his canteen from a sparkling brook. He brought it to his lips. As he began to drink, a ball tore through his chest and ruptured his heart. Stumbling back, he fell, his blood coloring the water red. The men with him panicked, scattered, and ran for their lives.

Colonel Smith sent riders racing to Boston. "We require immediate assistance," they reported to a shocked General Gage.

"Assistance? Why?" he demanded. "For what purpose?"

"Sir," replied a rider, "Colonel Smith is attempting to fight his way back to Boston. We are under attack by hundreds of colonials."

Gage understood what had happened. He had feared the colonials would respond, and they had struck back with a vengeance. His heart sank, but he did not hesitate. Infantry and cavalry were sent. Smith and his men were saved by the reinforcements. Bloodied and exhausted, they stumbled back to their bases. The sergeant majors made their counts and set them down.

The colonel reported the events to his general. As he finished, Smith almost wept, saying, "Those wretched people have succeeded in destroying my command. One third of my men are dead, wounded, or missing."

It took several weeks before London received the news. Newspapers sold out, as newsboys shouted the headlines. Both royalty and the public at large recognized that a major disaster had occurred.

Never before had a British Army been beaten by a mob of natives. The British lion was aroused. Citizenry, King, and Parliament demanded reprisal!

In Boston, General Gage sat at his desk pondering the events. "I had advised moderation in dealing with the colonists," he thought. "My advice has been ignored. This could have been avoided. Now we have a calamity. I am certain my views, as to how to achieve reconciliation, will again be put aside. Nevertheless, I am duty-bound to set them down. Both Minister North and King George must understand that a war in these colonies will be prolonged, bloody, and require vast numbers of troops. Far greater sums of money will be spent than raised by all the taxes they attempted to impose."

Upon receiving his report describing the events at Lexington and Concord, and General Gage's conclusions, the King yelled, "Gage is a fool and a defeatist."

"We must and will replace him," responded his Minister.

England was both shocked and angry. Very few citizens were prepared to consider reconciliation. Those who did were subjected to scorn and both verbal and physical attacks. A newspaper editorial concluded, by saying, "*The incident at Concord was an aberration. When the rebels feel the ungloved British fist, the slash of British steel, and Britain's massive military power, they will slink away like whipped dogs.*"

VI

Thursday, April 27, 1775

Jonathan was late. Dinner at the Rush house was served promptly at six, but problems at the hospital had resulted in a delayed departure. He walked quickly through the darkening streets, oblivious to the falling rain.

Ascending the steps to the house on Front Street, Wolfe knocked and was quickly admitted. Feeling the welcoming warmth within, he said, "Good evening, Alice. It's good to be out of the rain and cold."

An expression of relief appeared and she replied, "I was afraid you would be late, Doctor Jonathan. You know Miss Rebecca insists on promptness at the evening meal. Hurry now, you just have time to wash."

Snatching his hat and coat, the girl placed them on a rack, and led the way to a washstand. She gave him a bar of soap and poured water over his cupped hands. Wolfe washed, and then dried himself with a proffered towel.

"Alice, you are my guardian angel," he said.

She blushed. Her blue eyes, however, showed delight at his teasing compliment. Shyly, she said, "You had best go in. They are already seated."

Wolfe entered the dining room. "Good evening, Miss Rebecca," he said to his mentor's sister.

Peering at him, she replied, "Jonathan, it is always nice to see you." A gentle reproach was implied when she added," We have just begun to dine."

Jonathan thought, "She has really taken charge since her husband died and brother Benjamin invited her in." Turning to greet his mentor, Wolfe realized a guest was also present. He was a short portly gentleman, wearing spectacles that partly obscured his intelligent eyes. The man had a roundish pleasant face, the beginning of a double chin, and a balding head showing a periphery of graying hair.

"Jonathan," Rush said, "I would like you to meet Samuel Adams. Samuel, this is Jonathan Wolfe, my apprentice in physic."

"My pleasure, young man," and Adams reached across the table to shake hands.

"The pleasure is truly mine, sir," replied Jonathan.

Alice brought apple cider, preferred by Jonathan and Rebecca. Doctor Rush poured port for Adams and himself. They consumed the food in a slow deliberate manner and spoke about generalities.

Their conversation paused, and the lady of the house excused herself. "Benjamin, I am sure you wish to question Mister Adams about the recent events outside Boston," she said. "Please excuse me. I must oversee some matters."

The men rose as she did, and then resumed their seats.

Rush spoke first. "Jonathan, Mister Adams arrived today after journeying from Lexington. I happened to cross his path and insisted he stay with us. He has been providing the nature of the recent events to the newspapers. It is our good fortune to have him here and can question him at leisure. How say you, Samuel? We are waiting expectantly to learn of Paul Revere's ride, and the fighting on the nineteenth of April."

Adams took a sip of port from his glass, leaned forward and spoke. "It is quite a tale. I will not burden you with all the details. The newspapers will have them. I am tired of reciting the events, hoping the scribblers will get it right. I was careful to distinguish between what I witnessed, that which I am certain is true, and those events that are probably correct. However, I am sure the editors will make a hodgepodge of everything."

"Samuel, you speak as one who has had prior difficulties with newspaper editors. I know that many have not understood your true intentions," Rush said.

"Indeed, they have often misunderstood and misconstrued my political stance. Various editors have accused me of being a radical, a rabble-rouser, and Boston's political dictator. I am none of the above. I have always attempted to follow the rules of English common law, and those one assumes are provided by natural law merely because we are born. I detest rabble-rousing and any attempt to use violence for political ends. However, there comes a time when all measures of legitimate peaceful expression are exhausted. Then, it is one's duty to inform an intransigent government, which refuses to provide redress of honest grievances, that it is not only in the wrong but no longer has the right to govern."

"Jonathan, you have heard Samuel Adams at his best. He has appropriately summarized his political philosophy. He is a great patriot, an excellent pamphleteer, an organizer of the Sons of Liberty, and a constant thorn in the side of George III."

Adams smiled, nodded in acknowledgement, drained his glass and began. "At around midnight, Revere arrived at Lexington, roused the community and then rode on to Concord. He was stopped by a British patrol, but other riders carried the warning there."

"I will not go into all the details. Suffice to say that Lexington was a disaster for us. Parker did not have time to gather enough men and was vastly outnumbered. We do not know who fired first. It does not matter. Good men died that day. However, their sacrifice delayed the British arrival at Concord."

His voice rose slightly and Adam's eyes sparkled. His face became flushed and he began to perspire, warmed by both the wine consumed and the excitement of the telling. Rush filled his glass again. Adams took another sip and went on.

"Once warned, the minutemen from Concord and surrounding villages gathered. After Lexington, the British expected little opposition. Yet they were turned back at Concord, and then met steely resistance as they retreated to Boston. They have been badly bloodied, with heavy losses."

Jonathan blurted out, "But surely King George and Parliament will respond. I, for one, do not wish to see war between the colonies and the Crown. As a physician, as a thinking person, I know wars are terrible. Many will die, and more will sustain grievous wounds. There must still be an alternative. Is there no way we can find rapprochement?"

Adam's face became stern and serious, yet his tone was sympathetic and his voice measured. "It is not easy to enter into war. The risks are great for all involved. Jonathan, I respect your concerns. However, you know our people have been sore used. We appealed to the King as children to a father, and said we wished to maintain our relationship with the Crown. Despite our pleas, he has cast us out."

"I have come to Philadelphia for a second convention. We will be meeting shortly. Representatives from the thirteen colonies will gather and decide whether or not to join together in a confederation. Ultimately, I believe, we will proclaim our independence. Otherwise, it requires continued submission to the yoke of the Crown. I shall vote for confederation and subsequently for independence."

"The English will continue to pour troops into the colonies," said Wolfe.

"We will answer them. We will meet fire with fire. Hear me, Jonathan. Lexington was a defeat against overwhelming odds. Concord will be seen as a great victory. All the capitals of Europe must sit up and take notice. A ragtag group of colonials have mauled, and sent into grievous retreat, troops from the finest army in Europe. At Concord, our men fired a shot which will be heard around the world!"

Samuel Adams sat back and exhaled. He was smiling broadly.

"Amen," intoned Rush, as he raised his glass in salute.

Wolfe was subdued and thoughtful. He again recalled the French and Indian wars, the attacks and counterattacks. He remained fearful that coming events bore even greater hazards for the colonies and their people.

Jonathan had a sudden thought and spoke, "I may be fairly uninformed about the political situation. However, I do know there are thirteen different colonies and each has its own needs and desires. You mentioned a confederation but that is not easy to achieve."

"It will be done by slow steady persuasion," interjected Rush. "For example, many colonies are vying for their champion to be appointed Commander of our Continental Army. Virginia's George Washington is available. He led men in the French and Indian War. Mister Adams and his cousin, John, will persuade the New England delegations to vote for him. We believe his appointment will bring Virginia and other southern colonies into the fold. We shall work to convince each colony that its best interests lie in confederation. Whatever is required will be done. We are determined to succeed. Many delegates to the convention are lukewarm with respect to banding together and, certainly, to final separation and independence. But the war will proceed. As it does, we will ultimately also gain the votes for independence."

"Exactly so," Adams smiled. "Jonathan," he said, "Britain's citizens do not recognize the true significance of April's events. They fail to understand what the shots fired really mean. An ocean separates us from England. That ocean is not only physical but, more importantly, one of thought, attitude, and emotion."

Jonathan sat back, thinking, "Big words and well spoken. They have both hardened their minds." He felt exhausted and overwhelmed. To Adams, he said, "Sir, it has been my pleasure to have made your acquaintance. I have doubts as to the future, but you and Doctor Rush expressed yourselves well. I would enjoy continuing our friendship."

Adams responded. "Thoughtful men can disagree, but use rational debate to find an amicable conclusion. You speak honestly. I only ask you to honestly and completely evaluate our situation."

Wolfe turned to Doctor Rush, "Sir, as always, it has been my pleasure to dine at your table. The hour is late and I beg your indulgence to permit my leaving."

"Certainly Jonathan, sleep well. We will meet at breakfast tomorrow."

Wolfe left and climbed two flights of stairs. Once in his room, he disrobed, pulled on his nightgown, climbed into bed, and fell promptly to sleep.

VII

The next morning, Doctor Rush greeted Wolfe with a smile. "Good morning, Jonathan." His mentor said, "I hope you were not too troubled by Mister Adams' discourse last evening."

"Good morning, sir. In truth, it was fascinating. The colonial militias showed great bravery. However, I am still disturbed when thinking about the greater war sure to come. But where is Mister Adams this morning?"

"Adams left very early. He has much politicking to do. As for your feelings, they are fully understandable. However, you know I stand with Adams. War will lead to separation. But I wish to discuss a different issue. It's time I said how much I value you. You have been my star pupil. I was at first hesitant to accept your application. You were a bit older than the usual applicant, and your education had been rather rudimentary. A recommendation from one of your teachers swayed me. He said you showed a great passion for knowledge and you had repaired, and then released, an injured bird. Most of all, he wrote you learned quickly and well. Certainly, what he wrote has proven valid. Now, you are fully qualified. I am prepared to inform the medical establishment of your fitness to function as an independent physician."

"Sir, this is wonderful news."

Rush continued, "I am attempting to secure an appointment as a delegate to the coming Convention. If successful, it creates a problem. Serving two masters is difficult. Politics will demand both time and effort. That means I will be obliged to reduce the hours devoted to medicine. The patients have taken to you. I would very much enjoy continuing our relationship. It could lead to some form of partnership in the future."

"You overwhelm me, sir," Jonathan responded.

Doctor Rush looked pleased. "You will have to take on more patients," he said.

Wolfe nodded in understanding and his teacher added, "This morning I have scheduled a variolation. It's time you saw one performed."

Jonathan knew that variolation, was used to inoculate against smallpox or variola. Rush insisted that all medical practitioners should learn it.

His mentor went on, "One should also know the history surrounding a scientific discovery or procedure. What do you know concerning variolation?"

"Sir, I am aware it was imported into England and then traveled here. Unfortunately, I am not well read in that area."

"You must read more. The history is fascinating. The method has been practiced in the Middle East and India for centuries. It is said that, with their technique, a death rate as low as two persons in one hundred is achieved. Imagine, two percent! Compare that to a death rate of twenty, thirty, or forty percent during a variola epidemic."

"That is truly remarkable. Can we do the same?" Wolfe asked.

"Not quite. But our percentages with variolation are much better than with naturally contracted variola. Also, the induced illness and scarring is usually less severe. Yet protection against the pox is the same, whether acquired by variolation or by nature."

The Doctor continued. "When it comes to the history a wonderful story emerges. Lady Mary Wortley Montagu was both beautiful and extremely intelligent. Shortly after marrying Lord Montagu, she developed the pox. The Lady survived but was left with very noticeable facial scars."

Jonathan's interest was aroused. "What happened after her illness?" he asked.

"Well, several years later, her husband was appointed ambassador to Turkey."

"Turkey?" Wolfe interjected. "You mentioned the Middle East as a place where the technique was used. Turkey is there."

"Indeed," his mentor went on. "Madame Montagu discovered it was in widespread and effective use in that country. Women were the main practitioners, and she hired one to teach her the technique. The Lady's brother had died of the pox. That, and her own experience, caused her to have her son inoculated. Fortunately, the boy did well and, of course, was immune."

"How was the method brought to England?" asked Jonathan.

Rush went on. "The Montagues returned home. Several years later, a pox epidemic struck Britain. Lady Mary had given birth to a daughter, now three years of age, and had her variolated. Again, it proved successful. She then proselytized for its use."

"Her efforts persuaded the Royals to test it on prisoners. Once more, it proved itself. The Lords then had themselves and their families inoculated. With wider use, there were some deaths. Physicians and the Church railed against it. The doctors rejected it through ignorance and stupidity. The Church claimed variolation went against God's ordinances. Still, it has become the standard for protecting against the pox in England."

"So I understand," Wolfe interjected.

The Doctor continued, saying, "Unfortunately, negative aspects are present. Firstly, the procedure costs two to three dollars. The average farmer or journeyman can ill afford such a fee. Furthermore, those inoculated should be kept in quarantine until the scabs fall off and they can no longer infect others. Not all variolators even request such compliance. Many of those inoculated continue about their business during the days before feeling ill. They walk the streets, visit shops, and go to church. They may not know, or do not care, that they are silent carriers and spreaders of the disease."

Rush paused, took a sip of tea and went on. "The negative factors have caused rioting in many places and legislators have felt obliged to ban the practice. In Philadelphia, there is no prohibition to its use. I am a staunch advocate for variolation. If we could manage it for every person, it would be a great boon."

Several days later, Jonathan watched his mentor perform it at the nursing facility he used. The patient was a Mister Hugh Fenwick. He was seated at a table, upon which his left arm had been placed.

"Observe closely," Rush said. "I will make a two inch incision near the wrist just deep enough to draw a drop or two of blood." Then, speaking as he worked, the Doctor continued. "Now, I shall sprinkle finely ground scabs into the wound from someone previously inoculated. I prefer one who suffered only a mild infection." Placing a bit of cotton and a bandage, he added, "We will remove the dressing in one week and check the wound."

Rush then spoke to the patient. "My friend, I apologize for any discomfort you endured. You must now be confined until the scabs fall off, about four weeks. You will feel quite well for ten days. Then, you will have fever and become ill. Either Doctor Wolfe or I will come by to check your condition. The people here will attend to all your needs. They are very capable. We have been quite fortunate and have not lost anyone at this facility. You will get well, sir." He placed his hand on the man's shoulder and patted it gently.

Ten days later, the fever developed and shortly thereafter the vesicles showed on Fenwick's face, trunk and extremities. He was fortunate. The course of the illness was mild. He did well and left in the predicted time, having become fully immune to the dreaded smallpox.

VIII

Friday, April 28, 1775

Jonathan entered the Brave Pirate a few minutes after the time that he and Simon had agreed upon. Hunt was already there, sipping a cup of tea, and happily greeted Wolfe.

"You are very enthusiastic with your greeting," Jonathan said. "Your mood has changed completely. I gather you have avoided the marital noose."

"On the contrary," his friend exulted. "I am prepared to put my head in the noose and, have it tighten hard and forever, by springing the trapdoor beneath."

"What a startling change. Tell me, what have you been drinking, or what potion have you swallowed to bring about this change? It appears that some sorceress has you in thrall."

"You are exactly correct," Simon smiled. "I have met and fallen in love with the most beautiful, charming, elegant woman."

"The horror maiden your parents wanted you to meet? What about all the things that you must still learn, see, and do? Are you not much too young to let marriage act as a ball and chain against your future growth and development?"

As Jonathan recalled Hunt's prior concerns, his friend's face took on a sheepish look, but he answered bravely. "Those were the ravings of a callow youth," he said. "You must meet Gwendolyn. Only then will you understand the change she has brought about."

"And may I enquire as to whether or not she returns your ardor?"

"I am not sure," Simon answered, lowering his gaze and frowning. "I think she likes me, but it appears I am more smitten than she. You know women, Jonathan. They are far better at concealing their feelings than men."

"Yes, and better at toying with us and driving us to distraction."

Hunt gave Wolfe a quick glance. "I was not aware you had such a vast contact with the female gender."

"Mostly what I have gathered from men of experience," Jonathan demurred.

"Are you sure there is nothing closer to home?" Hunt queried, somehow sensing more existed than what was being acknowledged.

"No, nothing at all," Wolfe replied, and for a moment a vision of Grace flashed across his mind. "I do want to hear about your meeting with this fabulous lady, and all that transpired between you."

As Hunt started to speak, a waitress asked if they wished to order. They paused to examine the menu and place their requests. As she left, Simon began his tale.

"Of course you were right when you alluded to my fear that an unknown woman was being thrust upon me. However, as usual, I failed to appreciate my parents' abilities. We met at the Loring home. Quite a place, I must say. The pater is involved in the tobacco and rice trade. It is apparently very profitable, but war with England will surely interfere with it."

"To go on, my family and I arrived in the evening. We were ushered into a huge entryway and then a lovely parlor. It was there I met this beautiful apparition. Gwendolyn is seventeen and stands about five feet four inches in low-heeled shoes. She has blonde hair and wore it loosely, flowing down her back. Her lovely face is slightly rounded with deep blue eyes, long lashes, arched eyebrows, and the reddest lips I have ever seen. When she smiles I am overcome with joy. I tell you, Jonathan, no more smitten a man exists than Simon Hunt."

"Please continue," said Jonathan, sitting back and grinning. "I am enchanted."

Simon blushed and swallowed hard. "I must confess to being overwhelmed. We were seated together at dinner. I cannot remember the conversation, except to tell you I hung on every word she uttered. At some point, I retained enough wits to ask if she were free the following day, so as to go for a drive in the country. She replied there was to have been a meeting with another young lady, but her friend had become ill. I gratefully thanked the Lord! Her parents gave their permission. Alfred and my sister-in-law, Prudence, acted as chaperones. We rode about the countryside and picnicked in a charming meadow. I cannot tell you how exhilarated I was. Monday, it was back to work. Almost a week has passed and my heart aches to see her again."

Wolfe leaned forward and grasped his friend's hand. "Simon, I am truly happy you have met such a lovely young woman. The more Gwendolyn learns about you, she will realize what a wonderful person you are. Any woman would be fortunate with you as a husband."

Both remained silent for several moments. Then, Wolfe said, "Tell me what you think of the events at Lexington and Concord."

As though suddenly awakened from his reverie, Simon pushed back from the table. Unable to refrain from raising his voice, he blurted, "What do I think. I cannot think. I have to reject thought.

I can only react. Our world is filled with fools! Both Parliament and radical colonials have unleashed the dogs of war. I wish a plague upon Parliament, New England and a radicalized Continental Congress. Jonathan, thank God you and I are physicians, not politicians. Damn all the politicians! They are almost all self-serving men. If they do not have their hand out, or directly in the till, their vote almost always serves hidden interests of their own. Shakespeare said to kill all the lawyers. I say kill all the politicians! They provoke war, sending other men and other men's sons to fight. Others suffer wounds and death, while they hide behind their desks and sleep on feathered beds."

Simon quieted and moderated his tone. "I apologize for my rage," he continued. "It is partly that I am upset with myself. I believe both sides have something of the right. George III is our lawful king. I owe loyalty to him. Also, I doubt that Parliament deliberately means to subjugate us. Still, many of the laws and duties they have passed seem unfair, and the colonies have not had representation. That puts us in an untenable position. But my brain cannot decide which course to pursue, loyalty to the crown or opposition and separation. My only area of stability is to remain neutral, while I attempt to resolve this dilemma."

"I fully understand," Jonathan replied. "I am primarily moved by my hatred of war. But, in times like these, events often decide which road we take. True choice is rarely involved. However, whatever our roads, we must stay friends forever."

"Amen," said Simon.

They finished their meal in silence, thinking of the various factors about to encroach on their lives. Hunt broke the silence. "Jonathan, I appreciate your listening while I unburdened myself. I know

I sound a bit unhinged about Gwendolyn, obviously I am. As for war, you are correct. Events will determine our paths. My hope is there will not be too many twists and turns. Fortune smiles on us. In several weeks we will complete our apprenticeships and be able to function as independent physicians. At this time, we are both very busy. Hopefully, we will see one another soon. I suggest we meet here again in two weeks."

"Agreed," said Jonathan.

They shook hands, embraced warmly, and departed.

IX

It was a warm and sunny afternoon. Doctor Rush and Jonathan had been visiting homebound patients. His mentor had come along, explaining that only Wolfe might be seeing them in the near future.

"Jonathan," Rush said, "I believe we are in need of some refreshment. Nearby is a coffeehouse I know quite well." They proceeded to the shop. It was situated on a busy thoroughfare alive with both pedestrian and horse-drawn traffic. Entering the candlelit interior, a brief wait ensued and they were shown to a small table. Rush ordered coffee and small cakes.

"This is very good coffee," said Jonathan, "and the cakes are delicious."

"I thought you might enjoy the fare," the Doctor smiled. He then turned slightly and peered toward a far corner of the room. Jonathan followed his gaze. A candle had been placed on a table. The single figure there appeared to be at work, now and then sitting back as though in thought, then leaning forward and hurriedly writing with a quill.

Rush started to laugh and said, "Just the man I have been thinking about. Come, Jonathan, I want you to meet Tom Paine." Rising from his chair, he scooped Wolfe up and hurried him toward the writer. It was indeed Tom Paine.

Absorbed in his work, he paid no attention to their approach until they were almost upon him. Then, the sound of their oncoming boots penetrated his thoughts. Looking up, he smiled, rose, and held out a large hand. "Doctor Benjamin Rush," he said. "How good it is to see you."

"And glad I am to see you, Thomas. May I introduce you to my associate, Doctor Jonathan Wolfe."

Shaking hands with Jonathan, Paine said, "Sit down and join me. May I order anything for either of you?"

"We have just finished some refreshments," Rush responded. "I spied someone scribbling here. Your reddish hair and posture gave you away, and I hurried over. May I ask what you are writing about?"

"I am only scribbling, or more accurately ruminating over certain thoughts about the coming Continental Convention. I intend to use my notes for an editorial in the *Pennsylvania Magazine.* I am attempting to define what to say, and how to say it."

"Do you know, Thomas, that I hope to be a delegate?"

"I am aware of that," answered Paine.

"There will be great debates at the Convention. Intense argument will occur between those who still insist on going hat in hand to King George and those favoring partial or complete separation." Rush looked about the room and lowered his voice to a whisper. "Well, Mr. Paine, how do you feel about the colonies separating completely from England?"

"I am absolutely in favor of full separation," Paine answered, also keeping his voice very low. His face was serious, and he looked ready to challenge any contrary viewpoint.

Wolfe listened attentively. It was almost a continuation of the evening with Adams.

"As am I," Rush exclaimed.

Wolfe had always regarded Doctor Rush as being thoughtful and somewhat cautious. Although Rush supported the Sons of Liberty, until the evening with Adams, he had never known him to be radical in his political opinions. Jonathan thought to speak, but chose to keep silent and listen.

His mentor leaned forward and continued. "Lexington and Concord have added to my conviction that a total schism with England must occur. If we fail to rally those who are undecided, or change the thinking of those advocating acquiescence to the Crown, we are doomed to perpetual status as indentured servants or slaves. Thomas, you are an exceptionally fine writer. I cannot do it. Medicine and, hopefully, my forthcoming attendance at the Convention, will take all my energy. You have the ability, the understanding, and the fire from within required for this task. You must write a pamphlet arguing against continuation of our subservience to the Crown and for separation."

Paine appeared at once both thoughtful and excited. "I have been thinking along those lines. The shot has been fired, the conflict has erupted, and we most assuredly must go forward. If we succeed, we will be a light unto the world, creating something never before seen. I will undertake the task, but you must promise to advise and edit as I write."

"Agreed,“ Rush responded. "My first advice would be, you cannot use the words independence, republican, or republicanism in your dissertation. They are anathema to many of those you are trying to influence. I would also counsel you to be moderate in your forthcoming editorial. At this time, it is best not to draw undue attention to yourself."

Jonathan had listened to Samuel Adams, and had been thinking about what he had heard. The present conversation was additional heady material. Doctor Rush was asking Paine to preach seditious thoughts to the entire colonial population, and convert them to demand total separation from Britain. To Wolfe, the subdued voices served to further emphasize their feelings and their intent.

He managed to keep his voice low but blurted out, as he had with Adams, his concern with the idea of separation. "Gentlemen, we are English. England is our mother country. There must still be means for reconciliation. To attempt to separate will bring further war. War brings with it the other three horsemen of the apocalypse, death, hunger, and pestilence. All four will gallop through the land. Surely many will suffer and perish on both sides."

Paine responded, "Young man, first, you are totally off course as to England being our mother country. There are many mother countries from which the inhabitants of these colonies emanate. They are Dutch, English, German, Spanish, Scots, Irish, French, plus an assortment of other European states and duchies. Europe, not England, is our mother country. I can even include Africa, if we bring in the Negro people. I do not mention the native Indians, who were here before any of us. But fundamentally, we are from Europe."

"That is not good enough to satisfy me," Wolfe shot back. "You must provide me with cogent arguments." He was aroused, not quite hostile but determined to get real answers.

Tom Paine looked at him carefully and then spoke. "You are asking for quick answers. I can only give you some of my thoughts. I need more time to work everything out. But this will provide something of an outline for you to consider."

Paine leaned forward, eyes closed in thought. His words came slowly. "Society is produced by our wants and needs. Government is required because of our wickedness, our propensity to do harm to one another. Society promotes our happiness positively by uniting our affections, while government acts negatively by restraining our vices. Monarchy restrains our vices but adds vices of its own. It involves us in needless wars and is not interested in our happiness. To live under a total monarchy causes degradation. It results in a lessening of our very being. It does so by persistently encroaching on our rights and freedoms."

"To the evil of monarchy we have added that of hereditary succession. This is an abomination that has also been claimed by the Royals as a matter of right. It is an insult to us and, more importantly, it is an imposition on posterity. Even if a present monarch is competent, there is no guarantee that the progeny will be either competent or just. Furthermore, just as they cannot restore to prostitution its former innocence, those that tell us of the need to restore harmony and achieve reconciliation with England cannot return us to the time that is past."

"Jonathan, we are the King's chattel, available to be used at his discretion. We are being held on a tight leash. Our future growth, our children's future growth and security, surely fails to lie with continuation of the present relationship. Separation is the only answer. That is the gist of my thinking and that is what I shall write."

Jonathan remained silent for a moment, trying to assimilate Paine's points. "Your arguments are well stated, sir." he replied. "I must consider them with care. But war terrifies me. Its consequences are ruinous."

"I know," answered Paine,"but war has begun. I believe in my soul that it must, and will, result in victory for the colonies. Doctor Rush has requested that I write this pamphlet. I believe it is my responsibility to do so. I have only been in this country for a short time, but it has taken hold of me. My pen is at its service, as is my life."

Rush reached across the table and grabbed Paine's hand. "Thomas, you are a gem among men. I sincerely thank you for agreeing to embark on this enterprise."

They continued to speak for a time and then said their farewells.

During the weeks that followed, Paine was a frequent visitor to the Rush home. As editor, the Doctor continued to offer advice. One evening, as they were concluding their discussion, Rush said, "Thomas I am not quite happy with your title, "*Plain Truth.*" I thought "*Common Sense*" might be more interesting."

"*Common Sense*," Paine replied. "I like that very much. So it shall be."

X

Peter Loring was a shrewd trader. He knew the inner workings of the tobacco and rice markets. How weather, conflict, use of tobacco, or the need to feed Caribbean slaves altered prices. Techniques to outsmart others, and knowing how the markets could be manipulated, had been learned at an early age. He was also an astute observer of both English and colonial politics. Unlike many husbands, Loring had high regard for his wife's intelligence. He often confided his thoughts to her, and did so once more. They had dined with Gwendolyn and Simon. The young couple had gone for a walk and husband and wife were alone.

"Recent events have gone as I expected," he said. "The insurrection is definitely troubling our business. We depend on trade and the ability to secure loans from the great banks of London. Credit is the lifeblood of commerce. Those loans are no longer available and trade with England and the Caribbean has been disrupted."

"Fabric from our mother country is in short supply here, and the price rises almost weekly. On the other hand, American tobacco and rice cannot be easily exported. They merely accumulate in warehouses, so values decline in the colonies. Their short supply in Europe and the Indies increases values there. Meantime, our ships stay idle and serve only to add to expenses. However, I believe there are answers."

"You always manage to find answers to problems, Peter," Mrs. Loring smiled.

"Thank you, Emily," he said, raising his glass of port to salute her. "You are my best listener and adviser."

"What do you actually propose?" she queried.

"It is quite simple. For the immediate present we will do nothing. We must hope the colonies will return to their senses and yield to the King. If not, the vessels can be used to advantage in other enterprises. The risks are high, but the profits warrant them."

"Our three ships are all well fitted and fast for their size. Privateering should prove very profitable. I plan to arm one vessel, hire a captain with experience in naval tactics, and send it out to hunt for booty."

"In addition, there is a great shortage of arms and munitions on the colonial side. The French islands are available. Also, there is a tiny island called St. Eustatius. It is under Dutch control. They are neutral, but trade is in the Dutchman's blood. Consequently, they will trade with all who come their way. Almost no facility to produce gunpowder or quantities of arms exists in the colonies. We stand to benefit handsomely in this area. One ship will run the British blockade and sail to the island. It will carry tobacco and rice. The Dutchmen can profitably transport them to other West Indian Islands and Europe. It will return with war material which we can sell to the colonial army at good prices."

"And the third vessel?" asked his wife.

"The third will temporarily be held in reserve," he answered, "Until we decide how to best exploit it."

"I believe your plan is sound," she said. "But I would suggest further caution. It would be prudent to change the ships' names. Also, ownership of the vessels must be concealed, so neither side is aware of the true owner. If the colonies win, you can say that you helped the war effort. If the English win, your activities will be unknown."

"Adroit moves, indeed," the husband commented. "You have just reaffirmed my belief as to why you do so well when we play at whist. A sharp mind engenders clever moves. I will discuss the best means to achieve secrecy with William Hunt. He is an excellent attorney and possessed of the utmost discretion."

Emily raised her eyebrows and said, "Speaking of Hunt senior, how do you regard young Hunt with respect to our daughter? She has confided to me an increasing attachment to him. I believe she would be amenable to marriage, providing we approve."

"She is a bit young and there are many beaus who would wish to wed her," the husband answered. "Quite a few are from wealthy families or successful in their own right. A doctor's prospects are never equal to those of a successful trader or merchant. However, not every trader or merchant is successful. Fortunes may be made, but they can very quickly be lost. A good physician is able to count on a steady income. We are afflicted from birth to grave and illness is ever present. Simon appears to be quite intelligent. He is from a good family, and my inquiries indicate he has the makings of an excellent doctor. Most of all, he seems to be extremely devoted to Gwendolyn. We both know she can be prickly at times. A tolerant husband may be required. I would favor the marriage."

"So, it shall be," said the wife. "I am certain the Hunts will likewise approve."

After their conversation, they went to a card table and resumed a game of whist.

The Second Continental Convention was to be held in Philadelphia on the 10th of May. Benjamin Rush had focused on becoming a delegate. His appointment hinged on outfoxing the conservative anti-war Quakers and other elite who ruled Philadelphia and the Pennsylvania Assembly.

Committees of Observation had been set up by the rebels in cities and towns throughout the colonies to observe and ultimately control the political landscape. As a member of the Committee in Philadelphia, Rush maneuvered carefully. He encouraged outcries from the city's journeymen, and the farming areas beyond it, for more equitable representation. As a result, the Assembly was expanded to provide them additional voting power.

The Doctor was in high humor. "Jonathan," he proclaimed, "My friends in the Assembly can now appoint me a delegate."

As the Convention approached, Wolfe assumed more duties. Besides making home and hospital visits, he was seeing more office patients. He and Rush met each morning. Jonathan would indicate whether a change in someone's health had occurred and what medications should be added or deleted. His mentor always had the final decision.

The Doctor's favorite prescriptive was calomel, which he recommended for virtually every gastrointestinal problem. It was powdered mercury chloride, white and tasteless. "It is the perfect purgative," he would say, and almost all his patients had at one time or another suffered the benefits of having their bowels thoroughly purged.

As Wolfe assumed the additional work, his mentor proposed a new idea. "Jonathan," he said, "I have been thinking of training more apprentices. I believe we should take on six. You and I will teach them.

They could attend lectures at the medical school and assist in the practice, thereby receiving both didactic and practical education."

"Sir," replied Wolfe, "Your proposal has great merit, but presently we are both heavily burdened."

"We are still young and can surely bear an increased load," Rush responded. "The Convention will not last long. I have thought on it very carefully and have already secured a nearby barn for their accommodation. Advertisements will be placed in various newspapers, both in Philadelphia and elsewhere."

Jonathan thought, "Once he has a bit between his teeth, nothing can stop him. It does not pay to contest a decision already determined."

Rush added, "In my enthusiasm, I failed to mention that we would charge a reasonable fee for our services. Of course, you would receive half the fee. The barn and advertising costs will be mine alone."

Within a few weeks applications were received, reviewed, and candidates chosen. A new phase of medical education had begun.

The Convention ended, and Rush reported that several things were accomplished. "The Articles of Confederation have been written, approved by the delegates, sent to the thirteen colonies and await their consent," he said. "In addition, a Continental Army has been established and George Washington appointed its Commander in Chief."

XI

In Boston, before dawn on June 14th, General Gage was awakened from a sound sleep. "General," a colonel reported, "The colonials have fortified a hill on Charlestown Heights."

A conference was called and Gage asked for thoughts on the matter. Generals Clinton and Howe were at the meeting. Both had recently come from Europe.

Clinton spoke first, saying, "It should prove a simple task. The navy can bombard the hill and land troops at the neck of the peninsula whereon it stands. The colonials will be trapped and either surrender or die."

Howe felt otherwise. Eager for combat, he said, "Arriving here, I was informed that at Concord a mob of rebels had somehow managed to force a British retreat. The belief has spread that we are unable to crush their miserable attempt to defy our King. There is only one way to show the power of the English Throne. A direct assault by red-coated regulars will reveal the rebels' puniness and the might of our Monarch."

General Gage was also aroused. He agreed with Howe, saying, "You will be given 2,300 light infantry and grenadiers. The navy will begin shelling the hill immediately. Good luck, General."

"Thank you, sir," Howe answered, saluting.

Awaiting the British, the colonials were slightly fewer in numbers but well positioned. In the center, within a newly built wooden fort, were 300 men. Outside it, center, left, and right, were the remainder.

Upon landing, Howe was determined to move forward. "Our artillery is mired in mud near the shoreline and must be left behind," he told his aides. "However, we will begin the attack with 1,100 regulars on our right wing against the enemy left. It is their weakest point."

Advancing with his men, Howe called, "Take your time, we have a way to go."

The redcoats moved across flat and then ascending ground. At any moment they expected to receive fire from the American line. Advancing, Howe shouted, "Quicken the pace." His officers' calls echoed his. "Quicken your pace, men," they cried.

Moving at quickstep time, the regulars passed 200, and 100 yards. At 50 yards they would begin to charge with fixed bayonets. The colonial artillery had begun firing. At the 50 yards' mark, colonial muskets abruptly joined. "Fire now! Fire now!" shouted the American commanders. The redcoats staggered as gunfire erupted into sheets of flame and smoke. Rebel muskets were repeatedly reloaded and discharged. "Aim for where their white straps cross in the middle," they were told, and the advice was followed.

"Fill the ranks! Fill the ranks!" shouted Howe. At his call, thinning ranks of redcoats were brought together, and somehow maintained. Again and again, Howe demanded that the regulars attack. Each time, they were beaten back.

Casualties mounted and Howe realized his men could no longer respond.

Reinforcements requested earlier had still not arrived. "I have 1,200 regulars standing ready," Howe thought, as he moved to his center and left wing. "The able-bodied from our right are fairly spent but can fill the rear ranks." He drew his sword. "Forward," he ordered.

Now the terrain differed. It was a steady climb toward the great redoubt near the top of Breed's Hill. The response also differed. At 300 yards, American artillery commanders shouted, "Commence firing." Gaps began to appear in the English lines. At 200 yards, riflemen from the colonial right and left began to fire. "Look for the officers," one called, and the favorite target became English officers.

Absorbing the American fire and taking losses, the British came on, certain they would break the enemy. "The colonials were supposed to flee," the advancing lines thought. "Why in hell do they still stand fast?"

"Onward, men," Howe called. The English crossed beyond 100 yards, and some colonials began to fire their muskets. Their officers shouted, "Stop firing. Muskets are not accurate at a distance. Wait patiently, we will fire at 25 yards." Firing ceased and the men nervously awaited the oncoming foe.

Abruptly, at 25 yards, "Fire now!" was ordered. Again, sheets of flame sprang from the colonials. "My God," a British officer cried out, as he realized the carnage being suffered by the regulars. He had been struck by a musket ball but moved ahead. Then, shot again and mortally wounded, he fell, dying alongside his men who continued to be torn apart as the assault failed.

Unwounded, Howe ordered a retreat. "We must await fresh troops," he said. They finally arrived, and he called, "Advance, we will succeed!" The red lines again came up Breed's Hill. The colonials' ammunition was low and finally gone. The redoubt was stormed. Some of the Americans within fought to the end, dying by bayonet and sword. Others were shot down trying to escape.

Part of the rebel forces retreated to Bunker Hill, further back on the peninsula. Finally, all heeded the call, "To the boats." Both the wounded and able fled to the narrow tail of the peninsula. There, they were carried to safety by waiting skiffs and rowboats.

Howe, always in the midst of the battle and still unscathed, looked about him and gritted his teeth. He spoke almost aloud, "Devastation and destruction have befallen us. Gage sent reinforcements and victory was gained, but a hollow one. The Americans losses are far outnumbered by the dead and wounded among my regulars. Good officers and good men have been killed or severely wounded. It has been a terrible lesson. When they are dug in and well led, it appears the colonials can withstand repeated assaults."

At headquarters, General Gage was shaken to his core. General Clinton sipped a glass of his preferred wine. Taking a napkin, he dabbed his lips and softly whispered, "My plan was the better, Howe. Your victory was dear-bought, another such would ruin us."

For the English, disengagement and time to lick their wounds was necessary. During the weeks and months ahead, entrenchments were made to defend any attempt by the arriving General Washington to attack. He reached Cambridge on the 2nd of July. Colonial militia had gathered and awaited their new Commander. The British were confined to Boston, the Royal Navy their only means of supply.

Washington busied himself immediately. "We have 15,000 militiamen," he said, "Untrained, undisciplined, and often officered by equally poorly trained men and totally inadequate political appointees. Gage has far fewer troops, but they are highly trained and well fortified. Above all, he has heavy artillery and the British Navy. We lack both."

Into the beginning of 1776, a stalemate existed. The British held Boston but the surrounding area was under colonial control.

Despite the fighting's support in New England, the majority of the citizenry still desired accommodation with England. Many were totally uninvolved. Tories actively supported the Crown in New York. Germans favoring George III, a Hanoverian King, Scots and Quakers feeling allegiance to the Crown, conservative religious groups, and a majority of professionals were among those siding with the English. Many hearts were with the minutemen, but their minds had not yet determined to move toward supporting the war and full separation.

XII

The Second Convention completed its work in July 1775. A month later, Rush met the daughter of Richard Stockton, a New Jersey delegate. She was sixteen years old.

"Jonathan," he confessed, "I am a different man. I have met my lifetime mate. Her name is Julia. She is bright, lively and enchanting. I am many years her senior. But, when I am with her, I feel like a lad of twenty consumed by love."

Wolfe smiled, saying, "You have had good fortune, sir. You must continue to visit her."

"Yes, but I require your assistance," Rush answered. "The Convention is over but they will burden me with other duties. If I gain Stockton's approval to court her, I must prove myself a determined suitor. I will leave each Friday after seeing patients and travel to New Jersey, returning Monday. I trust you can adjust to the added load."

"Sir, you have my full support. I will manage," Wolfe answered.

Benjamin Rush's pursuit of Julia Stockton bore fruit. On January 11, 1776, they were married at her parents' estate. Apologizing for not inviting him to the wedding, Rush said, "You must remain here, Jonathan. Both of us cannot be away at the same time."

"Certainly, sir," Wolfe replied. "Time to move," he thought, and found quarters at Mrs. Appleton's boarding house.

Discussing it, Grace said, "You're making a wise decision, Jonathan. A point has been reached where some degree of separation is required. Doctor Rush and his wife need space to nurture their relationship. You need to feel more your own man. You do not have to live under the same roof to work together. However," she laughed, blushing at the same time, "You can always move to the McKenzie home."

"I hope that will be soon," he answered. "I want to marry you, Grace. However, I will not marry until my position is secure."

"Jonathan," she softly replied, "Doctor Rush is much older than you, and felt some urgency in his pursuit and marriage to Miss Stockton. Still, we met over eight months ago. In April, it will be a year. People often become engaged at that time. You must also consider my feelings. I love you and you love me. Please do not hesitate too long."

As their courtship continued, Jonathan and Grace stole every possible moment to be together, meeting at the McKenzie home, in coffee houses, or walking arm in arm through the streets. They engaged in long conversations about the war, teaching, medicine, and especially their feelings regarding one another. As the days and weeks turned into months, their love became deeper and continued to draw them closer.

Grace had become interested in Shakespeare. "Listen to his sonnets," she said, and Jonathan smiled as she read them. Afterward, she urged, "Now, we can read the plays together, I will do the female and you the male roles."

Jonathan loved hearing her voice and seeing Grace's eyes shining with delight, as they discussed a sonnet's meaning or a play's characters. He knew the time to broach engagement and marriage was at hand.

A letter interrupted any such discussion. Usually calm, he felt a sense of concern as he opened the envelope. His concern turned to anxiety as he read the contents.

"Dear Jonathan,

I am obliged to bring you difficult news. First, calm your fears. We are all safe. Rose and Ethan are here with me. She was several months with child and has miscarried. Urged on by the British, the Indians have attacked farms in the upper Mohawk, and they were forced to flee their home.

Ethan was able to slay one brave, but suffered a ball in the shoulder. He lost a large amount of blood and hid in the woods with Rose. You well know your sister. She was helping, loading one rifle as he fired a second. When he was wounded, she shot a charging savage. As he fell, he struck her in the belly. That, and the entire ordeal, caused her to lose the child. They are both weak, but very happy to be safe with us.

Samuel exploded with rage on learning what had happened. He has left to join volunteers fighting the Indians. I am concerned about him. He is now near fifty and not as robust as he claims. However, he has been on such campaigns before and returned without injury. I pray he again will be fortunate.

If you can come home for several days, it would be a great help to both Rose and Ethan. Her spirit is low. Seeing you would help restore it. Also, Ethan's wound is not doing well.

If you cannot come, we understand that circumstances do not allow it.

Your loving aunt, Isabel"

Wolfe recalled the wedding between Rose and Ethan Thorne. It had occurred just three weeks before he left for his apprenticeship. Rose was sixteen and Ethan twenty. They were deeply in love and it was not uncommon for couples to marry at even younger ages. After the wedding, Samuel and Jonathan had gone with them further up the Mohawk. Ethan had acquired one hundred acres of meadow and timber just beyond a tiny village and had almost completed building a cabin. All four worked hard and finished it quickly. It was small but tightly caulked, wind tight, and the chimney drew well. Best of all, the Indians nearby were peaceful and the area was considered safe.

Jonathan felt a wave of despair sweep over him. He was certain the severity of the injuries to Ethan and Rose was understated. He had obligations to Doctor Rush, to their patients, and to the apprentices. He was also supposed to dine with Grace in two days. Despite misgivings, Jonathan spoke to his mentor.

"Sir," he said, "News from home causes me concern."

The Doctor looked up. "What is happening?" he asked.

"Savages have attacked my sister and her husband at their farm. She was with child and miscarried and he was wounded. They are both now with my aunt. I must go to them."

"There is certainly reason to worry, Jonathan. But what is most important, they have reached safety. This is not an opportune time. However, I would be remiss if I did not advise you to leave for home in the morning. Tonight we will put together instruments and supplies. Is there a competent physician in the area?"

"There was," said Wolfe, "But Aunt Isabel had written that he passed away."

"Jonathan, you are no longer an apprentice but a fully vetted physician. You may be required to be with your family for some time. Fortunately, I no longer must spend time in Congress. Also, we started the new program and have the six apprentices. Several of them are reasonably competent at this stage and can assist in the practice. All will have to help. Actually, it may well improve their education."

"I can manage here. Realize that further attacks may occur. You could well be the only physician within fifty miles. Beside your relatives, others may need your assistance. I am requiring you to stay until the conflict subsides. Only then should you return."

"Truly, you are being more than generous, sir."

"Do not thank me so quickly. If all the tribes rise up, you could find yourself and your family in grave danger."

"I am aware of the possibility, but doubt it will happen."

"Pray to the Almighty it doesn't happen, Jonathan. Pray very hard."

"I will do that also," Wolfe smiled.

Lighting oil lanterns, they repaired to a shed adjacent to the house. Rush packed two large saddlebags, placing scalpels, scissors, a saw, forceps, clamps, needles and catgut into one. In the other, he stuffed bandages, cotton wadding, and miscellaneous supplies.

Jonathan, observing the material, stammered, "Sir, you know I have not been trained as a surgeon."

Rush laughed. "Neither have I, but this equipment is always kept for an emergency. If a battle gets hot and the wounded are bleeding and dying, none will ask whether or not you trained as a surgeon. All that will matter is that you are a doctor and available."

The usually solemn Rush now had a twinkle n his eyes. "You obviously do not know the secret code of surgeons. Dying, a surgical friend whispered it to me. *'See one, do one, teach one.'* You may not have seen a grievous wound repaired or an amputation performed, but you have studied anatomy and know it well. In my library is a treatise on the care and treatment of battle wounds by a French military surgeon, a man of copious experience. It makes good sense and excellent reading. I have translated it into English and possess but one copy. It is yours for the duration of come what may. So, unless you find a skilled surgeon to watch and thereby learn how to mend or amputate, you will be obliged to skip the see and start with the do."

Wolfe had turned pale during his mentor's discussion, but stiffened his spine and nodded acknowledgment. Later, he wrote a letter to Grace.

"Dearest Grace,

I am unable to keep our meeting. Family members have been injured during an Indian attack. I must leave forthwith for home and may be there for a time. I will write and keep you informed of the situation.

Please give my regards to your family.

I miss you already,

Jonathan."

Wolfe rose well before dawn, washed, shaved and dressed. At the Rush home, the Doctor was already awake and clothed. Together, they had a quick breakfast. Jonathan's horse, Cromwell, had been brought from a nearby hostelry and saddled. Behind it, rain gear and a blanket were neatly tied and the heavily filled saddlebags had been placed.

Rush grasped Jonathan's hand, his face slightly flushed with unusual emotion. He said, "Good luck, Jonathan, whatever happens, I have faith in God and your ability to see yourself through. Also, do not push the horse. A worn out horse is of no value."

"Yes, sir," Wolfe replied and gave a military salute.

From an upstairs window, Julia waved. Alice ran out of the house, hugged him, and kissed his cheek. "Take care, Doctor Jonathan. We know you will return safely," she said.

Jonathan waved, swung aboard his horse and started the journey. He had over two hundred and fifty miles to cover and was anxious to move quickly, but stopped at Grace's house. When he arrived, it was still before dawn. All was silent. He slipped the letter beneath the door, mounted his horse and moved ahead.

Three hours later, the family was readying for church. Grace found the letter. Recognizing Jonathan's hand, she tore the envelope open. Reading it, her eyes filled with tears. "Men are such fools," Grace cried to Martha, "particularly Jonathan Wolfe. There is trouble at home and he had to leave hurriedly. But he was here. How silly, to think he was doing me a service by not awakening me. I would much rather spend five minutes with him before daybreak then one or two hours in church at nine." Dropping the letter onto a table, she sank into a parlor chair.

Martha moved to comfort her. She hugged Grace saying, "I understand how you must feel but he will return to you."

"Martha, I am so in love with that silly man. Jonathan has been very occupied with medicine but has managed to be with me as often as possible. It has not been frequent enough. You know he has been at the house and at the Golden Eagle. But we have also been meeting at coffeehouses or just strolling about."

Martha frowned and looked worried.

"Oh, don't frown like some prude, Martha. Jonathan has been a perfect gentleman and I am too concerned with proprieties to do unladylike things. Sometimes I wish I had."

"Grace Lockhart, you scandalize me." Martha replied.

"Martha, I am sure you and Harold skipped about more than we knew. When people are in love, they want to be alone with one another."

Martha blushed and laughed. "My little sister is very clever. I love her dearly. I am sure your silly man will come back safe and sound, and anxious to be with you again."

Grace smiled, wiped her tears, and said, "It's wonderful to have a sister like you."

XIII

The trip North was difficult and slower than Jonathan had expected. Frequent rains turned roads into mud. A brook became a river and he was forced to wait till the waters subsided before crossing. Doctor Rush had insisted he bring heavy rain gear. It served effectively as protection from the elements and as a ground cover. Most nights he slept by the road, his horse tied to a tree. Sometimes he had been lucky to find a farmer willing to lend his barn and provide breakfast for a small fee. On two occasions payment was refused, after he had been asked in a neighborly way the purpose of his trip.

Wolfe arrived at the smithy and at once felt he was home. The sun was setting and the building shone in a golden light. The large doors had been bolted shut. Unaccustomed silence pressed around him. Jonathan stopped his horse and fell into a reverie of bygone days when he had worked side-by-side with his father. The buzzing of bees in a nearby stand of clover recalled him to the present. He urged the horse forward and rode to the house. Smoke rose from its single chimney. Almost immediately the door flew open and Isabel came running toward him. Wolfe sprang from the horse and caught her in his arms.

"Jonathan, Jonathan," she cried. "I was not sure you would come."

"I would never have hesitated," he said, hugging her tightly. They clung together for several minutes. Then Isabel exclaimed, "You must be hungry after your journey. Supper is almost ready. Come inside, Rose and Ethan will be anxious to see you."

"I want to see them as well. First, I must attend to the horse. It has carried me all this distance and is very tired."

After seeing to his mount, Jonathan entered the house. He started towards the stairs but Isabel stopped him.

"Jonathan, the situation is not the same as when I wrote you. Rose is still quite weak, but she is improving. Ethan is not well. The shoulder is inflamed and he has a high fever. I placed them in my and Samuel's bedroom."

Wolfe bounded up the stairs and entered the room. "Jonathan," Rose cried on seeing him. She stood up and started forward, but weakness overcame her. She stumbled and Wolfe caught her, brought her up against him and gave her a brotherly kiss.

"Oh, it's so good to see you," Rose said.

"I would have flown here if I could."

"Jonathan," she interrupted. "I am truly recovering. It is Ethan who has been getting sicker. The ball is still in his shoulder. There is no one nearby capable of removing it. He has been fevered and this morning was calling out nonsense. Please see to him."

Wolfe turned to the bed where his brother-in-law lay. Ethan was sweating profusely. His brow was hot, his face drawn and flushed, and he had a weak, rapid pulse. The entry wound was surrounded by ten inches of inflamed skin. Checking behind, he found no exit site. Ethan groaned as he was settled back. Opening his eyes momentarily, he appeared to recognize Jonathan, smiled weakly and was again asleep.

Looking at his sister, Wolfe said, "Ethan is very ill, Rose. We both know the ball must be removed. I am not a surgeon. Still, I will have to undertake it. Not tonight, however, it's growing dark and good light is required."

"Yes, I understand," Rose answered, "but will he survive?"

"He will till tomorrow. Then, it is up to surgery and God."

"He must live, Jonathan," she said, sinking back in her chair as tears ran down her cheeks. "I am certain you will do your best," Rose sobbed.

"Yes, I will," he answered and pressed her shoulder softly. "I have to go downstairs now," he said. "Aunt Isabel is waiting and I must eat. Please don't try to come down. We will bring dinner to you."

Wolfe and his aunt ate a hasty dinner. He explained the situation to her and the need to operate.

Gathering a tray for Rose, Isabel said, "I want to bring sugared water upstairs. Perhaps we can have Ethan drink some. It may be of help."

Returning to the bedroom, they urged Rose to eat. Wolfe went to Ethan. The ill man opened his eyes and mumbled. Jonathan snatched the water and brought it to his blistered lips. He started to drink and swallow as Wolfe slowly elevated the glass.

"A good sign," the doctor smiled. He kissed the women gently, saying, "I must retire to bed, my beloveds."

Jonathan did not immediately get into bed. As night descended, he lit a candle and unpacked the treatise Rush had given him. Turning the pages he came to the section labeled "Penetrating Battle Wounds" and commenced reading his mentor's translation.

It began, "What is essential in almost every instance is to remove the ball, shot, metal fragments or wooden splinters. An exception is where an exploded shell has cast multiple fragments into the body.

Removal of all may not be possible or even desirable. Attend to the major wounds. Small fragments, not involving vital structures, can be left for later or ignored. Remember, too great a time exploring, or too great a loss of blood by virtue of extensive surgery is not helpful. Think to consider the patient as a whole. Furthermore, during the surgery it is necessary to proceed quickly. Careful thoughts before the procedure are the ones most likely to assist."

"In contrast to multiple fragment injuries, gunshot wounds are often single. When several are present, an already dead patient usually presents."

"If the projectile has entered into the depths of the chest or abdomen there is no hope. A mortal injury is present. I have seen rare survivors, but always without interference by the surgeon. God has ordained the recovery."

"On the other hand, a penetrating injury to a limb can almost always be satisfactorily operated upon. If there are both entry and exit wounds, careful packing to control bleeding is the method of choice. Where no exit of the missile has occurred, it must be removed."

"A probe should be inserted into the wound. Carefully follow the tract. Do not push the probe too hard. Handle it gently, as you should a woman. It is essential not to create false tracts. With slow, delicate sounding, you will feel the ball or shot. Leave the probe in place. Use the knife. Enlarge the opening of the wound. Place a forceps and follow the probe. Once at its end, you can feel the forceps touch the object. Remove the probe. Grasp the object with the forceps, exiting it with care."

"Very often a bit of fabric or leather from a garment will also be removed. Look for this. It is important that nothing foreign to the body is permitted to stay behind. Excise any tissue that appears dead. Particularly debride the mouth of the wound. It must be added, that even after several attempts failure may persist. If so, wound enlargement must be done. Insert the forefinger and use it as both probe and extractor. Bleeding, however, will be greater and more tissue will be damaged."

"Packing can usually stop bleeding from either procedure. Indeed, packing the wound is essential, both to control bleeding and maintain wound drainage. Never close the wound. Leave the packing in place at least three days. Withdraw it slowly. If bleeding recurs, repack. On occasion, heavy bleeding obliges use of a flamed iron to sear the tract. Unfortunately, this is sometimes caused by erosion of a large vessel. If so, it is a harbinger of death."

Wolfe read the passages three times. Then, having committed them to memory, he placed the translation on his night table. Jonathan disrobed, blew out the candle, crawled beneath the covers, and was promptly asleep.

September's end brought a chill to the morning air. Wolfe did not awake until almost nine. The sun was already well above the horizon. He sprang from bed and washed, shaved, and dressed. Passing by the larger bedroom, he found the door slightly open. Ethan was tossing about and mumbling incoherently. Rose sipped coffee and was anxiously looking at her husband, but smiled bravely at her brother. He started to enter but, on hearing men's voices downstairs, threw a kiss and descended the stairs.

Two men were standing in the kitchen, drinking coffee with his aunt. "Good morning, Jonathan," she said. "Nathan Forest and Thad Driscoll have arrived early."

He remembered Forest from years before. They smiled at each other in recognition. Thad Driscoll was unfamiliar to him but also smiled back. The men shook hands. Both were in the fifties, sturdy and well muscled.

Isabel said, "These men are wonderful neighbors and came with no hesitation. They have already brought the dining table outdoors."

"I appreciate your coming on short notice," said Wolfe.

"Glad to help," they replied simultaneously.

"Permit me to have some coffee, and we can start. I must also get my instruments."

"I already unpacked them," Isabel said. "Sometime in your travels, those saddlebags were covered by muddy water. It seeped inside. In one, most of the wrappings were filthy but the things within were unharmed. Your instruments were in the other. They were soiled by dirt and mud. I washed them, but boiling was required to get them clean. I hope it did no harm."

"I am sure it caused no harm," Jonathan answered and, drinking down the last of his coffee, went outside. With Nathan and Thad, he positioned the table and a narrow board so Ethan would lie with his left arm extended outward and pointed at the sun.

"All possible light must be on the wound," Wolfe said. "I don't want even my shadow to interfere with seeing properly."

They carried the wounded man from his room and placed him on the table. He was groaning but, once there and covered by a blanket, the sun's warmth seemed to soothe him. He became quiet and slept.

"He must be held tightly," Wolfe said. "Any movement will cause problems."

"More help would prove useful," Thad opined.

The neighbors positioned themselves so as to restrain the patient. As Jonathan was preparing to begin the surgery, Robert Calder rode up, jumped from his horse and ran to help. "Just in time," they called, and he was assigned the arm belonging to the wounded shoulder. Aunt Isabel held the opposite one, and each of the other men a leg.

Jonathan began and tried to be as gentle as possible. Still, as the probe was pushed deeper, Thorne thrashed about.

Twice Wolfe tried, but on both attempts felt it necessary to withdraw the instrument. "I am afraid of creating a false passage," he said to his helpers.

Jonathan was perspiring heavily, sweat poured from the end of his nose and chin into the wound. He put the instrument down, straightened, and jiggled his back. Then he said, "Gentlemen, Aunt Isabel, please hold him very tightly."

The others were also covered with sweat, but they nodded and stood to the task. Again, the doctor grasped the probe and gently advanced it. This time he felt metal.

"We're there," he said.

They all gripped Ethan firmly. Jonathan incised the opening and placed the forceps. He removed the probe, closed the forceps and slowly withdrew it. The ball was in its grasp. Wolfe held it up for all to see, and then dropped it into a cup held by Isabel.

The wound started to bleed, but he recognized it as venous and it subsided. The doctor paused to think and realized no fabric had come with the missile. He tightened his jaw, urged his helpers to again hold Ethan, and repeated the procedure. This time he felt no metal, but placed the forceps, closed it and felt it grip something. He withdrew the instrument and with it a small bit of charred fabric. Further bleeding required packing and pressure, but it was controlled. He placed a bulky wad of cotton and cloth, securing them with wrapping.

Isabel and the men crowded about Jonathan, congratulating him. He was overjoyed at the success of the surgery. However, peering at his brother-in-law, he was not sure that it had been of much help. The signs were not good. Indeed, Ethan was very pale and not easily responsive. "Nevertheless," Wolfe thought, "He is alive and there is hope."

Thorne was wrapped in a blanket and brought to the bedroom. Rose insisted on staying at his bedside, kissing her husband's brow and holding his hand. Ethan started to shiver and more quilts were applied to keep him warm.

Once back in the kitchen, Isabel poured each neighbor a substantial amount of whiskey. Wolfe shook each man's hand and thanked him. As they departed, Isabel gave them a hug and kissed their cheek. As the door closed behind them, she said to Jonathan, "Good neighbors are one of God's treasures."

For the next seventy-two hours Ethan's condition deteriorated. The fevers were more extreme, his pallor took on a faint blue coloring, breathing became more rapid, and he was more difficult to awaken. On the fourth day, as Jonathan started to remove the pus-coated packing, he noted that Ethan was less fevered and the red discoloration about the wound had lessened.

Every day thereafter, improvement progressed. On the fifth day, he opened his eyes. On the sixth, Ethan was able to take some liquid. He lay in bed wasted, eyes sunken, lips parted slightly and covered with scabbed sores. He could barely whisper and was asleep almost constantly. But he was alive, and each succeeding day appeared stronger.

Seven days after the surgery, the packing was fully removed. Copious quantities of pus continued to exit the wound, but the swollen inflamed area had almost fully cleared. Jonathan decided to repack the wound and keep it open.

As the doctor began, his brother-in-law tried to watch. He bore the pain but, after a few moments, turned his head. Jonathan noticed and teased him gently. "Brother, your constitution has unique qualities of stamina and the ability to take a ball and survive. You hold still, but turn your head. Why does this small business trouble your sight?"

"It requires a strong stomach to do such work," Ethan responded. "I commend you, brother, on your stomach. While my constitution may be strong, my stomach churns to see such things, particularly when they are being done to me."

Wolfe laughed. He had no doubt his patient was well on the way to recovery.

Two weeks had passed since Jonathan's return. Ethan was making steady progress. Rose was fully recovered, though still mourning the lost child. Samuel had been gone for over four weeks with no word received. Then, news came of clashes between the settlers and the Indians. Casualties on both sides had occurred, but no details were available.

Wolfe spoke to his aunt at breakfast. "Aunt Isabel, we are both trying not to show our worry. There must be wounded and possibly dead. Some may be our neighbors or even Samuel. I would be derelict to not provide assistance."

He continued, "I have checked my horse. He seems in fine condition. Yesterday, I took the opportunity to open the smithy and shoe him. Upstairs, Rose is doing well. This morning, I plan to remove

Ethan's packing. If the wound looks healthy, I will not replace it. Under those circumstances, either you or Rose can change the dressings."

"I hate to see you leave, Jonathan. You have been in my sight for only a short time. However, you are correct. Let me see to Ethan's wound with you. Show me how to care for it. If satisfied with its appearance, you can leave with our blessing."

Jonathan spent the remainder of the morning writing to Grace and Doctor Rush. To his mentor, he attributed the operation's success to his excellent translation of the medical treatise. In closing, he noted the recent reports of battle and the need for him to help the wounded. To Grace, he said that he was still needed at home. Finally, he wrote,

"I do not know if you miss me as much as I miss you."

"Grace dearest, you are forever in my thoughts and in my heart."

Following letter writing and checking Ethan's wound, Wolfe said his goodbyes. As he was about to leave, Isabel confessed she had again boiled the instruments.

"I am not ordinarily a superstitious woman," she said. "But perhaps the boiling did something that helped Ethan. Perhaps it will help some other injured person. Please don't be upset with me, Jonathan."

"I can never be upset with you, Aunt Isabel," Wolfe said "Strange things sometimes happen." He mounted Cromwell and rode to the general store in their small village, added beef jerky to his supplies and posted the letters.

"Any more news regarding the conflict with the Indians?" Jonathan asked.

The proprietor shook his head, "We only know there was a fight to our northwest."

Wolfe left, and pointed his horse northwest. “Move forward,” he urged, and put the horse into a canter. As the road became a cart path and Cromwell started to breathe heavily, he recalled Rush’s advice and slowed the pace.

Following directions provided by those met along his way, he moved steadily over narrow paths, streams and thickly wooded terrain. On the third day, he and Cromwell were deep within a forest. Following a stream, he came to a small clearing. As he rode into it, two men dressed in homespun appeared. Their rifles were pointed at him and held ready to fire. Looking at them, they seemed much the worse for wear.

“Come ahead slowly,” said the taller of the two. Seeing Jonathan’s rifle slung alongside his saddle, the man relaxed slightly. “State your business, stranger,” he called. ”This is colonial territory.”

“I am Jonathan Wolfe,” he replied. “I am looking for my father.”

“You’re Samuel’s boy? I remember you as a tyke. I haven’t seen you since then. I’m Frederick Willow.” He grinned, came forward, reached out and grasped Jonathan’s hand. “Shorty, here, is Martin Packer. He doesn’t look like much, but he’s a good man in a fight. Your Pa is our captain. He’s up that path.”

“It’s good to meet an old friend, and make a new one,” Wolfe said, shaking each man’s hand. “I’m glad I came across you two. I gather you’re standing guard duty.”

“We are,” said Willow. “The Indians are probably close by. We have engaged them on and off for several weeks. It’s been a rough campaign. They’re well led and well armed. We are winning, but we’ve had losses also.”

“True enough,” Packer seconded.

Wolfe dismounted Cromwell and led the way through heavy undergrowth and between tall pine trees and huge oaks. At times, the forest was almost impenetrable. Eventually, an open area appeared. Men were scattered about, resting, whispering softly to one another, or cleaning weapons. They looked up as he entered the glen.

A stocky figure rose and wordlessly hurried toward him. It was Samuel and he signaled for silence. Reaching his son, he grabbed him in a bear hug not felt since adolescence. Samuel released him and stepped back. "You are the most welcome sight I have seen these past weeks," he whispered.

"And you are the dirtiest graybeard I have seen in six months," Jonathan whispered back, smiling at his father.

"I'm certain I am," the older man said. "This has been a hard several weeks. No chance to bathe, no fires, close engagements. We've been living on beef jerky, berries and nuts. I must have lost twenty pounds. But we have been pushing them back. In our last fight, I think we came near to breaking them. But why are you here, Jonathan?"

"I'm here because of you. We heard of battles, but nothing else. You've been gone these past four weeks. Isabel is very anxious about you. Besides, I am a doctor and thought I might prove useful."

"Of course, doctor," his father grinned. "You, your medical bag, and your rifle are all welcome. Am I permitted to ask if you still know how to shoot?"

Wolfe smiled in return and answered "Yes, I still know how, and I even cleaned my rifle before starting for here."

"Tell me about home, son," Samuel urged.

"Let me unload the horse and provide for him. Then we can talk."

Jonathan performed his tasks and rejoined his father. Word he was Samuel's son and a physician spread among the men. Several crowded close to where they were whispering. Jonathan told of his arrival at the house, that Isabel was fine, and Rose had almost fully recovered. Then he told of the surgery he had performed on Ethan.

"I was most fearful for him," Samuel said. "But I could not help there. I had to fight. Thank the Lord you came home and removed the ball. I am so proud of you, son. You have fulfilled our every dream."

The doctor blushed. "You are making too much of it. But since you now are aware of my capability, can I help with any of the wounded?"

"The men have some minor injuries which they usually care for themselves," Samuel replied, "but you can check them." Then, bowing his head added, "We started with sixty-five, so far we have lost five men, two yesterday. You might have saved them, but they had severe wounds and died during the night. We buried them early this morning."

As he finished speaking, Samuel suddenly held up his hand to signal for complete silence. He listened intently. "Too many bird-calls," he whispered to Jonathan. Again, he signaled. The men hurriedly recovered their weapons and supplies, and moved into the edges of the woods.

Sixty men were now standing with weapons readied. About a third faced the clearing, a similar number moved into the forest, the remainder held the mid-ground, prepared to reinforce in either direction. No specific orders had been given. Samuel had trained them well. Each man knew where and how to position himself. Jonathan brought Cromwell into the woods, tied him to a tree, removed the saddlebags and hid them under fallen hemlock branches. Taking his rifle from the horse's side, he rejoined his father.

Three braves cautiously entered the glen. The men remained silent. The Indian scouts explored the site, judging how recently it had been evacuated. For several minutes they stayed bent over, close to the ground and circling slowly. Then they exited where they had entered. Birdcalls soon followed.

Suddenly, a large party burst into the clearing. They were almost directly opposite the colonists and perhaps fifty yards away. "Fire now," Samuel called. He was the first to discharge his weapon, and a fusillade from his men's rifles immediately followed. Several braves fell. The others spread out, hugging the fringes of the woods or moving deeper into the forest. Taking advantage of available cover, they moved forward.

Samuel's men were assigned in pairs. One fired and reloaded as the second stood ready to shoot. A hiding Indian might charge after he heard the first shot, thinking the enemy was busy reloading. The second colonist would bring him down. In this way, they maintained an almost continuous fire. But the braves still came on, reinforced by more warriors.

"Watch the woods," Samuel shouted. Half the reinforcements shifted to strengthen that perimeter. The Indians continued to add more warriors to their wood-side attack. Samuel and Jonathan moved to confront the onslaught from that quarter, and his father signaled the remainder to follow.

The fight in the forest hung in the balance. The Indians surged forward, attacking with courage, determination, and ferocity. The battle raged for two long hours. The red men rallied and pressed forward three times, but on each occasion were forced to give way. On the fourth charge, it became close combat. Both sides were wielding rifle butts, tomahawks, axes, and knives. Some were fighting with bare fists, clawing and ripping at one another. There was a crescendo of curses and howls, of fighting bodies and flowing blood.

Three Indians came at Samuel as he was in the midst of reloading his rifle. Seeing them about to close, he reached for his axe and flung it with great strength, striking the nearest brave full in the chest. The force of the blow stopped the man in his tracks and he fell to the ground mortally wounded. Jonathan fired and took down the second warrior. Raising his rifle, Samuel struck with its butt at the third just a moment too late. The blow could not fully stop the charge. His opponent swung his tomahawk hard. Although partially deflected by the rifle, it smashed deeply into Samuel's left shoulder. He fell backward, bleeding profusely, and was pushed to the ground with his enemy atop him.

The Indian paused momentarily, readying to swing the weapon once more. Fighting was everywhere, but Jonathan focused on his father barely ten feet away. Racing to Samuel, the discharged rifle's butt held high, he struck with all his power at the head of the brave. The raised tomahawk had begun to descend, but Jonathan's blow felled the warrior. He fell to the side, his weapon lying alongside him. As the older Wolfe crawled away, his son continued to viciously pound at the red man. Finally, as though suddenly seeing his foe's bloodied, smashed head, he stopped and sank to the ground.

The battle continued about them. Impervious to it, Jonathan sat, slowly recovering his composure. He moved to his father's side and cradled the older man's head in his arms. Samuel was alert, though bleeding heavily. Wolfe examined the wound. It was to the bone, slicing deeply through the shoulder muscle. Ripping apart his own shirt, he pushed portions into the wound. Positioning his father's right hand over the improvised packing, he said, "Press as hard as you can."

Samuel nodded with understanding, as his son turned to survey the scene and reload their weapons.

The engagement drew to a close. Those Indians able to force hand-to-hand combat had been beaten back. Most had never penetrated so closely. Despite the braves' prowess at using the woods as cover to advance, they had been halted by the colonists' effective gunfire and skill in close quarters battle. His father, convinced the fighting had ended, signaled the men to move back into the clearing.

"Count the bodies of the Indian dead and tally our losses," Samuel ordered.

Using the supplies he had brought, Jonathan tended the more seriously injured. Opening the instruments, he used clamps to stop large vessel bleeding, catgut for ties, and packing for less active blood loss. Heavy packing and pressure were employed where he was unable to secure larger bleeding vessels.

Wolfe returned to his father. Samuel slumped against a saddlebag, and Jonathan used fresh packing to redo the wound. Wearily looking at his son, the older man said, "I believe there were well over one hundred savages." Receiving his men's reports, he added, "We recovered the bodies of eight braves, and perhaps four times that number have been wounded. Their dying and wounded have been carried away. They left behind their dead. For the time being, they are broken."

Samuel continued, "We have lost four dead, six are badly wounded. Ten, like me, are less damaged and many have small wounds. We are all exhausted."

Looking at his shoulder's bloody dressings and then at his son, he said, "You saved my life today, Jonathan. Your father owes you a great debt. Certainly, the whole frontier owes a great debt to the men who stood, fought, and died here this day and during these past four weeks. I have been examining an axe we found. It is undoubtedly English and newly made. We know King George has armed the Indians. Only two rifles have been recovered. They were made in the colonies, but they too could have come from British hands. Setting this area aflame is a mean but effective policy. It is meant to divert us from the more important fight. The Indians think that by attacking us, they are defending their territory. But, if we are obliged to, we will kill every one of them without mercy."

Peering across the clearing, he pointed and said, "I have lost many friends in this struggle. Frederick Willow was cut to pieces. Across there is Shorty Packer, leaning over his comrade's body. He is mourning and I am mourning. But what are we to tell Frederick's widow and children? What are we to tell all the widows? What shall we say to all the children? I am not a man given to weeping, but it tears my heart to think of telling them their men are dead. We will fight to avenge our dead. Of that King George can be certain. I have been a peaceable man but what has happened to Rose and Ethan, and all the people along the Mohawk, has changed everything. Hate has replaced moderation. Vengeance is no longer the Lord's alone. It is also ours."

Samuel, having rested, and now with his arm in a sling, stood and said, "Jonathan, walk with me among the men." His father shook each man's hand and said, "Thank you, good work today." He took a poll, asking, "What about the savages, do you think they are broken and will stop their attacks?" He followed with, "For how long a time will they stop attacking?"

They returned to their places and Samuel slumped down. Drawing a blanket over his body, he lay back on a bed of hemlock branches covered with a thin cloth.

His father spoke softly, saying, "They are all so tired. Still, they would fight tomorrow and the next day if needed. They are longing for home, but I know they speak what they believe. You heard their answers. Two think the red men will strike soon again. The rest hold that they are finished for at least six to eight months. I am with the majority. What do you think, son?"

"Father, come look at the dead Indians. I wonder if they are local or come from a distance. Viewing their bodies, I noted that the paint on their faces had two red stripes. The body markings showed three white circles. Those are different from the local tribe."

"Of course," Samuel said, sitting upright, and rose.

They walked to where his father's three attackers lay and examined the bodies.

"You are very correct, Jonathan," he said. "We were all too tired. You saw what we failed to notice. They are not local. The British could not entice the local tribes to attack. They bought allegiance from a more distant one. Son, you are a keen observer. Those braves will not soon return. Now, I feel more confident in deciding to go home. I will sleep well tonight."

The day was drawing to a close. Jonathan sat beside his father and relived the battle. He thought of the harm done to his sister and

Ethan. He bowed his head and recalled the crime committed against Martha and Harold. The attacks by the Indians were part of the same pattern. Doctor Rush was right, sides had to be chosen. Jonathan looked toward the setting sun. It was blood red. Revolution was at hand and he would join it!

As always, guards were posted while the men slept. In the morning they buried the dead. Taking up their meager belongings, they started homeward. Samuel refused to mount Cromwell and had Jonathan place the more seriously wounded on the horse. Others were placed on stretchers, constructed on the spot and borne by teams of those healthy enough to carry them.

It took four days before they came to the first sizable village. Once more, Samuel thanked each man, promised to arrange payment for their services, and sent them to their homes. Jonathan checked each of the wounded. He insisted that the three most seriously injured be brought to the Wolfe home. Two days later they were there. Ethan stood at the door and waved. Isabel and Rose came running to greet them. Samuel, exhausted, fell into their arms.

Ten days later, Jonathan felt it was time to leave and spoke to Isabel. "Ethan's wound is almost fully healed. He has regained his weight and is helping tend the wounded. They are also recovering. Father is able to partially raise his injured shoulder and it will recover further."

However, Samuel, who had always prided himself as fit and vigorous, was not same man who had embarked on the struggle to protect the frontier. He recognized his limits and at dinner said, "I am becoming fit enough to reopen the smithy, but it is the turn of other men to take up the fights which lie ahead. I, and most of the men who served with me, have become too old to continue in woodland battles. New and younger men must come forward."

"They will join the fight," his son responded. "I am returning to Philadelphia tomorrow. I plan to discuss my situation with Doctor Rush, and inform him that it is my solemn duty to join the Continental Army."

XIV

October-December 1775

Wolfe arrived in Philadelphia before the sun awakened the city. It was Saturday. "We are almost back, Cromwell," he murmured, urging his mount forward. The horse responded and they made good time. Jonathan left the saddlebags and his rifle near the shed, rode Cromwell to the livery and walked back to the Rush home.

When he knocked, the door was opened and Wolfe received a warm welcome. Everyone grasped him, gave a hug or kiss and said how much he had been missed. At breakfast, Jonathan told of his adventures, how he had removed the musket ball from Ethan, and the battle with the Indians.

Afterward, when he and Doctor Rush were alone, Wolfe broached his intention to enlist. "Jonathan," Rush said, "I am in full agreement with your desire to join the Continentals. When you described removing the ball from Ethan's shoulder, it showed your ability to save wounded men. However, I ask you to stay a few more weeks. Knowing of my chemistry lectures, Congress requested that I create a factory to produce gunpowder. Presently, almost no manufacture of saltpeter occurs in the colonies."

"Very well," Jonathan replied, "but only for a few more weeks."

Wolfe's mind drifted toward thoughts of Grace. In a passing

moment, Rush mentioned the Sons of Liberty were meeting that evening. "I don't know why I brought that up," he said, "I have begun to ramble. There are so many things happening lately that I sometimes volunteer any matter crossing my mind."

"I may wish to attend, sir," Wolfe replied, "if only to hear the latest scuttlebutt. But please excuse me, I must unpack the saddlebags and return the supplies. Also, I still possess your wonderful translation of the French surgeon's manuscript."

Rush rose from his seat. "Of course, Jonathan, I will help. I am delighted you made good use of everything. As for the treatise, keep it with you. When you are with the Army, you may wish to refer to it."

They worked quickly and then spent time seeing office patients. Two apprentices sat with each of them as they listened, questioned, examined and prescribed. Afterward, the novices accompanied Wolfe as he made rounds at the hospital and visited homebound patients. Their progress was slowed by the welcome Jonathan received at every stop they made. Finally, he was able to deposit them at the barn where the other apprentices welcomed him.

"Tell us about your adventures," they all demanded.

"I thought you were only interested in medicine," he laughed, and related what had happened during his northern journey.

Leaving, Wolfe walked to the boardinghouse. It was late in the afternoon. Lying on his bed, he rested and fell asleep. Suddenly awakening, Jonathan whispered, "I am late." He rose, lit a lamp, quickly washed, freshened himself and straightened his clothing.

Descending the stairs, he exited and paced rapidly into the chilly night. Clouds were thick, but a three quarter moon occasionally peered through and helped show the way. Entering the tavern,

Jonathan realized the evening meal had ended and the meeting had begun. Tables had been cleared, and Grace was cleaning the bar with a cloth. Hearing the door open, she looked to see who the late visitor might be. Recognizing him as he came into the light, Grace froze for a moment. Wordlessly, she opened her mouth and clutched her throat. Then, dropping the cloth, she ran to him.

"Jonathan," Grace cried, "I have missed you so much. Thank God, you are safe. Thank God, you are here!"

Wolfe opened his arms to receive her. Holding her tightly, he whispered, "I missed you always, Grace. You never left my thoughts. I cannot express how good it feels to hold you in my arms, feel your cheek against mine, and know that I am truly home."

They continued holding and kissing one another for several minutes and then went to a table in a dark area of the room. As they sat, Grace wiped at her tears. Suddenly remembering the past, she said, "You may be good at doctoring, Jonathan Wolfe, but you have had no education where women are concerned." Then, abruptly smiling, told him how she had responded to the letter slipped beneath her door.

"I apologize for my ignorance," he said. "I would be most happy for you to educate me as to the proper way to treat a lady."

She began to laugh and they sat absorbed in one another, speaking of how much each had missed the other. The Sons of Liberty meeting completed, men filed down from above. They left the tavern, unaware of the two figures embracing in the semi-darkness.

McKenzie was the last to descend. Surprised at not immediately seeing Grace, he peered about and finally saw them. Approaching, he recognized Wolfe and seized him in a welcoming embrace.

Stepping back, he gazed at Jonathan and said, "You have been greatly missed. I am glad to see that you appear unscathed by your adventures. I am anxious to hear of them." Then, remembering his manners added, "I hope all is well at home."

"Yes, the situation has been resolved and everyone is fine."

"I am glad to learn that," Elias said. "I would be very interested in your telling of the journey. But I wonder whether you have eaten dinner?"

"No, I have not," he replied. "However, I am not really hungry, a cup of coffee would suffice."

"A cup of coffee? Grace, you are not taking proper care of our friend. Surely he can use more than coffee."

"Of course, Uncle," she answered, and hurried to the kitchen.

While they waited, McKenzie impatiently asked him to begin his story.

Jonathan had reached the point of describing the surgery on Ethan when Grace returned. She carried a small tray holding cold meat, a slice of apple pie and coffee. Setting them before him, she said, "I hope this is satisfactory, there were many in attendance tonight. The larder is bare."

"This is more than enough. It will well satisfy my appetite."

Taking a fork and knife, he began to eat. After consuming the meat, Wolfe sat back, wiped his mouth with a napkin and completed the telling. He left out the more gory details of the surgery and only briefly touched on the fight with the Indians.

When he finished, he took a piece of the pie and a sip of coffee. Then, in the ensuing silence, looking from one to the other, said, "Those events have changed my thinking. I am now committed to the colonial cause and plan to join the army."

McKenzie, exultant, grabbed Jonathan's hand and gave a hearty whoop.

Hearing the intake of Grace's breath, Wolfe added, "There is no need for concern, doctors are always far to the rear. Besides, for the present I am needed here. Doctor Rush is busy producing gunpowder. The practice still requires me."

Grace sank back, "How soon do you think?" she queried.

"Not for at least four and possibly eight weeks. He knows I am anxious to serve."

"Jonathan, you have just returned from a difficult journey. You provided aid to your family and fought the savages. I am sure that you have not told the full story. Truly a respite is required. Wars continue on. Do not be so fast to jump into the fire."

Wolfe recognized her anxiety and attempted to sooth it. "I understand and will be cautious. But isn't it true that Harold is already under arms. Should I not also serve?"

"No, the choice is clearly yours," she murmured.

"Please be of good cheer, Grace. Permit me to walk home with you and Elias. I want to see you frequently in the time ahead."

She smiled and nodded agreement.

Elias clasped them in his arms and proceeded to close the tavern. They walked to the McKenzie home, Wolfe holding tight to Grace's hand. They found the occupants already asleep. Elias went to bed. The two lovers remained in the parlor. They continued to speak, declare their love and embrace each other. Later, they arranged a meeting, kissed and said goodnight.

There was no doubt that they were deeply committed to one another. However, Wolfe never proposed marriage or even an engagement. At the same time, Doctor Rush continued to claim a need for him to stay on.

On a bright Sunday in early December, Jonathan arrived at the McKenzie home. Grace welcomed him and he joined the family for the late afternoon dinner. As it concluded, Wolfe turned to Grace, saying, "There is some business we should discuss." To the others, he said, "Please excuse us."

Taking her by the hand, he led Grace to the parlor and faced her as she sat. Wolfe began, "Grace, I wish with all my heart to become engaged and married, but my head speaks otherwise. Last evening I made a list of the reasons for and against. They seemed of equal weight, but my head says the negatives plead reality. You have my full devotion. However, I have seen men die or be terribly maimed in battle. If I am killed or lose a limb, you will either be widowed or tied to a man unable to properly provide for you. If with child, it will be even worse. I feel I would be placing you at a disadvantage. The war will end and then we can always be together."

Grace listened with increasing emotion, then the volcano within her erupted. "Jonathan, you have not learned one thing since you placed that letter beneath the door. I am not some fragile female dependent on the male species. I am able to earn my keep."

"Furthermore, I think your heart speaks the truth and your male brain is out of order. I love you, and you said you love me. That is what counts. Anything can happen to either of us at any time. Death or injury is ever present. Did Shakespeare's plays not teach you anything? Frankly, I do not know how I can be so in love with such a foolish man."

At the end, her voice rose, so that the entire household could clearly hear the anger and frustration she expressed. Elias and Evelyn sat looking at one another, determined not to interfere. Joshua hunkered down, not quite understanding what was happening. Martha fully comprehended what had occurred. She sprang up and came into the parlor, ran to her sister and placed a comforting arm about her.

Wolfe stood, his face flushed and not able to adequately answer Grace's response. He reached into a pocket and withdrew a small box. Opening it, he exposed two gold rings. "I purchased these yesterday. I am placing one on my right forefinger as a pledge to you. The other I place before you on this table." Saying so, he set the ring down. "I would be honored if you would do the same," and gazed at her expectantly.

Tears filled her eyes as she said, "Jonathan, I love you but you are breaking my heart. Please leave. I will consider answering in a few days."

Wolfe said quick goodbyes to Martha and the others. He left the house not merely unhappy but depressed by the vehemence of Grace's response. He had anticipated some reaction, but believed the rings would provide a solution. Walking to the street, Wolfe mumbled to himself, "I am a rational man and my points were well thought out. Why could she not understand?" Then, "I have never understood women and doubt I ever will. They are overcome by emotion. Their thinking is often directly opposed to a man's. If you stand firm you are unreasonable. If you agree in any way, they press the advantage."

Finding a carriage, he directed it to Mrs. Appleton's. As it rumbled forward, a great sorrow possessed him. "How can I arrange an agreement with the person I care for so deeply?" he whispered. "I am at my wits end." He stared at the ring the entire trip. Reaching home, Wolfe paid the driver, entered the boardinghouse, climbed to his room, and discarded his boots. Fully clothed, he lay on the covers and ruminated through the night.

Wolfe did not hear from Grace, and the following Sunday went to her home. He came to the door and knocked. Martha answered. She looked at him with sadness and said, "Grace asked me to say that she has not yet decided. Oh, Jonathan, I feel so terrible for you both. I must tell you that Grace is despondent one moment and then fired up the next. It has been very difficult for her. Please be patient and understanding."

"I do understand," he replied. "I love Grace and will be patient. Please tell her that." He smiled bleakly, said goodbye, and returned home more depressed than before.

XV

In the following days, Wolfe tried to become fully engrossed in the practice. He did anything to avoid thinking about Grace and their opposing views.

It was now early December, and having completed house visits, Jonathan came upon the coffeehouse where he first met Tom Paine. Remembering the cakes and coffee enjoyed with Doctor Rush, he entered. The smell of fresh baked pastry and brewing coffee brought a smile. Looking toward the corner where the penman had sat, Wolfe broke into a broad grin. Paine was there, scribbling and hunched over in the exact posture as before. Jonathan quickly strode toward him, and the writer rose to greet him.

"Thomas, it's good to see you," Wolfe said. "I was under the impression you were away, serving with the Army."

Paine shook his hand and answered. "I was serving, and still am. I am in a militia unit from Philadelphia and saw some action. We have suffered severe reverses. A miasma of doubt now envelops both the Army and the citizenry. I was asked to write another pamphlet, something to provide inspiration and rally our people to continue onward, and began doing so. Whenever we bivouacked during our retreat across New Jersey, my scribbling progressed. I came to Philadelphia to complete the writing. It is just finished. I intend to call it *The Crisis.* It will be the first in a series of pamphlets I will publish during the course of our fight." Paine pointed to what he had written, and said, "The pages are out of order. However, this is the opening page. Would you like to read it?"

"It would be my great honor," Wolfe answered. He sat with Tom and began to read by the candle's light.

"These are the times that try men's souls. The summer soldier and the sunshine patriot will, in this crisis, shrink from the service of their country; but he that stands it now, deserves the love and thanks of men and women. Tyranny, like hell, is not easily conquered; yet we have this consolation with us, that the harder the conflict, the more glorious the triumph."

Wolfe read the entire pamphlet, as Paine continued to pass him pages. Finishing, he looked at him, saying, "Thomas, this is wonderful. The writing is very much to the point and sure to inspire anyone who reads it. Your choice of words and the cadence truly serve its purpose. When will it be published?"

"In just a few days," the author replied. "It has already been arranged, and there is hope it will be widely circulated."

Jonathan went on, "Your pamphlet has further inspired me to join the Continentals. I have been speaking to Doctor Rush. Delays in releasing me have been the order of the day. I will brook no further ones. Where is the Army now?"

"Still in New Jersey, but they are going to cross the Delaware and come into Pennsylvania. I possess a map, and will show you where the encampment will be sited."

He drew out the map and carefully explained it. Wolfe discussed some of the details, sat for a time and savored anew the different cakes and strong coffee. As he wiped the last crumb from his lips he leaned forward and said, "Tom Paine, I sincerely thank you for coming to America. You have inspired us all. I do not doubt that you will continue to do so."

Paine produced a huge smile, "Thank you, Jonathan, I am overwhelmed and encouraged by your kind words." Shaking hands, they said farewell.

Wolfe had a long discussion with his teacher. At the conclusion, Rush agreed he should be free to join the Continentals.

That night, tossing and turning, he thought of Grace. Her face and tear-filled eyes haunted him. Jonathan awoke in the predawn stillness. He hurriedly groomed himself, clothed, left and started for the McKenzie home. Reaching it, Wolfe peered through a window and saw Grace sitting in the parlor, a blanket wrapped about her. Moving to the entry, he knocked softly. She responded, opened the door, smiled wanly and motioned him in.

"It's very cold outside," she said. "Come into the kitchen. I started a fire and you can warm yourself."

He stamped the snow from his boots, removed them, and followed her. Grace remained silent as he stood and received the fire's warmth. Even when he turned to face her, nothing further than silence presented.

Wolfe spoke softly and said, "I did not mean to hurt you in any way. My intent was to protect you."

Breaking her silence, she answered, "What men call honorable intentions or protecting are often misplaced or misused expressions. Jonathan, I know that love does not provide all the answers or shield us from war or life's realities, but it does offer respite and requires nurturing. The world survives by virtue of a man and his wife creating the future. Separation does not often keep love's flame alive. Just as this fire requires fuel and stoking to maintain it, so does love. I have said that I love you and still do. I will keep your ring, but will not wear it. It does not provide the love I require. There is no guarantee that I will be here at war's end. Women are also subject to its destruction or find others with whom to share love. Truly, I do wish to be here for you. But, as you have said, war provides no guarantees. Now, you must go before I fling myself at you in frustration and despair."

She led him to the front door and watched silently as Wolfe put on his boots, outer coat and hat. Opening the door, Grace suddenly embraced him and then very gently eased him outside. "I wish you Godspeed. Come back safely," she called as the door closed.

Crestfallen, Jonathan stood motionless as snow fell about him. Then, as the sun rose above the horizon, he mounted Cromwell, rode to the street and on to Mrs. Appleton's. Once inside, weariness overcame him. He sat in the parlor and kept remembering Grace's words. Her love had been declared, her despair obvious. Above all, his mind kept recalling her warning that, if other men pursued her, she might be available. She had every right to do so, he concluded. What he had offered was not a commitment but a promise, and promises were not always kept. Jonathan began his day feeling a great weight on his heart that persisted throughout its remainder.

The following morning, Wolfe, who had been appointed a captain at his recruitment, said his goodbyes to the Rush household. Saddlebags had been packed and were secured. Once again mounted on Cromwell, he traveled toward Washington's battered army. It was now in Pennsylvania, having retreated across New Jersey before the victorious English. New York had been lost. The colonials had been required to defend too much territory with too few inadequately trained men. Poor choices had been made. Washington had been outgeneraled on numerous occasions. The Royal Navy's control of the waters surrounding Manhattan enabled General Howe to land his forces above the colonial positions on several occasions, almost trapping the American army.

General Lee, who had been a professional soldier in Europe, arrived at the last moment. "General Washington," he exclaimed. "The English are about to close their jaws about us. You must abandon Manhattan or lose the Army."

"Agreed," Washington answered, "But we will hold Fort Washington. It is a strategic strongpoint. The garrison can hold out for months and inflict heavy losses on attacking troops. When necessary, they can retreat across the Hudson's ice."

The General was wrong. English and Hessian forces took only three hours to storm the fort. As a result, 2,900 Americans surrendered and would face the horror of rotting in prison ships anchored in New York's harbor.

Despite setbacks, the bulk of the colonial army had been preserved. Following the battles for New York and Westchester Heights, Washington divided his forces. He sent half his men to defend New England. The rest remained with him. Retreating across New Jersey, trees were felled and bridges destroyed, slowing the pace of General Howe's advancing troops. On December 2nd as winter approached, the tattered and ill-fed colonials crossed the Delaware and encamped in Pennsylvania. Their opponents went into winter quarters, units being dispersed among various towns and villages.

Washington called a meeting of his closest advisers. "I have determined that we must adopt Fabian warfare," he said. "It will be a war of posts, based on the strategy of the Roman general Fabius Maximus, which proved successful in Rome's war against Hannibal. Surprise and overwhelming force will be used against smaller enemy encampments. Major engagements will be avoided. Men and supplies are limited. They must be husbanded and carefully used."

Wolfe arrived in the Continental's encampment on December 20th, quickly learning the duties of a military physician and surgeon. Only days after his arrival, the General, using the Fabian strategy, determined to attack Trenton.

On Christmas night of 1776, Washington was aboard his gray horse at the banks of the Delaware. "We will cross here and move on Trenton," he said.

Behind him, the troops shivered in the cold. Fog obscured the scene.

"Sir, the river is filled with ice floes. Crossing will be hazardous," a colonel advised.

"The boatmen from Marblehead and from along the Delaware will get us across," he replied. "We must surprise and defeat the Hessians."

"What of Colonel Cadwalader's men and the troops under Ewing."

"Hopefully, they will also cross successfully. With or without them, we will attack. It must be done. Success will restore confidence in our men and throughout the colonies."

Fortune smiled on the Continentals. Crossing points and roads had been left unguarded. The men advanced in bitter cold and over icy roads. Wolfe, on horse in the rear, saw bloody footsteps left by those without shoes. "After the battle, I will be treating both wounds and frostbite," he thought.

Reaching their objective, the colonials moved to their designated positions, firing cannon and small arms at the surprised Hessian garrison. No matter where they turned, American muskets, rifles, and artillery cut them down. Colonel Rall, the Hessian Commander, died while trying to rally his men. As he fell, the bulk of the green-coated enemy surrendered. Some, however, escaped. Ewing and Cadwalader were unable to cross the Delaware to block a southern retreat, and a way had been left open for some enemy troops to flee to Bordentown.

Upon receiving the news at his Princeton headquarters, General Cornwallis was shocked, but then said, "I must respond to the Trenton attack. We will take 8,000 men from the garrison, move south and crush the rebels."

As they marched, sharpshooters sent by Washington repeatedly fired on them. Harassed and slowed, Cornwallis arrived at Trenton near dusk.

Informed the British were nearby, Washington replied, "Let them come. We are now well entrenched."

"General," an aide said, "Our backs are against the Delaware."

"Yes," he replied, "But in front of us flows Assunpink Creek. The enemy can only cross at the stone bridge or a few other places. All are already ranged by our artillery and well covered by our muskets and rifles."

"Dusk and night are approaching," Cornwallis thought. "Still, we will begin the engagement. Forward men! Storm the bridge and crush the enemy!" Again and again, the English and Hessians flung themselves onto the bridge. Cut down by cannon and small arms fire, bodies piled atop one another and the bridge could not be crossed.

During the night, the Americans silently moved across the Assunpink. Washington exulted, "We have succeeded in slipping past them. To the east, there is a side road to Princeton. We will attack the garrison Cornwallis left behind."

Marching quickly, the Continentals reached Princeton and overwhelmed its redcoats. Victorious, Washington remained in New Jersey and established quarters in Morristown.

XVI

Winter's winds howled through the Morristown encampment. Cabins erected to protect the troops from exposure to the cold were grossly overcrowded. That plus inadequate nutrition, improper sanitation, poor hygiene, and weary men, led to dysentery, typhus, and other diseases. Finally, smallpox struck and rapidly spread through the ranks.

It was the 20th of January. The sky was a dull gray. A deep snow had fallen during the night. Mist shrouded the morning air. It was becoming colder and, though snow had ceased falling, one sensed more was on its way. Fierce gusts of bone-chilling winds blew from the northwest. Their sudden bite caught the unwary by surprise and produced an involuntary shudder.

Despite the elements, Wolfe walked with a rapid pace, his boots making deep tracks in the fallen snow. Approaching the cabin he sought, he slowed. Despite or perhaps because of his profession, a feeling of dread arose from his subconscious mind. Within was the fifth young recruit in his unit falling ill during the past ten days. Two were under the care of another physician. Two for whom Wolfe was responsible had died very quickly. He feared that this boy might well join them in the same burial ground.

Jonathan opened the door and quickly closed it behind him. As he did, the heat provided by a small potbellied stove embraced him.

A man within the cabin rose from his stool. Jonathan returned a salute. The corporal's tired bloodshot eyes stared at him.

Anticipating Wolfe's query, he said, "He is still very feverish, sir."

"Yes," Jonathan replied, "The rash has not yet shown. When it does, the fever should break."

The corporal was only in his thirty-fifth year but appeared older. He continued, "Indeed, sir, I well know the signs and their progress. On Deer Isle we had the evil thing. My family and the whole town had it. My wife, the two oldest and I survived. We lost little Lucy. Only three years old she was. At night, I still weep for her and pray she is with God. Yes, we carry on, but we bear the scars of the small pox upon our bodies and in our souls."

So saying, he touched his face where several deep pockmarks disfigured it. The doctor unconsciously touched his own which also bore the telltale signs.

The cabin still retained the odor of recently cut logs. Mud had served to caulk gaps between them. The room had a dirt floor and was barely six feet in height. A small window provided little external light. In addition to the stool and a tiny table, it housed four narrow cots. Three were empty. Jonathan walked to where his patient lay. The boy was seventeen. Lack of adequate and proper food had taken its toll. His blonde hair was disheveled, hanging down over scrawny shoulders. A gaunt face held a slackly open jaw, showing already yellowing teeth.

The doctor placed his hat and overcoat near the small stove and turned to examine the soldier more closely. Covered by a threadbare blue blanket and sweating profusely, the boy picked at the coverings with small uneasy motions. His eyes were glazed over, his head slowly tossed from side to side, and he muttered incoherently.

Taking the young soldier's thin wrist, Wolfe found the pulse to be strong and bounding, characteristic of the early stage of smallpox. He removed a cloth with its enclosed ice from the boy's forehead. Placing his hand there, the high fever was still obvious. The corporal helped him roll down the blanket and raise a much-used nightgown. There was a slight flush to the skin, but the pox had still not appeared.

"How do you find him, doctor?" asked the aide.

"Much as I expected. Until the pox show, the fever will remain. Even then, it will be uncertain. But I must compliment you, Miller, on the attention you have given this lad."

"I was glad to be of help, and always will be," said the corporal. "You saved my feet after they froze at Trenton. I am truly in your debt, sir. Indeed, so many of us are. Besides, he is a valuable recruit. After Trenton and Princeton, many enlistments were ending. Few would sign again. The ten dollars in hard money offered by General Washington caused some of the men to stay on for a time. With this cold winter and the pox, not enough are joining or even staying. We need every last one. This boy is special. He brought his own weapon. The barrel is rifled so it can fire the long shot. I have seen him shoot and he has fine aim."

Jonathan sat on the stool, evaluating the situation. Stirred by Miller's words, he responded, "We shall do our best to carry him through this dreadful illness. But physicians are still helpless before it. We can only aid by attempting to bring down the fever, and provide liquids and whatever food they are able to take. There is only the hope that time and God will bring a successful outcome. Miller, it is your turn to rest. Please tell private Jameson to relieve me in an hour. I will stay and observe our patient." And, he added to himself, "Think about the plague that has befallen us."

"Aye, sir, by your leave." Miller saluted and left. It had again begun to snow.

Wolfe remained deep in thought. It was early winter, the usual time for the appearance of variola. But longer winters fostered longer outbreaks. The disease held serious consequences for the Army. Indian tribes had already been decimated by it. Half aloud, he said, "Only by variolation can we succeed in stemming the outbreak. Otherwise, deaths among the troops will continue, as more uninfected farm boys come into camp."

Jonathan thought of conversations with his mentor. "Doctor Rush warned that poor sanitation, lack of proper nutrition, and pestilence would do more harm to our army than English or Hessian troops. So far, he has been proven correct. The military must be convinced to move ahead with inoculation. I am certain the risks can be avoided. Even if it means going to General Washington, variolation must be initiated."

The following day, he sought out Major Cartwright his immediate superior. Saluting and invited into the Major's quarters, Jonathan spoke. "Sir, I have given much thought to our problem with the pox. I believe it would benefit the Army to institute variolation. It would protect our men and halt spread of the disease. The hazards can be overcome."

Cartwright responded forcefully and disparagingly, "You are barely out of training, yet you presume to tell your more knowing elders how to respond to the pox. It is not your place to do so. You may believe your intentions are honorable, but they smack of youthful presumption and indiscretion. I do not approve of variolation. I never will."

Jonathan stood, saluted and left. Visiting the ill private, he saw the pox blebs had begun to show and, feeling the boy's forehead, the fever had declined. He was hopeful, but not convinced the crisis was over. Looking at the young recruit as he struggled against death, Wolfe determined to pursue his efforts.

He approached Colonel Henderson, the regiment's commander. Henderson had shown unusual concern for his injured men. While his subordinates neglected to see how they fared, Henderson often visited them. He was shown to the colonel who nodded in recognition, and invited him to be seated.

Beginning his story again, he said, "Sir, I believe there is a means to prevent further spread of the pox among our troops. The English have long used variolation to safeguard their forces. Major Cartwright has refused any attempt to carry it forward. Bypassing him is irregular and unpleasant for me, but I felt it necessary to do so."

The colonel was an educated lawyer turned soldier. As a youth, he had suffered smallpox. Attuned to Jonathan's plea, he said, "I am not concerned about your going above Major Cartwright. At times, I find him involved in his duties, at other times he seems unaware of problems around him. General Washington is quite concerned about the situation. I am going to ensure that he sees you."

The following day a lieutenant took him to the colonel, who then brought him to Washington's headquarters. Once admitted, he came before the General. Salutes were exchanged. Although Washington was seated, Jonathan was struck by his great height. Rising from his chair, he grasped Wolfe's hand. He was a handsome, powerfully built man, and smiled in a polite greeting. Jonathan noted that his face was slightly pockmarked.

"Well, Captain Wolfe I have heard much about you. Your mentor, Doctor Rush, was briefly with us immediately after Trenton. You missed one another by just a few hours. He mentioned you had joined our forces and highly recommended you to me. What have you to say with respect to this scourge among our men?"

"Sir," Wolfe replied, "Variolation must be carried out. The risks can be circumvented. The benefits far outweigh them."

"Variolation has been mentioned before," Washington replied. "I have consulted with our senior physicians and even with Doctor Rush. Most of them are against its use. Even your mentor has been vacillating in this regard. It is difficult for me, not a physician, to make such a uniquely medical decision. Still, I am commander of this army, and it is being destroyed by the pox. Tell me how you would carry out the inoculations."

Jonathan described the technique and added, "Sir, we can perform the work throughout the winter. As the men leave quarantine they can slowly resume their duties. The British are in winter quarters and therefore most unlikely to attack during this time."

"It appears you have thought carefully about your proposal. I will consider it," said the General. He shook Jonathan's hand with a firm grip, and indicated the interview was concluded. Wolfe saluted and left for his post. Two days later, February 5, 1777, Washington ordered the commencement of variolation.

Major Cartwright had Jonathan report to him. Rumors had circulated that the major had political connections. It served to explain how an unpleasant and rather ignorant physician had been appointed his superior officer. The conversation opened in a friendly manner, "Captain Wolfe, I have received orders that we are to begin variolating the troops," Cartwright said. "As I had mentioned, the concept does not appeal to me. However, one must follow the dictates of our superiors. You seem quite familiar with its use and I appoint you in charge of the inoculations."

"Thank you, sir, I will do my best to deserve the honor," Jonathan replied. "The men will require isolation and nursing care after inoculation. I suggest that we recruit the men's wives or sweethearts from among the camp followers and pay a small fee for their services. We can screen them as to their prior pox exposure."

Cartwright responded, "Captain Wolfe, those women are foul mouthed, ignorant and slovenly at best. You can hire some to do cooking and scrubbing. Our men deserve the more cultivated and appealing local ladies as caretakers. I have made the arrangements and do not wish you to interfere with them. Keep with the duties already assigned you."

"Also, I have spoken to the pastor of the local church. He has agreed to its use as the quarantine center. Consult with him as to moving the pews and setting up cots. If necessary, use only mattresses. As for blankets, God only knows where to acquire them."

Somewhat chastised, Jonathan left. But once begun, the inoculations proceeded satisfactorily. Every day Wolfe and his friend, Farnsworth, processed thirty men and other physicians were also inoculating. More could have been handled, but the nursing facilities were inadequate to provide the space and care required.

Nevertheless, rapid progress ensued. Wolfe became deeply involved and neglected his concern about exposing the women not already immune. After several weeks, however, he was suddenly wrought with anxiety and approached Major Cartwright. Despite disliking the man and inwardly rebelling, Jonathan always treated him with respect.

After saluting, he said, "Sir, if possible, I would appreciate a word with you."

"Of course, Captain Wolfe. Always nice to have a chat with you."

Although it was early in the day, Cartwright was already consuming his Madeira. Despite the low temperature of the cabin, his corpulent face was flushed and perspiring. The major's large stomach bulged forward, requiring his uniform's vest to lay open.

"Sir, I am increasingly concerned about the Morristown ladies," Jonathan said. "Experience teaches us that it is best to employ only those already immune to the pox as caregivers. I have spoken to them. Several have not had it and can become ill."

"Captain Wolfe, as I have previously told you, those charming ladies have freely offered their services. The troops enjoy seeing nicely dressed females attending to them. I personally informed the women of the possible dangers. I see no purpose in going over this matter. Please do not again come to me about it. I trust you fully comprehend me."

So saying, he reached for his glass and took another sip of wine.

Jonathan was astounded at Cartwright's response. It was almost as though, either through ignorance or malice, he was going to cause some of the women to develop the pox. He had gone over the major's head previously. Though aware he was again violating the chain of command, preserving lives demanded he do so once more.

Wolfe approached Colonel Henderson, and said, "Colonel, I come with concern for the ladies who are nursing our men. Among them are several who have never had this illness. They may themselves become victims and face an unreasonable hazard. Major Cartwright fails to understand how serious the situation is, and does not wish to remedy it. I am distraught at what is bound be a calamity."

Henderson became angry. "Dammit," he said, "I am concerned for the women at large, also, several of the younger ones are engaged to officers under my command. I am ordering you to attend to this matter. Leave Cartwright to me."

"Thank you, Colonel," Wolfe replied, saluted and left.

Jonathan immediately went to the church. The women were milling about in distress. Mary Anderson, an elderly lady with a kind face and graying hair approached him. "Doctor Wolfe, I must inform you that one of the ladies, Catherine Tompkins, has come down with a fever and is at home. I, as well as my family, have had the pox. I know the signs, and am concerned she may be harboring it. What do you suggest we do?"

He looked at her and a great fear possessed him. "Mrs. Anderson, I think we must discuss this with the other ladies. It is my belief that those who have not had the pox should be individually quarantined. I suspect that some of them may fall ill with it. The quarantine can be at home, provided all there have had the disease. Otherwise, I will ensure proper placement of everyone. My apologies, madam, I am overcome that this has been allowed to happen. It has been against my wishes."

"I understand your purpose," replied Mrs. Anderson. "I am certain the women will abide by your advice. But what about Catherine Tompkins?"

"I will go to her home, if you tell me how to find it," Jonathan answered.

Prior to leaving, Wolfe explained the problem to the women. He and Mrs. Anderson arranged for isolation of the endangered ones at various Morristown homes. He then rode to the home of Miss Tompkins. Her father opened the door as he dismounted.

Raising a hand, Tompkins cautioned, "Stay away, there is plague within."

"I am a doctor and have had the pox," he replied and continued to advance. "I hope Catherine is not too ill. She was very brave in volunteering to nurse the troops. I was most distressed to learn she had not previously had the illness and was vulnerable. May I assist in any way?"

"You are kind to have come," he said. "However, my wife and I have both had it and are able to care for our daughter. There is snow about, available to cool the fever. We know the pox's movements. If necessary, I will call upon you. A sad day, though we are proud of our daughter. Our two boys are with the Army. She was determined to serve by nursing the men."

Wolfe had already mounted when another rider appeared. Captain Warren had courted Catherine since arriving at Morristown. He had been stricken with variola in his youth. The Captain waved at him and sprang from his horse. He was welcomed by Tompkins and shown to her bedroom.

Overcome with emotion, he knelt at the bedside and kissed her forehead, saying. "Catherine, I implore you to recover from this illness. I wish to wed you, above all else. Get well. If you do, I will somehow manage to survive this war. I will act honorably in all my endeavors. I will remain faithful to you forever." So saying, he kissed her again and wept.

Warren came every day to sit with her, hold Catherine's hand, and sponge or kiss her brow. In the ensuing weeks, she went through the phases of the pox and recovered. As healing progressed, her sunken face and scarecrow frame slowly began to regain weight. Although pockmarked, she seemed more beautiful to her captain. In April, they became engaged and were married, just prior to the troops leaving Morristown.

Two other women were not so fortunate. One, a middle-aged spinster, succumbed to hemorrhagic smallpox. The second, a young woman of twenty, died just as they believed she was on the road to recovery. Morristown, afflicted, mourned their deaths.

A funeral was held for the nurses taken by the pox. The minister had delivered a sermon about Christ and his sacrifice, and of the need to be observant Christians and attend church. He closed with the following remarks.

"I have spoken about your duties to God and His Church. But, there are obligations we ignore. Louise Carmichael and Hope Grenville, who we lay to rest today, did not ignore their earthly obligations. They gave of themselves far beyond that which most of us do. They frequently worshipped in church but ritual did not suffice, nor should it ever suffice. Christ said, love thy neighbor as thyself, and the two lying here have given that love."

"We are presently engaged in a war wherein the English are killing colonials and colonials are killing them. I cringe at the blood being shed and mourn for all who lie wounded or dead. God appears to stand above the fray and both sides pray for his assistance. I must side with those struggling for just laws and liberties. We can only hope that our brethren succeed in this great endeavor and achieve true justice. Louise and Hope have served in that effort and taught us that being a hermit, hidden away, is not enough. Service to God and the community are both required. Such true service is their memorial. May the Lord receive their souls with His utmost mercy."

During February, frost and snow continued. Graves for Louise Carmichael and Hope Grenville were dug with difficulty through frozen soil.

Washington was frequently out of doors during inclement weather.

"General, you must spare yourself," said an aide.

Nevertheless, he persisted until one of his recurrent sore throats struck. "I can barely speak," he hoarsely moaned, "I burn with fever and can hardly stand."

The General took to his bed in Arnold's Tavern. As his condition deteriorated, Doctor Cochran, his physician, performed frequent small bloodlettings.

"I require Martha's formula of hot molasses and onions." Washington insisted. It was provided, but not in the exact mixture she used, and Cochran continued taking blood.

News of their General's illness spread through the camp. Officers and men prayed for his recovery.

"Our prayers will do more good than the bloodlettings that are being used," Wolfe said to Farnsworth. "They will only weaken him."

"I was not aware you were opposed to the taking of blood," Farnsworth replied. "I still use it and believe it helpful."

"One day we will sit down and have a discussion on its pros and cons," Jonathan answered. "At the conclusion, I think you will agree with me."

"I look forward to our discourse," Farnsworth answered.

As Washington's condition worsened, word went out to high officers and public officials that the General might die. They gathered about his bed, their heads bowed, praying for his recovery.

The news was also sent to Mount Vernon. Martha Washington responded immediately.

"Lord," she said, "speed my journey," and set forth on a hazardous dash to her husband. Reaching Philadelphia, Martha attended a reception held in her honor and played the happy guest. The same night, she changed into warm clothing and raced with accompanying cavalry toward Morristown. The wind blew already fallen snow from pine trees and oaks into the narrow roadways. The coach, converted into to a sled, sped through the brooding forests. Dawn broke as she arrived at Arnold's Tavern, and Martha quickly went to her husband's bedroom.

"The General is slightly improved, Madame Washington," Doctor Cochran said.

"Thank God," she answered, and sped past him. "You have given me a terrible fright, George," she said, kissing him. "I plan to douse you with enormous quantities of molasses and onions."

"My love," Washington replied in a hoarse voice, "I am prepared to do anything you wish." He reached up and pulled her down to him.

"George," she whispered, "Restrain yourself, we are almost in public."

"Martha, I am so glad to see you that I want to jump out of bed and dance."

"I know you love to dance, George, but for now bed rest is required."

"Yes, my dear, but with your ministrations, I shall shortly dance to many a tune. The thought of having you as my partner provides great stimulation."

"It shall be my pleasure to follow your lead, dear. However, you must drink this warm molasses and onion mix now. I sent my formula ahead and it has been prepared as requested." So saying, she handed him a large mug of her concoction and Washington drank it down.

Molasses and onions were frequently consumed. Within a week, Washington was well on the mend. He insisted on leaving the bed and dictating orders to Hamilton, his aide-de-camp. Word went out that the General was recovering and he was again on his great gray stallion. He rode about camp observing everything and issuing commands. In the evening, he spent his time with Martha discussing Mount Vernon and his hope to visit it soon. Always, the diminutive Martha was warm and enthusiastic.

"I have urged the officers to bring their wives to Morristown," she said. "When they arrive, I shall organize socials and dances. The young women of the village will be invited. We will have a gay time and lift everyone's spirits."

"Indeed, we will," Washington lightheartedly replied, "But you and I shall out-dance them all." He rose from his chair, bent down and kissed his five-foot wife.

Arnold's Tavern glowed on many nights. Music, dance, and song were present, as the officers and their ladies enjoyed the warmth of Martha Washington's parties. Good food and drink were frequently available. The enlisted men, however, partook in none of it. Their food was inadequate, consisting of low quality stew, rarely potatoes, and no green vegetables. From afar, they heard the music and dreamed of home.

XVII

On December 26th, as Washington's troops were moving toward Trenton, Grace exited the McKenzie house before dawn. She left a letter explaining her decision to spy, of her intent to enter New York and gather intelligence at the very heart of the British Army. Her hastily scrawled last sentence read, "If a man can go to war, a woman can be a spy."

Two weeks earlier, knowing Leonard Peabody, her school's headmaster, was a leading figure in the Sons of Liberty, Grace went to him. "I want to be a spy and go to New York," she said.

At first startled, he attempted to discourage her. "Grace, there are great risks, and little or no intelligence may be gained. Spies are executed. In September, Nathan Hale was hanged. This is not a woman's calling."

"Why not," she replied. "A woman will be least suspected. She can go where a man cannot and gain more information. With or without your help, I will manage to enter New York. I love my family, but will still go. As for the school, Martha can take my place."

Peabody thought, "She is fully capable of attempting such a mission unaided. Spying by herself, she is more likely to be caught. I must agree to assist her. It will better ensure her safe return." He replied, "Think this over for several days and then come back."

On returning, Grace still expressed her determination to spy.

"Very well," Peabody reluctantly said, "I will assist you."

Leaving the house, Grace wore the oldest, least conspicuous clothing available, a long gray cloak and old sturdy boots. Once on the street, she walked to a carriage driven by the Master of the Ben Franklin School. She climbed in and Peabody pulled a warm robe over her. He held the reins firmly but did not start the horse. Looking at her, he said in a low serious voice, "Grace, you are of great value to your family. The children, indeed all at the school, love you. You can turn back now, or at any time on the journey, or even after you enter New York. Neither I, nor anyone at any time, will think less of you."

Grace replied, equally serious, "It is getting late, Doctor Peabody. Please start the horse." Her adventure had begun.

Only the most trusted members of the Sons of Liberty were permitted into Washington's intelligence service. Other recruits were carefully screened men and women, all staunch supporters of the revolution. Grace was moved across New Jersey in stages. No one was privy to her mission or her destination. The object was to create no suspicion when Tory or British checkpoints barred the way. Her dress and appearance changed. Sometimes she was a farmer's wife or daughter, sometimes a merchant's.

The passage into New York was as a farm boy. The woman cutting her hair kept repeating, "It's such a shame to remove your beautiful curls and leave you without them."

Afterward Grace sat somberly, thinking, "It's not the loss of my hair. I question whether the disguise will succeed. But now, I will bind my breasts and dress in farm clothing. This woolen hat will serve to hide my remaining hair."

Later, she sat aboard a wagon. A warm jacket had been added to her clothing. Her boots were now encrusted with mud. The farmer was bringing late-harvested hay to British horses, providing her with virtually unchallenged entry into the city. Once there, Grace was deposited at a house belonging to a merchant. The wagon traveled on with its load of hay. After he unloaded it, the farmer turned his wagon and left for home. The enemy was not aware that two had entered the city, but only one had departed.

XVIII

February-April 1777

Simon and Gwendolyn had seen each other almost every weekend. Their romance flowered. He was progressively more smitten, and she more loving. Her respect and care for him grew. Though continuously chaperoned, hidden kisses had occurred.

In February, they became engaged and a marriage date set for early April. Jonathan, quartered at Morristown and in the midst of carrying out the variolations, received an announcement and an accompanying note from Hunt.

"Dear Jonathan,

I hope the enclosed missive finds you in good health and decent spirits. You can see from this that I have conquered Gwendolyn's heart, and already know she has conquered mine. I hope you will be able to attend our wedding. If not, I understand the exigencies of war demand your first attention.

As always, you are my best and closest friend,

Simon"

Wolfe thought carefully. "If we can complete a good portion of the inoculations several days prior to the wedding, I might be able to return to Philadelphia and attend."

Jonathan spoke to Farnsworth who agreed it could be done and wrote a response.

"Dear Simon,
Congratulations! Looking forward to kissing the bride.
Jonathan"

Thinking about his friend's wedding brought thoughts of Grace. Realization had come that work could not fill the void within him. With a prayer, Wolfe determined to resume their courtship and marry her. He had written but not received a reply. He wrote:

"Dearest Grace,

I have not heard from you in response to my letters. I hope you are well and happily teaching at Ben Franklin's. I think about you a thousand times a day. When I dream, it is always about you. My love and affection are unabated. The situation here is quite stable, and my position is proving very satisfactory. I look forward to seeing you soon and have much to say.

With all my love, Jonathan"

As the weeks went by, Wolfe and the other physicians continued the inoculations. It was well into March and only seven days prior to his friend's wedding. He sought out Major Cartwright and requested a ten days leave. The major readily approved the request.

"Weddings are very special," said Cartwright. "I believe they should be celebrated to the fullest extent possible. I remember my own with great fondness. I wish your friend, and his wife-to-be, the best of good fortune."

Philadelphia was not far, but Jonathan felt it wise to start two days prior to the wedding. It would give him additional time to avoid British patrols, find quarters and properly groom and refresh. Arriving in the city, he again lodged at Mrs. Appleton's.

It had taken just over twenty-four hours to complete his journey. During it, Wolfe's thoughts continued to focus on Grace. Once rested, he rode to the McKenzie home. Aunt Evelyn opened the door. She greeted him warmly, but did not look her usual self.

Suddenly, Evelyn broke down and became openly distraught. She pulled him to the kitchen and began speaking. Jonathan listened, stunned by her revelations. "Grace has gone to New York," she sobbed. "She has joined Washington's intelligence service. That young fool left in the middle of the night, only leaving a note. Grace must have contacted some madman in the Sons of Liberty. Elias is beside himself, as is Martha. And, bye-the-bye, she wrote that if you could be away in the army, she could be a spy."

Evelyn sat down, blew her nose, and continued. "You know how her brain works. Grace always thinks ahead. Her note said that Doctor Peabody had been told she had urgent business elsewhere, and Martha was perfectly able to replace her. Then the girl wrote that the holiday recess would provide time for Martha to learn what was required."

"We heard from Peabody and he agreed to it. I suspect he is part of the whole scheme. Imagine, Martha has become a schoolmistress. The man actually stopped by to speak to her, even though they always see those seeking employment at the school."

Once started, the normally reticent Evelyn continued. "Well, after weeks of anxiety we finally heard news about her. It was three days ago. A note was slipped beneath the door. She is employed as a waitress in a tavern frequented by British officers, sniffing around for information. Sometimes, that girl has more nerve than sense."

Sighing, she went on, "I am sorry to be the bearer of bad news, Jonathan. Usually, I am a calm person. This business has overwhelmed me. You surely understand my fright for Grace's safety. She can be hanged as a spy. Being a woman is no protection. My niece thinks she can secure information more easily than a man. That may be true, but she is exposed to constant peril. God help us, it appears this war is forcing us to do things of which we never dreamed. But you must be hungry and tired. May I offer you something?"

Wolfe stood, mesmerized as she related Grace's story. Stunned, he grasped the back of a chair for support and blurted, "I am overwhelmed. I believed Grace was teaching, that I would see her, and we would enjoy each other's company. I thought of the wonderful times we have all had. My friend, Simon Hunt, is to be married. I hoped to surprise Grace and ask her to accompany me to the wedding. I have come to realize that I have been a fool. We two should also marry. Truly, Aunt Evelyn, I am shaken to my core. Permit me to sit for a moment and collect myself."

Jonathan took the chair he was holding and sat. He slowly became calm, and put a hand on Evelyn's arm. Looking at her, he said, "Without doubt, the situation causes great concern. Grace is involved in a dangerous enterprise. Still, we both know she is very resourceful. Also, there must be a network of our spies within New York. She should be able to call on them for assistance. As for myself, I have certainly been thrown off balance and require some moments to recover. A cup of coffee would be appreciated. While

I drink it, you can tell me about the rest of the family. Have you heard from Howard?"

"We have," and her face brightened. Pouring coffee, she said, "He is with a Virginia regiment under the name Thomas Lowell. He fears that, if captured and knowing his real name, they could learn of the charges still pending. Howard has written as to how much he missed and loved Martha and Joshua. We were so happy to learn he is alive and well."

"I also," Wolfe answered and hastily swallowed the coffee. "I must be on my way," he said. "Give my regards to all. If you are able to, please send my love to Grace. Tell her I said she was, as always, correct. She will understand."

"I will do that. Stay safe, Jonathan. We all care deeply for you."

Wolfe left, mounted his horse, and disconsolately returned to his quarters. He could not keep Grace and her decision to spy from his thoughts. But, aware of the approaching wedding, he used the remaining hours to buy a new shirt and have his best clothing properly cleaned and ironed. He also spent time purchasing small gifts for Joshua and Rush's household.

XIX

On a Tuesday morning, considered the lucky day for a colonial wedding, it was cloudy and chilly. Still, Wolfe felt warmed by anticipation. He went to the church, showed his invitation, and was admitted to the special service. Jonathan looked about for anyone whom he might know, and except for Hunt's family, saw only unfamiliar faces. He was able to garner an aisle seat and watched as the wedding proceeded.

Three minstrels played as the couple came down the aisle. Simon's face was pale and he appeared anxious. Gwendolyn was veiled and her figure clothed in a magnificent white gown. She walked in a manner that indicated complete composure. Reverend Melrose led the way. Behind them came her and then his parents. The remainder of the wedding party followed. Jonathan waved to Hunt, who smiled and nodded in acknowledgement. At the ceremony's end, the couple said their oaths and exchanged rings. The previously stern minister smiled and pronounced them man and wife. Simon lifted Gwendolyn's veil. Looking into each other's eyes, they embraced and kissed, as everyone applauded.

Exiting the church, the wedding party and guests departed for the home of the bride's parents. Wolfe secured a carriage and traveled by himself. Entering the stately mansion, he found it exactly as Simon had described. Jonathan savored a wine and various hors d'oeuvres.

The hosts appeared, bid their guests welcome, and invited them to dinner. The largest room on the first floor had been converted into a dining hall. Jonathan went to his assigned seat. Looking about, he found the wedding party's table.

At Wolfe's approach, Simon and Gwendolyn rose to meet him. Grasping him, Hunt said, "I am overcome by your being here." He turned to his bride, "Gwendolyn, this is Jonathan Wolfe, my best friend. He is as loyal at the end of the day, as at the beginning. You have not met previously, but he is now with us. I wish that he should also become your friend. The three of us must live our futures in the warmth of each other's company."

"I say amen to that," Wolfe responded, and added, "With your permission, Simon." He leaned forward and kissed the bride's cheek.

Gwendolyn gave him a hug. "It is a pleasure to at last meet you. Simon has been telling me how much he admires and cares for you. I am sure we will be close friends, and look forward to seeing you frequently."

Wolfe introduced himself to the Lorings whom he had not previously met. "It was a magnificent wedding," he said. "I am certain of your daughter's future happiness with my friend." He embraced Simon's parents, congratulated them, and shook hands with Hunt's stepbrother and sister-in-law. A gong sounded, and the guests were asked to take their seats.

Hunt and Wolfe embraced once more. Jonathan softly said, "Gwendolyn is truly beautiful, love her well. I am sure she adores you as much as you do her. Now, you must pay proper attention to your bride. I will go to my table, so as not to distract you." He took Gwendolyn's hand, kissed it politely, and returned to his seat.

As the meal was about to be served, the chair next to him, previously unoccupied, was filled by a late arriving guest. He heard the rustle of silk and inhaled an intoxicating perfume. Jonathan turned to find Agnes Stiles, dressed in a pale blue gown, staring at him. Instantly, he recalled the death of her husband and her lashing out at Doctor Rush.

"Well, Doctor Wolfe, it appears we are to be seated together," she said, and coyly smiled. "As a forgiving woman, I believe we should be able to overcome past differences."

Jonathan blushed and stammered slightly, as he replied, "I am certain we will do so."

The meal progressed with each stealing furtive glances at one another. Finally, she turned to him and said, "I have spent a great deal of time these past months revisiting what transpired during my husband's illness. I understand he was extremely ill when you first called, and almost surely would have succumbed to his illness. However, Doctor Rush's use of bloodletting hastened his death. Of that, I am certain. It seems to me, as a mere woman totally ignorant of medicine, that removing blood is almost pagan in its concept. Do we not need blood to function? I recall personal instances where everything was done to stop bleeding. Has not your own experience in this war taught you that?"

At first, Wolf felt at a loss for words. He was taken by surprise at the change from her prior appearance and behavior. She had been downcast and despondent at his visits to her home, functioning as though half asleep. At the last, she had been overwrought, excited, and vehement in her attack against his mentor. Now, she was calm, very collected, and quite logical.

Finally, Wolfe answered, "In many ways, I must agree with you. Both personal and battlefield experience cause me to conclude it is essential to stop bleeding. Previously, I had been taught that taking blood improves the ability to overcome a serious ailment. In the case of Mister Stiles, I thought removing the first half-pint helped. Following his second bleeding, I was uncertain as to whether we had assisted or caused harm."

"Your willingness to admit this is admirable and reflects positively on your character. I wish Doctor Rush was capable of the same."

"Doctor Rush is a man of principle. He has worked hard to acquire medical knowledge, and pass it on to younger men. He is always attempting to learn, so as to improve the lot of his patients. At times, he may persist in holding onto ideas beyond their usefulness. Perhaps we all do. But, above all, he is a man of science. Such men discard beliefs which prove erroneous."

Agnes closed her eyes for a moment. Opening them, she looked at him and said, "I hear your words, but in the meantime he has become Doctor Dracula."

Jonathan was startled anew by the intensity of her statement. They both remained quiet during the meal. However, as their food was almost consumed, she again spoke, "I am Gwendolyn's first cousin via our mothers. I understand you are a friend of Simon."

"Yes," Wolfe responded, "We have become very good friends since we met at the beginning of our apprenticeships. It is a great pleasure for me to be here today."

"Wasn't it difficult for you to come. I heard you had joined the Continental Army. Are you with them now at Morristown?"

"I have come from there. I was fortunate in being granted leave for the wedding."

Looking at him, she said, "Simon must be delighted you were able to do so. I truly hope you enjoy whatever leave has been given you."

"Thank you," he replied and returned her gaze. As he did so, he again noted how much her appearance had changed. Mrs. Stiles showed a small amount of rouge on her cheeks and lips. Her hair was swept up and tied in a manner permitting the overlapping curls to hang in a lovely way. She no longer possessed a wan expression or downcast eyes. Her eyebrows were arched and her eyes sparkled. Wolfe had not been in such close proximity to a woman for some time. Her perfume again drifted toward him and he felt aroused.

Jonathan looked at his plate and took another sip of the excellent wine their hosts had provided. As tea, coffee, and dessert were served, the guests were invited into another large room. It had been cleared of furniture, save for a few lounges set at the periphery. The minstrels began playing a dance tune. Suddenly, Agnes Stiles exclaimed, "I have been in mourning long enough. It is time I danced again."

Taking Jonathan's hand, she urged him to his feet and onto the dance floor. It was a familiar tune. Although he did not consider himself even an average dancer, he recalled dancing it as a schoolboy and was able to negotiate the floor with her successfully.

Perspiring from his effort, he smiled and said, "I am really not an adequate dancer. However, when I was about twelve years old, my schoolmaster insisted we learn reels and other dances. He played a fiddle while calling out instructions. Those were happy times."

"Your telling how you learned to dance is delightful. But truly, you are doing quite well," she replied. "Oh, now they are playing a minuet. I would like to try it with you."

Despite his judgment, Wolfe was overtaken by a desire to please her. With great trepidation, he embarked on the floor, and once again managed to struggle through.

Agnes smiled at him and said, "You have successfully negotiated the dances. I am delighted to have been your partner. However, it may be wise for us to quietly relax for the remainder of the evening."

They began conversing on a love seat, and, from time to time, observe the whirling dancers. Wolfe asked about her children. She replied it had been difficult, but they were both slowly recovering from the loss of their father.

"Children seem able to overcome the worst of disasters," she said. "Scars are left, but fade with time. I do not intend to hide facts from my children. They must grow up unspoiled and aware of what is happening about them. Only then, can they develop the maturity required in times as difficult as these. I miss my husband greatly. He was always loving and kind to me. His departure has left a great empty space. He tried to protect me from the true world. My parents were wiser and taught me how to look out for myself. You met my brother, Stephen. He is examining our finances, and has encouraged me to learn about money and investing. Despite being a woman, I am slowly becoming adept in those areas. I intend to continue to do so. It may be contrary to a woman's accepted mode of behavior, but death and war combine to make changes imperative."

Wolfe found himself more and more engrossed and fascinated by this lady. She certainly looked like a women of the Philadelphia gentry, but her perception and conversation sounded as though a man were speaking. He was reminded of days spent with Grace, when she had expressed some of her opinions. Certainly the decision to join Washington's intelligence service was most unusual for a woman. It seemed the world was indeed changing. He felt it would not surprise him to find a woman masquerading as a man within the Continental Army.

As they talked, the newlyweds approached. Jonathan and Agnes stood to greet them.

Gwendolyn said, "I can see you have enjoyed being placed with one another. I deliberately seated you together. I must add that Simon was not sure what would occur. As usual, men are often wrong when dealing with social situations."

"My dear," Simon interjected, "I plead guilty to the charge. You are quite correct. Men fail to understand the subtleties of peoples' responses to each other, in particular those between men and women." Hunt smiled blandly at Jonathan and then shrugged his shoulders, thereby indicating a total inability to comprehend what was occurring. Knowing the history, he had clearly feared their being seated together would produce an explosive situation.

Agnes smiled, "I think we have both enjoyed a marvelous experience at your wedding, Gwendolyn. As for you, Simon, you are without a doubt the luckiest man in the world. My cousin is not only beautiful, but she also adores you completely. You can be certain she will be a wonderful wife. But the hour is becoming late and I must leave. Doctor Wolfe, I wonder if you would be kind enough to accompany me home."

Jonathan managed to cover his astonishment at her request. Once again, he felt outmaneuvered. He was obviously not a very good general when it came to tactics involving women. He smiled and signaled his agreement, saying, "Of course, it has been my pleasure to enjoy your company. It is only proper I escort you home."

Leaving the house, the early April night chilled them and each shivered slightly. Wolfe assisted Agnes into her carriage and then followed. Sitting together, she moved close to him and drew a fur-lined quilt over them.

"I do not enjoy cold weather," Agnes said.

"Neither do I, nor do the British, nor our own army."

They remained silent thereafter, each trying to analyze the evening.

Arriving at the Stiles' home, Jonathan helped her from the carriage. It had begun to snow. As Wolfe accompanied Agnes to the door, the coachman started up and was quickly down the road.

She laughed. "I just engaged that carriage for the evening. The coachman must have assumed you were my husband and therefore departed. Please, come inside. I will send someone to obtain another."

As they spoke the snowfall became much heavier. Agnes opened the door with a key. "I told the servants they could go to bed early. Only Abigail is still awake, seeing to the children. You should go to the parlor fire and warm yourself."

Wolfe removed his overcoat, already covered with a thin layer of snow. He shook it quickly, hung it on a rack and removed his boots. Entering the parlor, he stretched out his hands toward the fire. It took several minutes for him to feel warm. In the meantime, Agnes had gone to check the sleeping children and send her servant to bed. She returned, and in each hand held a small glass of sherry.

"This will help warm you," she said.

Jonathan took the glass and they saluted each other and drank.

Too much alcohol had already been consumed at the wedding, he thought, but its warmth was required.

Agnes put her glass down and came toward him. "You have been very sweet to put up with me and accompany me home this evening," she said. Then, placing her hand behind his neck, Agnes kissed his lips with great tenderness. She maintained her embrace. Jonathan felt himself aroused and overwhelmed. He took her in his arms and felt her body respond to his.

Grasping his right hand, she placed it on her left breast. Desire overcame him. Jonathan lowered the upper portion of Agnes's dress and, tearing away any impediments, exposed her breasts. He placed a hand on each, so as to cover the nipples and slowly massaged them. She seemed almost in a trance, also stimulated and aroused.

Wolfe carried Agnes to a grizzly bear rug in the center of the parlor. Her eyes looked at him as he placed her upon it. She lay there, discarding her gown and underclothes, as he stood above her stripping the clothing from his body. Looking down, he saw how beautiful and desirable she was, and lowered himself beside her.

Taking Agnes in his arms, he caressed her face and neck, and kissed her softly. She responded to his touch, and began to stroke and then kiss his breasts. For twenty minutes they explored one another's body. Then, his hand slowly sought her lower abdomen and moved to where tufts of blonde hair covered her pubis. Jonathan felt the moisture accumulating over her vagina, and began to fondle her clitoris. There was a sharp intake of breath. "That feels so good," she whispered. He continued further and her passion responded in kind. The moisture became a stream and her legs spread to welcome his expanded penis. They clutched, kissed and moved together, coming to a crescendo of lust, desire, and passion.

Exhausted by their pleasuring, they sank back, and now felt the effects of the long day and consumed wine. Agnes looked at him and whispered. "Jonathan, I believe I have seduced you, but it was not quite intentional. I miss my husband. It is a long time since I felt a man's body next to mine. I may be too bold when I say that you are a wonderful lover. It has been quite a while since I have felt so passionate."

Saying this, she kissed him gently, and then rose to put on her underclothes and gown. When she had finished, she said, "Even without looking outside, I am certain the snow will prevent my servants from gaining the attention of a carriage, particularly at this hour. There is a guest bedroom available. I will make sure it is properly arranged for you."

After Wolfe had put on his own underclothing and trousers, Agnes led him up the stairs and showed him to a well-appointed bedroom. She inspected it and, satisfied, wished him goodnight and started for her own quarters.

Turning back, she said, "Have breakfast here. When you leave, I will make sure a carriage is waiting for you. Come back on Friday evening. I will expect you."

Jonathan nodded in agreement.

XX

In bed, Jonathan lay awake, thinking over the evening's encounter. He recalled the ghosts of women from his past. Wolfe was not quite an innocent regarding them. He did not have broad experience but he knew more than the essentials. Somehow, he had always been shy in approaching females. They had usually been the ones who initiated both friendships and more intimate relations.

During a warm spring day, when he was fourteen, a slightly older neighbor with long blond hair, blue eyes, and a sweet smile had seen him walking near her home. Occasionally they had spoken before and often seen one another at church.

She approached him, saying, "Hello, Jonathan. It's such a pretty day. May I walk with you for a bit?"

Surprised, he had murmured, "Sure, Juliet." Walking beside her, he had been silent, his head slightly down, but somehow proud to be walking with a girl who was not his sister.

Despite his silence, Juliet kept speaking. Coming closer, she took his hand in hers. It felt warm and, walking hand in hand, Jonathan became very comfortable. They came to a meadow where early spring flowers were starting to bloom.

"Will you pick flowers with me?" she asked.

Wolfe and his sister often picked flowers, and the freshly opened ones in the lush meadow called to him.

Together they gathered an armload and Juliet said, "I want to lie down for a moment. Sit beside me." As he did, she drew him to her and kissed him. Her lips felt soft and inviting as they pressed against his. She released him and then pulled him back. Her kiss was more passionate and Jonathan felt warmth spreading through him. Juliet let go and, looking into his eyes, said, "The older boys and some of your friends have tried to get close to me. They are all rough and raucous. You are the nicest boy around and the handsomest." She kissed him again. Lying back, she said, "Lay down by my side and stroke my hair, Jonathan. Then stroke my neck, but be slow and gentle. My mother does that sometimes. I like it very much."

They spent an hour lying in the midst of the meadow's flowers, kissing each other while he stroked Juliet's hair and neck. They met there frequently through the summer. No one saw the two, as they lay side-by-side, happy in their secret trysts.

Fall harvest was ending, when Juliet said, "I have sad news, Jonathan. I am moving away very soon. We have become good friends and I will greatly miss you. My father has been offered a position at a big mill. I must help with the packing. I love being with you, but I cannot even stay today." She kissed him and stepped away. Tears appeared in her eyes as she turned and started running for home.

He remembered kisses with other girls, but they never tasted as sweet or as fresh as those with Juliet. They were all very short romances, not meaningful to either party.

Several months before leaving to begin his apprenticeship, Jonathan and his father built a small iron gate for a local shopkeeper.

Wolfe was installing it by himself. The gate was heavy and, when he finished, Jonathan was sweating and tired.

Elizabeth Wellesley had stepped from behind the store's counter and watched as he checked the swing of the gate. Then she also tested it. "You've done a good job, Jonathan. The gate looks attractive and moves nicely," she said. "It's been a warm day and you look like you need some refreshment. Come in and have tea and something to eat." He followed her, as she continued, "The shop is slow today. If someone comes, I can easily hear the bell when they enter."

The store had been built onto the front of the house. Wolfe followed her to the kitchen. It contained a small table, two chairs, counters, and cabinets. The fireplace was to one side and served as the oven.

"Here is some tea, milk, bread and cold meat," she said, setting them before him.

He ate quickly and, his appetite satisfied, leaned back. Jonathan raised his arms overhead and gave a contented smile.

While he was eating, Elizabeth had left and returned at that moment. Startled to see that the woman was clad only in undergarments, Wolfe hurriedly stood. She came close to him, took his hand and placed it on her bosom. He felt a soft breast with a firm nipple and became confused but also aroused. Taking his hand away, she gently pushed him back into his seat and drew the other chair next to him.

Leaning toward him and speaking with intensity, Elizabeth said, "Jonathan, I am aware that my behavior has unnerved you. Despite appearances, I am not a loose woman. What I say may seem unusual and startle you even more, but I need your help."

She stood up, quickly replacing her dress. Again sitting down, Elizabeth continued, "You must listen closely. Tobias and I have been married for six years and remain childless. His prior wife also bore no children. I was married before. We were together for just over a year when my husband died in an accident. I was early with child when they brought the news. I fell where I stood and some days later miscarried. I could not bear the two losses, and for a year was in despair. In truth, I still mourn my lost love and our unborn child."

"By the end of that year, I used up the little money we had. With no other family, I sought employment, and went from one dreary job to another. When his wife passed, Tobias needed help in the store. He was looking for a man, but I approached him and he agreed to a trial. I believe he then hired me not just because I was satisfactory, but also because he could pay me less than a man. I worked with him for a year. He became used to me being about and offered marriage."

Elizabeth sat back gathering her thoughts and went on, as Wolfe became fully engrossed in her story. "I had begun to feel comfortable near him and also sought security for myself and for a child I hoped would come. I have gained security but not a child. Tobias was already well into his fortieth year when we married and is now nearing his fiftieth. I am still not yet in my thirtieth year. I believe that I am still able to bear a child and Tobias would be a happy father. However, we are not often consorting as man and wife. I am certain it is because he is frightened of his aging and is concerned about his capability. But when he returns from a trip, he has missed me and always desires me. Still, considering the failure of both his wives to conceive, I believe he is barren."

She paused, and said, "I am still a somewhat attractive woman, Jonathan. What I propose may be unusual but I need you to father my child."

Wolfe jumped back and stood, prepared to run from the store.

Elizabeth also rose, grabbed his shoulders and put her face close to his. "Jonathan," she said, "Be calm. Listen to me, I beg you. Desperate people do desperate things. Such doings may be uncommon, but they are done. Realize this, you would be providing a child both to me and to a man empty by its absence. Tobias would gain as much as I. Two people would be the happier and you would be bringing a life into the world. Besides, I have observed you. You are shy around women and, I am certain, unknowing of how to satisfy one. My husband, Mathew, and I were young. We enjoyed each other and made love frequently. There are many things I can teach you."

She stepped back. The pupils in her eyes were dilated, her face imploring, and her overall appearance quite attractive. "Jonathan, you may go but, shaken as you may be, think carefully on what I have proposed. Tobias is not due home for a week. If you decide to pursue it, you may return any evening after I close the store. It can only be for three days or four at the most. I would not want my husband to be home early and find us together."

Wolfe left on unsteady legs. He gathered his tools and reached home at the same time as Samuel. Rose and Isabel had prepared dinner and, after washing, the men came to the table. Jonathan was quiet throughout the meal.

"You are unusually silent this evening," Isabel said.

"Oh," he answered, "Somehow I keep thinking of how well that gate at the shop swung. Tell me how your work went, father."

His quick change of the subject went unnoticed. Later, he remained awake, thinking of Elizabeth Wellesley's proposal. "I am both frightened and eager," he whispered. "Save for the time with Juliet, I have not been very close with a woman. Fathering a child fills me with apprehension, but learning about intimate love excites me."

Wolfe remained thoughtful for two days. On the evening of the third, he returned to the shop as it was closing. Elizabeth smiled almost shyly, and said, "Thank you for coming back, Jonathan."

Taking his hand she led him to her bedroom, had him disrobe and did so herself. She drew him to the bed. Lying together, she kissed him softly several times. Their closeness and her kisses began to arouse him. He stroked her hair and neck, as he had with Juliet.

Elizabeth said, "That feels very soothing. Kiss my neck now, Jonathan." Later, she added, "Lick it, I find that very exciting." Further on, Elizabeth whispered, "You are wonderful, Jonathan. I am feeling much more relaxed. Now, hold my breasts and fondle them." After some moments, she said, "Kiss my nipples very gently."

He kissed the erect nipples and felt them swell even more. With no urging, he began taking more of the breast in his mouth, sucking gently on the nipple as he withdrew it.

"I am becoming more aroused," Elizabeth sighed. "Keep doing that, Jonathan, it makes me tingle." He lay beside her and continued sucking her breast. Elizabeth spread her thighs and took hold of Wolfe's right hand. She placed it on the inner side of her thigh, and said, "Stroke me there very slowly and then stroke the other thigh."

Jonathan moved even closer. His left arm was beneath her back and he reached with his hand and began fondling Elizabeth's left breast. She started to arch her back and took his right hand and moved it to her pubis. He felt the strangeness of a woman's pubic hair, as she began to carefully bring his hand back and forth. Elizabeth brought it lower, and he could feel the moisture between the lips that engulfed his fingers. Again, she slowly moved the hand and he felt the small protuberance there begin to engorge. As he continued she became more aroused, closing her thighs slightly and then opening them ever wider.

"Oh" she moaned, clutching him. "I feel so wonderfully young again. Now, Jonathan, mount me and ride."

He did her bidding. Fully aroused he moved to top her and they continued on for many moments. He climaxed before Elizabeth. "Please go on, Jonathan," she cried, and he was able to sustain his motion until she fell back having also climaxed.

Afterward, she hugged him to her and said, "Jonathan, you have made me a happy woman. I hope you have also enjoyed our being together." Still overwhelmed by their lovemaking, he could only nod in response.

Elizabeth smiled, saying, "I do not know whether or not our first encounter will bear fruit. I hope you will agree to continue being together like this." Wolfe nodded again.

Her smile widened and she drew him closer. "Tobias goes monthly to the city for supplies," she said. "You can return the next two nights and then count four weeks. It may well be a few days afterward, but I will signal you by placing an oil lamp directly in this window. When you see it, wait another day and then come to me. Now you should dress and return home."

Wolfe descended the stairs behind her, as she carried the lamp before them. Shielding the light, Elizabeth had him quickly exit. He used a circular path to reach his house. On questioning, Jonathan said that he had been with some friends. In bed, his mind recalled the initiation into intimate love. "It is thrilling," he said, and lay exulting in his manhood, considering himself the luckiest of men to have struck such an agreement.

They continued their relationship the next two nights. Thereafter, for several months Wolfe and Elizabeth met together for three or four nights, each time more eager to engage their bodies. One month before he was to leave, she signaled and they again had relations. As they lay together, she said, "This is the last time, Jonathan." He sat upright but she brought him down and hugged him close. "You have planted your seed and it has taken root," Elizabeth whispered into his ear. "I have not shown blood these past two months. Thank God, there is life within my womb. I am certain that I can sustain and nourish it. My breasts have begun to swell. They are preparing to feed a newborn babe."

She drew back slightly, smiled and peered into his eyes. "It may sound like blasphemy but you have been our Lord's instrument. They say he acts in mysterious ways and that Child Jesus was born of virgin birth. An angel informed Mary that a child would be born. Well, to me you are God's true Angel. Be happy for me, Jonathan. You have made me love you and should feel proud to father a child. Truthfully, I believe Tobias will be overjoyed to claim fatherhood."

They remained together for an hour, holding one another tightly. Wolfe could not quite realize he had helped create a new life. They finally rose and dressed. Before the door downstairs opened, they embraced for the last time. "Take care, Jonathan," she said. "You will be leaving soon to learn physic. I wish you Godspeed. You will go on to become a fine doctor. Wherever you are, know that my heart holds you within it."

He went home and never saw Elizabeth again. Almost a year later, one of Isabel's letters related the local news. *"People here are smiling and shaking their heads in wonder. Tobias Wellesley's wife has recently borne him a son. He is like a man reborn and struts about, boasting that a man near fifty and his thirty-year old wife can still bring life into the world. Indeed, miracles do happen. They have named the babe James Mathew, James for Tobias's father, Mathew for her first husband."*

Wolfe felt warmed by his recollections. As sleep came to him, he wondered how Elizabeth and his son were fairing.

Jonathan rose early the next morning. A servant was already cooking food and provided him a hearty breakfast. A carriage was waiting at the door. His coat was dry. The boots, which he had left the previous night in the doorway, had been cleaned and polished. He thanked the servant, exited, and entered the coach. The snowfall had been significant, but they made good progress and arrived at his destination in thirty minutes.

Entering the boarding house, Jonathan ascended the stairs to his room. He removed his coat, sat down, drew off his boots and, fully clothed, collapsed onto his bed. He did not attempt to analyze the previous day and night, but slept and awakened in the afternoon. He had eggs, toast, and coffee at a nearby tavern and decided to visit Doctor Rush.

It was not far to Front Street. He entered the familiar area, came to the house and knocked on the door. Alice opened it, shrieked, "Doctor Jonathan," gave him a great hug and kissed his cheek. "Welcome back," she said. "Doctor and Mrs. Rush are not here and Miss Rebecca has again married and moved away."

"Good for Miss Rebecca," he smiled, "But I am sorry the Rush's are away. I was hoping to see them. Do you know where they might be?"

"I am not sure of their whereabouts. He and the missus left hurriedly this morning. There has been misfortune. While visiting his estate in New Jersey the British captured her father, the congressman. Word is that he has been abused and thrown into prison. Doctor and Mrs. Rush are trying to obtain more information."

"I sincerely hope they will be successful," Wolfe replied. "I am at the Appleton House. When they return, tell them I called and hope to see them." He hugged Alice, kissed her cheek and went to the office area of the house. Wolfe spent the remainder of the day speaking to the apprentices and seeing patients with them.

The following day, Jonathan breakfasted at the boarding house. Later, he went to the hostelry where his horse was stabled. Mounting, he rode through the streets looking about. "Philadelphia grows ever larger," he thought. "The war and the presence of Congress make it an even more important center of commerce and government. It seems that everyone is benefiting from the need to supply the Army, even if it is not being properly supplied."

XXI

After riding about the city, Jonathan set off to the Lorings. On his arrival, Simon and Gwendolyn greeted him. The three embraced and entered the house.

They spoke of the wedding, and the newlyweds smiled, saying they could not be happier. Later, Simon said, "Jonathan, you serve the colonial cause in the manner you deem appropriate. Gwendolyn and I desire to remain neutral. It is not possible to do so under the conditions prevailing in the colonies. We are gong to England. Doctor Rush studied in Edinburgh and I wish to continue my medical studies in London. I also want to learn whether Parliament is truly intent on imposing acts designed to keep the colonies subservient."

Gwendolyn interjected, "Simon really cares about your opinion, Jonathan. He worries that you will think him a Tory or as turning his back on the colonies. Please understand that we have reached this decision after much thought and discussion. It will not be easy to break the bonds of friendship and parental closeness we presently enjoy."

"My friends, my very best friends, I have no doubt you have considered this with great care," Wolfe replied. "Your decision holds much merit. Simon, I sincerely wish you a great educational experience. As for you, Gwendolyn, I am certain you will have a wonderful life with this fellow. England will prove new and exciting. But it appears we three have little time left to savor one another's company. Today is Wednesday. I know you are very occupied. May I return on Friday and spend the day with you?"

"Jonathan, you are the most understanding person I have ever met," Hunt said, "That is after Gwendolyn, of course." He smiled at his wife and placed a kiss on her brow. "How about Friday?" he asked her.

"Friday, is fine," she replied, and kissed him in return, this time on his lips.

Wolfe laughed. "It is wonderful to see your love for each other. I will be off and come around noon on Friday."

The newlyweds accompanied him to the door. He secured his horse, mounted, waved, and rode away. Their happiness remained with him, providing warmth that the chilly air failed to diminish.

Once again, Wolfe rode through Philadelphia. Tom Paine's *The Crisis* had been published and was being distributed. He bought a copy at a roadside bookseller. Placing it in his pocket, Jonathan smiled, thinking of the scene in the tavern. "There was Paine," he whispered, "Scribbling to reinvigorate the struggle for freedom. This pamphlet should be widely circulated among the troops." He stopped, and bought five more copies.

Returning to the Rush house, Alice answered and drew him in. "No escape this time, Doctor Jonathan," she said. "Have some coffee and cakes. The Doctor has taken Mrs. Rush to a country house."

Surprised, Wolfe understood. Julia's father was a British prisoner and their army was not far from Philadelphia. It was necessary that she feel secure and in a peaceful place.

Jonathan remained, telling Alice about army life, and the variolations. He did not speak of the illness and deaths among the women. Alice would have nightmares, if told of unfortunate events. He took the girl's hand and said, "You have been very kind to me, Alice. I may not have expressed it, but being away has made me recall all your efforts and kindness."

She showed her usual blush, saying, "You have deserved every kindness and returned kindness in full measure."

They stood together in the kitchen, hugged each other, and Jonathan started to leave.

Alice called out, "Wait, Doctor Jonathan. I forgot Doctor Rush left something for you."

She withdrew and quickly returned. In her hand she carried a wrapped book and said, "This is the Doctor's chemistry book. He wanted you to have a copy."

Wolfe opened his mouth in astonishment. "Please say that he has been wonderful to me. I receive this with great admiration for him and am most appreciative of his generosity."

"He cares for you, Doctor Jonathan," Alice replied. "Take care. Come through this war unharmed."

Smiling, he said, "I will do my best," and, stopping in mid-sentence, added, "Heavens, I have also forgotten something." Opening the door, he ran to his horse and went to a saddlebag. He placed the chemistry book inside and withdrew several packages. Returning to the house, he gave one to Alice and set two on the hall table.

"Please open yours," Wolfe said. "The others are for the Rush's." Doing so, her eyes lit with joy. "What a lovely, colorful shawl," she said. Alice hugged him again, saying, "Thank you for thinking of me." Final goodbyes were said and Jonathan departed.

Wolfe returned his horse to the stable and had dinner at a tavern near the boarding house. Once again, he spent the evening reading, on this occasion an anatomy text. Satisfied with his review of the material, and after close examination of cross-sectional views of the limbs, he removed his clothing and climbed into bed.

He slept fitfully, with dreams of young men dying of smallpox, losing limbs to frostbite, or succumbing to terrible battle injuries. He also dreamed of Grace and how much he missed her. Twice he was awakened in the belief the English had discovered her mission. He became frightened that an Atlantic storm had crushed the ship bringing Simon and Gwendolyn to England. Finally, he dreamed of the wedding and Agnes Stiles. This last dream did not cause him to awaken. He slept deeply in the following hours and awakened surprisingly refreshed. For a few moments, Wolfe sat on the side of the bed. Then he washed, dressed, went down to breakfast, and consumed a hearty meal.

Jonathan retrieved his horse and rode into the countryside. "I need fresh air and exercise," he said. He arrived at the Loring home shortly after twelve. Gwendolyn and Simon greeted him. Mr. and Mrs. Loring invited him in.

As they drank tea and ate sandwiches and cakes, Peter Loring turned to Wolfe. "Well, my boy," he said, "How fares the army? After Trenton and Princeton, the men must be quite proud."

There was a tone in his voice that Jonathan did not like. He detected a note of looking down at those in service.

Nevertheless, he responded in an even manner, "Our spirits are high, we are well armed, and the problem with variola is being successfully handled. However, the government and the army are being cheated at every turn. Suppliers are holding back, thinking that continued inflation of paper money will bring even higher prices. Rancid meat and poor quality flour is being shipped. When I ride through Philadelphia, I sense that prosperity is being driven by the war. In the meantime the soldiers suffer, poorly clad and with inadequate food."

"Unfortunately," Peter replied, "Things like that happen in every war. I understand your feelings, Jonathan. You are serving our country well. It's difficult to see those involved improperly cared for."

"Enough of the war and me," Wolfe said, lifting his cup and draining the last of the tea. "I want to hear more about Simon's and Gwendolyn's plans for England."

Simon put down a half-eaten sweet and said, "I mentioned London. I have arranged with a Doctor Hilton, a very illustrious physician, to make rounds with him at St. Barnabas Hospital. There are also lectures on chemistry and discussions of different diseases. I believe it will prove both an adventure and a great learning experience. Gwendolyn will be busy in her our own way," he added, looking at his wife.

"First, I intend to see that we have a proper home," she began. "That seems to be the most important thing a wife can do. After it is appropriately furnished, I will study the fashions. Also, I have friends there and received letters of introduction from several ladies in Philadelphia to their London friends. I do not believe we will have any difficulty in becoming socially engaged. That may prove quite important, especially if we are obliged to stay in England for any length of time. We certainly do not know how long this conflict may last."

Wolfe smiled, "You two appear to have well laid plans. I truly hope the war ends very soon. You both will be greatly missed by me, and by all who love you."

The Lorings excused themselves. The three who remained spoke quietly. They spent another hour together, reminiscing over the past and encouraging one another about the future. Finally, feeling he had imposed on the young couple longer than he should, Jonathan bid farewell, mounted his horse and rode to his quarters.

Wolfe kept thinking about the opportunities awaiting his friend in England. "Simon will return a highly qualified physician," he thought. "Here in the colonies, I remain in a backwater, relatively ignorant in both medicine and the world. However, there is Doctor Rush's chemistry book. I am determined to memorize the contents from cover to cover."

Feeling renewed, Jonathan sprang from the bed. Whistling softly, he dressed for the evening. Once on his horse, Wolfe rode to Agnes' home. Any hesitation brought on by thoughts of Grace was overcome by loneliness and his need to feel a woman's company. He arrived in a morose mood with thoughts of past and coming battles, injured bodies, and dying men and women. Agnes opened the door and greeted him. Seeing her instantly restored him. She was dressed in simple black, contrasting with her blonde hair. Together with her smile, it provided an immediately refreshing picture.

"Good evening, Jonathan, it's good to see you," Agnes said, as Adelaide took his outer garments. She added, "I hope your day has been pleasant," and extended her hand. He took it in his and felt its warmth and softness. The fragrance of her perfume excited him anew.

"I spent the afternoon visiting Simon and Gwendolyn," Wolfe answered. "They are off to England quite soon. Simon, I will dearly miss, and I am just beginning to become acquainted with Gwendolyn."

She listened, smiled again, and led the way to the dining room. The table was laid with fine china, sterling silver utensils, and sparkling crystal. It provided an additional glimpse into the good taste and wealth of the house. After they were seated, fresh oysters accompanied by a pleasant wine were served. Conversation during the meal lingered over the departing couple.

"It's really not my business," Wolfe said, "but expenses in London will certainly prove substantial. Simon's educational costs will be moderate, but Gwendolyn mentioned buying and furnishing a house, and spoke of expeditions into female fashions. A dowry was given the bride, but wartime prices in London must be exorbitant. Where will they obtain the funds?"

Replying, Agnes said, "Do not worry about their funds, Jonathan. Gwendolyn is the only child the Lorings possess. They will see she lacks for nothing. Do not misperceive the new bride. She is young and may seem frivolous. However, I know her well. At one time we spent a great deal of time together. She will accommodate to Simon's situation and ensure that, wherever he practices, he will succeed. You may think her unaware of monetary values. I can assure you she has been well schooled by her parents. My cousin is quite familiar with the ways of commerce and finance. She is neither dull nor ignorant. Remember that well."

She said this with obvious emphasis. Wolfe felt the force of its delivery, and concluded Agnes had experienced some difficulty with her cousin in the past.

The meal over, they moved to the parlor and conversed quietly for a time. Then, taking his hand, she brought him to her bedroom. A single candle glowed at the bedside.

Looking at him, Agnes slowly removed the black dress. She was completely naked beneath it. Jonathan was again astonished. Her body's beauty enthralled him. He kept focusing on the pinkish brown areola surrounding her erect nipples. She came forward and slowly undressed him. Coming closer, Agnes pressed against his body, softly kissing his lips, and then licking and caressing his nipples. The warmth of her body, its continued pressure, and the manipulations of Agnes's hands, lips, and tongue, continued to raise his passion. He took her in a tight embrace and kissed her. She returned the kiss and placed her tongue against his. Tongue against tongue, they continued exciting one another. Finally, she whispered, "Let's use the bed, Jonathan." They tumbled upon it, still locked in an embrace.

Separating for a moment, Agnes blew out the candle, and returned to his waiting arms.

Jonathan caressed her hair, and kissed her lips and neck. She placed his hand on her lower abdomen. "Massage very slowly and gently," she said. A bit later, she moved it over her pubic hair, opened her legs, and brought it over the clitoris. "Very slow, Jonathan, slow is good." He followed her command and, as he gently caressed, it slowly enlarged. The moisture began to flow and he inserted several fingers into her vagina, still using his thumb to continue the stimulation. She opened her thighs widely, breathing became deeper, and she started to moan his name. His penis had grown hard and to its maximum size. He moved on top of her, inserted it, and they made love passionately, reaching a climax almost simultaneously.

They lay together, enjoying the closeness of their bodies. After a time, she rolled onto him, began to stimulate him, and mounted him for a second encounter. Finally exhausted, they lay in each other's perspiration, tightly embracing.

Agnes stretched out and relit the candle. "I am certain, I appear a woman knowledgeable about sex and quite forward," she whispered. "I was sixteen and Stiles was fourteen years older when we married. I was quite innocent. He had been to England and France and was very handsome. There were many dalliances with upper-class women. He became quite experienced in the arts of love, and insisted I learn them all. He was my only partner and lover. I still mourn him, but he is gone. You are the first man to pleasure me since his death. I do not believe you have had very much experience with women, but you learn quickly, and make me feel wonderful." She leaned toward him and kissed him tenderly. Taking in a breath, she added, "Jonathan, I have learned to enjoy being with a man. While I restrain from being wanton, lovemaking is a real necessity for me."

As dawn broke they awakened. Agnes washed first and now appeared rather shy, secreting herself while putting on under garments and a robe. Wolfe groomed himself and dressed quickly. Agnes reappeared, smiled, and said, "Daylight brings back our lost modesty."

They entered the breakfast room and had eggs, coffee and biscuits. "Jonathan, you had mentioned variolating the Continentals," she said. "The pox is not only in Morristown but also in Philadelphia. I, and my children, have not had it, my servants have. If you were able to perform inoculation, they could care for us."

"I have been carrying a vial of ground scabs in my saddlebag. Let me ride about for a time. You can awaken the children and the servants. I will return, and perform them."

Two hours later, Wolfe carried out his promise. Agnes went first. The children watched as she unflinchingly kept her arm and wrist steady. With some encouragement from their mother and the servants, they bravely took their turns.

"You are both wonderful patients," Jonathan said to them. "You followed your mother's example very well. I wish the soldiers would be as courageous as you."

He said goodbye to the children and thanked the servants. Agnes accompanied him to his horse. As Wolfe mounted, she looked up and said, "Take care, Jonathan. I fear you have a habit of being in places where trouble happens."

He leaned down, took her hand and kissed it. "I want to thank you for the hospitality and warmth shown me. You are a beautiful woman, Agnes, and have offered a great deal of yourself. I will be thinking about you frequently." So saying, he straightened, nudged his horse and rode toward Morristown.

XXII

Grace spent two weeks secluded in the house of the merchant. During that time, his wife provided details of the city. The information was carefully absorbed. "Still," the would-be spy thought, "This lady speaks in a way more upper class than commoners. I must walk outdoors and through shops and markets to acquire a common tongue and become aware of local sayings."

When they were young, Grace and Martha played a game in which they attempted to mimic neighbors' speech. During the following weeks, she learned a commoner's manner of speaking and the colloquialisms used, taking on a New York voice. Later, she was introduced to Uriah Pinckney, assigned as her contact and adviser.

"I came to New York to gather intelligence," she said. "I am ready to begin."

"You appear both willing and able," he replied. "We were informed that you are familiar with serving in taverns. I have arranged to place you in The King's Arms, a tavern favored by British officers. Two of the waitresses have taken ill. I know the owner. He was happy to learn you were competent and available."

Work began and she learned terms such as, "M'lord, how may I serve you?" rather than using a patron's rank. Also, "Dearie, you are just too much," was a reply to an officer's joke. The waitresses frequently said, "Move your rear," during a busy evening, as they pushed one another aside to reach a table.

The officers were generally polite. When tipsy, they might try to pull a girl onto their lap or fondle a breast, but it usually stopped there. Often, they would try to arrange an assignation and, speaking sweetly, flatter some of the prettier ones into doing so. Grace would smile or laugh and fend them off.

Contact with Pinckney occurred daily. An accident had crushed his left leg. Using a crutch, he hobbled along, passing by the tavern to his nearby tiny tailoring shop. In the early evening, before the tavern filled, he would arrive. Uriah would order a pint of ale and a small amount of food, often sitting at a table served by Grace.

Several days after she began, he said to her, "Do you have a knife?"

"No," she answered. "Do I need one?"

"Speak to the other barmaids," Uriah said. "All of them carry one during work and when they go walking in the city. This can be a dangerous place. British patrols keep order, but they are not everywhere. Women have been accosted and injured."

She became more familiar with her co-workers, and sounded them out about carrying a concealed blade. "Of course we all carry one," said Lilith. "It is our only real protection. If you do not have a knife, I will help you get one. This is what I carry." She reached beneath her skirt and withdrew a thin eight-inch stiletto.

The next day, Lilith went with her to a shop handling hunting clothing. The proprietor took them to a rear room and showed various knives suitable for the purpose. "That one," Grace said, pointing to a twin of Lilith's blade. "A good choice," smiled the proprietor, "and this is the sheath."

He left the room and Lilith showed her how to strap the sheath-bearing knife to her thigh. "This is how to remove the blade," she said, and did so with a swift sweeping motion. "You have to practice. The quick movement does not come easily."

She paid for the purchase and walked with Lilith to the tavern. Approaching the other barmaids, her companion nodded. It signaled, "She is armed."

Grace worked avidly to gather information. Although gleaning small bits and pieces, nothing of importance was obtained. By April, she was becoming disillusioned, and thoughts of her family kept intruding as she worked.

"No information," she would signal by a slight shake of her head.

"Can't do this much longer," she whispered to Pinckney one evening. "No results."

"Patience is required," he whispered back.

Grace swung between, "Time to go home," and "You must be firm. The spying will bear fruit." However, "Time to go home" rose to prominence.

As April ended, a gray-haired colonel who often dined at the tavern asked her to take a seat opposite him. It was late and the tavern was almost empty.

"Miss Grace," Colonel Edwards began, "do not take offense." Then, sensing some concern, he added, "I am not going to do you harm. I want to tell you that I have observed your quickness and good service. I noted how you gently rebuffed advances, and especially the care you gave to serving the officers and cleaning tables. You have a nice way about you."

"I must explain that my work is at General Howe's headquarters. We are sometimes doing business in his home. Few servants have been brought from England. The matron in charge has employed some local women. She is demanding, requires good service, and is unhappy with several of them. This, of course, is not my bailiwick, but there was unfortunately some disturbance that invaded our work area. Given the situation, I believe my interference would actually be welcomed. After watching you here, I thought you might be suitable. Consider it. If you agree, I will approach the matron. Naturally, an interview and references will be needed. No hurry, but what is your present thinking?"

Grace had difficulty in containing herself, but answered calmly, "Sir, I am most grateful you have offered this to me. At first thought, I am unsure as to whether I can properly fill the position. I can clean and serve well, but it is such a fine house. Do you think I am truly qualified?"

"It is not for me to make the decision. I think you might chance it. Once hired, you should manage quite well."

"Yes, sir. Thank you, sir. It would certainly mean a rise in my station. I do feel a desire to try for the position."

"Then I will mention you to the matron. If she is inclined, you will be informed."

The next evening she whispered to Pinckney, "I may obtain a position at Howe's residence."

Incredulous, he stared at her but said nothing.

Two days later, she was informed that an interview was at hand. Wearing appropriate clothing, Grace was seen by the matron. "Well girl," she said after questioning her, "Stand and turn around several times. I wish to see you from all sides." Satisfied, she concluded with, "You seem adequate. I will verify your references. If proper, we will try you out. Now, you may leave."

Pinckney provided bona fide references and she was hired. At first, her duties involved heavy cleaning, but she was quickly placed in one requiring serving at table or at large parties. At night, when General Howe and upper echelon officers were working late, she brought sandwiches, wine, and whiskey. Colonel Edwards was usually there and offered a quick smile. He had received word that the matron was pleased with her performance. When Grace entered the room, the conversation would abruptly cease. However, growing accustomed to her comings, she might still hear a few words.

In June, news came that, led by General Burgoyne, the British had begun an invasion of the northeast from Canada. He expected to be joined by an army striking from New York. Washington was uncertain whether Howe would push north to join Burgoyne or thrust in another direction. He positioned the Continentals west of the Hudson, midway between Albany and Philadelphia.

Grace assumed Jonathan was with him, "I pray for his safety," she whispered.

"Burgoyne has taken Fort Ticonderoga and is continuing to advance," an aide informed General Howe. At a conference with his staff, Howe said, "General Burgoyne does not require our assistance. We will move on Philadelphia."

At month's end, the harbor was filled with ships. Grace thought, "A major attack must be planned."

On the evening of July 22, 1777, when entering the area where Howe and his officers were working, she heard, " … and their Congress will scatter to the wind." It was followed by laughter. Silence ensued as the officers quaffed their wine and saluted General Howe.

The assembled fleet began departing the following day. It slipped over the horizon as Grace, finding an excuse, left her position and hurried to Uriah Pinckney's shop. She entered just as he was finishing with a customer.

As the man was leaving, Uriah said, "Yes, miss, how may I help you?"

She waited until the door closed and the customer was already several feet away. "Philadelphia is their destination!" she burst out. "It has to be there." Quieting herself, she explained what she had heard.

"Yes, that must be so," Pinckney responded. "You have done good work, Grace. Remain in your present situation. Other valuable material may become available. In the meantime, word must be sent to General Washington."

Grace returned to the Howe residence and resumed her duties until close to midnight. Completing them, she went to her quarters. That night she awakened frequently, wondering when and whether Washington would receive the intelligence.

Her information was delivered on the 28th of July. "This could be valuable," the General said, "but we need confirmation." On the 31st reports reached him that Howe's armada had been sited off Delaware. "This verifies the prior intelligence," he told his aides. "Philadelphia is indeed their goal."

Washington started the Army south. He was aware that Clinton, left behind in New York, still had a large number of troops and could attempt to assist Burgoyne. Nevertheless, his first thoughts were to protect the center of colonial government.

Howe's fleet was delayed by numerous storms. "At last," he exclaimed, as the British began landing in Maryland. "It is over four weeks since setting sail. Our men and horses have suffered storms and illness. They are in far worse condition than when we began."

It took several weeks for his forces to recover. Finally, the British general felt able to start forward. He then moved rapidly, beating Washington in several battles. On September 26, 1777, the English and Hessians entered Philadelphia.

Howe was exultant. "We outflanked Washington at Brandywine and almost crushed his army," he said. "He barely escaped there. Then, he was not positioned to prevent us from crossing the Schuylkill River. Now, we enter the city with our bands playing and colors high. The Tories will turn out to welcome us with open arms."

However, the great Tory reception the triumphant legions expected did not materialize. Tories hesitated to reveal themselves. Congressmen had scattered and many citizens fled before the city fell. As Philadelphia was occupied, almost all those remaining were stunned and kept silent.

At first, the English and Hessian troops were well behaved. Soon, however, the conquerors behaved as many armies did. They invaded and plundered houses or robbed citizens on the streets. The Army of Occupation rapidly became hated by most of Philadelphia's residents.

Five months earlier, at April's end, Simon and Gwendolyn left Philadelphia.

Peter Loring spoke to them, saying, "You should have a smooth journey. The authorities expect a Tory couple to arrive and depart for England. You must behave as Tories. Do not express otherwise throughout your stay in England. Simon, they have been informed you are a doctor who will be studying and possibly practicing there. Gwendolyn, your mother and I, along with Simon's parents, have provided some gold. It will suffice for the immediate future. Rent quarters for the present. If you later desire to purchase something, it will be managed. A merchant in London owes me money. He has been instructed to offer it to you."

"Also, the St. Eustatius voyage has become too hazardous. The Dutch captain and his crew are highly grateful for their employment and are loyal fellows. The ship is now trading between Holland and England. The captain will deposit all funds with my agent in Antwerp. He is an honest man, and I have ordered him to send you all money above that required for the crew and himself. As for letters, all parties must communicate through my Tory friends in New York."

Emily Loring sat, quietly listening. She rose and, after hugging them both, took Gwendolyn aside. Always in control of her emotions, she burst into tears and grasped her daughter in a tight hold. "You are my darling girl," she wept. "I will think about you every waking moment and in my dreams. Please come back to us safely." She continued to kiss Gwendolyn's lips and cheeks. Afterward, she stepped back, once more her composed self.

In June, after a storm tossed voyage, the couple arrived in London. They left the ship somewhat debilitated but eager to venture into their new life.

"London at last," beamed Simon, hugging his wife. "Yes," she smiled back. "I know it will be wonderful. We have much to do and learn. The friends from Philadelphia now living here, and also the friends of friends are Tories. They will provide us with bona fides as to our loyalty to the Crown."

For months they moved in a dream world. The war had made prices expensive but their funds seemed unlimited. Gwendolyn found a house and they bought it. Surprisingly, she was not extravagant on its furnishings. Her clothing was within the current fashion but of moderate expense. Together, she and Simon moved in a circle of young people who were wealthy and clever. All of them supported the King and his Minister.

Howe had brought his army ashore in Maryland at the end of August. On learning of the British landing, Peter Loring and his wife spent several hours devising their plans. "The city will fall," he said. "I would assume our house is to become occupied by some general and his staff. Anything of value is certain to disappear. You, my dear, must arrange to pack the silver and the most valuable furniture and paintings. Replace them with a few common goods."

"What about transportation, and where are they to go?" she asked.

"I will arrange for transit and have already purchased a place to the west, near to Lancaster. As for our gold, I have buried some of it here, working at night."

Emily raised her eyebrows, silently questioning that he had done the work himself.

"Yes, is my answer to you," he smiled in a satisfied manner. "This body is still capable of doing what is required of it."

She smiled in return, saying, "Peter, you certainly remain the man I married."

He rose from his chair and went to his wife. After kissing her, he said, "I must add that the burial locations have been carefully mapped. The remainder of the gold I shall carry to Lancaster and bury it there."

"What of the ships? How will you manage them?"

"Presently they are safe. One, as you know, is now trading between Holland and England. The privateer is at sea. I am relying on its captain to make safe harbor in some port. The third is already in South Carolina at Charleston and is quite secure."

"Have you told any of our friends of our plans to leave Philadelphia?"

"Only cousin Agnes. She has chosen a place north of Germantown. It is a good selection and she is moving there with the children and her valuables. You know she is a clever investor. Her St. Eustatius investment did very well."

"Good," she said. "Agnes Stiles is one of the people I truly like."

XXIII

Following Burgoyne's success at Ticonderoga his Canadian forces and their Indian allies continued to advance. But they were slowed, and finally stopped well short of the intended Albany destination. Howe had struck at Philadelphia, unaware that the Continentals confronting the descending British and Hessians had been joined by thousands of militiamen. The army from Canada was virtually surrounded and running short of food and supplies. Their numbers diminished by illness and injury, Indian allies melting away, they attacked at Freeman's Farm near Saratoga on September 19th. The attack failed and heavy losses were sustained.

The Hessian commander, von Riedesel, spoke to Burgoyne, saying, "I advise a retreat to Canada, General."

"No, we will strike again and break through their lines," the British general replied.

On October 7th, the attack was launched. It was Burgoyne's last desperate attempt to achieve success and reach Albany.

General Gates, the American commander, had resolved to use a defensive strategy. Following a dispute over tactics, and despite being ordered by Gates off the field, primed by whiskey, General Benedict Arnold rode into the battle. "Forward men!" he cried. Seizing a flag, plunging his horse ahead, urging the Americans to follow, his daring swept the field. English and Hessian troops fled before him and enemy opposition collapsed.

Closing on his opponents, Arnold was again shot in the same leg as in the failed American attack on Quebec. His horse was also struck and fell on him, crushing the wounded leg. But his action had proven decisive. At days end, the Battle of Saratoga had been fought and the Americans stood victorious.

Burgoyne sat in his quarters. "Generals Howe or Clinton were to strike from New York up the Hudson," he said to his commanders. "Together we could break the American lines. Now, we are surrounded but must delay surrender. I still hope for relief."

His hopes were in vain. Clinton, now in charge of New York, never came. On October 17, 1777, Burgoyne surrendered with almost 5,900 English and Hessian troops. Horatio Gates took full credit for the victory. In his report to Congress, he failed to mention Arnold's bravery and effectiveness in the battle.

In Philadelphia, General Howe had initially posted almost half his forces in Germantown. Subsequently, some were withdrawn south into the city. Washington became aware that the number positioned to the north at Germantown had been significantly reduced. The news from Saratoga had been received and the General was warmed by the information. Nevertheless, he thought, "Gates has achieved a great triumph and is in high esteem. I have only had defeat since Trenton and Princeton. I must also gain a victory. Germantown seems the way. Its garrison has fewer troops than we. A quick strike can bring success."

His plan was complicated, required close coordination, and

doomed to fail. Fog, delayed attacks, and lost regiments combined to snatch defeat from the jaws of victory.

Wolfe sat with Miller. Now a sergeant, he drove the first of two wagons. On the second was Jameson, recently promoted to corporal. "We have painted DOCTOR on both sides and the rear of our wagons," Miller said. "Also, on the banner above us. We hope that when they see it, the English and Hessians will not shoot. How do the signs strike you, sir?" the sergeant asked. "Jameson and I completed them just this morning."

"They are well placed and can be seen from a distance," Wolfe answered. "The question remains as to whether or not they will be honored. I harbor doubts about their effectiveness. Its best I carry a pistol and we keep loaded muskets in the wagons."

"So far, it appears the results of the early fighting are encouraging," he added. "Our men are pressing the enemy back. You and Jameson should gather the wounded. I will triage and treat them. Men able to ambulate are to be sent to the rear. Those seriously injured and capable of surviving are to be placed in the wagons. The ones beyond help must be set aside."

As the fighting progressed, British reinforcements arrived and the Continental's right wing collapsed. Retreat became necessary. Exploding shells and cannon balls fell about the wagons. The smell of gunpowder from muskets and rifles hung in the air. The terrible sounds of battle rose to a crescendo and wounded, dying and retreating men milled about them. "Turn the wagons," Jonathan called. The wagons were turned about and they joined the retreat.

General Washington rode into the fray, exposing himself to enemy gunfire and rallying his men. "Stand fast! Stand fast!" he called, and the Americans rallied and fought to stem the enemy's advance. Once more the Army escaped.

The fighting ebbed and flowed, and Wolfe would call, "Stop, we have room for more wounded."

Later, Miller said, "The wagons are fully loaded, sir. Each has eight wounded. The weight is tiring the horses."

They moved slowly, the moans of the wounded accompanying them. Then a wheel on Jameson's wagon loosened and he yelled, "Halt! Halt!" Jonathan and Miller went to aid him, but the weight of the injured men was too great. The three could not raise the wagon sufficiently to permit pushing the wheel into place. "Help us! Stop for a moment and help!" they called to the retreating men. But those fleeing were anxious to get safely away and failed to respond to their entreaties.

The sounds of battle had subsided when six redcoats appeared. They had come silently and were now only ninety feet away. Moving forward, their muskets were held low, positioned to use the attached bayonets. The knife-like daggers reflected the setting sun and glinted a reddish gold.

Miller began pointing at the signs, yelling "Doctor! Doctor!" Momentarily hesitating, the grenadiers suddenly surged forward. Their intention to take no prisoners was apparent. To them, the Americans were unarmed and easy targets.

At fifty feet, Wolfe shouted "Arms out!" He drew his pistol and fired at twenty-five, bringing down the sergeant in the lead. Miller and Jameson each retrieved a musket, fired and two more fell. There was no chance to reload and the remaining grenadiers quickly closed the gap.

Death hovered above them, when shots rang out. The charging English toppled to the ground. Stunned, Jonathan and the others turned to where the firing had come. From the woods fifty yards away, five men appeared. They were in buckskin, carried rifles, and were obviously snipers sent to pick off enemy troops. The central figure raised his rifle in triumph and salute. As he came closer, they recognized his face. It was Tim, the boy they had cared for when he was ill with the pox.

"Tim," exclaimed Wolfe, "Your skill saved us from a bayonet stick. We owe our lives to you and your friends."

"We were just in time, I guess," he answered with a grin.

"Just in time and very accurate," whooped Miller as he hugged him.

"We have been searching for this group," said one of Tim's fellows, pointing to the dead bodies. "We heard there were English going about and killing our wounded. It was lucky we picked up their trail and were here just as they charged."

"Yes, thankfully you arrived at the right moment," Wolfe said, mopping his brow.

Another man pointed to the loose wheel. "I see why you were stopped," he said. "That wheel is about to come free." Seeing the wounded and hearing their groans, he added, "You have a full load. We will have to use all of us to raise the wagon, even then it will be difficult."

"There is a way," said a third. "Come with me." Leaving Tim as a guard, Miller, Jameson and four of the men ran into the woods, returning with logs and a sturdy pole.

"Now," said the organizer, "Pile the logs. They will serve as what is called a fulcrum. Using the pole as our lever, we can place it over the logs and under the wagon. All but one will pull down to raise it. The free man can push the wheel into place and secure it."

Following his instructions, success was achieved. As dusk descended, they were again moving, the riflemen following as a rear guard. An hour later, surrounded by darkness, the army was rejoined. Wolfe and his aides spent most of the night and the next day tending the wounded. Afterwards, wherever the Continentals moved they followed.

Across the ocean, France received word of the victory at Saratoga on December 3rd. The next day, Benjamin Franklin strode from his Paris mansion rejuvenated. He moved with a quicker step and felt years younger than he had only two days before. He and his fellow commissioners, Arthur Lee and Silas Deane, had celebrated the colonials' victory. Today, the good news absorbed, they met again.

"I'm certain Foreign Minister Vergennes and the King will quickly bring France into our war against England," Franklin said.

Deane demurred, saying, "I am not sure it will be quick. They may continue to secretly supply us with funds and arms, but England has thrashed them in recent battles. I suspect they will still hesitate. Before doing so, Louis XVI may desire Spain to enter the conflict alongside him. It would provide a larger fleet and strength in numbers."

"I agree with Deane," added Lee. "Vergennes will offer some aid, but may not feel France is ready for direct action. Still, our negotiating position has improved. England is sure to offer some compromise. France is in a position to recoup the prestige it lost in the French and Indian Wars. We can play them against one another. Their spies are everywhere and they will learn of the advances each make to us."

"Benjamin," smiled Deane, "You can shed those plain suits and fur hat you have been wearing. Your portrayal of the innocent American is not accomplishing much."

Franklin laughed and responded, "France has an autocratic King, but the opinion of the people and particularly the aristocracy bear weight. If Louis XVI believes there is extensive support for a war against England, he will more readily move in that direction. My velvet suits can be resumed in America. The fur hat will definitely be discarded."

Laughing along with Franklin, they plotted future strategy.

Foreign Minister Vergennes discussed the situation with his King, "Sire, we have been most circumspect in providing money and arms to the Americans. However, we are both aware England knows of our activities. The rebels' victory at Saratoga convinces me they will be the ultimate victors. We must ask what France has to gain by joining the conflict. We may not regain Canada, but the Caribbean islands are very valuable. To gain them would offer us vast stores of sugar. More importantly, an independent America would be grateful for our help and prove a profitable trading partner. England would no longer have sole access to the wealth available in its former colonies."

"All very well," replied the King. "What about their Royal Navy?"

Vergennes was ready with the answer, "If we secure Spanish support, our two fleets would overwhelm the Royal Navy. Spain is desperate to regain Gibraltar from England. We can offer a joint force to secure it."

"And what will you offer the American delegates?" asked Louis XVI.

"With your approval, sire, I will offer them two alliances, both in secrecy. The first will be a treaty of commerce. The second will be a military alliance. It will stipulate that France chooses the time we actively join the conflict. To satisfy them, it will state that any peace treaty must recognize the independence of the colonies."

"So," said the King, "I am assisting a rebel movement to secure victory over one of God's legitimate monarchs."

"Not at all your highness," replied Vergennes. "George III has not been crowned by a priest and does not follow the faith. He is an enemy of France. The honor of your realm will be restored by our victory, and the Royal Treasury reimbursed by our conquests."

On February 6, 1778, both treaties of alliance were signed at the offices of the French Foreign Minister.

XXIV

After Germantown, the Continentals encamped at a place called Valley Forge. Washington called his generals and aides together. “Gentlemen,” he said, “This was not my first choice for wintering the Army. Smaller, somewhat separated sites would be better. In that way, we could feed and supply the men far easier than in one large encampment. However, Congress demanded that we keep together and not too far from Philadelphia. They fear that disbursal into smaller units could result in a reverse of Trenton and Princeton. In addition, they actually want us to attack Howe. What are we to attack with?”

“Mon General,” Lafayette interjected, “we will be resupplied and more men will join the cause.”

Behind their hands, others smiled knowingly. One general spoke out, “Since General Mifflin resigned as head of the quartermasters, no one has been appointed to replace him. The private contractors have failed to deliver on time or provided goods of low quality. Spoiled meat and rancid flour are the norm. Valley Forge will become a place of privation and death.”

Nevertheless, construction of the camp proceeded. Wolfe helped stock a hastily built hospital. Cold air leaked in through gaps between the logs, but potbellied stoves provided some warmth. Cots were crowded together and ragged or naked men slept beneath a tattered blanket or with none at all.

Wolfe and Farnsworth had worked together since Morristown and were now close friends. As the winter moved forward, freezing cold and lack of boots and clothing created new problems.

One evening, working by the light of several oil lamps, Jonathan completed the amputation of a private's two frozen and blackened legs. He was exhausted and dejected. With a bitter tone, he began a diatribe. "Oliver, we trained to be physicians and they have turned us into surgeons. No, not surgeons, rather butchers. We bear knives and saws, removing the black fingers, toes and legs of both young and old. They, like us, are trapped in this frigid winter. I have lost count of the amputations done, and cannot recall the faces of the men on whom I have performed the butchery. It has all been so unnecessary. Clothing, socks and boots could have prevented it. These unfortunate men will be sent home. Their wives and sweethearts will receive three quarters or one half of the man who left them, or perhaps nothing at all."

Farnsworth recognized the exhaustion in his friend, and said, "Jonathan, you have been deprived of sleep and worked beyond reason. Please, go to our cabin and get some rest."

Wolfe became calmer and rose as though to leave, but paused and started again. "Yes, I will return to our cabin. We officers sleep six together and are housed in a two-roomed structure. We are warmed by two fireplaces and covered by a blanket. Over there, Miller and Jameson are working just as hard as we do. They sleep with ten others in a drafty cabin with but one fireplace. I have been inside that cabin. The fireplace is poorly built and does not draw properly. Smoke pervades the room."

Recognizing the near hysteria of his friend, Oliver called to the aides as Wolfe continued. "Our men are covered with lice, poorly fed, and ill clothed. Typhus and dysentery have become rampant among them. Thousands of our soldiers are in hospital, sick and dying. We officers still receive meat and bread, even some vegetables. Yet, just yesterday, one complained he was merely receiving weak beer and low quality ale. Poor fellow, his store of wine and whiskey had been consumed and he could not replenish it."

Miller and Jameson started toward them. Jonathan's voice rose and he became aware that he was beginning to attract attention. He lowered it and almost whispered, "Farnsworth, you and I are cut from similar cloth. Both our families were not poor but by no means wealthy. Both struggled to provide funds to educate us. We are physicians because of their struggles. We fully understand class distinction and live with it each day. I accept it reluctantly, but I accept it. Many of the officers are wealthy or from wealthy families. Some are political appointees foisted on General Washington. Some have proven competent and many have failed the test of battle. We require a system of merit."

The two aides were now at hand. Oliver turned to them and said, "Doctor Wolfe is exhausted. It is snowing heavily and you must assist him to his cabin. Afterward, since you both have worked till nightfall, go to your cabin and rest."

Securing their threadbare coats, they assisted Wolfe into his. Placing him between them, they left and struggled through the snow. Entering his cabin, they saluted the officers there. One of them stepped forward to help and they deposited Jonathan, fully clothed, onto his bed.

"Thank you," he murmured, as they covered him with a blanket.

Departing, Miller and Jameson went to their cabin. Before retiring, they spoke together, bemoaning how hard their doctor was working. "A good man," they kept repeating.

Later, Farnsworth also returned to the cabin. Wolfe was fast asleep and Oliver felt his friend's forehead. "There is no evidence of fever," he whispered. Once during the night, Oliver awakened and found Jonathan half off the cot. He rose, repositioned him, and returned to his own bed.

The morning brought another day of cold weather. The officers were rising. Most had slept in their clothes. The night's freeze had penetrated the cabin. Using only slightly warmed water, they scratched away at scraggly beards in an attempt to present a small measure of appropriate military appearance.

During breakfast, Jonathan assured Farnsworth he was again able to perform his duties. Suddenly, he whispered, "I am fully recovered and thank you for helping me last evening. However, I slept fitfully and dreamed about our wounded troops. In my dreams, I saw them fall and how their comrades, on occasion, tried to carry back the severely injured. On dying, these men were hastily buried by friendly hands in shallow, poorly marked graves. Many others were left behind. They lay on their backs, their unseeing eyes staring at an unfeeling sky. I tell you that I saw the birds of the air circle above them. They would swoop down and those eyes would be plucked out. Lying there, the bodies were torn by wild dogs and beasts of the field. The skeletons were bleached beneath the sun."

"I dreamed of farmers in years to come toiling in fields previously untilled. They would find the bones. Some, having served with us, would recognize a Continental buckle or another sign that it was the remains of a comrade in arms. They would bury those bones with reverence. Others would cast them aside or plow over them."

Farnsworth put his arm about Wolfe's shoulders. "Jonathan," he whispered, "You do no good to carry on like this. Please stop, you are unsettling me as well as yourself."

Wolfe persisted, but was calmer and spoke slowly. "Doctor Rush, who was my teacher, much admires the British system. After every battle, they attempt to recover both their wounded and their dead. They bury the dead in marked graves and record their names. Even if the bodies are not recovered, the names of the missing must be set down. Their officers, unlike ours, are obliged to write letters of consolation to families of the dead. In addition, whether a man is wounded or ill, officers must visit them in hospital to ensure they are properly treated."

"When General Mercer was gravely wounded and taken captive by the enemy near Princeton, Washington sent Doctor Rush to aid him. Taken through the lines, he assisted in his care. The English doctors treated Mercer well and accorded Rush every courtesy. Impressed by their ability and concern for the injured, he studied their methods. He convinced me that we should be following in their footsteps."

Oliver sighed and said, "Jonathan we are a young army and an even younger medical service. Both require more training, more experience, and better organization. With time and patience we will improve in all our affairs."

"Amen to the last," Wolfe replied, "but my patience is being tried and I fear time may be running out." They finished their meal in silence. When they stood, Jonathan took his friend in a great hug and whispered, "Oliver, it has been my pleasure to serve with you. No matter how long this war, my sincerest wish is to continue at your side." Releasing him, Wolfe jumped up and rose well off the floor. His spirit was obviously renewed. On landing, he said, "Doctor Farnsworth, I am fit for duty once more."

Despite attempts to improve conditions, the enlisted men continued to suffer through the winter. Desertions became commonplace and ill clothed disgruntled men entered the British lines. Sickness and death further shrunk the army's ranks and replacements were few in number.

At a meeting with his aides, Washington said, "Gentlemen, our situation appears bleak, but we must maintain a positive attitude. Congress has been meeting in Lancaster. I have been assured of further efforts to increase recruitment. Conscription has been instituted with terms increased to three years or till we achieve victory."

"What manner of men will we obtain?" asked Alexander Hamilton. "Wealthy men have avoided entry into the army by paying the poor to do their service. Those conscripted will constitute a poor man's army."

"Poor men can fight as well as rich men," said another aide. "They require encouragement and we must instill the belief that better times lie ahead for them."

"Gentlemen," said the General, "Irrespective of rich or poor, recruits will be coming. Variolation must continue. It has eliminated the fear of the small pox. Thankfully, that horror has been lifted from us. Some good news, I have secured blankets and shoes. Also, Congress has ordered that promotions below the rank of Major General will require my approval. They will be based solely on merit."

Whispered conversations began. Washington interrupted them, saying, "Thank you, gentlemen, you are dismissed."

Several weeks into February, Martha again joined him. Her arrival buoyed the spirits of her husband and the troops. Washington assumed a more relaxed demeanor. The General's wife organized dances and parties. Once settled into his private quarters, they renewed their romance and love making.

Later, Wolfe and Farnsworth stood together, observing the performance of General von Steuben. He was in a field drilling one hundred men, attempting to teach them close order maneuvers. The "Baron" only spoke German. Watching, it was obvious von Steuben was actively cursing in his native tongue, relying on a translator and body language to communicate.

"Well," said Oliver, "what is your opinion of the new drillmaster? Apparently he has claimed that, within a few months, the Continentals will be marching as well as English or Hessian soldiers. Shall we place a small wager as to his success?"

"Agreed," laughed Jonathan. "Would you mind if I take the negative side? I really cannot fathom how that man can succeed."

"Not at all," Farnsworth answered. "I rather like the old campaigner. I believe he will succeed, though I must confess not having any idea as to how he shall do so."

By the weeks end, von Steuben said through his translator, "You are marching as well as any troops. Now go out, each man will train an additional one hundred. The entire army will learn how to march and maneuver." Beneath his breath he added, "More importantly, they will learn to follow orders."

In May, word was received that Congress had approved the Franco-American alliance treaties. Washington organized a Day of Joy. On May 6th, the two doctors again stood near the drill field. As the sun shone on the green grass, a cannon roared. The Continentals started to march. Wolfe and Farnsworth watched as the General reviewed the newly trained troops. Company after company passed by in perfect order. Oliver stuck out his hand. "Well done," Jonathan laughed and deposited a large coin into it.

XXV

The Penn mansion, the largest home in the city, was chosen by General Howe for use as both his headquarters and personal dwelling. Because of doubt as to the loyalty of the locals, the matron of the New York residence was ordered to provide competent, loyal staff. Grace was one of those approached.

"I would prefer to stay in New York, ma'am," she said. "However, I value my position and wish to please you. Philadelphia will certainly be a new experience. I will go ma'am, and thank you for asking me."

"Very good, my dear," she replied. "Pack your things. You will leave in the morning."

To herself, Grace said, "I cannot inform Uriah of my new location. I must contact the intelligence service after arriving in Philadelphia."

The servants travelled by wagon and cart over both good and poor roads. It took ten days to reach Philadelphia. By then, all were covered in dust and eagerly awaited reaching the city. As they did, a torrential rain fell, providing an unwelcome greeting.

"Oh, Grace," said Matilda Parson, a young scullery maid, "I am so frightened by the storm. I came along fearing my position might otherwise be lost. I have family in New York and miss them already."

"You can always come to me when you are lonely or frightened," Grace replied.

Over the next months, Matilda often said, "Grace, you are my newest and best friend. Somehow, I will repay your kindness."

Once established in her new position, Grace thought, "I must inform the spy network of my whereabouts. I may again be able to learn General Howe's plans."

Her free period was Thursday afternoon, and she walked to the Ben Franklin School. A new sign had been placed in front of the building reading "School for Children."

School hours had ended. As Grace approached, the schoolmaster was leaving. Seeing her, his expression never changed. He entered his carriage, started the horse, and gave the barest of nods.

Two days later, Martha came down the stairs at an early hour. She found a note beneath the door. Opening it, she sat down and tears came to her eyes. "She is in Philadelphia," it read. Awakening the others, Martha excitedly divulged the good news. At breakfast, Elias said, "Grace is most probably among General Howe's servants. She must still be a spy. If by chance we come upon her, our familiarity must not be indicated. Joshua, you must remember this. It is very important."

"I will remember, uncle," said the boy. Each time he left the house, he whispered to himself, "Remember."

General Howe named Joseph Galloway as Police Commissioner of Philadelphia. He was also charged with organizing an intelligence network. Galloway spoke to his wife, "I failed to succeed in turning aside the radicals when I was a delegate to the First Convention. I merely slowed their progress toward this foolish war. Now, I will seek out each one. They and any Sons of Liberty member will be thrown in prison. I hope to hang them all."

Doctor Peabody's leadership of the organization had always been kept secret. As a respected scholar, he continued as headmaster of the school. Known members of the Sons of Liberty hid or left the city. Elias McKenzie stayed on and continued to run his tavern, now favored by sergeants and corporals of the enemy army.

As the British occupation continued, Galloway improved his intelligence gathering. The decline in the number of able-bodied Continentals at Valley Forge became well known. "General Howe," reported Galloway, "The rebel army is in a sorry state. Sir, I would urge that now is the time to destroy those malcontents."

Howe remained immobile. His officers grumbled about their commander's lack of aggressiveness. Galloway, the leader of the city's Tories, complained to his fellows, "Howe chooses to remain safe in Philadelphia. It is shameful he does so. He should be confronting the malnourished and sick remnants of the rebel army."

Working at Penn House, Grace was frequently called upon to serve food and drink inside headquarters. She readily became aware of the Howe's refusal to move against Washington. Each Thursday afternoon, she walked to the School for Children. Doctor Peabody would be by his carriage, pretending to be busy loading books or school papers. On the first two occasions, Grace moved her head slightly to indicate there was no news. On their third encounter, passing the headmaster, she whispered, "All is safe. No attack planned." Thereafter, she would signal "No attack," by a slight movement of her head.

Within Valley Forge, General Washington spoke to his confidants, "Howe has a numerically superior army. I continue to wonder why he fails to strike. Yet, intelligence indicates the British do not plan to attack."

XXVI

In August, two months after arriving in London, Simon and Gwendolyn, having finished dinner, were enjoying an evening at home.

Feeling the glow of her company, he said, “Sweetheart, I am truly a fortunate man. You encourage me to pursue my studies and are always smiling. I feel loved and very comfortable.” He took her in his arms and kissed her.

“I love and admire you more each day,” Gwendolyn replied, kissing him. “You continue courting me, but I want to hear about your studies. I am truly interested in your telling me about them.”

Hunt began, “I have found English medicine more advanced than in the colonies. The lectures are excellent. Doctor Hilton arranged for me to accompany senior physicians on visits to hospitalized patients and examine them. We discuss findings, diagnosis, and treatment. It is all very exciting and I am learning new things each day. Being here has been wonderful for me and I hope for you.”

“Also, for me,” Gwendolyn replied. He kissed her again. She put her head in his lap, thought for a moment and said, “What about your visits to Parliament?”

Simon frowned. “There’s the rub,” he replied. “Listening to North and his cohorts, I am becoming convinced the colonies will never gain representation. However, there is opposition to the war. Some officers in both the army and navy have refused to fight their American cousins. A small minority in Parliament is calling for negotiations and even freedom for the colonies. Still, the King seems increasingly intransigent in his determination to bring the rebels to heel."

"I was wondering about that," Gwendolyn said, taking his hand and playfully licking the palm. Hunt felt a thrill run through him. She smiled and looked at him, saying, "We must be careful to maintain ourselves as Tories."

"Yes," he replied, "You are right," and kissed her passionately.

Gwendolyn whispered, "Husband, I am over four months with child. My nausea during our voyage was part of the morning sickness, but it is gone. I am now at ease."

Stunned, Simon yelled exultantly, "With child! With child! I am to be a father and you a mother!" He took her hands in his and kissed them, saying, "Gwendolyn, my darling Gwendolyn, you continue to make me very happy. You are the most beautiful and most adorable woman in the world." Suddenly, his thoughts altered and he became concerned. "But are you all right? Are you comfortable? Can I help you to bed?"

"Simon," she laughed, "I am perfectly fine and will deliver a healthy and lovely child. Please take hold of yourself. You are behaving like the proverbial expectant father."

"Yes, indeed I am," he laughed. "I will assume a more dignified approach." He suddenly took her in his arms and repeatedly kissed her lips as they laughed in joy.

Over the next several months, as Gwendolyn showed and her belly swelled, they partied less and spent more time together in quiet evenings at home. They became even more loving, conversing about their futures and what to name a son or daughter.

"Simon," declared Gwendolyn one evening, "The baby's name is best determined after it is born. I have hired a midwife who has birthed many of my friends. I must still arrange for a proper nursery and nursemaid. I am due in three months."

They had written to their parents. The Hunts and Lorings became closer as they anticipated a new grandchild. Alfred and Prudence had a two-year old boy and were delighted that he would have a cousin as a playmate.

February 1778 was cold and bleak. Simon had asked a physician who sometimes consulted on female problems to be available. On a drab Tuesday morning, Gwendolyn went into labor. Over the next eight hours all went well and that afternoon the child was born. Simon was outside the door, alternately sitting in a chair and then pacing in circles. The nursemaid stuck her head out the door and said, "You have a beautiful little girl, Doctor Hunt. She is robust and cries well. Mrs. Hunt is also doing nicely."

Simon relaxed and sat quietly, expecting to soon be called in to see Gwendolyn and the child. After thirty minutes, he became apprehensive and started for the door. It opened and the nursemaid appeared. Her face was ashen.

"Doctor," she sobbed, "The bleeding will not stop. The afterbirth came out nicely, but your wife is bleeding fiercely."

Hunt raced to Gwendolyn's side. She lay on the bed, exhausted from her labors. Her face was very pale but she showed a sweet smile and said, "There seems to be a problem, my darling Simon. However, I have given you a daughter. You must love her as you love me."

Leaning forward, he kissed her lips and took hold of her hand, trying to remain calm as he saw the red blood extend further on the white sheets. The midwife was still working beneath them. The consultant doctor had entered the room and he stooped down to join her. After several minutes, he stood erect and motioned Simon to accompany him.

In the hall, the elderly doctor appeared distressed. "Doctor Hunt, I am overwhelmed by what is happening. In truth, I have never seen such a case. Several colleagues mentioned encountering such a problem and found no solution. I became interested in learning about this manner of hemorrhaging. I wrote to doctors in Glasgow, Edinburgh, and Paris. Several answered, saying they had seen or heard of this type of bleeding. None offered a solution, except one doctor from Glasgow who had seen two such cases. Thereafter, he carefully studied female anatomy. He wrote that the only possible solution was to remove the womb. That we cannot do."

The consultant was concerned for his colleague. He put his hand on Hunt's shoulder and said, "I have been of no assistance in your hour of need, Doctor Hunt. I have, however, been truthful. You have an excellent reputation, and I hope you will continue your studies. Now you must be with your wife. I heard her words as I entered the room. She is a brave woman." He gently patted Simon's shoulder and departed.

Returning to the room, Hunt recalled Wolfe's telling of the young man shot in the groin. The midwife was still working beneath the sheets. The nursemaid was taking the newborn child to the nursery. Simon looked at his daughter for barely a moment. He could only think of Gwendolyn. He sat by her side, holding her hand and whispering his love.

The midwife stood up. Tears ran down her cheeks as she left. Gwendolyn stared at him, pale and silent as a marble statue. Then she closed her eyes and drifted away.

Simon did not release her hand, but continued holding it into the next afternoon. A physician friend, hearing Gwendolyn was in labor, stopped by to congratulate the couple on their new baby. Shocked at the news of her death, he inquired about Simon and the newborn.

"Sir," said the servant, "The child is fine. It is a girl. She cries well and appears healthy. We are concerned about the master. He has not left the room where Mrs. Hunt lies. We do not know what to do."

For a moment Bartholomew Graham stood silent. Then, he said, "I believe it might be wise if I saw Doctor Hunt."

The woman hesitated, but replied, "Yes, sir. It is this way."

She led him to the birthing room. He knocked on the door. There was no reply. On opening it, he briefly gazed at Gwendolyn, now lying in a pool of congealed blood. Graham went to his friend and very softly said, "It is time to leave this room, Simon."

There was no response. Hunt continued to stare blankly ahead. Graham separated his friend's and Gwendolyn's hands. He grasped Simon and lifted him to an erect position.

Hunt suddenly focused his eyes on his friend. "Hello, Bartholomew," he said. "Gwendolyn is dead," and proceeded to sob uncontrollably.

"Is there a guest bedroom?" Graham asked the servant.

"Yes, sir. It is always made ready. Please follow me."

Bartholomew helped Simon to the room, placed him upon the bed and covered him with quilts. He weakly resisted but fell asleep. Graham sat at the bedside. Remembering the couple's solicitor, he wrote a note and had the servant bring it to him.

Nicholas Allendale responded quickly. He came to the house and spoke with Graham. "I am familiar with their church," he said.

"I will make arrangements for the funeral. Mrs. Allendale is coming. She will arrive shortly and see that the servants clean Mrs. Hunt and properly dress her. They must also dispose of whatever is unsightly. Doctor Graham, you have done this house a great service. Permit me to relieve you."

Gwendolyn was buried several days later. It was a Sunday. Her funeral was well attended by their young friends and Simon's colleagues. He managed to thank everyone who came, but was inconsolable. For several weeks, he sat in his study staring blankly ahead. He ate little and failed to groom himself. He ignored the child, who had not yet been named, and never saw her. One day, as he passed the nursery, he heard her laugh. It reminded him of Gwendolyn's and he entered the room. The nursemaid was playing with her and the infant was responding. He looked at the tiny being and saw in her his departed wife. "Your name is Gwendolyn," he said and took her in his arms.

Simon Hunt was reborn. He returned to his room, washed, and looking in the mirror saw he now possessed a red beard. "I will not shave," he whispered. "I will keep it."

He resumed his medical education, but always played with his tiny daughter each morning and evening. Nevertheless, something within him remained dissatisfied. It was not only the absence of his wife. Hunt kept thinking of how she died and how ignorant male physicians were of females and the birthing process. He sought out the few dissections being performed on women and studied their internal organs and blood supply. He saw normal and diseased organs but determined to also learn about childbirth.

Simon found the midwife who delivered Gwendolyn. "I want to accompany you on your birthings and learn about the process," he said.

"Doctor," she answered, "I am unable to help you, even though I may wish to do so. The women I serve and their husbands would never permit a male to attend."

"I will pay to learn," Hunt replied.

"Sir, I will ask the other midwives. Possibly one may be able to teach you."

"Why is a gentleman trying to learn a woman's occupation?" the midwives asked. "He must be a peculiar fellow," they laughed. Nevertheless, word was passed about. The higher ranks refused. Finally, one midwife stepped forward.

"I work among the poorer folk, Doctor," Charity Peters said, when shown to him. She was poorly clothed, heavy in body, and missing several teeth, but presented a clean appearance. "They may allow you to see the birthing, if you will pay them a small fee," she added.

"That will be satisfactory." Hunt said.

Simon observed ten deliveries and inquired whether he could do one. The answer was an emphatic no. But an offer of even more money gained permission.

He was taken to a hovel where a woman lay on a table in full labor. Simon discarded his jacket and rolled up his shirtsleeves.

"Wait for the crowning," Charity said, as the top of the infant's head appeared. "Now bring it forth."

"There is tearing of the surrounding tissues," Simon said.

"Not to worry," came the answer. "Turn the head and bring forth the shoulders."

As he delivered one shoulder and then the other, she added, "Let the child come forth." The newborn fully descended from its mother's womb but did not cry.

"Hand me the child," Charity said. Receiving it, she smacked its buttocks and it began to wail. Satisfied, Charity placed it on the tired mother's abdomen, saying, "A boy for you, dearie." Then she used a bit of string, tied the umbilical cord and divided it. "Now we await the afterbirth," the midwife said. When the placenta delivered, she threw it into a waiting bucket. Again Charity turned to the child, wiped the birth fluids off and handed it to a woman standing by. "Swaddle your grandson, Mary," she said in a kindly voice.

"Charity," Simon said, "The tissues have been torn almost to her anus."

"I have seen far worse," she answered. "Most often it heals. Healed or not, they still bear more children. Children are the blessing and curse of the poor."

Hunt persisted in his acquisition of the newfound knowledge. On two occasions he helped turn a transverse lying fetus. On a third, he persisted when Charity had ceased her efforts. She smiled and said, "You are learning well, Doctor." They could not solve the most difficult problem of turning a fetus descending feet first. It was destructive to the newborn from birth injuries, and to the mother from tears to her vagina that often extended into the rectum and anus.

Finally, Charity said, "Doctor, I can teach you nothing more. You are now my better."

Hunt decided to strike out on his own and descended into the heart of London's slums, offering his services for no payment. Several desperate women, unable to pay a midwife and delivering either alone or with a relative, sought him out. As his reputation spread among the poorest, more called on him.

He had instructed the servants to always answer the door and hear the message. Often it would be the middle of the night. "The doctor is needed," was the usual statement. Simon would be awakened and go to the bedside. He began to be accompanied by several strong men, sent by leaders of local gangs. They would precede him into the bowels of the most violent slums, ensuring his safe passage to and from a delivery.

His tall lean figure and flaming red beard earned him the name "Doctor Redbeard." On hearing of it, he smiled, delighted at his new title.

Moving past his fiftieth delivery, Hunt continued to consider the tearing of the tissues about the vaginal opening. "I must act to prevent a tear into the rectum and anus," he thought.

His next delivery was a young girl's first pregnancy. The delivery progressed rapidly and, as the head crowned, Simon saw the surrounding tissues thin out. "A tear is beginning in the midline," he said. Quickly, he inserted two fingers from his left hand beneath the tissues on her right. "Now, cut," Hunt exclaimed, and with a scalpel cut through the stretched out tissue, thereby enlarging the vaginal opening and preventing a midline tear.

"Not too much bleeding," Simon said. "Now the head comes nicely. Push hard, Mrs. Latham. Now here are the shoulders and the baby."

He cleared material from the newborn's mouth, tapped it lightly on the buttock and it cried loudly. "A sturdy boy," Hunt sang out. "Now tie and cut the cord. Next comes the afterbirth and the sewing," Hunt whispered. The placenta delivered, he prepared a curved needle and catgut. With a running stitch, he closed the wound.

Several days later, Simon stopped by to examine his patient and the baby. “Your wound is healing well, Mrs. Latham, and your boy is fine,” he said.

“It hurts some. Doctor, but not too bad,” she replied. “My mother was watching and says I was starting to tear and you cut me. She was torn into her asshole while birthing and never healed. She says you saved me from such and I thank you again. But I know you as Doctor Redbeard, what is your true name?”

“Simon Hunt,” he answered.

“The boy will be christened Simon Hunt Latham,” she said. “It sounds nice and I believe my husband will agree.”

“You do me a great honor,” Simon smiled, and left the house in a happy mood.

The months passed and Hunt continued his studies and the deliveries. Through it all, he did not neglect his daughter. He squired Gwendolyn about, taking her stroller into the streets and parks of London. At home, he would spend hours playing and giggling along with her. They would lie together on a rug, bouncing a ball or playing with a toy, and he took solace in being with her.

XXVII

The loss at Saratoga in October 1777 struck hard in London. The news was received in early December. General Howe was castigated in Parliament and throughout the country.

Minister North railed to the King, "Burgoyne's defeat is due to Howe's failure to assist him. Together, they could have isolated the New England colonies from the others. There was a plan and he failed to follow it. A magnificent opportunity was lost."

North was bitter and dejected. "My government is teetering on the edge," he said to his colleagues. "Opposition to the war increases, but the King wishes me to continue. The northern colonies seem lost to us. Nevertheless, we will hold fast, but a different strategy is required."

After months of deliberation between the politicians and military, his Minister again sought audience with George III. "Sire," he said, "A new strategy has been determined. We must look to the South. It is where the greatest value lies for England. Canada is safe. The colonials have tried to invade it on multiple occasions. Each time, they have been beaten back with heavy losses. New England holds little value for us. It can be abandoned to the rebels. New York City and its environs will be held. It is highly defensible. Our Navy protects it and the harbor is a perfect berth for their ships."

The King was determined to continue his war and listened intently as North continued. "Sire, the South furnishes the cotton needed by English mills. It supplies the masts, tar, and pitch for our navy. Its tobacco and rice have great value. They are also growing indigo. Many Tories await us and will join their King's cause. General Howe and his brother, the Admiral, will be replaced. Philadelphia offers us nothing. It will be abandoned. The troops there are better used in the Caribbean and to reclaim the southern colonies."

General Clinton received orders and left New York, arriving in Philadelphia the second week in May. With him, he brought details of the new strategy. Grace learned all and wrote the information on a small piece of paper. "Clinton now commander in America. General and Admiral Howe relieved. War with France anticipated. Philadelphia is to be abandoned. New strategy aims to conquer the South."

On the afternoon of May 14th, Grace left Penn House. She moved slowly, stopping to shop at several stores and checking that no one was following. Eventually she came to the School for Children. Passing the Doctor's carriage, she stumbled. He reached out and caught her. "I have you, Miss," he said.

The note passed between them as Grace replied, "Thank you, sir. You saved me from a bad fall."

He held her for another moment and said, "You must be careful, Miss."

"I will, sir," Grace answered.

Two days later the information was in Washington's hands. He knew Clinton would withdraw to New York, but not whether his troops would leave by sea or by marching across New Jersey.

In the following weeks, the English general discussed the situation with his staff officers, "Gentlemen, you have had pleasant duty in Philadelphia. However, we do have a war to fight. I have explained the new strategy to you. Our goals are elsewhere and we must withdraw. Our problem in leaving is the city's Loyalists. They have stood fast with their King. If we abandon them and leave them to the mercy of the rebels, they will suffer severe retribution. England's reputation will be damaged."

Clinton went on, "This is not merely a humanitarian view. It is politically and militarily necessary. There are large Tory groups in the south. They will not support us, if we abandon those here. We will use every ship available to get these people to New York. The army will go there by a long march. I expect General Washington to attempt an attack on our rearguard. I hope he tries. If so, we will destroy him."

Grace became aware of the final plans and the route, but was continuously busy. She and the other servants were pressed into service to pack military records and supplies. By June 15th the Loyalist population had brought whatever they could and were gone. With them sailed John Galloway and his daughter. He left behind his wife, telling her to defend their home and property. British patrols were less frequent, but still on guard.

On the night of June 16th, Grace whispered, "It is midnight and time to leave." She dressed in dark clothing and tucked her hair beneath a hat. Then, she strapped the ever-present knife to her thigh, saying, "I will save this blade for my grandchildren. It will add to my tale of being a spy."

As she quietly left her room, Matilda Parsons suddenly appeared. "Oh, Grace," she said, "All the noise and commotion of today is upsetting me. I was coming to ask if I might spend the night with you." Suddenly aware of her friend's clothing, she said, "But why are you dressed to go out at this late hour?"

"Come into my room, Matilda," Grace said. Once inside she put a hand on the girl's shoulder. "I must leave Matilda," she said. "I will not be back, and you must help me."

"Oh, Grace, You make me even more frightened," exclaimed Matilda.

"Your time to be frightened has past," Grace answered. "You are no longer a child. I have been a good friend and am asking for your help."

Matilda replied, "I was being silly, Grace. You have helped me grow up. Thanks to you, I am no longer a scullery maid but do regular cleaning. How can I help you?"

"I told you it is necessary for me to leave. They will wonder where I have gone and why. You must say, I had mentioned meeting a young carpenter. Tell them, I said he was nice to me and I liked him. If they question you further, say you know nothing more and keep saying it. Do not try to add to the story. Do not worry, Matilda. If you do as I say, you will not get into trouble."

"I will do as you ask," the girl said. "I will always remember you, Grace."

They left together. Matilda returned to her room. Grace slowly descended the staircase from the servants' quarters and reached the door exiting to the rear. It was unguarded and she moved across the backyard into the shelter of neighboring trees.

Intermittently, a sliver of moon showed. Clouds scudded across it and added to the darkness of the hour. The streets were deserted.

Grace progressed from one doorway to the next. Carefully checking at every corner, she dashed across each street. It was a warm night and Grace unbuttoned her coat to lessen the accumulating perspiration.

Suddenly, a British patrol appeared, carrying torches and moving toward her.

"How do I avoid detection?" the fleeing spy thought. She was standing in front of a large tavern. Retreating, an alley appeared alongside it. "This looks dark and inviting," Grace said, and crept further into the alley. The tavern's side door was securely bolted. High up was a small, unbarred window.

"Maybe," she thought. Hurriedly piling some boxes, she climbed up and pushed the window open. "Almost too small," she said. "Off with the hat, coat, and skirt." Removing them, she pushed the clothing through the opening and proceeded to follow. "First my head," Grace muttered. "The shoulders are the problem."

She succeeded in crossing the sill and tumbled into a pantry. Just in time, Grace closed the open window. The patrol stopped and the men raised their torches at the alley's entryway. They paused for a few moments but, seeing nothing, continued on. Grace saw the flash of light and its disappearance. "Safe for now," she breathed.

Opening the pantry door, Grace crept to the tavern's main room and sat in the farthest corner from the front door. The spy dozed through the night. The predawn light was entering the tavern's eastern windows when Grace awoke and started to the front. Suddenly, she felt a hand on her shoulder and was spun about.

"Where are you going, my pretty?" said a large figure, emitting the stench of alcohol. "I slept the night here and find you when I waken."

The man was dressed as an officer, but his uniform was totally disordered. Gray and black whiskers covered his unshaven face. Saliva spilled from his mouth and he staggered slightly, saying, "Well, my girl, speak up or has the cat got your tongue. I am Major Winston, formerly a warrior and now reduced to serving with the quartermasters of His Majesty's Army. You look like a whore, though a young and pretty one. What do you charge? No answer? Good, then it will be freely given. Here on this table will do."

Grace stood still, almost paralyzed at the realization that the man responsible for Martha and Harold's problems was now about to rape her. Recovering her poise, she took a step back. "You misunderstand, sir," Grace said. "I am this tavern owner's daughter and came early to prepare for a busy day."

Winston stopped for a moment. "No," he said, "I come often to this place and have never seen you."

Her left hand reached into a coat pocket and withdrew the keys to her house. "Here are the keys," she said waving them at Winston to distract him. Grace's right hand crept beneath her skirt, found the knife and withdrew it. As he came forward again, she plunged it upward and tilted slightly to his left. "This is how Lilith told me to do it," Grace whispered.

The Major felt a sudden stab, as the blade entered just left of the breastbone's lowest protrusion. It passed upward beneath the rib cage, penetrating the diaphragm and the base of the heart's muscular left ventricle. The knife's point continued up and to the left, piercing the ventricle's outer wall. It entered the pericardial sac, the space between the heart and its surrounding fibrous pericardium, and stopped there. With each ventricular contraction, blood was propelled out the aorta to the brain and body. It also exited the ventricle's opened base into the abdomen and, through its pierced wall, into the pericardial sac.

Winston raised his arms. "Witch," he shouted and reached out in an attempt to grasp her. He was already a dying man. In only one minute, two ounces of blood entered the pericardial sac. As it continued to accumulate, the ventricle was compressed. It could no longer expand to receive oxygenated blood returning from the lungs, nor provide adequate output. Neck veins swelled. Brain and body failed and the major collapsed.

Grace looked down at his corpse, carefully withdrew the knife and wiped it on a rag from behind the bar. Placing it back in its sheath, she examined him carefully. The narrow blade had caused only a small slit in Winston's uniform. No blood seeped through. She found the place where he had been sleeping, dragged him there, and overturned two chairs. After placing a small cloth beneath the knife's tear, she buttoned his vest to cover it. Grace wiped away any traces of dragging. She went to the side door. A bar had been placed across it. She slid the bar to permit the door's opening and exited into the daylight. Two streets away, Grace tossed the bloody rag into some garbage.

Later, the tavern owner came to the front door. He placed his key and entered. Walking toward the pantry, the man noted the bar on the side door was not in place. "I must be getting old," he said. "I am certain I locked it." A barmaid came and started checking that the tables had been properly cleaned. Seeing the overturned chairs, she went to straighten them. Coming upon Winston's body, the girl screamed. The proprietor ran to her. "My God," he uttered.

"That is Major Winston. Sometimes he sleeps here after drinking heavily. I never disturb him. Not to speak ill of the dead, but the man could be ugly when drunk. He must have had some sort of apoplexy. I best inform the authorities."

It was quickstep time for the British. Orders dictated they were to leave early the following morning. Winston's body was collected. The surgeon on duty viewed it. "Look at the swollen blue face and distended neck veins," he said. "The major drank heavily. We must conclude he suffered an apoplectic fit. Further examination is unnecessary. We are readying to depart. The burial detail will barely have time to provide a decent funeral."

"I must walk in an unhurried way," Grace thought, as she left the tavern. "The night's curfew is over." Further on, she said, "Patrols are few and people are beginning to fill the streets. The Tories are gone. Everyone is awaiting the end of the British occupation. But it is still a long way home."

Grace came to the alley leading to the house and looked about. Seeing no English troops, she entered it. First walking quickly, she broke into a run to the front door. Too anxious to use her key, Grace pounded with the knocker.

Joshua opened the door. "Hello, Auntie Grace," he said. "I remembered not to tell."

"I am sure you did," Grace laughed and took him in her arms.

"Auntie Grace is home," he shouted, and all came running to see.

They gathered around her, and she fielded their questions as best she could. Aunt Evelyn brought a cup of coffee. "Permit Grace a moment to rest and catch her breath," she said. "She needs some peace to recover from her recent adventures."

"Thank you, Aunt Evelyn," Grace smiled. "Coffee is just what I need. I am fine, but why are you and Joshua not at school, Martha?"

"Doctor Peabody closed the school for today," Martha answered. "He was concerned that, with the English leaving, some incident might occur."

"Oh," Grace said, "I was thinking I might speak to him about some future employment."

"Actually, one of the teachers is leaving and he is looking to hire a replacement," her sister said.

"Perhaps I should stop by this afternoon and see if he is there."

"In the meantime you can tell us about your exploits as a spy," Elias interjected.

Between bites of blueberry pie and sips of coffee, Grace told of her activities. As she came to the end, her hand rested over the sheathed knife. She did not mention Winston's sudden appearance or how she had stabbed him. Her tale ended at almost the same time that the major was being placed in his grave.

Elias left for the Golden Eagle. Grace walked with him for a way and then struck out for the school. Arriving there, it seemed deserted. She pounded on the door and finally Doctor Peabody came and opened it. "Grace," he said, "Come inside, I am delighted to see you." She entered and followed him to his office. "You have been amazingly successful," he continued. "I am almost sorry you are not returning to New York with General Clinton."

"My days as a spy are over," Grace answered. "Leaving as I did will create suspicion. Martha mentioned there might be an opening for a teacher."

"You are hired," he answered. "Heather Byron has sent word she will not return. Her husband has been with the Philadelphia militia. He lost his left arm during a scuffle with some English foragers, but he is home. As a bookkeeper he can still earn a living with his good right hand. I plan to use his services at the school."

"I am happy he is able to work," she replied. "But before I fully retire as a spy, I must give you my final report. General Clinton will return to New York by land. This paper shows his route and the disposition of his forces."

"Grace, " Peabody smiled, as he saluted her, "You are, without a doubt, the perfect spy."

XXVIII

General Clinton began the march to New York with the forward elements. Behind was a long baggage train, then the rearguard under the command of General Cornwallis. Knowing their route, Washington sent Charles Lee to attack Clinton's rear.

As Lee struck, the British responded in force. The Continentals, despite heavy pressure, were maintaining their position. Lafayette gave orders to his men, "We must withdraw slightly to a more defensible site," and slowly moved back. It was misinterpreted. The adjoining ranks shouted, "Lafayette is retreating," and Lee's entire force was thrown into a disorganized run to the rear.

"Our men are in full flight," Wolfe called to Farnsworth. They were in separate wagons drawn up behind what would prove the final position of the Americans' attempt to stem the enemy's counterstroke. "Here comes General Washington," Oliver called back.

The General rode up and reorganized the defense. The line became stabilized, but fighting continued. Cannon fire was all about them. The horse pulling Farnsworth's wagon suddenly bolted. It lurched forward, its movement unable to be controlled. A wheel struck a boulder and shattered. Oliver was flung beneath the wagon as it overturned.

Seeing what occurred, Jonathan and his helpers rushed to assist. "You men, help here," he called to several soldiers. "All together now," Wolfe exhorted, as they heaved it over and found Farnsworth. He was unconscious. A large gash was evident across the crown of his head. Blood oozed into his hair and over his forehead. Jonathan kneeled and examined him. He placed a finger within the head wound. "His skull is intact," he said. Raising Oliver's eyelids, he added, "The pupils are even, a good sign." Later, he said, "The rest of him seems intact, except for the left thigh and leg." There, Farnsworth's pants had been torn apart and a deep gash extended from the hip to below the knee.

"The thigh muscles are rent open," Jonathan noted. "Place Doctor Farnsworth aboard my wagon. Jameson, apply a compress to the head wound." Jonathan examined the thigh further. "The muscles are still actively bleeding and portions of the bone are exposed," he said. "Sergeant Miller, bring my instruments."

With the instruments available, Wolfe proceeded to clamp the larger vessels. "Fortunately, we have prepared a large amount of catgut," he said to the sergeant, as he tied off the clamped structures. "Packing and applying pressure will control the smaller bleeders. The thigh wound is best left open, but I will suture the head."

Farnsworth's wounds were bandaged. The fighting had ended. The English again moved toward New York and the battered Continentals ceased the pursuit.

"A detachment of the army will head for Philadelphia and reclaim the city," Washington ordered. "The majority will move cautiously and encamp near Manhattan."

"Captain Farnsworth needs close care and seclusion," Wolfe reported to a superior. "We cannot provide that here and are far from Philadelphia. But I know of a closer house."

Given permission, he and the aides climbed aboard their wagon. Jonathan rode in the back with Oliver. "I will give directions," he said. The sergeant and corporal drove. As dusk fell, they arrived at a large, dimly lit farmhouse.

Jonathan descended and knocked on the door. "Who is there?" asked a voice. "Jonathan Wolfe," he replied. The door was opened, a lantern held high. "Jonathan," Agnes exclaimed. "You are an unexpected visitor."

"Good evening, Agnes, I trust everything is well here. My apologies for this sudden intrusion but we need your help." He turned to indicate the wagon standing in the shadows.

Initially flustered, she quickly recovered. "We are all fine, Jonathan. What is the problem?" Agnes asked, looking at the horse-drawn wagon and the aides.

"A good friend has been badly injured," Wolfe answered. "He is not conscious and his thigh has been badly damaged. His injuries will not permit a journey to Philadelphia. I thought you might be willing to provide a place for him."

"My brother is serving with the Virginia cavalry, Jonathan. I am happy to aid any American soldier."

"His name is Oliver Farnsworth," Wolfe added. "He is a doctor and very special to me. Can we bring him in?"

"Of course," she replied. "There is a room available."

Farnsworth was carried into the house and up a staircase to the assigned space. Jonathan checked him again, as Agnes and his aides watched.

"There is no change in consciousness," he said. "But the bleeding from the scalp and thigh have stopped."

"Can he recover?" Agnes asked, her concern evident.

"He can, and he will," Wolfe answered.

They descended the stairs and Agnes said. "You must all be famished. Sit in the kitchen and have something to eat."

Adelaide and Laurel were gathering blankets. Agnes cooked eggs, and added bread, butter and coffee. Jonathan again admired her ability to quickly adapt to circumstances. When they were finishing the food, she addressed Wolfe.

"I assume you and your men are planning to stay. There are no other rooms. We have blankets and the three of you can sleep on the floor of the great room or in the barn. The nights are warm and we no longer need the fireplace."

"What would you prefer?" Jonathan asked his aides.

They looked at one another. "The barn will be fine, Captain," Sergeant Miller answered, and Jameson nodded his assent.

"Adelaide will bring blankets for you, in case the weather turns." Agnes said. "But the barn should prove comfortable. The British missed this place when they were scavenging and there is plentiful straw."

"Thank you, ma'am," they said and followed Adelaide to the barn.

"The floor is for me," Jonathan smiled. "We may indeed be here for a time."

"You are welcome to stay for as long as required," Agnes said. "I do believe we might find a stuffed mattress for you. The great room should prove comfortable."

Agnes sat with him as he drank more coffee. Wolfe inquired about her situation. "The children are doing well," she replied. "They are very happy here. We have some horses, cows, pigs and chickens. There is an old farmer up the road. His one boy is with the

Continentals. He helps with the animals and teaches the children how to care for them. As for myself, I am quite content. Leaving that big house is a relief. Things are more contained here and simpler. Tell me about you."

"A good question," Wolfe said. "The war has served to harden me, but I am unsure whether or not that is good. We younger physicians have been used as barber surgeons. I flinch less at bad wounds but, thankfully, still retain an empathy with the wounded. Being a doctor puts me well behind the front lines. It is relatively safe, but Oliver is an example of what may happen. Now, its time to examine him once more."

"Of course. You go upstairs, Jonathan. I must see that the children are asleep."

Arriving at Farnsworth's room, he found Laurel sitting at the bedside holding his hand. "It's warm," she said. "Mother said that was good."

"Yes, but let me check him, Laurel," Jonathan answered, and proceeded to examine his friend. "There is no change," he frowned.

The next day, Wolfe sent Miller and Jameson back to the Continentals. The following forty-eight hours showed no alteration in Farnsworth's state of consciousness.

Jonathan, who had been almost steadily at his bedside, was asleep when Oliver opened his eyes. Confused, he stared about him. Agnes was sitting alongside, holding a cool compress to his forehead. Seeing her, he smiled and whispered, "I must be in heaven for a beautiful angel is with me. Tell me your name, angel."

Agnes was suddenly overcome with emotion, "My name is Agnes," she said, leaned forward and kissed his forehead.

Farnsworth smiled again, closed his eyes and fell asleep. From then onward, his consciousness improved and he made steady progress toward recovery. Within several days, he was taking liquid, then semisolid and finally solid food.

On the seventh day of their arrival, Wolfe said, “It’s time to change our patient’s dressings, Agnes. I will need you and Adelaide to assist me.” Arriving at Farnsworth’s room, he said, “Time to assess the wounds, Oliver.”

Farnsworth nodded and replied, “Forge ahead, my friend. The patient is ready.”

Removing the dressings from his head, Wolfe reassured him, “The scalp wound is clean and healing nicely”. He then turned to the thigh and wet down the dried, blood-caked packing with water. It was discolored by a greenish tinge and had a peculiar odor. Jonathan slowly removed the packing from the depths of the thigh muscles.

Oliver bit down on a cloth as the procedure became painful. Agnes and Adelaide stood behind Jonathan. The women momentarily looked away while Wolfe removed the deepest packing. The wound looked very ugly.

“There is no bleeding, Oliver,” Wolfe said, wiping away a collection of green foul material. “The muscle looks healthy. There were areas of bone previously exposed. Now good muscle covers the entire femur. The wound will heal and you will enjoy a good leg.” Agnes handed him fresh dressings. The deep gash was again packed and bandaged.

“Thanks to you, Jonathan, I will heal,” his patient murmured, as perspiration rolled down his face and neck. “You have always been the best with wounds.”

"You have always been there with me, Oliver," Wolfe replied, feeling his friend's forehead and then checking his pulse. He gave a confident smile and added, "You are quite stable."

Jonathan chatted with him for several more minutes. Oliver lay back, closed his eyes and dozed off. Wolfe signaled to Agnes to accompany him. They left the room, leaving Adelaide at the bedside.

"Tell me what is happening," Agnes said.

"He has a fever and a rapid, thin pulse. That greenish, smelly pus is not good. The muscle does look healthy. However, I suspect he will get worse, maybe much worse. I have seen this so-called laudable pus carry a man away and very little can be done to help."

"I will not let him die, and I will not permit you to let him die," Agnes cried.

"Agnes, I will do everything possible to get Oliver well. I know he would do the same for me. You and I will work together to heal him."

She reached out. "Thank you, Jonathan. He must be special for you to hold him as a friend. It may sound unnatural, but somehow I feel it is my mission to help save this man."

"It's wonderful you express such feelings," Wolfe replied. "For now, you should get some rest. The next several days will tell the tale."

Jonathan returned to the bedside in time to see a febrile shudder. He felt Oliver's hot forehead and rapid pulse. He looked at the wound packing, already showing a tinge of the blue green ooze. The peculiar odor also rose from it.

"The smell almost speaks of kitchen odors Aunt Isabel clears with vinegar," he whispered. "I am going to soak the packing with vinegar and, if changing it every few days is helpful, why not change it every day or even more often?"

He sought out Adelaide. "I require vinegar," Wolfe said. "Is any available?"

"Yes, doctor," she answered. "We make our own from apples and use it to clean the kitchen."

She returned in a few minutes with a jug and accompanied Jonathan to Oliver's room. They turned the patient onto his right side. "Now," said Wolfe, "I will remove the wound's packing. As I place the new one, pour a small amount of vinegar to moisten it."

"I understand," Adelaide replied.

Every twelve hours the procedure was repeated. Either Agnes or Adelaide would assist in pouring the vinegar. Five days after the new technique was begun, the blue green pus started to clear and the odor was diminishing.

"It looks much better," Agnes commented, "and his forehead is cooler. Thanks to you, he is going to get well, Jonathan."

"I believe he will. You and Adelaide have been a great help. But I fear you may be neglecting the children."

"Not at all," she replied. ""I am with them several hours each day. We read together and I teach them arithmetic, grammar, and penmanship. I relate some small information about the war and news of their uncle in the cavalry. Randall and Sally are well aware of why you and Doctor Farnsworth are here. They ask every day about his progress and always want to see you. I have held them at bay, so you may devote your attention to our patient and also rest."

"Well, I am rested. I would like to spend some time with them."

Agnes led the way to where her children were studying. "Doctor Jonathan," they shouted, and ran to him. Jonathan stretched out his arms and embraced them.

"We have been very patient," Randall said in a most serious voice. "Mother told us about Doctor Oliver. She said we must not disturb you."

"But now you are here and can tell us he is getting better," Sally interjected, "and all about General Washington and the Army."

Wolfe laughed, "That is a lot to tell, Sally. I think it may be time for a butter cookie and some milk. I will sit with all of you and tell everything."

The four of them sat a small table in the kitchen. Jonathan regaled them with his adventures. Thereafter, each day he spent an hour or more telling his stories or going about the farm with them and the old farmer. They would feed the animals and pet them. The farmer came across some new horseshoes, and Wolfe reshod the farm's two horses.

"You know how to doctor people and horses, Doctor Jonathan," Randall said. "I would very much like to do that."

"Me, too," Sally chimed in.

"Doctoring is not for girls," Randall exclaimed.

"Why not?" she retorted and started to cry.

Wolfe picked her up. "Sally," he said, "If you wish, I will be happy to teach both you and Randall how to be doctors."

She wiped at her tears. "Doctor Jonathan, you are the best doctor in the whole world," she said. "But I have never seen a lady doctor. Are there any such?"

"Truly, Sally, I am not sure. But you can become the very first lady doctor."

She put her arms around his neck and hugged him. "I will be," she said.

As the new wound therapy reduced the pus, Farnsworth's fever broke. He opened his eyes and, though a haze still shrouded his vision, he saw Agnes. "My angel has returned," he whispered through parched lips. "Are you here to save my soul?"

"Both your body and your soul," she replied.

"If my body is to be saved, why am I in heaven?"

"The angels are circling about you, but God desires that you still remain on earth," she answered. "He has other things in store for you. Since it is He who desires it, you must fight very hard to recover."

"And what do the angels say?" he asked.

"The angels side with God," Agnes answered.

"Since both God and the angels wish me to recover, I will do my best," he whispered, closed his eyes and fell asleep.

"I know you will," she whispered back, and once more kissed his brow. Then, feeling it was of normal temperature, she smiled and said, "Thank you, God."

Oliver's recovery was slow but steady. His lucid moments lasted longer and he again began to take liquids. He had lost a great deal of weight and become very gaunt, but his good spirits returned quickly. He began to joke with Jonathan and Agnes. Even Adelaide remarked on his good nature.

Two weeks later, Agnes said, "Jonathan, Adelaide and I have been observing how the packing and wound dressings are done. I believe that we can manage them. You can leave and come back in one or two weeks. Just let me know how to reach you. If something untoward should happen, I will send for you."

"We must discuss it with Oliver," Wolfe responded. "He must agree to my leaving or I would not feel comfortable. Let us speak to him about it."

The next morning, they entered Farnsworth's room. "Good morning, Oliver," he began. "The sun is up and the day looks bright. How are you feeling?"

"Thanks to you and my angel, I am definitely in recovery. I should say my three angels, since Adelaide and Lauren have joined Agnes on the list of angels known to me. As always, Jonathan, you were there when most needed."

"Oliver, you would do the same for me. But a question has arisen. Agnes believes she and Adelaide can now care for the wound by themselves. What is your response to that?"

"It is about time you asked me," Farnsworth smiled. "I see no reason why they cannot do the dressings. They have both watched you long enough. Why not let them try this morning. If it proves satisfactory, they can continue. You have been with me long enough. As I, you are beginning to smell like vinegar itself. It is time you had an airing out. By the way, how did you arrive at such an idea as to use vinegar to clean the wound?"

Grinning, Wolfe said, "The smell somehow reminded me of my Aunt Isabel's kitchen at home, just before she would clean it with vinegar."

"My friend, you are remarkable," Farnsworth said and laughed along with him.

Jonathan supervised, as Agnes proceeded to remove the old packing and replace it. Adelaide poured the vinegar.

"Adelaide, in the event Mrs. Stiles is unavailable, you can do the packing, and your daughter can pour the vinegar," said Wolfe. "But what do you think, Oliver?"

"I think that both are far more gentle than you, my friend. They have women's hands and not the rough hands of a butcher."

"Well then," Jonathan responded affably. "I see no other course but to abandon you. Certainly, sir, you are a most ungrateful wretch."

"Guilty, as charged," Farnsworth answered, laughing and clearly in good humor.

In the morning, Wolfe said his goodbyes He visited with his patient and assured him he would return in a week. Then, he took Agnes aside and they spoke together.

"Agnes, Farnsworth and I are both in your debt. You have done more than I. You gave him the will to fight for survival and he is falling in love with his caretaker."

"His caretaker has already fallen in love with him, Jonathan. It's strange, but from the beginning I sensed a kinship, a feeling of mutual destiny with Oliver. You know me quite well. But except for the time with you, I am very wary of sudden involvements. Still, I did become involved with you and I believe we both benefitted. We were not in love, but we needed and respected each other. It is different with him. There is intensity to my feelings I have truly never before experienced, not even with Silas. God help me, I am in love with this man and I barely know him."

"I understand, Agnes, I confess that the same also happened to me."

"Then you had better return to her quickly."

"I am not sure she will be there when I do return."

"Then you had best search for her," Agnes smiled.

"I will," Jonathan replied. "But to get back to you and Oliver. He regards you as his saving angel. I said he is falling in love with you, but you must treat him very gently. I became quite close to him, and believe he has been damaged by love in the past."

She said, "You once told me how an injured bird was nursed and then released. Oliver is my injured bird. I will nurse him back to health and release him, but I hope and pray he will choose to stay with me. Now, it is time for you to seek your own true love."

"Thank you for everything, Agnes. He is fortunate to have you as his angel."

Wolfe went to a horse she lent him and mounted it. Waving goodbye, he set off for Philadelphia. There were no British patrols to avoid and the Continentals had taken charge of the city. The Pennsylvania Assembly and Congress had returned from their hiding place in Lancaster. The military governor was now General Benedict Arnold.

Jonathan searched for the army's medical headquarters. After a fruitless hour, a fellow medical officer saw him ride by. "Jonathan Wolfe," he called out.

Hearing the voice, he immediately turned to its source. Major Charles Evans was waving at him. Jonathan dismounted and they embraced one another. Evans anxiously looked at Wolfe and said, "I heard that Oliver Farnsworth was badly injured and you were caring for him. If you are here, who is supervising his care? Is he alive? How is he?"

"Slowly, Charles," Jonathan laughed. "All is well. Our friend was not conscious but his senses have fully returned. The injury to his thigh is healing. I brought him to a friend's home. The people there are dealing with the wound. I plan to see him in a week."

"Wonderful news," said the major. "But I heard the thigh wound was deep and bone was exposed. How did you manage that?"

"I will reveal my secrets to you. But you must show me to our base. If I do not report for duty, they may charge me as a deserter."

"Never," laughed Evans and led the way. Jonathan accompanied him on foot. As they walked, he spoke. "I believe in always boiling my instruments for each patient. Despite it, his wound became filled by pus. I then hit on the idea of using vinegar to clear the purulence. I changed the packing and wet it with vinegar twice a day. It worked."

"Amazing," Evans smiled. "I might try it, though it seems like witchery."

Shortly, they came to the area housing the medical service. Seeing Jonathan, the doctors crowded about. He waved them off. Pointing to Evans, Wolfe indicated that he had been appointed to answer questions, continued on to the headquarters tent and reported for duty. When done, he whispered, "Now, I must find Grace."

XXIX

It was late in the afternoon. Jonathan rode to the lane leading to the McKenzie home. His heart lifted as the house came into view, smoke rising from the chimney.

"Thank God," he thought. "Now to learn if Grace is here, and whether she is still available and cares for me."

The sound of his horse's hoofs caused Grace to glance out the window. "It's Jonathan," she called and ran to the door. Flinging it open and running to him, she cried, "I have been waiting for you."

"And I have been a fool to make you wait," he answered, gathered her into his arms and kissed her.

"Do it again," Grace whispered. "I do not care who sees us."

Wolfe kissed her again. Then, peering past her, he whispered back. "The only one watching is Aunt Evelyn, and she is crying and smiling at the same time."

"Jonathan Wolfe, you must learn to be more romantic," Grace replied.

"Will you teach me?" he responded.

"I certainly plan to do that," and kissed his lips. "Can the doctor stay for dinner?"

"Yes," Jonathan answered, "He can, providing Aunt Evelyn agrees."

"Of course I agree," Evelyn laughed, opening her arms to welcome him. "We were all concerned about you, Jonathan. It will be a great treat to have you at dinner tonight."

Martha and Joshua had been shopping but arrived within the hour, and later Elias came home. They were excited to find Jonathan there and each expressed their happiness at seeing him. The meal having been eaten, McKenzie pushed back his chair and said, "Now, we would like to hear about your latest adventures, Doctor Wolfe."

"I will be happy to tell them," Jonathan replied. "But before that, since you are in a sense Grace's guardian, I wish to ask you for her hand in marriage."

"I readily and happily agree," Elias smiled and everyone clapped hands. "But what say you, Grace? You are the one this fellow is asking to marry."

"Oh, uncle, you know what my answer will be," Grace laughed, showing the gold ring on her right hand. "Of course I shall wed him."

Again they all clapped, Wolfe the loudest.

"We must post banns at the church to announce the wedding. When shall it be?" her uncle asked.

"As soon as possible," Grace and Jonathan said simultaneously, and everyone laughed.

"With your permission, Jonathan," McKenzie said, "I will speak to Reverend Godfrey at the New Congregational Church. It is where Martha and Harold were married."

"Certainly," Wolfe replied. "But I must inform my family of the wedding. It will be difficult for them to come to Philadelphia. If Grace agrees, we can visit them afterward."

"I look forward to meeting your people, Jonathan," Grace smiled.

"Then it is settled," he grinned. "Marriage is at hand."

McKenzie arranged for the banns and a date was set for the wedding.

Wolfe wrote a letter to his family.

"Dear Father, Aunt Isabel, Rose and Ethan,

I miss you all very much. This letter bears good news. I am to be married in less than three weeks to a wonderful lady. Her name is Grace Lockhart. Aside from Aunt Isabel and Rose, she is the loveliest woman I know. We have been keeping company for some time and are very compatible. I know it may come as a surprise, but war often requires quick action.

The marriage will occur in the morning of Tuesday, the 21st. I realize it may well be a hardship for you to come. Grace and I will visit you afterward.

My love to you all, Jonathan"

Wolfe received four weeks leave and congratulations from many colleagues. A notice was circulated through the medical department that everyone would be welcome at the service. Doctor Rush and Julia were again in the house at Front Street. He sent an invitation to them and Alice. A prompt return indicated all would come.

Miller and Jameson came forward and saluted. "Sir," Miller said, "We congratulate you on your coming wedding and look forward to attending. May we kiss the bride?"

"Well," replied Wolfe, "You ruffians must wash, shave and wear your best clothing. My future bride is a very delicate lady. I am not sure she can bear a kiss from such bedraggled men." Seeing their crestfallen faces, Jonathan smiled. "I was being a terrible tease," he said. "I am certain Grace will be happy to have you kiss her. She has already heard about you when I spoke of our adventures."

The aides saluted and left. Outside they jostled one another, happily speaking of the wedding and kissing the bride.

Five days before the event, Jonathan received a letter from his Aunt.

"Dearest Jonathan,

Congratulations from us all. Give our love to Grace. Samuel and I will not miss the wedding. We are anxious to meet your bride-to-be and her family, and plan to be in Philadelphia on Friday, September17th. We were given directions to the Old Oak Coffee House and hope to be there by one in the afternoon. Please look for us at about that time.

Rose and Ethan are not able to attend. Happily, she is about four months with child and unable to travel. They send their love.

Looking forward to our meeting, Isabel"

Wolfe read the letter and gave a loud huzzah. Excited that his father and aunt were coming, he hurried to the McKenzie home. All were delighted on learning the news.

"That's wonderful," Grace exclaimed. "We are all thrilled your people will stand for you at the ceremony."

"They and apparently a large number of physicians and aides," he laughed. "We may have half the medical department."

"If so, we will move to the Lutheran Church. It is far larger," Elias joked.

"New Congregational, please," responded Grace.

"I did not know you were so committed," Wolfe said.

"Well," she answered, "That is how we were raised. You, my love, have been highly influenced by the free thinkers and are becoming a deist."

"In doing so, I am in good company," Jonathan answered. "Ben Franklin, Thomas Jefferson, Tom Paine, and possibly General Washington fall into that camp. The English are praying for victory, just as we are. To whom will the Almighty render favor? When you are at war and see good men pray but still starve and die horrible deaths, one wonders about the value of prayer. Deists believe in a God who has created natural laws by which the world functions and by which we must live. God is not available to listen to our prayers. Rather, it is for us to behave honorably and create heaven here on earth. However, I do occasionally say a prayer. I prayed every night you would be here when I returned."

"Jonathan, that is the sweetest and most beautiful thing to say," Grace replied. "You have always been in my prayers. I prefer to think they helped bring you safely back to me." Saying this, she came close to him. They embraced and kissed to cheers from all.

Stopping by to wish her well, several friends hinted at being included among the bridesmaids. Grace busily sewed her wedding dress. Following custom, it was white to express joy and a blue ribbon encircled the bottom to indicate purity.

At one o'clock on the appointed Friday, Wolfe waited in front of the Old Oak Coffee House. The end-of-summer sun warmed him as he peered at the roadways. Shortly past the hour a carriage drew up and Samuel assisted Isabel to descend. Tears clouded their eyes as Jonathan ran to them, and the three enfolded arms about one another.

"It's wonderful that you have come for the wedding," said Jonathan. "The family is expecting us for luncheon at the Golden Eagle. You will like Uncle Elias, father, and Aunt Evelyn is very much your type, Aunt Isabel. Best of all, you will at last meet my lovely Grace. Let me help you back into the carriage. I will lead the way on my horse."

Arriving at the tavern, Elias ushered them inside. Wolfe made the introductions. Samuel held Grace's waist with outstretched arms. He smiled and gallantly said, "Jonathan indicated you were pretty, but you are far prettier than he mentioned."

She blushed in delight, stepped forward and kissed his cheek. Then, it was Aunt Isabel's turn to hug and kiss her. The pleasantries and formalities over, all were seated, engaged in conversation and ate.

"My sister, Martha, is teaching school and her son, Joshua, is also there. Please come to the house this evening and you can meet them," Grace said. She added, "Martha's husband, Harold, is with the Continentals in Virginia. We are quite proud of him."

"As well you should be," Samuel replied. Then he turned to McKenzie and said, "Bye-the-bye Elias, we had the banns posted at our church and brought a certificate."

"Samuel," Elias responded, "Have no fear. The banns have also been posted here." He continued on, "The Golden Eagle is not far from our home. I have taken the liberty of having a room made up for you. You and Isabel will have time to rest and refresh before dinner. If you agree, my people will bring your things to the room."

Isabel and Samuel exchanged glances and nodded. "We appreciate your offer," Samuel smiled. "You are going beyond duty to make us feel like family."

That evening, they gathered at the McKenzie home. Martha and Joshua joined the festivities. The pleasant aroma of Evelyn's cooking whetted their appetites. A knocking at the door interrupted the conversation. Martha rose to see who it was.

Seated in the parlor, they heard her shout, "Harold! Harold!"

Joshua was first to respond. He raced to the door, "Father!" he cried.

Elias and Evelyn followed Joshua. The Wolfe family stood with Grace and waited. A gaunt, bearded Continental officer hobbled forward on crutches. His uniform was threadbare and his coat dirty and torn. Despite his appearance, he radiated happiness.

"I am Harold Goode," he said. Leaning on his crutches, he extended a hand to each Wolfe as they were introduced. "It's my pleasure to meet you. Forgive my appearance. I have been away quite some time and it has been a long journey home. But I seem to be interrupting your visit."

Martha's eyes filled with tears. "Harold Goode," she exclaimed, "We are all overjoyed to see you. There is no need to apologize for your appearance." Her eyes streaming tears of happiness, she embraced him, saying, "Everyone is delighted to see you, silly man. Harold, you are safe and home with us. We can discuss your injury later. Right now, you look very tired. You need a bath and decent clothes. However, you should know that Grace and Doctor Wolfe are to be married Tuesday. You have arrived in time to celebrate their wedding."

Goode focused his gaze on the doctor. "Congratulations," he said. "You are marrying a fine lady. It will be a pleasure to have you as a member of the family."

"Thank you," Jonathan answered. "It is an honor to meet a man who is serving his country. But you should sit and rest."

All echoed his words. Harold sat on the settee and hugged Martha and Joshua. The little boy blurted out, "Are you badly hurt, father?"

Harold drew him close and held the boy tightly, stroked his head and kissed his cheek. "Not too badly, Joshua. I will heal nicely in a short time."

There was an intake of Martha's breath and the others looked at him. He only smiled and lifted a hand slightly to indicate no further discussion. "Do I smell McKenzie cooking?" Harold asked. "I would gladly pay a month's wages to merely taste it."

"You can not only taste it, you may also eat some," Aunt Evelyn said, came forward and kissed his bearded cheek. "Harold, that beard needs cultivation," she laughed. "Please, let us have dinner before the food spoils," and led the way into the dining room.

Dinner was a celebration of both the coming wedding and Harold's return. Over the next few days the Wolfe family easily integrated with the McKenzie clan. Harold, once fully shaved, washed and properly dressed assumed a new persona. His weariness rapidly disappeared and he quickly became friends with Wolfe.

Monday afternoon Harold and Jonathan were sitting in the McKenzie parlor. Goode spoke of his injury. "In the army, being a surveyor was helpful. I could rapidly understand maps, scout out and sketch roads and terrain. I knew where and how to position our men to attack or hold off an enemy. I was steadily promoted up the ranks and commissioned a captain. Last month, we were in North Carolina doing well against a somewhat larger body of English troops. Unfortunately, they had more and better cannon. A cannon ball exploded and sent shrapnel into my left thigh and leg. My men held the line and the fighting ended in a draw. Later, they carried me to safety. My good luck was to have a competent surgeon who removed many of the fragments. Still, I continue to drain at two sites. There is less discomfort now, but bearing full weight is painful. At any rate the war is over for me."

"Your surgeon must have been very busy that day," Jonathan said. "He did fine work, but fragments still present are causing the drainage. I have had some experience with these wounds. Let me examine you, but it would be best at the army medical post."

"Why not here?" Goode smiled. "Close the parlor doors and I will strip down." Wolfe drew the pocket doors closed and Harold quickly became naked.

Jonathan carefully exposed the wounds and examined them. Replacing the dressings, he said, "The drainage is certainly from retained pieces of shrapnel. Sometimes they come to the surface, but usually require removal."

"If you will do it, I will have it done," Harold said. "But after the wedding, when you are settled. Martha told me you operated on your brother-in-law with great success."

"Yes, but luck is always a factor. There are no guarantees."

"As in war, luck is always a factor. But I have observed that competency in tactics, knowing where and how to fight, when to retreat and when and how to attack are most important. We make our own luck. I believe you are quite lucky, Jonathan," Harold smiled.

"I have been lucky to find and love Grace."

"And I, Martha. But tomorrow is your wedding day. Grace is busy preparing and you should be doing the same."

"I had hoped to see Grace, but the women have engulfed her. It is not safe for me to brave their ranks," Wolfe smiled. "I had best leave and follow your advice."

It rained lightly Monday evening, but the next morning the sun shone and the sky was a bright blue. Autumn had arrived, but the air still retained some of summer's warmth. For good luck, Grace placed a final stitch in her gown. She came down the stairs to the family's applause, as they admired her and her handiwork.

By ten o'clock the pews of The New Congregational Church were filled with friends and acquaintances. As the church bell tolled the hour, Minister Godfrey led the wedding procession down the central aisle. Behind him came Grace and Jonathan. Elias and Evelyn followed them, and then Samuel and Isabel. Lastly, side-by-side the bridesmaids and groomsmen joined the ceremonial party.

Godfrey intoned their vows and the couple repeated them. Jonathan moved the gold ring from Grace's right hand to her left forefinger. She did the same to him and the minister pronounced them man and wife. They embraced and kissed, as cheers erupted.

The wedding procession turned about. Bridesmaids and groomsmen leading, they exited the church and stood to each side. The newlyweds walked between them, entering a coach to which was tied an old boot for good luck. The attendees surged about, offering good wishes. Then, all set off for the Golden Eagle.

At the tavern, white tablecloths festooned with garlands of cut white paper had been placed. Grace and Jonathan sat at a large table with the entire family. "What beautiful cakes," Isabel exclaimed, pointing to a nearby small table.

"The large white one is the groom's cake, and we and the guests will enjoy it," said Evelyn. "The small one is for the newlyweds. After the party, we will place it in a tin with a little spirits. Our bride and groom may have some each anniversary until it is gone."

"It looks so good, it may not survive the first one," Jonathan laughed.

About them, the room was alive with good fellowship. Courtship was actively manifest. People came to the bridal table to express their best wishes. Doctor and Mrs. Rush were the first and the bride and groom rose to greet them.

"Jonathan," Rush said, "You have been successful in every way. Above all you are now wed to a lovely lady. Julia and I wish love and happiness to you both." Turning to Grace, he smiled, "Your husband is very fortunate to have found you. I was told of your brave service to our cause. He should be very proud of you."

Rush shook Wolfe's hand and kissed Grace's cheek. Julia hugged Jonathan, then embraced and kissed Grace. She said, "We are delighted to be here. The wedding was joyful and this room is also filled with joy. Sadly, we are only able to remain for a short time. The children require us at home."

Immediately afterward, Alice came, "Doctor Jonathan," she said. "I am so happy for you that I have begun to cry." She held him tightly, then kissed him and Grace, smiled and wiped her tears.

Just then a cheer went up from the medical attendees as Oliver Farnsworth came into the room. Using a crutch and accompanied by Agnes, he was moving toward them. With a whoop of joy, Wolfe exclaimed, "Oliver, Agnes, I did not think you two could come."

The two doctors embraced for several moments and Farnsworth said, "We are here thanks to Miller and Jameson. They bundled us aboard a cart and brought us to the church and here. It was a wonderful ceremony. We were delighted to attend. Agnes, Adelaide, and Laurel have been excellent nurses. The wound is almost fully healed."

"I was certain they would prove competent and take good care of you, but let me introduce you to my bride."

As it was being done and kisses exchanged, Agnes whispered to Wolfe, "I noticed Doctor Dracula is present. Fear not, I will be good." To Grace, she said, "I am delighted to meet you. Your husband did Oliver and myself a great service. We are keeping company."

Grace saw before her a beautiful blonde woman. Dressed in a modest blue dress, Agnes still looked an elegant lady. "How did Jonathan meet this woman," she thought, "and what has been their relationship?"

They continued exchanging pleasantries and a fiddler began a reel. "Excuse us," Wolfe said. "It is customary for the bridal couple to lead the first dance." Taking Grace by the hand, he brought her into the center of the floor. Others lined up behind them.

The reel proceeded in quickstep fashion and, as they danced, Grace began an interrogation. "Mrs. Stiles is a beautiful woman. How did you meet her, Jonathan?"

"Doctor Rush and I attended her husband when he was very ill. Rush bled him several times. He did not survive and she partly blamed us."

Another question came. "How then is she friendly with you?"

"We happened to meet again at Simon and Gwendolyn's wedding. You were away on your spying and they somehow seated us together."

"Is there more?" Grace asked, raising her eyebrows.

Beginning to perspire, Wolfe replied, "She apologized for her behavior toward me and said Rush was really the culprit. I accepted the apology."

"There must be more," she said as the reel progressed.

"I had mentioned that we were variolating the troops. Shortly afterward, she requested me to inoculate her and her two children. A smallpox outbreak had begun and she was grateful I had the material with me to perform them."

The reel ended and as they stood together, she asked, "How did you know she was close by when Doctor Farnsworth was injured?"

"Grace, you are asking many questions," he answered somewhat petulantly. "I had visited the Lorings to inquire about Simon and Gwendolyn. That is when I learned Gwendolyn had died in childbirth. They had left Philadelphia and were terribly downcast. In speaking of their move, they mentioned that their cousin Agnes had also moved and described her location. When Oliver was injured he needed a quiet place, and I remembered she was nearby."

For the moment Grace was contrite. "Oh," she said, "Forgive me. I was too long a spy and suspicion is ever in a spy's thoughts."

"Mrs. Wolfe, you are now a former spy, suspicion is no longer requisite," he replied.

"Husband," she answered, "Suspicion may be laid to rest but, like the Phoenix bird, it can always be reborn." She smiled, took his hand and led him to their table.

Miller and Jameson, freshly bathed and beards trimmed, approached. They saluted the couple. Jonathan and Grace saluted back.

"These two creatures are my aides," Wolfe said. "They have come to beg a kiss, but I am not certain if they really deserve one."

The aides' faces showed disappointment. Grace smiled and said, "Surely Major Wolfe, if they have served with you, they must be kissed."

"Well, since in truth they are the finest aides in the medical department and have helped many injured men, a slight peck may be in order."

Grace laughed, hugged and kissed each of them and said, "I have heard many wonderful things about you two. It is my pleasure to at last meet such brave men."

Wolfe hugged them both and said, "I thank you for bringing Doctor Farnsworth and Mrs. Stiles to the wedding. You are both good men and I am delighted you are here."

"Thank you, sir," they jointly said. Miller added," We wish to continue to serve with you, major." They again saluted and returned to their table.

After many reels and minuets, the music paused. A waitress brought them to the cake table. The crowd shouted, "Feed him! Feed him!" Grace cut a portion and fed it to Jonathan. "Feed her! Feed her!" they shouted and Wolfe did so. They kissed as those assembled cheered.

"We must dance late into the night," Grace laughed, as she again pulled Jonathan to the dance floor.

"If we continue dancing, we will lack energy when we are alone," he whispered.

"They tell me, Doctor Wolfe, that, after a battle wherein there have been many wounded, your energy has been extraordinary. On this night, I surely expect you to again provide all your energy."

"Madame," he answered, "I shall provide quite sufficient resources."

They laughed together and danced on.

After midnight the pace slowed. Wolfe stepped forward and said, "My bride and I wish to thank you all for being here. It is time for us to leave you." Grace and Jonathan clasped hands and began ascending the staircase to their room. The crowd cheered them with whoops, huzzahs, and clapping. At the top of the stairs, they waved back, and were then lost to view from those below.

The couple entered their wedding chamber. A single candle glowed at the bedside.

Embracing Grace, Jonathan said, "You are my one true love."

"And you are mine," she answered.

They kissed and hurriedly undressed. Grace stood before him fully exposed. Her skin glowed in the candlelight.

He picked her up, gently placed her on their bed, and quickly followed her. Once more kissing and holding close, they felt the urgency in each other.

"I have not been with a man like this before," she said.

"I know, my darling. I will be very slow and gentle," he answered, and began to stroke her hair. Wolfe kissed her lips and massaged her back with slow soft motions. His hand moved to her buttocks and she responded with an intake of breath.

"I am becoming warm and very relaxed," she whispered.

"You are the most beautiful woman," he whispered back.

Turning Grace on her back, Jonathan stroked her lower abdomen with his right hand, encircled her with his left arm and lovingly held the left breast.

She suddenly kissed him passionately, "You are my wonderful

lover," Grace said, and spread her legs slightly.

He moved his hand into the hair over her pubis. Slowly and gently he probed with his forefinger to find the clitoris. Grace sighed and pushed upward. Wolfe spread his hand and stroked the vulva's lips. She relaxed and placed her left hand on his, moving it slightly. He responded by massaging the breast and felt the nipple grow firm and full.

"Jonathan, I love you," she breathed.

"And I you," he answered.

Once again, Wolfe began stroking the clitoris, and the vulva. He probed her hymen and felt its thinness. Very slowly, he continued to massage her clitoris and felt the juices begin to flow. He mouthed her right breast and sucked at the nipple. She gasped with pleasure.

Jonathan continued his stroking. Grace spread her legs widely and lifted her thighs, saying, "Oh Jonathan, I am ready for you."

He mounted her, his penis fully engorged, and with several urgent thrusts penetrated the hymen. Pushing deeper, he felt the tightness of her vagina relax about him. The warmth of her body engulfed him, and her breathing became heavier. Their bodies shoved together and moved faster.

"Jonathan, Jonathan," she repeated and surged upward.

Wrapping her legs around him, Grace emphasized his thrusts, pulling him deeper and pushing hard against him. Her breathing was accompanied by moans of pleasure. Grasping him tighter, she made a final thrust and he ejaculated his sperm into her. Grace fell back, reached up and pulled him down. Kissing him with soft, full, and passionate lips, she whispered into his ear, "Jonathan Wolfe you have made me a woman tonight."

"And you have made me a very happy husband," he softly responded.

Wolfe moved off her. They embraced and kissed several more times. Clinging together, they fell asleep in each other's arms. In the middle of the night, it became cold and Jonathan awoke. The moon was shining through the window and sent its soft light into the room. He found their nightgowns and pulled his on. Shaking Grace half awake, he sat her up. Wolfe placed the gown over her, kissed her and laid her back. When he was again beside her, she stirred, snuggled close to him, and remained so through the night.

The sun had been up for several hours, when they heard a knock on the door. Wolfe opened it slightly. A tray was on the floor. It contained a pot of coffee, milk, toasted bread and strawberry jelly. He brought it into their chamber and placed it on a table.

Grace sprang out of bed. "Jonathan, today is our first anniversary," she laughed and hugged him. She poured coffee and, while they sipped it, jellied the bread. He watched with anticipation. "Open wide, husband," Grace said. As he did, she began to feed it to him.

After several bites, he leaned forward and kissed her. "I can see you are prepared to fatten me with food and love," he said.

"Exactly so," she answered and returned his kiss, saying, "A wife must cater to a husband who loves like you. I am prepared to do just that. But now we should dress. It is a glorious day and I want to ride through the countryside seeing the fall colors."

They washed and quickly clothed. Descending the stairs, they found Samuel and Isabel waiting and smiling happily.

"You look so wonderful as a married couple," Isabel said, hugging them.

"You surely do," Samuel chimed in. He added, "We decided to stay another few days. It is too pleasant being with you and Grace's family to leave abruptly. Besides, Philadelphia is new to us and we wish to see the scalawags in Congress debate."

"You will probably be either bored or wish to pound heads," Wolfe laughed. "We are going for a drive in the countryside and will see you this evening." Turning to Grace, he said, "I have a surprise for you. I know a lovely inn. It is twenty miles away and on a small lake. It is secluded and not too visited at this time. I think we will enjoy a week there."

"Jonathan," she glowed, "You are the perfect husband."

They stayed at the inn for the week, each night cuddling and exploring one another's body. Upon returning, several days were spent with Grace's family. Then they travelled north to the Mohawk Valley where Grace met Rose and Ethan.

Rose and Grace quickly bonded. As October drew to a close, an early snow fell. Wolfe's leave was expiring, and the newlyweds journeyed back to Philadelphia.

During the following months, Jonathan was able to return every second weekend. They made love, feeling their bodies join together in perfect harmony. The war seemed far away. In the North it was desultory. In the South, England began its new strategy by attacking Savannah. The city fell quickly and 1778 drew to a close.

February arrived and the Wolfe's visited the Rush's. The women were conversing in the parlor, and Rush and Wolfe sat in the study.

"Jonathan," Rush said, "You have matured greatly. I learned you were the one who convinced Washington to initiate variolation and it has proven very successful. I am proud to claim you as a pupil, a colleague, and a friend. Tell me about your current situation."

"Presently, I am at a large hospital. It is not pleasant. Beyond my immediate area and one or two others, the place is a pigsty. Even worse, the patients are poorly cared for, on filthy beds with putrid sheets. The other day I stumbled on a man who was cold, stiff, and dead for at least two days. The only saving feature is that it lies fairly close to Grace."

"I fully understand," the Doctor replied. "I inspected many army hospitals. They showed the same filth and poor care. Men died of diseases acquired in the hospital. Several head physicians had ordered enough rum for the patients to last two rather than one year. They were selling it, and pocketing the money. We still have mismanagement and greed."

"Furthermore," Rush continued, "The nation is losing its will to continue on. Even I am starting to feel we shall fail. Only by France sending us troops can we be saved."

"The army still stands fast with General Washington," Jonathan said. "So long as we have an army, the fight continues. The English will ultimately tire of the struggle."

"Yes, but for how long must we fight and to what purpose. The General is a great patriot and a man of character, but on larger battlefields, against British and Hessian professionals, he has not done well. Now, the enemy is moving into the South, the weakest link in our chain. They took Savannah and have a navy capable of putting men ashore at any point from Georgia northward. Lose the South and they win. To the North will be Canada, to the West the Indians and, to the South, British occupied colonies. Only New England,

and parts of New York, Pennsylvania, and New Jersey may remain in our hands. We will no longer be a viable country."

Rush, obviously distraught, ran a hand through his hair and said, "Washington remains focused on New York where the enemy is strongest. He should look after the South where we are the weakest and most vulnerable."

"I am still hopeful of our success, "Wolfe replied. "The General may lack professional training but he is cool and holds firm to our cause. The English must bring men across 3,000 miles of ocean and spend huge sums to maintain their army. I still believe we can win." Jonathan paused and then said, "Sir, it is always a pleasure to be in your home, but we should leave. Tomorrow, I must be early at my post."

"Jonathan, it is a joy for Julia and me to have you and Mrs. Wolfe here. Maintain your good spirits. Let us both pray for the success of our enterprise."

Rush's forebodings were realized. In April, General Augustine Prevost took 2,100 men from Savannah and quickly overran towns and villages along his way to Charleston. Outside the city, he threatened its total destruction. Frightened, Governor Rutledge offered to withdraw South Carolina from the rebellion. His aides prevented it. Prevost had been bluffing, knowing he did not have the army needed to take Charleston, and returned to Savannah.

In the North, Washington continued to focus on New York and maintained his army close to it. South, skirmishes between rebel and tory backcountry units were occurring.

XXX

February- November 1779

Gwendolyn's death devastated the Lorings. They sat in mourning for days. Simon's family visited them repeatedly. On each occasion, Peter Loring was colder and more distant, finally saying, "You have been kind to visit us, but I would prefer you no longer come. The marriage has resulted in my daughter's death. It is too painful to see you."

Later, he told his wife, "Simon bears the blame for Gwendolyn's death. Our ship may conduct trade with England, but we will sever communication with him."

"What of our grandchild, Gwendolyn?" Mrs. Loring replied.

"She cannot replace our daughter," he answered.

Slowly, Emily Loring attempted to soften his view. It took months for her to bring him out of his depression and hostility toward his son-in-law. Finally, she said, "Simon is not to blame for Gwendolyn's death. I do not know what caused her hemorrhage. He did not. Do not continue to harden your heart. I am aching to see our grandchild."

She had never seen tears in his eyes, now they appeared. "I never told you that my mother also died giving birth to me," he said. "I had no siblings and my father was often away. There were no grandparents and I was very much alone. No child should feel alone. Yes, I also wish to see our daughter's child."

"Then we should re-establish communication with Simon. We must tell him our feelings and that we hold him blameless."

"If you write it, I will send a message through our Dutch captain," Peter replied.

Captain Meerbrandt came to Simon's home. "From America," he said, handed him an envelope and left. Hunt opened it and read Emily Loring's letter. It stated they bore no ill feelings toward him and were looking forward to seeing Gwendolyn. One from his parents was also enclosed. All was well, and they hoped to see him and Gwendolyn when the war ended.

As time advanced, Simon became increasingly lonesome for his family and concerned with the ongoing war in the colonies. Plotting his return to America, he calculated his best way was via Holland. "I will say that I am going to study microscopy," he said. "Some microscopes are being built in England, but those made in Holland are far superior. The Dutch are also the most expert in using and teaching them. That will be my reason."

A Professor Selziger at Leiden University was communicating his microscopic studies to the Royal Society. Writing to him, Hunt was informed that the professor would assist in his learning microscopy.

Gwendolyn was fourteen months old, when they sailed for Holland. With them was Mrs. Kirkland, a widow who had been hired as a nursemaid.

"I do not look forward to going, Doctor," she said. "But I love Gwendolyn, the pay is good, and they say the Dutch are a clean people."

It was a two-day voyage to Amsterdam. Surprisingly, the English Channel was fairly calm. The next day, a coach brought them to Leiden. They procured rooms at an inn. The following morning,

Simon set off for Selziger's house. Arriving there, he used the knocker. A young woman opened the door and looked at him inquiringly.

"Guten morgen," he said in German. *"Ich bin Doktor Simon Hunt."* Stumbling on, he added, *"Bitte, Herr Professor Selziger?"*

She smiled and answered in perfect English. "Yes, this is his house and he is in, Doctor Hunt."

Simon also smiled, saying, "You speak English far better than my poor German, dear lady. My Dutch is nonexistent."

"Your German was quite adequate," she replied. "I am Jacqueline, his daughter. Please come in. We have been expecting you." Preceding him to her father's study, she whispered, "He also speaks English well." Then, knocking and entering, Jacqueline said, "Doctor Hunt is here, father," and left the room.

Selziger rose to greet him. "Welcome, Doctor," he smiled and extended a hand.

The professor was an inch or two shorter than he, but still tall. He was portly but appeared vigorous. A blonde head of hair and nicely trimmed beard adorned his features. His nose was somewhat long with a slight curve. Behind spectacles sparkled intelligent pale blue eyes. Ruddy cheeks bordered wide red lips and his smile showed excellent teeth.

"Thank you," Hunt responded. "It is a pleasure to meet you."

"Please sit with me," said Selziger. "Tell me about your medical studies and why you are interested in microscopy."

Simon told of his education in America and England, and noted his recent interest in birthing. In closing, he said, "I believe microscopy opens new areas for study and will add to medical knowledge. I wish to begin learning while it is still in its infancy."

"Well answered," said the professor. "I wrote that I would help you, but presently work at the university consumes my time. However, I can recommend a fine teacher."

"Who might that be?" queried Hunt.

Jacqueline had appeared with tea and cookies. "Here is your tutor," her father smiled. Simon's jaw dropped. Seeing him obviously surprised, Selziger added, "Jacqueline is well versed in all aspects of microscopy and has had many students. She prepares all my samples. In fact, she builds and sells microscope. Her university examinations are this week, but she will then be free to teach you."

Hunt looked at the girl who was pouring tea for them. He wondered about a woman attending a university but said nothing.

"Sugar, doctor?" she asked in a soft, pleasant voice.

"Yes, please," he answered.

As Jacqueline poured the tea, he looked at her face and saw how lovely it was. Initially, he had not paid much attention to her appearance. Now, he took more notice. Jacqueline's blonde hair was pulled back into a single long braid. She had a high forehead, arched blonde eyebrows, and her father's eyes. Her nose was straight and not too long. Wide red lips and colored cheeks were also present. She appeared confident, self-assured, and very pleasant to look at.

"I would like to begin as soon as possible," Simon said. "When might that be?"

Jacqueline was sipping her tea. "Today is Thursday and examinations are Monday and Tuesday," she said. "Wednesday morning would be fine. What time would you like?"

"Half eight would be good," he answered. "But what fee do you wish?"

She named a reasonable charge and Hunt readily accepted it.

The professor stood and said, "We should go to the study area."

They followed him to a room adjacent to the kitchen. It had previously served as the dining area. "Here we are," Selziger said. "Notice both van Leeuwenhoek and Huygens microscopes. Jacqueline will train you to use them. However, there is a rule. The door must always be kept open and Olga, our maid, will serve as chaperone."

His daughter nodded, as Hunt said, "Agreed."

They spoke for several more minutes. Then, Simon departed and went to the inn. He had dinner with Gwendolyn and Mrs. Kirkland. The child ate bits of meat, mashed peas and applesauce. She drank milk from a glass, and handled it competently. Afterward, they put her to bed and Simon tucked her in. Still tired from the trip, he went to bed early.

Friday afternoon was warm with a bright sun. The nursemaid placed Gwendolyn in her carriage and Hunt started off. She laughed and giggled, occasionally saying words, as he pushed and spoke to her. Seeing the university buildings, he said, "We shall visit school, Gwendolyn."

As they drew near the buildings, a young woman waved. Still at a distance, she had recognized his red beard.

He smiled and waved back as he realized it was Jacqueline.

Meeting, she said, "Doctor Hunt, I did not expect to find you at the university pushing a carriage." Looking within, she added, "And with such a beautiful little girl. She must be yours, but where is your wife?"

"My wife is in heaven," he answered with a subdued voice.

Jacqueline felt embarrassed and her cheeks became even redder.

Disconcerted, she said, "I am so sorry." She stood silent and then again peered into the carriage. The baby smiled at her and giggled. "What a lovely child," Jacqueline said, and remained with her face near Gwendolyn's. "Tell me her name and how old she is."

"Her name is Gwendolyn," Simon said, "And she is almost fifteen months." Smiling, he added, "She is an excellent companion for one so small and seems quite bright. Though that, of course, is a father's opinion."

Jacqueline laughed. The atmosphere had changed. "Since you are here," she said, "I would like to show you about and explain the university's history. However, we are not chaperoned and I will have to walk apart from you."

"Agreed," he replied. "I must say the structures seem old."

"We are very proud of our university. William of Orange established it in 1575. The Dutch had revolted against their Spanish oppressors and in 1574 the city was besieged."

Gwendolyn interrupted by starting to cry. Simon took her from the carriage and comforted the infant. She quieted and he asked, "And what saved them?"

Jacqueline took a cookie from a bag she was holding. Handing it to Gwendolyn, she said, "I baked this cookie, please enjoy it."

The little girl took it, smiled, and began eating.

"They were saved by a Dutch fleet," Jacqueline replied. "The dikes were cut and the meadows flooded. The fleet sailed to the city and drove the Spaniards off. The next year, William came and thanked the people. To show his gratitude, he established the school. It has become famous throughout Europe and many scholars come here."

"A wonderful story, and you told it well," he smiled.

"You must be wondering how a woman is at university," she added. "I am father's assistant and so they allowed my entry. There are two other women here." Jacqueline paused and glanced at a clock tower. She said, "Please excuse me Doctor Hunt, it has been nice speaking with you and meeting Gwendolyn, but I must go home and study."

"I will see you Wednesday," he answered, "Good luck on your examinations."

It rained the entire weekend. Monday and Tuesday were cloudy with intermittent drizzles. He read to Gwendolyn and played with her. She was continuing to progress in speaking and Simon was overjoyed.

Wednesday morning was clear and sunny. Hunt arrived at the professor's home ready to begin his entry into the microscopic world. Olga opened the door, took his hat, and led him to the microscopy room. His teacher was already there.

"Good morning," Simon said. "I hope your examinations went well."

"Good morning," Jacqueline replied. "Yes, it seems I studied appropriately. You are right on time, doctor. Let us begin by discussing the different microscopes."

She led him to the table where two of the instruments were placed. Teacher and student sat next to one another. In the adjacent kitchen, Olga peeled potatoes and silently observed them.

Jacqueline began, "We will use Leeuwenhoek's microscope today. It only has a single small lens, but it is thick and he found a way to grind it to a very convex shape. That gives it great magnification. Huygens' instrument uses two lenses. They are easier to make and work well, but there are colored rings because of dissimilar glass or grinding."

"Now, scratch your teeth with a fingernail, add saliva and place it on this glass." He did so and she placed the glass over a hole on the microscope's platform. Adjusting a small mirror below, so the outdoor light was sent up the instrument, she said, "Now, look."

"The view seems fuzzy."

"It is out of focus," Jacqueline replied. "Turn the knob to move the tube up or down."

Doing so, he suddenly jumped back, saying, "There are tiny creatures swimming about." Again looking, Simon added, "This is truly marvelous." He turned to his teacher, saying, "Those tiny things are moving by means of fine fibrils. They are like oars."

"Yes," she answered, "and we never knew they were in our mouths, seemingly harmless. But there are many other things to see, Doctor Hunt."

"Please call me Simon," he said.

"As you wish," she replied. "Then you may call me Jacqueline."

"Excellent" he smiled. "I prefer less formality."

They worked through the morning, Olga always hovering in the background.

Walking home Hunt thought about what he had learned. His thinking turned to his teacher, "She is very competent," he whispered.

Jacqueline began teaching him to make very thin slices of specimens and mount them on glass. "I am having difficulty learning this," Simon said. "You are so quick."

"It takes time to acquire the skill. Women are used to needlework and handling small objects, skills men do not possess. You will make progress. Oh, my father asked if you would like to join us for dinner Sunday. You can bring Gwendolyn, he loves children."

"It would be my pleasure and I am certain she will enjoy the visit."

"Good," she smiled, "Would three in the afternoon be good?"

"We will be here at three," and he also smiled

Sunday, Simon arrived with his daughter at the appointed time. Jacqueline answered his knock, welcomed them, and he carried Gwendolyn into the house.

Coming to the study, the professor rose. "Welcome to you both," he said. "I am delighted to have you here." He shook Hunt's free hand and looked carefully at Gwendolyn. "Young lady," he said, "You are very pretty and I am charmed to meet you."

Taking her hand, Selziger kissed it. The child reached out and patted his beard. He roared with laughter, saying, "Little girl, you certainly know how to charm an old man."

Olga indicated dinner was ready and they entered a small room.

"Our new dining area," Jacqueline said. "It is small but cozy."

The food came and the professor sliced the meat, cutting a portion into very small pieces. He added mashed potatoes and peas. Placing the plate before Gwendolyn, he said, "Enjoy your dinner, child."

Several pillows had been put beneath her, so that she was at table height. Taking a spoon, she began to happily eat. "Food," she said and they all applauded.

Afterward, as they drank tea and Gwendolyn slept in Simon's lap, they spoke about Holland. Later, the conversation shifted to the conflict between England and America.

"It is most uncharacteristic for a Hollander to pry into other's affairs,“ the Professor said. “Still, you know we revolted against Spain to gain our freedom. I wonder what your feelings are about the American war?”

Hunt replied, “I do not mind your asking. My wife and I wished to remain neutral, but I also desired to study medicine in London. It was best to pose as Tories. I visited Parliament, heard the members speak, and discussed their attitude toward the colonies with her. We became convinced that our people would never secure representation and determined to support the revolution. After my studies here, I will return to America.”

Over the following months, his instruction continued. On frequent Sundays, he and Gwendolyn were asked to dinner. Jacqueline would walk part way home with them. As summer came and Jacqueline was free from classes, they spent more time with the microscope. Afterward, they sat together and began to discuss various things.

Occasionally, she would question something about different medicines and he would have to justify their use. They would speak about European politics and the war in America, then music, about which she was passionate. As the summer progressed, both expressed more of their inner feelings. Student and teacher continued to draw closer. She also began to walk further with him. Olga was always behind and watchful.

Simon thought, “I am feeling aroused when near her.”

Jacqueline kept thinking, “I feel so comfortable with him. His hair color is strange at first, but he is quite good looking and very nice.”

By October, Selziger realized his daughter was quite taken with her student. He said, “You appear to show more interest in Doctor Hunt than for prior men. Tell me your thoughts.”

She answered. "Father, I am more and more attracted to him, and think he feels the same toward me. He has not really courted me, but I am interested in him."

"And the child?" he asked.

Jacqueline smiled and replied, "I am as taken with her as you are. She is still very young and would benefit by having a mother."

Her father nodded and said, "Doctor Hunt said he wishes to return to America."

"Yes, that is something I must consider," she replied, and hugged him. He kissed her forehead, patted her gently and their conversation ended.

"I know that love is again rising in my heart," Simon thought. "I am of two minds. Gwendolyn has been gone for twenty months, but I still think and dream about her. Jacqueline is a marvelous woman, and I am in love with her. She certainly likes little Gwendolyn and I believe she cares for me, but would she marry and go to America."

They continued to become more involved. Despite Olga, she would take his hand and walk close. He felt its warmth spread over him, his interest in her even more provoked. One day, turning a corner, she kissed his cheek. Overwhelmed, he kissed her lips. When Olga sighted them, they had moved on but knew they were in love.

He spoke to the professor saying, "I love Jacqueline, and believe she cares for me. I ask your permission to court her."

"I respect your asking," he answered. "What exactly are your intentions?"

"They are to treat her with respect, and hopefully have her agree to marry me."

"What of your wish to return to America?"

"I have an obligation to do so. My wife died giving life to our child. I owe her parents and mine the opportunity to see their grandchild. Jacqueline and I must discuss this. It would be difficult at first, but I believe she will like America."

"Let us ask Jacqueline," Selziger replied, and called out to her.

She entered the study and her father said. "Doctor Hunt asks my permission to court you, Jacqueline. He says, if you marry, he will want to take you to America. How say you?"

"Courtship first, papa, decisions later," she replied.

Courting began in earnest with them spending hours talking, and with locked arms taking long walks. Olga followed, but frequent kisses were stolen. Both understood that they had the compatibility needed for a happy marriage.

November ended, and Hunt knew they were both deeply in love. He proposed marriage to Jacqueline. She had already given it serious thought and said, "I am in love with you, Simon, and also love Gwendolyn. You wish to return to America. I would marry you and go, but you must ask my father's permission, and he must agree to my leaving."

"I understand," he replied and spoke to Selziger. Hunt nervously said, "Sir, you have permitted me to court your daughter. Now, I ask for her hand in marriage."

"I have been expecting this," the professor replied. "Observing you both, I was reminded of courting my wife. Let me hear what Jacqueline has to say." He rose from his chair, opened the door and called out to her.

She was in the kitchen, helping Olga prepare dinner. Suspecting the question had been asked, she dried her hands and came to them.

Her father said, "Simon has asked to marry you. It means leaving your family and going to America."

"Father, we are in love and he is a good man. I know he will care for me and keep me safe. With your permission we can marry in January. Beside you and Olga, there is room here for me, Simon, and Gwendolyn. In that way, we will be close to you until April or May when we will sail for America."

For a moment her father looked unhappy. Then he smiled, saying, "I will miss you greatly, also Simon and Gwendolyn. If your sister were not nearby my answer might be different. Somehow, God and fate have brought you together and I bless your marriage."

She started to cry and took hold of her father, "Bless you, papa. You have made me very happy," she murmured, and wept even more. The professor gently kissed her forehead and reached a hand toward Simon's. Taking it, he said, "Welcome into our family."

XXXI

Jonathan had been assigned to a hospital in Morristown and came home for the weekend. Finishing breakfast, Grace softly said, "Husband, you should know I am with child. I have not shown blood for two months and morning sickness has begun."

Overcome with joy and concern, Wolfe took her hands, saying, "Sweetheart, this is wonderful news. But are you all right?"

Grace smiled happily, saying, "I am fine, Jonathan. There is no need to worry."

"Well then, hurrah," he shouted, embracing and kissing her.

Wolfe gently sat her down, and drew his chair close. Keeping her hand in his, he spoke of his love for her. They discussed their hopes for the coming child. The hours drifted by and the conversation turned to their families and finally Agnes and Oliver.

"Do you think they will marry?" Grace asked.

"They are obviously in love," Jonathan answered, "His hesitation to move ahead is related to prior experience. Oliver confessed he had been previously engaged. It was his great love and she deserted him for a very wealthy man. He fears Agnes's wealth."

"Agnes is not unknowing and certainly realizes love and patience will eventually bring him to the altar."

"Wise women seem to recognize one another," he laughed, kissing her.

In early November, Farnsworth and Wolfe were at the hospital. Oliver, clearly unhappy, said, "News from the South brings only reports of disaster. The attempt to recapture Savannah has failed. Pulaski and many of his cavalry were slaughtered by enemy artillery. It is a grim time for the rebellion."

"I too feel discouraged," Jonathan replied. "But we are fortunate to frequently be with our ladies. I am aware that I pry, Oliver, but what is happening with you and Agnes."

Oliver grinned. "My hesitation has been overcome. I plan to ask her to wed me."

"That is the best news I have heard in a long time," Wolfe said.

"Please do not tell Grace, Jonathan. I hope Agnes will accept my proposal. We have become very close. However, one never truly knows what might be the response."

"Do not fear, Oliver. I believe she will accept you with a joyful heart."

In early December, Farnsworth proposed marriage. They were sitting in the great room feeling the warmth of the fireplace flames. He softly said, "Agnes, the country is at war and I do not know what my future prospects may be. I love you and believe you love me. You would do me great honor, if you will marry me."

Tears showed in Agnes's eyes. She wiped at them and said, "Oliver, I love you with all my being. I will marry you gladly."

Clinging to each other, they kissed. "Christmas is not far. Would that day be agreeable?" Agnes said.

"Christmas Day is perfect," he replied.

"There is a Presbyterian church in the village. Is that acceptable?" she asked.

"My darling, I will marry you anywhere you choose," Farnsworth answered.

"It will only be a small wedding, Oliver."

"Agnes dear, my eyes will only be on you."

She hugged him tightly, saying, "Will you always be such an agreeable husband?"

"I will obey you in all things, save returning to my post. Your love will keep me safe."

They kissed once more, spoke of their love and stayed close.

Snow had fallen through the month, but December 24th dawned clear and bright. Grace and Jonathan arrived at the farm in the afternoon, as did Peter and Emily Loring. They were still recovering from Gwendolyn's death, but put on a brave face. At dinner, Peter said to Farnsworth, "Doctor, I am sure you know that our cousin is both a beautiful and caring woman. Doctor Wolfe assures me that you are a fine individual and skilled in your profession. My wife and I congratulate you on the coming marriage. We wish you both great happiness." He raised his glass and the others joined him.

"Agnes and I truly appreciate you and Mrs. Loring being here, sir. As you know, her brother is with the cavalry. His family is still in the South and unable to be here. She is happy that relatives are present."

Agnes rose from her chair and came to her aunt and uncle. Kissing them warmly she said, "Oliver speaks well for me. I, also, thank you for coming. You both, of course, know Doctor Wolfe and have now become acquainted with his wife."

They nodded and Emily said, "Mrs. Wolfe, your husband has been serving our country well. You are as lovely as Agnes and, I am certain, a perfect wife. Forgive me for noticing that you appear to be with child. I mention this only to offer sincere best wishes for the future." Tears brimmed in her eyes, but she held them back and smiled.

Grace blushed, but said, "It is sweet of you to notice and say such nice things. Yes, I am almost four months on my way, possibly June or July for the baby's arrival. Jonathan and I are looking forward to the event."

Oliver raised his glass and toasted Wolfe and Grace. Then he said, "To the coming newborn. Tomorrow is Christ's Day and our wedding. Let us be joyful."

Peter leaned toward Jonathan, saying, "I thought you should know, Simon is in Holland with baby Gwendolyn and intends to return to America. Keep the information close. British spies are everywhere."

Wolfe grasped his hand, saying, "Thank you for telling me, sir."

After a pleasant evening, the farmer drove them to their quarters at an inn. Helping the ladies down, he said to Grace," You have married a good man, missus. He knows doctoring, but even better he can shoe a horse." He laughed and bid them goodnight.

In their room and lying together, Jonathan told her what Loring had revealed. "We must not speak of it," he said. "Still, it is peculiar, he spoke of Simon and the baby. Neither he nor his wife mentioned their daughter. It is over a year since she died."

"Jonathan," Grace answered. "They lost their only child. People never quite recover from such a tragedy. Eventually, they will embrace their granddaughter and be able to speak of her mother. We must be kind to them."

"Mrs. Wolfe, you are right, as always. Somehow, your perception of a difficult situation always exceeds mine. It must be womanly intuition." He hugged her and then placed his hand so as to feel the unborn babe.

They stayed this way for several minutes. Then Grace rolled away and fell asleep. Jonathan remained awake, thinking of the coming birth and whether it would be a boy or girl. "Either will be fine," he said softly, "So long as it and Grace are well." He turned to see their quilt properly covered her and promptly fell asleep.

On Christmas Day, 1779, the church was filled with local worshippers and festooned with holly leaves and red berries. Agnes wore a simple white dress with an encircling blue ribbon. Like Grace, she applied a last stitch that morning.

Minister MacDonald started the service and spoke of Christ's Glory and the need to follow his teachings. Concluding, he spoke of the war. "War is a terrible thing," he said. "Even so, the present confrontation is necessary. All of us should now kneel and pray we achieve those most valued entities, freedom and peace."

The congregation knelt. With bowed heads, they heard him say, "Peace to all this Christmas Day. Let mercy and truth meet together; righteousness and peace kiss each other." The minister rose, "Please be seated," he said. "Today, we are blessed to witness a marriage. Doctor Farnsworth of our Continental Army, and Mrs. Agnes Stiles, a resident of our village, are to be wed."

MacDonald led the procession down the aisle. The couple said their vows, rings were exchanged and he pronounced them husband and wife. They kissed and some called out in joy. Randall and Sally hugged their mother tightly and turned to Oliver. Lifting them, he kissed their cheeks and invited the small congregation to a local tavern.

Almost all came to imbibe some Christmas cheer. After offering good wishes, they left. The wedding party stayed on, enjoying a bountiful meal. Later, the Wolfes and Lorings departed and the newlyweds returned to the farmhouse with the children and servants.

A three-day honeymoon ensued. Oliver and Agnes made love passionately. On their return, intimacy continued with even greater intensity. In January, he rejoined the army.

Simon and Jacqueline met with Reverend Arnheim at a nearby Dutch Reformed Church. Religious obligations were discussed and banns posted. Numerous dinners were held to introduce distant relatives, Jacqueline's friends and the professor's colleagues to the bridegroom. He had met Ava, her husband Hendrik Boerhaave, and their boys Pieter and Ludwig. Now they were frequently at the house.

A thaw arrived in early January, one week before the wedding. Hendrik said, "We must follow tradition," and revealed a can of green paint. Removing his jacket and replacing it with an apron, Boerhaave proceeded to paint the door of the house. Shaking their hands, he said, "Now all who pass will know this is the house of a lady soon to be married."

In mid-January, they wed. Jacqueline looked radiant in her white dress and carried a basket of forced white narcissus. On her head she wore a silver crown.

Arnheim performed a short but meaningful service, and the newlyweds embraced and kissed. Gwendolyn sat between Pieter and Ludwig in a front pew. Mrs. Kirkland and Olga were alongside. The church was filled with relatives, friends and colleagues. As the couple exited, flowers bombarded them.

The celebration was at a local tavern. Simon and Jacqueline sat at a table next to a tree branch. "That is for us," she said. "Each guest has a paper leaf. They will write good wishes, and tie the leaf to the tree. Then we shake hands and the men will kiss me."

Simon smiled, "Me first," he said, and kissed her as she laughed.

Jacqueline fed him, saying, "The sweetbreads are called bridal sugar and the spiced wine is bridal tears."

"I am enjoying both," he replied, kissing her again, "But far more, being married to you."

"You are warming me, even more than the wine," she smiled.

Beer flowed freely and everyone was joyous. The wedding cake, proudly baked and decorated by Olga, was cut. The bride served her groom and he served her. They kissed to cheers. As the reception concluded, Jacqueline tossed her crown to a group of single women. The one catching it would be the next bride.

That night they stayed at a nearby inn. Jacqueline was not shy. Undressing, she appeared naked before him. Seeing her body in the light of the fireplace fire, he felt immediately aroused. Also naked, Simon took her in his arms, kissing her gently.

They moved to the bed. "You are the loveliest woman and I have been fortunate to find you," he whispered. She hugged him and tenderly kissed his lips. Slowly they stroked one another and, as their passion increased, brought their bodies together. Moving slowly and then with greater intensity they climaxed, as the fireplace became dark.

In the morning, they awoke early. Kissing him, she said "I am very much in love with you, husband." They cuddled and, after Simon made a fire, again had intimacy and fell asleep. Later they awoke, dressed, had an early lunch, and left for The Hague.

They visited buildings that were the seat of Holland's government, walked the snowy streets, entered shops and dined in fine restaurants. After several days, Jacqueline smiled and said, "You are spending too much money, dear husband."

"I must continue to court my bride," he responded.

Friday, they returned to Leiden. The Boerhaave's came with Gwendolyn. She ran to her father with tears in her eyes. "Papa," she cried. He picked her up, hugging and kissing her. Professor Selziger embraced them. Olga, ordinarily self-contained, seized Jacqueline and Simon. She kissed them warmly and said, "Welcome home." At dinner, the Professor and Hendrik each rose to toast the couple. Gwendolyn sat in Hunt's lap. Later, she reached out to her new mother. Jacqueline took her and held her close. Happy, the child fell asleep. The Boerhaave's departed and Selziger said, "Goodnight my beloved daughter and son."

XXXII

As December 1779 drew to a close, it was bitter cold. General Washington addressed his generals and aides. "Gentlemen, we have divided our army among several sites, the better to feed them. None are too far from New York. General Clinton has detached some of his forces to fight the French in the Caribbean. Still, we lack the ability to launch an attack against him. He is now camped behind the city's defenses. The Royal Navy is available to him and secures the waters around Manhattan. We can only watch, anticipate, and counter his next move."

"There are reports the British are planning another assault in the South, very possibly Charleston," Hamilton remarked.

"We cannot rely on rumors," another interjected. "Besides, the South is not so important to our cause. South Carolina has never put forth great effort to meet the recruiting goals set for it. Governor Rutledge may have signed the Declaration of Independence, but he refused to send his militias north when they were most needed and was ready to surrender the state to Prevost. Laurens raised the possibility of recruiting three thousand Negroes from the colony. Several northern states have actively done so, but South Carolinians shuddered at the thought. Now, the British have offered freedom to blacks who enter their lines and many do so."

"South Carolina's poor performance in supporting the rebellion is well known, but everyplace is important to us," a general replied. "North or South, we must hold every inch of ground. Peace settlements often end with each side keeping the area they occupy. No territory should be ceded to the enemy."

"General, you make good sense," Washington said. "We will evaluate the options that Clinton has at his disposal and prepare to respond."

As they spoke, an armada was gathering in New York's harbor. Learning of it, Washington thought, "I still do not know what it means. If Charleston is the target, General Lincoln will determine how to act. If his choice is to defend the city, he must ensure a route for retreat. Like New York, it is less important than the army."

On Christmas Day, 1779, coincident with the wedding of Oliver and Agnes, General Clinton and his staff boarded the flagship of the assembled fleet. "We are off to new adventures, gentlemen," he said to his aides. To the admiral in command, he added. "Admiral, shortly your captains will open their orders and learn we sail for Charleston. Let us wish for good winds to quickly speed us there."

On the Atlantic, storms buffeted the invasion fleet. During the voyage, both men and horses suffered illness and death. Not till February 11th was a landing made on Simmons Island, twenty miles below Charleston.

General Lincoln sat with his aides at breakfast. "So Clinton has landed," he said. "We have erected formidable defenses and will continue to bolster them. I had expected more South Carolinians to turn out. But our problem in defending Charleston is not just the British Army. Their fleet lies outside the sand bar at the entry into the harbor. It is high, but if they cross it, we will be in difficulty. We are at the end of a peninsula and between the Ashley River to our west and the Cooper River to our east. Their ships must be held away from the Cooper. If retreat becomes necessary, its control is critical."

Charleston's mayor had joined him and said, "Do not even think of retreat. I am recruiting every man in the city to stand with you. As for the Royal Navy, there are only several ways through the sand bar. Admiral Whipple, even with his smaller frigates, can defend those passages. The British can only come through in single file. Standing broadside, Whipple outguns each ship."

Lincoln responded. "Whipple has determined not to do so. The fool has refused to hazard his ships. He will only stand near Fort Moultrie and add his guns to theirs. Also, I expected the backcountry men to join us but they have not come."

"I do not know why they have not yet arrived," the Mayor frowned, anxiously mopping his forehead.

One of Lincoln's aides spoke out in an angry tone. "They will not come, General. They will not come, because they refuse to risk their necks for people who have put them down and scorned them for years and years. They will not come to save Charleston's wealthy merchants and plantation owners. I have attempted to rally them and that has been their universal response. Frankly, I believe they will be happy to see the city fall."

"They are ignorant fools," the mayor exploded. "If we fall, what is their fate?"

"Well asked," replied the aide. "I queried the same. Those fellows are already fighting the local Tories. If the British Army comes, smaller units will be attacked as they venture into the interior. The leaders of the backcountry folk are well versed in the swamps and hideaways of the territory. They impressed me as strong, rough, capable men, and seem to have their heads about them."

"Bother to them," answered the Mayor. "We can defend Charlestown without their assistance."

"Yes, we can and we will," Lincoln echoed.

In April, speaking to his aides, Howe said, "Our Army and Navy are tightening the noose about the Americans. We have crossed the Ashley and begun the siege. Our ships have passed the barrier bar and run past Fort Moultrie. Only Whipple's small frigates hold the Cooper River. Now we will move to control it and spring the trap on Lincoln's army."

Inside Charleston, an aide reported to General Lincoln, "Sir, Admiral Whipple states he is unable to lay a boom across the entry to the Cooper. If their navy gains control, it reduces our ability to retreat. Our army is essential to the rebellion. If we are trapped, it will suffer great damage."

Lincoln listened but was slow to move. Clinton was not. "Colonel Webster," he ordered, "Take your men and cross the Cooper. Strike the rebel cavalry stationed at Monck's Corner. They guard the enemy's last line of retreat."

"I will move directly, Sir," the Colonel replied, and quietly crossed the river. Tarleton's cavalry was with him." Colonel Tarleton," Webster said. "Attack the enemy's cavalry and hold the area until reinforced."

"Yes, Sir," he responded and pushed his men forward. In the dead of night, they approached the unsuspecting Americans. "We will surprise and cut them to pieces," Tarleton said. And, as dawn broke, the charge was launched. For the English, it was a great success. Their enemy was overwhelmed, and the last line of retreat for Lincoln's Army was severed.

General Lincoln held a council of war with his officers and civilian leaders. "We can cross the Cooper and attempt to break through to the east," a Colonel said. "In that way we might be able to free the Army."

"We will not permit you to abandon us," shouted a civilian. "Is it not better that you die in a glorious cause, than slink away from your duty?"

"Who will do the dying?" replied the Colonel, "Certainly not you, sir. General, we are in dire straits, but we may be able to fight our way through. At least part of the army may be preserved."

"We will stay," Lincoln said, caving to the civilian demands.

General Clinton glowed with joy. "Our siege guns are moving closer to Charleston," he said. "American resistance will soon be over."

On May 11, 1780, Lincoln surrendered. It was the greatest disaster in the course of the rebellion. Imprisonment loomed for 5,700 American soldiers and the 1,000 sailors from Whipple's flotilla. Loring's vessel and many others along Charleston's wharves were taken. Other generals were also prisoners but they, like Lincoln, were paroled, as were all his officers. As such, until exchanged for an officer of equal rank, they were free but sworn not to fight again. While the officers moved about and lived a fairly easy life, the enlisted men, militia, and sailors faced hard times, disease, and death in prisons and prison ships.

A month after Charleston fell, Clinton spoke to General Cornwallis. "We have done well here," he said. "Now, I will return to New York. Your task is to secure all of South Carolina. Move at your discretion, but always leave sufficient forces to hold Charleston against any attack."

"Very well, Sir, your orders will be carried out," Cornwallis answered. Under his breath, he whispered, "But you are departing with 4,500 of our best regulars and South Carolina occupies a very large space."

XXXIII

In the months after the marriage, Selziger did everything he could to make the newlyweds feel comfortable. Jacqueline was happy, but concerned about the move to America. Hunt reassured her, saying, "Do not worry, sweetheart. You speak excellent English and my family will welcome you. Furthermore, there are people in the area who speak Dutch. If you wish, we can go to a Reformed Church. You will quickly be content."

She smiled, saying, "I am certain you are right, husband." Within, she continued to worry about the new world she would soon enter. Also, her father, despite his brave talk, would be left with Olga in a large house.

To her and Simon's surprise, the professor began coming home later than usual and often left for several hours in the evening. His step was lighter and he smiled more. As February ended, he said, "Do not worry. I have met a charming and intelligent widow. Actually, she had been married to a colleague. A friend introduced us and we are quite taken with one another. She has put new vigor in me. We may not marry but we will keep company."

"Oh, papa," Jacqueline said, "I am so happy for you. Can we meet her?"

"I mentioned you were shortly leaving for America. Mrs. Hofbrandt said she would enjoy meeting you. We can ask her to come for dinner."

"That would be very nice," his daughter said.

In March, Selziger escorted Ingrid Hofbrandt to his house. She was a robust lady who, at forty-five, still retained good looks and was quite intelligent. The professor and she seemed to make a good couple.

Later, Simon and Jacqueline spoke. "What was your impression?" he asked.

"Mrs. Hofbrandt made a nice impression, but she would try her best to do so," Jacqueline answered. "Father is an important man and would be a good catch."

"True," Hunt answered. "Jacqueline, I may not have mentioned that my mother was a widow and my father had never married when they met. They have had a happy marriage and here I am," he smiled.

"Yes, you are," she said, kissing him. "Let us hope for the best."

The professor reassured Jacqueline that he would be fine. Olga would stay on. The house would be managed, and he was planning to continue teaching and exploring the microscopic world. Mrs. Hofbrandt was available and time would determine their future.

Over the next few weeks, Jacqueline packed her clothing and microscopes. She helped Simon with his and Gwendolyn's things. It became a whirlwind of visits by and to friends. The Boerhaaves came frequently and the sisters drew even closer. Tears were shed, and each knew they might never see one another again.

As April ended, the Hunt family boarded a Dutch ship bound for New York. It carried passengers, Leiden linens, wines and other goods for wealthy Tories and British officers. The seas were turbulent at times and the voyage took six weeks. Jacqueline and Simon were frequently seasick but Gwendolyn's sea legs quickly developed.

On landing the first week in June, they passed through customs and were questioned. "You left for England, doctor," Captain MacIver said, "You have come from Holland. Our records show your wife had a different name than this lady. An explanation is required."

Jacqueline drew Gwendolyn out of earshot. Hunt began, "My wife and I being Loyalists, went to England for me to further study medicine. She died birthing our daughter who you see here. Later, the child travelled with me to Holland. I wished to study the microscope. I met my present wife there and married her. We return now to introduce my wife to my family and the child to her grandparents."

The captain seemed sympathetic and also homesick. "I understand your feelings. As for your wife, the English and Dutch are at peace. There is no problem with her entry."

"Thank you, Captain," Simon said.

"However," MacIver continued, "Leaving New York requires special permission."

"Who must I see to obtain it?" Hunt asked.

"Colonel Ashcroft, is in charge," he said. "The sergeant at the next desk can help you."

"Thank you, Captain," he replied.

The sergeant arranged for an interview in three days. Their entry papers signed as acceptable, they entered the city and found quarters.

Three days later, they were at the office of Colonel Ashcroft. He was lean and clean-shaven. Hunt's red beard initially startled him. Simon again explained their story. Irascible, the Colonel listened and said, "I have reviewed the captain's findings. My uncle was a doctor. How did you find English medical practices?"

"Very much advanced over the colonies, sir," Hunt replied.

"I would expect so," said the Colonel, pleased by the answer. "And why go to study in Holland? We have those microscope things in England."

"Yes, sir," he answered, "But truthfully, most have been imported from the Lowlands. The best teachers seem to be there and many English go there to learn."

"That may be," he shot back, "But you agree we have the best doctors."

"Absolutely," Simon said.

Jacqueline had been sitting by Simon, holding Gwendolyn in her lap. Periodically Ashcroft glanced at her and the child. As he looked again, Gwendolyn smiled, put a hand to her mouth and blew a kiss. Having three daughters at home, the Colonel was overcome.

"You have a charming child," he said. His mood suddenly altered, he added, "I can understand your desire to go to Philadelphia. Will you be safe there as a Tory?"

"My sympathies are not really known. They merely know I left to study medicine. Since my wife is Dutch, I do not anticipate problems."

"I must mull over your request, come back in two days," he said.

Hunt thanked him and returned two days later. Shown to his office, Ashcroft looked up and said, "I have decided to permit you to leave New York. Here is your pass. However, you must sign this form. It states that you will never join the rebels nor assist them in any way."

Expecting this might be required, Simon immediately signed.

Ashcroft leaned back, saying, "I suggest you quickly find and purchase a horse and carriage. You have a long journey to Philadelphia. I will be visiting an old friend commanding the garrison at Sandy Hook. A cargo ship sails there in four days. Room aboard might be available. Meet me at this pier and I will see if you can come."

The Colonel handed him the pass and pier number. "I have a warm spot for doctors and little girls," he smiled. Hunt thanked him effusively.

It took three days but Simon was able to buy a used carriage and a rather old horse. "I paid an exorbitant amount for them," he said to Jacqueline, "But they should get us to Philadelphia. We must pack and be early at the wharf."

Ashcroft was there when they arrived. "You are fortunate," he said. "Captain Malcolm informs me that cargo is light. There will be room and he has agreed to take you."

"Sir, you have been extremely helpful," Simon said.

Jacqueline smiled and said, "Say thank you, Gwendolyn."

The child also smiled, saying, "Thank you, sir," in a soft voice.

The Colonel picked her up, kissed her cheek and said, "It is a pleasure to help such a lovely lady, Gwendolyn." Putting her down, he addressed the adults. "We will defeat Washington and his army. Stay loyal to our King and you will be rewarded."

Shortly afterward, they boarded the boat and it sailed across the harbor to New Jersey. Arriving in Sandy Hook, Ashcroft wished them well and helped expedite their departure. The carriage had travelled several miles when armed men suddenly stopped them.

"Halt," one of them called. "You were seen leaving the British camp. You must be questioned by our captain." Climbing onto the carriage, he took the reins. Simon and Jacqueline were blindfolded.

After thirty minutes over rutted roads, the carriage stopped. They were helped off and taken into a cabin.

"Your names and business here," a voice said. Hunt and Jacqueline gave their names. Simon related their story and the voice said, "The lady claims to be Dutch, but answers in English. What town are you from?" came the question in Dutch.

"Leiden, I was born and lived there all my life," she replied in Dutch.

The blindfolds were removed and they saw a thirty year old, tall, bearded man. He began conversing in her native language. Finally he smiled and said, "My name is Anton Schpeerboeck. You speak far better Dutch than I do. My grandparents came from Holland and we still speak it at home. Welcome to America."

Shaking hands with them and switching to English, he added, "We are New Jersey militia and you are free to go. I will provide a pass stating you have been interviewed and cleared. They know me well for the next fifty miles. I will ask them to give further passes."

"Thank you," both Simon and Jacqueline said.

The man who brought them led them out. Mounting the carriage he drove to the road from which they had come. Dismounting, he gave directions, said goodbye, and disappeared. The three continued on, stopping at inns for the night and moving during daylight. Progress was slow but steady. Schpeerboeck's pass paved their way.

Nearing Philadelphia, Hunt said, "We are almost home."

In the afternoon they reached his parents' home. Overjoyed, Simon's father and mother ran out to greet them. Jacqueline and Gwendolyn were introduced. Hugs and kisses were exchanged, and all happily entered the house.

Several days later, Hunt sent a note to Peter and Emily Loring. Simon wrote of his marriage to Jacqueline, that she was a good mother to Gwendolyn, and he looked forward to meeting them with his family. A quick reply received, they travelled to Lancaster.

Arriving at the house, the Lorings looked at Gwendolyn and saw in her a picture of their daughter. Almost overcome, Peter said, "Thank you for coming," and shook Simon's hand. To Jacqueline, he added, "It is a pleasure to meet you, Mrs. Hunt." Lastly, he gently picked up the child and kissed her cheek. "We are your grandparents," he said, bringing her to Emily.

Emily Loring took Gwendolyn and kissed her. Jacqueline had tried to explain the situation to the child. Still befuddled, the little girl kissed her grandmother. The woman's eyes filled with tears. She clutched the child tightly and placed Gwendolyn on her lap.

The adults spoke for a time, and then went to the dining room. Initially, the conversation was formal, but slowly warmed. Gwendolyn's mannerisms further rekindled memories of their daughter. Simon told how he had met Jacqueline, and she spoke of her background in Holland. Over dessert and coffee, both grandparents placed cookies before Gwendolyn. She gobbled them down, alternately smiling at Emily and then Peter.

As the Hunts were leaving, the Lorings hugged and kissed the little girl. Overcome with emotion, Emily grasped Jacqueline and said, "We can see that you have been a good mother to Gwendolyn. Thank you, for caring so much. I hope we see all of you frequently." Peter, close to breaking down, echoed her sentiments and again shook Simon's hand.

Later, the Lorings sat together, thoughts of the past and today's events drifted through their minds. "Peter," Emily said, "Simon's new wife struck me as a good person. She speaks excellent English, is intelligent, and cares for the child. In that sense, we are fortunate. Best of all, little Gwendolyn is here and has taken hold of us. We should move back to Philadelphia."

Her husband kissed her hand. "Back we shall go," he smiled. "We will sell this house, return to Philadelphia, and recover the gold there. I do not think the old house is right for us. It holds too many memories. We should sell it and buy a smaller one."

"Thank you, dear," Emily replied and began to weep.

XXXIV

After their arrival in Philadelphia, Simon was occupied, helping Jacqueline and Gwendolyn adjust to their new surroundings. Then, he sought out Jonathan. Uncertain as to his friend's whereabouts, Hunt went to Doctor Rush. Ushered into his office, he was warmly greeted. "Doctor Wolfe spoke of you often," Rush said. "It's good to find you back in America. He is serving with the army, but comes to Philadelphia often." Then, he added, "He has married a lovely lady and she will soon give birth."

Totally surprised, Simon said, "You give me wonderful news, sir. Where are they living?"

Rush wrote down an address and directions. He handed it to him and said, "Give them my best wishes, doctor."

It was Thursday, but Hunt was anxious to renew his and Jonathan's friendship. On a whim he rode to the address. It was a warm day and he perspired as he approached the house. Smoke rose from the chimney. Descending from his horse, he knocked on the door. A pretty young woman with a swollen belly opened it.

Lifting his hat, he said, "Good afternoon, Mrs. Wolfe. I am Simon Hunt an old friend of your husband. I am most pleased to meet you and also bring good wishes from Doctor Rush."

Amused that he failed to recognize her, Grace answered, "Of

course, Jonathan often spoke of you. I recall he mentioned your red hair but not your beard," she smiled. "He is not here, but is due home this weekend. Please come in."

Hunt followed her into a small parlor and sat as she indicated. "Would you like some coffee or ale," she asked.

He failed to follow the ale part, but thought it might be a custom in her family. "Thank you, but nothing is needed," Simon replied. "I am happy to learn my good friend is married and you are soon to give birth. How did you and Jonathan meet?"

"Oh," she smiled, "We first met at a tavern called The Golden Eagle. I was a waitress there."

Suddenly, recognition came, and Hunt jumped up. His face flushed, he stammered, "You were our waitress and spilled ale on me." Then, recalling how he had patted her buttock, Simon blurted, "My Lord. I behaved like a boor and am terribly embarrassed."

Grace laughed and said, "You were the instrument of my first meeting with Jonathan. All was forgiven long ago. Please sit down. I promise not to spill ale on you ever again."

Calmed by her good nature, Hunt sat as requested, eager to learn the details of the courtship. Discussing the events, Grace made light of her spying and never mentioned Major Winston. As Simon left, she said, "Jonathan will be on furlough for the coming birth. He will certainly visit you when I tell him you are home."

Aunt Evelyn came to stay for the expected birthing, and Wolfe arrived Friday night. By Saturday, the anxious father-to-be kept pacing about. Grace finally said, "Go visit Simon. You will be glad to see each other and it will ease your worries."

Relieved to be away for a time, Jonathan rode to the Hunt home.

A servant directed him to behind the house. Simon and Jacqueline were playing with Gwendolyn on the lawn. Seeing Wolfe, Simon took them in each hand. Coming to him, he grasped his old comrade, saying, "Welcome, Jonathan. Meet my family."

"With great pleasure," Wolfe replied.

Introductions made, Jonathan kissed each of Jacqueline's cheeks. He picked Gwendolyn up and hugged her. For a time they spoke outside, and then entered the house for coffee and cookies. Wolfe could hardly take his eyes off Gwendolyn. He kept thinking of her mother and how she had died. They talked of old times, how Simon met Jacqueline, and the present war.

Hunt accompanied Jonathan when he left, and quietly said, "My decision to learn about birthing was the result of Gwendolyn's death. I cannot stop that type of bleeding, but learned whatever the midwives could teach me. I also devised a way to prevent tears and learned to turn a fetus in utero. I become skilled in doing so. In short, I am an expert in the field."

Wolfe knew that Hunt was not boasting but rather stating facts. "You have become educated in not just medicine. I am very proud of you," he replied, embraced his friend and started home.

Two days later, Grace's experienced contractions and her water broke. Jonathan alerted the midwife who quickly arrived. As he paced the hallway, Mrs. Gable and Aunt Evelyn attended his wife. Two hours later, the aunt came to him. Her face was drawn and pale. She reached out and said, "Jonathan, there is trouble. Mrs. Gable says the baby has turned. It lies across, where before it was properly positioned. She cannot put it right. What shall we do?"

Wolfe felt his heart give a great thump, as it first slowed and then began to rapidly beat. A chill came over him and perspiration formed on his brow. He began to feel unsteady, sat down and mopped his face and forehead. For several minutes, Jonathan was unsure and sunk in thought. Suddenly, he sprang up and started for the door. Over his shoulder, he called out, "I will soon be back."

"Where are you going," Evelyn cried.

"To get help," he shouted, as he pulled open the door and ran for his horse. Mounting it, Wolfe sent the animal rapidly ahead. Thirty minutes later, at full gallop, he arrived at the Hunt home.

Simon was in front of the house, speaking to a neighbor. The man had arrived on horseback. Startled, they saw Jonathan riding toward them. His horse was spent and foaming at the mouth. Leaping off, he shouted, "Simon, we need you now." Grabbing his friend, he seized the bridle of the neighbor's horse, swung aboard and pulled Hunt behind him.

"Sorry," he called to the stunned owner as they galloped away.

The wind whistling about them, Simon yelled, "What is happening?"

"Grace is in labor," he shouted back. "The babe lies across."

"For how long?" Hunt called.

"Several hours," Wolfe cried.

"There is time," Simon shouted. "Slow down or you will kill both the horse and us."

Jonathan slowed the animal to a rapid canter. Arriving at the house, Simon jumped off and entered. He took off his dusty jacket, grabbed an apron from the kitchen, and went to the labor room. "Grace, I am here to help," he said.

Between her contractions, she looked at him, a question forming on her lips. Simon said, "Jonathan brought me. I am skilled in this area." Looking at the midwife, he added, "Permit me to assist you."

She stepped aside and Hunt took her place. He leaned over, put his ear to Grace's abdomen, and listened. Straightening up, Simon said, "The babe's heart beats well, Grace." He put his hands on her belly, felt the fetus, and between contractions began slow manipulations. Periodically, Hunt paused, listened for the heartbeat, and assured his patient that all was well.

Forty minutes later, after moving the unborn infant one way and the other, he listened again. As Grace's next strong contraction came, he pushed down. Holding his hand steady, he listened as before, smiled and said, "The heart is good and the head is in the pelvis. Now the birthing can proceed."

To Evelyn, he said, "Tell Jonathan, all is well and I will need the following instruments."

As Simon listed them, the aunt wondered at their purpose. She left and a few moments later stuck her head back into the room. "Is there time to boil them?" she asked.

"As he chooses," Simon answered.

Over the next hours, he alternated with Mrs. Gable. Each left the room twice to drink coffee and reassure his friend that the birthing was moving along.

Nine hours after arriving, Simon prepared to make the incision he had devised. But the birthing had proceeded slowly and the head delivered without any tearing. Turning it cautiously, he faced the head sideways and said, "Push, Grace."

With the next contraction, she bore down. He brought out one shoulder and then the other. The rest of the newborn readily followed. The midwife cleared its mouth and nostrils, and smacked its buttock. It cried out lustily and she placed the babe on Grace's abdomen, saying, "You have a lovely boy, missus."

In the hall, Wolfe heard the cries and ceased pacing. He sat down, still concerned that his wife and child were safe. Inside the room, Mrs. Gable tied and cut the cord. She handed the baby to Aunt Evelyn who swaddled it and placed the child next to an exhausted Grace.

Hunt delivered the placenta. Discarding the bloody apron, Simon kissed Grace's cheek. "You were very brave and both you and the babe are fine," he said.

She smiled and murmured, "Thank you, Simon."

He left the room and came to Jonathan who anxiously stood as he approached. "Your wife and son are both fine," Hunt smiled.

"Thank God," Jonathan said, and fainted into his friend's arms.

XXXV

During the early months of 1780, Franklin and his colleagues repeatedly met and spoke with one another. In early June, he said, "Only bad news comes to us from America. Charleston is under attack and we await news. If it falls and the Southern Army is lost, our cause becomes desperate. Vergennes has continued to refuse our requests for more funds and, particularly, French troops."

To the surprise of the American delegation, the Minister called Franklin to his office. After proper exchanges, Vergennes said, "In his grace, His Majesty, Louis XVI, has decided to send 6,500 of our finest troops to America. More will follow. They will be under the command of Comte de Rochambeau. Also, the King will grant generous loans to your country and a gift of money directly to General Washington for his army."

Momentarily, Benjamin Franklin was dumbfounded. He could barely conceal his joy and excitement. "America thanks both the King of France and you, Minister. Your country's efforts will not be forgotten by America."

He left and reported the good news to his colleagues. They drank toasts to the King, Vergennes, Rochambeau, and the French Army.

In July, Rochambeau's troops landed in Rhode Island to a joyous welcome and were royally entertained.

September leaves were turning red and gold when Washington travelled north to meet the French Commander. Doctor Cochran, his physician-in-waiting, had become too old to travel and Wolfe was called as a temporary replacement. "We will stop at West Point," the General said. "I wish to speak with General Arnold and inspect the facility."

Benedict Arnold, believing himself mistreated and in debt, had turned traitor. Because of his leg injury, Washington felt he was unavailable for battle and had appointed him Commander of West Point. With Peggy Arnold's assistance, Major Andre, one of her former admirers, was contacted and acted as intermediary with General Clinton. Money and a general's rank would be Arnold's reward.

"George Washington will be dining here September, 18th," he informed the British. The information arrived too late for action. Unmolested, the General continued on. Meeting with the French Commander and Admiral Ternay, he urged, "We should plan to attack New York. That is their key base."

"Our manpower, even combined, is inadequate to the task," Rochambeau replied. "Also, Admiral Ternay does not have the ships to overcome the British fleet. General, your endeavors have earned our respect, but we need time and patience to sort things out. This is our first meeting, we will continue to work together and plan for future events."

"I am bedeviled with disappointment," Washington said to his aides. "I expected more and sooner French action." He journeyed back to West Point. Again, Arnold made arrangements to capture or kill his Commander. This time a British raiding party stood ready.

The day before Washington's arrival, Andre cautiously approached West Point. Stopped by militia he thought loyalist, he said, "I am an English officer."

"Happy to meet you, sir," they replied, and took him into custody. On searching Andre, incriminating papers were found and he was brought before General Arnold. "All is discovered," Arnold realized and, leaving his wife and children behind, fled to a nearby British warship.

General Washington's party arrived the following day. Peggy Arnold was screaming hysterically. "What ails Mrs. Arnold?" he asked. "Major Wolfe, please attend to her. Determine why she appears so distraught. Where is General Arnold? Why is he not here to meet us?"

Jonathan took Arnold's wife in hand, "What is the matter, madam?" he said in a soft voice, trying to calm her. "Is there a problem with one of your children?" She shook her head and ran from the room.

Washington was shown the papers taken from Andre. "Arnold has plotted to turn West Point over to the British and capture or kill me," he thought. Aloud, he cried, "Arnold has betrayed me," and sank into a chair, anguished and dismayed. "He has fled because of these papers, leaving his wife and children to our mercy. He was a bold fighter, and was badly used by Gates. Congressional rules of apportioning major generalships among the colonies foolishly resulted in his not being promoted. In Philadelphia, he abused the power of his office to accumulate wealth and I had to reprimand him. But I decorated him, believed in him, and gave him this important post. We must apprehend and hang him! But who else plots with the English behind our backs?"

Major Andre, a protégé of General Clinton, was never considered a battlefield warrior. He was a poet, playwright, and artist. Caught in civilian clothing with incriminating evidence, there was no option but to try him as a spy. An offer to exchange him for Arnold was refused. His conduct as a prisoner, before and during his one-day trial, and particularly the bravery he exhibited at his hanging, showed him to be a man of great courage.

In England, the newspapers proclaimed Andre a national hero. King and country mourned his death. Arnold was considered by most a turncoat, purchased with money and someone not to be trusted. The military, however, viewed him as Washington's best and most aggressive general.

In America, Clinton was devastated by Andre's fate. He had regarded him as almost a son. His death appeared to sap some of the general's strength and eagerness for war. Multiple attempts to capture Arnold were made, but all failed. He would remain a thorn in the side of Washington and the rebellion throughout the remainder of the war.

During the next several months, almost all fighting was confined to the South. In South Carolina, loyalists came out to aid the British, and rebels organized in opposition. Tory and rebel neighbors fought for dominance of their cause, raiding and burning each other's farms.

Cornwallis established new posts, moving part of his forces into the interior. Guerrilla bands fought to turn the tide of British successes. Marion, a leader of the backcountry rebels, rallied his followers, saying, "The English have to provision their outposts. We will ride out, strike swiftly, and capture the supply trains. Then we will disappear back into the swamps and woods."

In Philadelphia, congressmen wrung their hands, saying, "The loss of Charleston and the Southern Army is appalling. We have nothing with which to oppose Cornwallis."

Others replied, "We need a new, bold commander in the South, and General Gates is the answer."

Once appointed, Gates rode to North Carolina. Arriving at Charlotte, he put together the limited forces available and planned his strategy. He thought, "I must evaluate my options. General Washington has attempted to backwater me. Many doubt I was truly responsible for our victory at Saratoga, but I will show them what Horatio Gates can accomplish. There are only 1,400 Continentals available, but I have 2,600 militiamen to bolster them. General Cornwallis remains in Charleston. Beyond, his forces are spread thinly. This is my chance, and now is the time to move. Camden is the place to strike."

Unbeknown to Gates, the enemy's intelligence gave warning of his army's movement. Cornwallis quickly responded. "Form up," he ordered. "Battle and victory await us." He arrived at Camden well before Gates. The armies made contact on August 15th.

"Cornwallis is here in force," a surprised Gates said. He was perspiring from the heat, and sweat stained his uniform "Fall back and entrench," he ordered, but there was little time and no high ground to defend.

As the sun continued to rise, the redcoats advanced. Bayonets on their Brown Betsy muskets glistened. Fear enveloped Gates' militiamen. They turned and ran. With their flank exposed, the Continentals fell back. A rout ensued. General Gates was swept along by his troops. Dispirited and in despair, he galloped back to Charlotte.

Disaster had again befallen the rebellion and the hero of Saratoga faced ignominy and disgrace.

The victory at Camden further buoyed Cornwallis, but the actions of the rebel guerrillas caused him to think further. Discussing the situation with his officers he said, "Our victories have brought the Tories out to join us. At the same time, the rebels increase. I am convinced that, to secure South Carolina, we must conquer North Carolina. Thereby, we cut off the rebels' northern supplies and their ability to continue fighting."

In September, Cornwallis was confident. "We have crossed into North Carolina and taken Charlotte with ease," he said. "Loyalists continue coming out to join our militias. Major Ferguson is to the west, and his Tories are being rapidly augmented as more volunteers join him."

By month's end, Ferguson had recruited hundreds of loyalists. Still, he knew the backcountry rebels were gathering to oppose him. "We must not be cut off from General Cornwallis," he said. "We will move to join him."

The Major led his men east toward Charlotte. The rebels followed. Brought together under Colonel William Campbell, the backwoodsmen's army now outnumbered the loyalists.

At Kings Mountain, Ferguson announced, "This is a perfect place to stand and fight. Its steep slopes and rocks will impede the rebels. We will turn it into our own Bunker Hill. I have requested reinforcements from General Cornwallis and they will soon arrive. Atop the mountain, we can hold out until they come."

At dawn on October 8th, Campbell shouted, "This is our day for victory. Move up the slopes." Firing as they climbed and using Indian tactics, the attackers moved from rock to rock and tree to tree. Each time they neared the top, the Loyalists charged down, shooting and bayoneting their opponents. But again and again, the backwoodsmen pushed upward, finally sweeping to the top. As they did, Major Ferguson suddenly raced his horse downward. “Kill him,” shouted the rebels. Shots rang out and Ferguson died, falling from his charger as he plunged into their ranks.

The shooting and killing did not stop until well after white flags were raised. In the end, over three hundred Tories were killed or wounded. The dead were left unburied and the wounded left to die. Seven hundred were captured and led away, as their Major was placed in his grave.

Cornwallis groaned when he learned the news. Commiserating with himself, he thought, “I have lost a good portion of my army. I must regroup and consider my next move.”

XXXVI

Following Gates' defeat, Washington wrote to Congress, stating, "General Greene is the only man who can manage the war in the South. You must appoint him to that post."

Nathanael Greene answered the call and travelled to North Carolina. He slowly restored the morale of the surviving Continentals and secured more militia. Greene wrote to his Commander, "I have few men and fewer resources. Fabian tactics will be the rule. Our partisans have been very active behind the enemy's lines and they are good fighters. General Morgan leads them and has joined me. It may not accord with the rules of warfare, but I have divided my army. Morgan goes west with six hundred men. I go east with eight hundred. Cornwallis has no option but to also divide his forces."

"Dividing one's army is dangerous," Washington said. "Nevertheless, I rely on Greene's judgment. He must stop Cornwallis."

The British general took up Greene's challenge. "We will also divide our forces," he said. "Colonel Tarleton, take your men and go after Morgan. I will pursue Greene."

Tarleton quickly began the pursuit. Morgan responded, saying, "We must stay ahead and draw the enemy deep into North Carolina's backcountry. Wearing him out is our purpose. Later, the time to turn about will come." On January 16th Morgan stopped at Cowpens.

"This is a good place to stand and fight," he declared.

In February, Agnes received a letter from her cavalryman brother. Farnsworth was home on a short furlough. He listened as his wife stood by a window in the sunlight of a bright autumn day. She had opened the envelope and read it aloud to him and the children.

"Dear Sister Agnes,

I trust you, Oliver, and the children are well. I expect Eugenia and baby Lawrence to shortly join you from Virginia and know you will keep them safe.

I have been serving with Colonel Charles Washington's cavalry and we were assigned to Morgan's army. Colonel Tarleton's Tory cavalry and his troops have been chasing us. We ran before them, but at Cowpens we turned, fought and, using general Morgan's plan, achieved a great victory.

Fortunately, I suffered no injury, and will write to you again when possible.

My love to all, Stephen"

When she finished, Farnsworth said, "Stephen is a very brave officer. As for details of the fighting, there is a more complete account. On my way here, I stopped to buy a newspaper. Fortunately, it had a report of the battle. Let me read it to you." Agnes and the children remained quiet as he began to read.

"The following is an eyewitness account by a courier who brought the news of Cowpens to Congress:

The battle occurred on January17th. Morgan had placed us in three lines, each separated by many yards.

The British advanced with fifes, drums, and loud huzzahs. We responded with our own Indian battle cries.

First, they encountered our sharpshooters. The riflemen fired, taking many down, and withdrew into the woods. The oft-timid militia made up our second line. This time they did not run, but unleashed three terrible volleys. Again, many of the enemy fell. The militia turned and ran to join the third rank.

The British thought we were in full retreat and charged after them. But the third line was waiting, our sturdy Continentals. Their troops charged with bayonets and our men fired and countercharged. A terrible struggle ensued.

At that moment, General Morgan signaled Colonel Washington to join the fight. The cavalry had been hidden behind a hill. Out we came, our sabers flashing in the sun, slashing at the enemy, cutting them down, and devastating them. The sharpshooters and militia rejoined the fighting. It was short quick work and we exacted severe payment from Colonel Tarleton's forces. Surprisingly, his loyalist cavalry never really entered the battle. Two hundred of them ran away. Their Colonel rode about trying to rally his men. He and Colonel Washington fought at close quarters. They were both unscathed, and Tarleton was the last of the English to flee the field.

We took many prisoners and killed over one hundred. Sadly, some of their troops were slaughtered after surrendering. Our men were screaming, "Buford's revenge!" It was a reprisal for Tarleton's cavalry slaughtering Buford and his men. Those at Cowpens paid their debt.

Our men are proud of the way we fought and are ready to fight again."

Farnsworth finished reading, as the others remained spellbound. "This victory is the first good news we have had from the South," Oliver said. "Stephen and the others have fought well and deserve great credit."

"I and the children are very proud of him," Agnes replied. "I often worry that he may come to harm. Still, he is a good horseman and, in close battle, that always helps. His letter also mentions that Eugenia and the baby are coming here. We have not heard from her and it causes concern."

"If he says they are on their way, they will arrive," said Farnsworth. "Many things can delay people. You are always calm, Agnes. Why are you so unsettled?"

She smiled, kissed Oliver and said, "It's because I am married to a wonderful man who deeply cares for Sally and Randall as well as me. I fear something untoward might happen to him."

"There is nothing to fear. I have told you my orders are to serve here. Jonathan is the one we should worry about. He has been ordered south. It means being in his wagon. It may be behind the lines, but still close to combat."

"I do not see how Grace manages," she said. "Little George is an infant. His father is now close by and sees him often. In the South, he will be far away and where there is fighting."

"Jonathan has always had luck," Oliver replied. "He has managed to survive all situations unharmed."

"Let us pray his luck continues and also ours." She kissed him again, saying, "You will be returning to the army on Monday. I plan to go to Philadelphia this coming weekend, visit the old house and see to selling it."

"Are you certain you wish to?" he asked.

"Yes, too many bad memories. Time to shed the past and look only to the present and our future." Agnes came closer, her eyes bright with joy. "Furthermore, husband, I am three months with child," she smiled.

"My Lord," cried Oliver. "How can I be happier than now," and took his wife in his arms. They sank back, embracing one another.

XXXVII

General Greene's task was to stay out of Cornwallis' grasp while separated from Morgan. He and his weary men retreated north, slogging along muddy roads and crossing each river barely ahead of their pursuer. Cornwallis was determined to overtake his enemy. "Burn the wagon train and supplies," he ordered. "Speed is essential, we must push forward." He drove his men harder and came near to his enemy, but failed to close the gap.

Wolfe and Grace argued about his orders to go south. "You have been in enough danger for two lifetimes, Jonathan," she said. "George is barely six months and his father will again risk life and limb. Have you not done enough? I cannot prevent you from going but, once more, you are breaking my heart." Grace picked up the sleeping baby and tears filled her eyes. "Husband, you are abandoning us for war and whatever foolish duty you feel necessary," she cried. "We are both bereft."

Wolfe reached out to her. "I love you both," he said.

"But not enough to try getting the orders countermanded and stay," Grace answered, and turned away.

"I must go," Wolfe cried. "Many wounded are there and it is where I am most needed. Grace, I swear to stay safe, well behind the fighting."

Her back to him, she whispered, "That is what Oliver Farnsworth believed. He would be behind the battle and safe."

Jonathan left the house and returned to Morristown. From there, he started south. Jameson and Miller were no longer with him. They had become too old for the hardship of working in the field. Two new aides accompanied him, Francis Ditmar and Clyde Champion. Both had been trained by him and eagerly awaited their assignment.

Moving north toward Virginia, Morgan successfully rejoined Greene. "I must leave the fighting," Morgan said. "I am no longer young and not physically able to continue leading. It is time for me to go home."

"General, you have performed magnificently," Greene answered. "Cowpens has sapped their strength and our armies have been brought together. Still, we are too weak to challenge Cornwallis. The wise move is to stay ahead of him and cross the Dan River into Virginia."

As the second week of February 1781 ended, the Americans crossed the Dan. Once again they had eluded the enemy.

"I am totally frustrated," Cornwallis groaned. To his lieutenants, he said. "Our men are exhausted. We will move to Hillsborough. There, we can reinvigorate the troops, and recruit more Tories."

Wolfe met the army as it was marching north. On arriving, a Colonel Wilkinson welcomed him. "We are desperately in need of a doctor," he said. "Do you and your aides have battlefield experience?"

"I do," Jonathan replied. "My aides do not, but they are well trained."

"Excellent," Wilkinson said. "We have several men who need your immediate attention."

Wolfe examined and treated eleven wounded. One man had been shot near the ankle but continued to march with his unit. "Corporal Bourne, that is an ugly wound," Jonathan said. "The ball missed the bone and exited, but the site is inflamed. Red streaks are moving up your leg. You also have fever," he added, feeling the corporal's brow.

The soldier looked at Wolfe with pleading eyes. "Can you save my leg, sir? I would rather die than lose it. I can't farm otherwise."

"It might be best to lose the leg," the doctor answered. "You might still be able to farm with a peg leg."

"Not walking through a muddy field," sobbed the corporal. "Please, I will risk everything if you try something else."

"I will try for a very short time," Wolfe said, finally agreeing. "But, if the leg worsens, you must agree to amputation."

"I will," doctor. "I will rely on you and God."

Wolfe had his instruments opened and the aides boiled them. Several men watched and wondered among themselves at the reason. "It is some sort of Indian method," said one. The others nodded in agreement.

The aides plied the corporal with liquor. As he became drowsy, men took hold of his arms and legs. Wolfe cut into the wound and debrided the shaggy tract. Bourne awoke and screamed, biting down hard on a cloth soaked with whiskey.

"It is almost over, corporal," Jonathan said. "Just a few moments more." Turning to Ditmar, he spoke calmly, "Packing and the jug of vinegar."

"Yes, sir," his aide answered. Those watching continued to wonder.

Wolfe wet the packing with vinegar and placed it into the tract. Then he bandaged the leg. "Apply pressure," he said to Champion.

The aide took his place and the doctor spoke to Bourne. "I have done my best to clean the wound. Careful observation is needed. Those red streaks worry me. If they continue to advance, we must amputate."

The corporal was sweating and exhausted. The alcohol again made him groggy. He managed to say, "Thank you, doctor," and fell asleep.

Over the following two days, the army moved north. Bourne had been placed in the medical wagon and every twelve hours the packing was changed. The red streaks did not subside but advanced slightly further. The corporal was more feverish and Wolfe realized they had failed.

"There is no other choice but to amputate," he said to Bourne. "It is hard to accept this, nevertheless you must. We can still save the knee, later amputation will be above the joint and you will never walk."

"I have prayed and God has decided my fate," Bourne said. "I accept his decision. You may proceed, doctor. I still thank you for trying."

That afternoon the leg was amputated. "The wound is best left open," Jonathan told his aides. "Those red streaks still worry me. We will wait a day for the bleeding to quiet. Then we will resume the vinegar therapy."

They began the vinegar treatment and observed the open wound. It remained clean and the fever cleared. "Now the stump will slowly close," Wolfe said to the corporal. "You will be able to walk, albeit with a peg leg. I truly believe that a vigorous man such as you will farm again."

"I will certainly try, doctor," Bourne replied, taking Wolfe's hand in a firm grip. "My family may be sad to see me so injured, but will rejoice that I am alive and again home."

In Virginia, Greene rested his men and then reentered North Carolina. "My little army is growing," he whispered. "Virginia Continentals, militia, and backcountry men are joining us. The time approaches for a real battle."

At Guilford Courthouse the American commander said, "Cornwallis continues to come after us. He is drawing close. It is time to fight, and this is the place."

Cornwallis spoke to his officers. "The long chase is over," he proclaimed. "We must destroy Greene's army here. It will clear the Carolinas of all effective opposition."

"General," said Colonel Webster, "He possesses more troops than we. Our men are tired. We must rest them before the battle."

"No rest," Cornwallis replied. "On to Guilford Courthouse. They have mostly worthless militia and not many hardened Continentals. We have our English and Hessian regulars. One of them is worth ten of their militia."

"We will deploy our men in a similar fashion to Morgan at Cowpens," Greene said. "But, I believe we should place the lines further apart. It gives more time to get off another shot before the enemy closes. We will rest tonight, have breakfast and await our foe."

"Will we keep men in reserve, General?" asked an aide.

"No reserves," Greene replied. "All our troops are to be committed at the outset. We have no cavalry available and must stand fast."

On the morning of March 15th, the Ides of March, a high

noon sun was shining as the British and Hessians came forward. The American sharpshooters fired and enemy fell, but their lines came ahead. As they continued to advance, several militiamen fired early and ran, but most stood firm. At musket range, a terrible volley erupted from their line and tore at the enemy ranks. The red and green clothed units stopped, discharged their weapons at the Americans, and then moved ahead. Once more the militia fired. Again, their fire was deadly.

Despite heavy losses, the enemy lines were reformed. They surged forward, but the militia had disappeared into the woods. Some quit the fight, but most stayed on.

The British troops believed victory was theirs. Suddenly, they realized a line of Continentals stood ready to confront them. The Americans fired and moved into an area of scattered brush and trees. The fight became a tangle of groups and individuals, struggling, grappling, bayoneting and shooting at one another. The rebels started to move back on their right but then counter-attacked. On their left, they fell back and held. In the middle, the fight surged back and forth.

Cornwallis rode about the field, impervious to the danger. His horse was shot from beneath him, and he mounted another. "Our center is giving way," he said. "We must disrupt the fight and reform." With steel in his voice, he ordered, "Load the six pounder with grapeshot and fire."

"Those are our men out there, General," an aide gasped.

"Dammit, try to aim above them. There is no alternative," shouted Cornwallis. "Fire! I said fire!"

The grapeshot flew into the center of the battle, killing and maiming friend and foe alike. Despite their losses, it gave the British time to regroup and prevent a rout. Once again they advanced, this time cautiously, but the Americans were gone.

"We have done what I wished," Greene said. "They may have the field, but we have punished them immeasurably. They paid heavily for the territory and we avoided an unexpected blow. The new Southern Army has been preserved. It is stronger and prepared to fight again."

"Victory has been achieved and the field is ours," the British General boasted. Inwardly, he said, "It has been a Pyrrhic triumph. Our losses far exceed the American's. Another costly battle and we will no longer be a viable army."

In the aftermath of the fighting, Wolfe and his aides were faced with the task of caring for the wounded. He retrieved lead balls and fragments of grapeshot from arms and legs. Stabs and gashes from bayonet and sword wounds were also attended. Those to the chest and abdomen were often beyond help.

Many amputations were also required. In each case they were left open. Men screamed and cried as Jonathan moved to quickly do the work. After the limb was removed, he or an aide seared the exposed muscle with a white-hot iron. The agony was unbearable and most of the amputees fainted. "Liquor is insufficient," Wolfe said to his helpers. "There must be a better way."

By the end of the third day, Jonathan and the aides were exhausted. They slept twelve hours that night. It was well into late morning when they awoke. General Greene also succumbed to stress and fatigue. It took weeks for him to recover. In both the North and South, colonial newspapers applauded him. Hope arose that the Americans had truly turned the tide of battle.

The British General withdrew his battered forces to the North Carolina coast. To his aides, Cornwallis said, "We must rest, recuperate, and determine our future action. Possibly, we can still recruit Tories and induce the Negro slaves to join our ranks."

XXXVIII

After Guilford Courthouse, additional physicians joined Greene's army. Wolfe and his aides headed north. Spring came and the trees were again showing leaves. As April ended, flowers were starting to bloom, and their wagon reached Philadelphia.

Jonathan was given leave and arrived home in the midst of a heavy rain. Grace opened the door, readying a tart remark. But, seeing him soaking wet, she said, "Welcome home, husband. You look drenched and tired. Take off your clothes and get dry."

Wet as he was, Wolfe drew Grace to him and kissed her. She did not resist and clutched him closely. He held her for several minutes, then let go, stripped, dried himself, and went to find dry clothing. Dressed, Wolfe returned to the kitchen where coffee and Grace awaited him.

"I missed you and the baby," he said, taking her in his arms.

Grace pushed him away. "You have to do more than say I missed you and the baby, Jonathan. I know there were orders, but you could have appealed them. You wanted to go. I was here, desperate for news about you and worried beyond measure. When I heard about the battle at Guilford Courthouse, I feared you were injured or, even worse, dead. Finally a letter came and answered my prayers, you were safe and coming home. Now, I do not know whether to hit or kiss you," she sobbed, and broke into tears.

Wolfe again took her in his arms, stroked her hair and whispered words of comfort. She stayed there but periodically stepped back and struck him softly in the chest. Afterward, still crying, Grace kissed him. "You must be hungry," she smiled. "I will make dinner."

Jonathan sat and watched as Grace worked. Baby George awoke and she picked him up and nursed him. George finished suckling and Wolfe took him, held him close, and rocked him to sleep. Twice, the infant briefly opened his eyes and his father kissed him. At dinner, he told of the battle and his adventures, and asked about the family and friends.

"I will begin with your family," she said. "I had a letter from Rose and all is well with her, Ethan, and baby Samuel. They have returned to their farm. She says your father and aunt are fine and he is busy at the forge."

"As for the Farnsworths, Oliver is working at the hospital. Agnes is very swollen with child and they are both extremely happy. She sold the house in the city and they are at the farmhouse. It has become quite crowded. Eugenia, Agnes' sister-in-law, has arrived from Virginia with her child. Captain Wainwright is well and with the cavalry in Carolina."

"He is a good man," Wolfe interrupted, "I hope he remains well."

"As do I," she answered and gave a salute, saying, "Permit me to continue with my report Major Wolfe. The Hunts have found a house and Simon has started a practice. He is doing medicine, but several midwives have called upon him when they encountered difficulty. His ability in birthing is becoming known."

"That is good news, Sergeant Grace," Jonathan smiled. "Tell me about Jacqueline and Gwendolyn. How are they accommodating to America?"

"Gwendolyn is doing very well. Both sets of grandparents adore her. In particular, she has been a Godsend to the Lorings. The little girl is finally bringing them joy."

"And Jacqueline?" Wolfe asked.

"I am not sure about her, Jonathan. After England declared war on Holland, she became very worried about her family. Jacqueline misses them and, despite Simon's attention, she appears unhappy. Fortunately she brought the microscopes with her. Several doctors have shown interest, and she is grinding lenses and building what she calls the Huygens type. Actually, Jacqueline showed me how they work and I saw tiny creatures swimming about. It was quite wonderful. You should ask for a demonstration."

"I will, dear wife. But, right now, I am thinking of bedding with you." He picked up the baby, took Grace's hand, and they climbed the stairs to their bedroom. Cuddling together and making love, they fell asleep.

The next morning, Grace was eating while nursing George. She finished and handed the baby to Jonathan, saying, "Play with him, husband, so that he may get to know his father."

"With pleasure," Jonathan replied, took the infant and kissed him. Then, sitting in a rocking chair, he rocked back and forth. Suddenly the baby began to spit up. "Good Lord," he said, and hastily handed George back to Grace.

"I forgot to burp him," she laughed, and held the child to her shoulder while tapping his back. A great burp shortly erupted and Grace laughed again. "Here," she said to Jonathan, "Wipe yourself with this cloth and I will give George back to you."

Wolfe cleaned himself, tentatively took the baby and began to walk about. As he began to gently bounce him, the infant looked at him and started to giggle. Jonathan felt the joy of fatherhood and, holding George tightly, kissed him.

"It's good to have you home, husband, and see you frolic with your son," Grace said. She came to him and, with George between them, they kissed.

"And wonderful to be here with you and our little boy," Wolfe said. "From now on, I will stay as close as possible."

"Yes," she replied, frowning. "Until the next call to duty takes you away."

Again, he took her and the infant in his arms, saying, "Dear wife, whatever happens, I will always return to you and George."

"I shall have to live with that," she answered and kissed his lips.

Sunday afternoon, they travelled to the McKenzie home for dinner. The family crowded around the table. Martha had given birth to a baby girl named Amy, now fifteen months old. Elias asked God's blessing, cut the bread and carved several chickens. He gazed about and said, "It is my great joy to see our family united once more. Fortunately all of us are safe and in good health." Pointing at Joshua, his grand uncle said, "You are the oldest of the new generation. We count on you to be kind and generous to your sister, Amy, and cousin, George."

Joshua puffed up his chest and said, "I will, sir."

All applauded, raised their glasses in a toast and began to eat Aunt Evelyn's cooking.

Wolfe turned to Harold and asked, "How is your leg?"

"Thanks to your surgery, there is no drainage, but it still aches and causes me to limp," he answered. "I am working in the tavern, helping Elias."

"And he is an excellent helper," Elias chimed in.

"And a good husband," Martha added. Blushing, she said, "I am again with child."

They all congratulated Martha and Howard except Joshua. "Another baby," he moaned. "I will be surrounded."

Harold took Joshua and hugged him. He said, "You are the big brother. Amy and the new baby will love you. Your mother and I will never stop loving you. Son, the more there are people who love you, the happier you shall be."

The boy nodded, brushed away a tear, and took his seat.

They finished the meal with cookies and coffee, sat and chatted. Later, the Wolfe family departed for home.

"I had a very pleasant time with your family," Jonathan said.

"Yes," Grace answered, "But they are yours too, and they truly care about you. The more we see them, the closer they feel to you."

"I know," he answered and said, "Grace, I would like to visit the family in the Mohawk. I miss them."

"Certainly, Jonathan, they must miss you also. I too would like to go."

They were in a small coach, driving into the setting sun. Jonathan said, "We should visit Simon, Jacqueline and Gwendolyn. You voiced concern about her and I have not seen them in some time. I would like to look through the microscope at this new little world."

"Yes," Grace answered, "I will send a note to ask a satisfactory day."

The following weekend, they travelled to the small house the Hunts now owned. Gwendolyn ran to greet them and Jacqueline seemed radiant. "I am with child," she said, patting a slightly enlarged abdomen. "Also a young couple took a house close by. He is from America and she arrived here from Holland five years ago. We happened to meet and often speak together in Dutch. My homesickness is much relieved, although I am still concerned about the war here, and between England and Holland. The Dutch navy is no match for Britain's."

"The Devil take the war," Simon said, "Happily, Jacqueline and Gwendolyn are fine and our family is due to expand. As for me, I am content. The practice has started and it is growing. I am proud to say, my wife is also a breadwinner. She has built and sold two microscopes."

"Excellent," Wolfe said, "May I have a demonstration?"

"Simon can show you," Jacqueline said. "He has become skilled in its use. I would like to spend time with Grace and the children."

Hunt nodded, took him to a microscope, and demonstrated its use and the tiny creatures now visible.

"Amazing," Jonathan said. Fascinated, he kept staring down. Afterward, they rejoined the others. During lunch they spoke of old times and new events. Later, their friendship renewed, the Wolfe family left for home.

After Guilford Courthouse, Cornwallis encamped in Wilmington, a town near the coast of North Carolina. Sitting at his desk, he pondered his next move. "Virginia is the answer to subduing the southern colonies," he thought. "My orders were to stay in the Carolinas and secure them, but that can only be done by taking Virginia. General Clinton does not see the big picture. He only thinks of New York. Once in Virginia, the armies of Phillips and Arnold can join me. I will urge Clinton to bring an army south. The Americans and French will respond, be drawn into open conflict, and we can crush them."

Clinton was horrified on learning his subordinate's plans. "New York will be the final battlefield," he said. "His move into Virginia will cost us the Carolinas and Georgia." Still, he made no effort to countermand Cornwallis's decision.

Von Steuben, now in Virginia, drew up his own plan. "Call out the state's militia, Governor Jefferson," he said through a translator. "We can send most of the men to Greene and the others to Lafayette. With additional troops, Greene will be strong enough to defeat Cornwallis and Lafayette can prevent Phillips from aiding him."

Several of the governor's aides supported the idea, as did many in the House of Burgesses. Thomas Jefferson and his Council rejected it.

"Governor," von Steuben again urged, "You helped write the Declaration of Independence that cited the reasons for separating from England. Think large! Our country hangs in the balance!"

"The militia is needed to protect our port cities and those along the waterways," Jefferson said. "They can not be left undefended."

The Governor was wrong. The British navy controlled the coastal rivers and sailed them with impunity. Their frigates marauded up and down the waters, devastating shipping and towns, while the militia proved totally inadequate to prevent it.

As Cornwallis continued to march north, General Greene turned south. "This is our chance to reclaim the Carolinas and Georgia," he told his aides. They readily concurred and, as they marched south, more backcountry men joined them.

"The dominos are falling," Greene exulted. "One by one, British outposts will be overcome. Finally, they will be confined to Charleston and Savannah."

In Virginia, Cornwallis joined with General Phillips's troops. "My old friend has died," he said, on learning of the general's death. "Arnold has left and is raiding Connecticut, but his men are here. I possess a substantial army. Still, General Clinton has not responded to my messages asking him to join me."

Clinton's orders were confused and varying. One of them, to Phillips, had indicated he should establish a naval base on the coast. "That makes the most sense," said Cornwallis. "Yorktown appears the best site. From there we can be reinforced and resupplied while awaiting Clinton's further orders."

XXXIX

Half of 1781 had passed when Rochambeau, acceding to Washington's request, brought his forces south from Rhode Island. They joined with the Continentals in Connecticut and the two generals conferred. Washington still believed New York should be attacked and they moved closer to Manhattan. Careful probing, however, failed to reveal any weakness in its defenses.

A report from Lafayette reached them. "Cornwallis is moving toward the Virginia coast," it read.

Rochambeau added, "Letters from the Admiral reveal he is sailing toward Chesapeake Bay with a large fleet. It appears that Virginia is the place to gain victory."

Washington rethought his plans, "General Rochambeau," he said, "We have found the defenses here well placed. This new information causes me to agree that our armies should best go to Virginia. With de Grasse controlling the water as we attack by land, Cornwallis will be cornered and forced to surrender."

"General, I am in complete agreement," replied the Frenchman.

"The question remains as to how Clinton will react when he realizes our intention," said Washington. "He may come after us from New York, and direct Cornwallis to overcome Lafayette's small force and move north. If so, we will be caught between two British armies."

"He may also evacuate the Virginia army by sea, before de Grasse has sealed the Chesapeake," Rochambeau replied. "There are many possibilities but we must act on the moment. Our moment is now, General!"

The French and Americans crossed the Hudson into New Jersey. Secrecy was the word and only senior officers knew the plan. They marched south, paralleling the river, and came opposite the city. Observing their movement, Clinton said, "I still believe New York is the target. They may wish to establish bases, bombard us from the west side of the Hudson, or cross from Staten Island. It is best to sit and watch."

The two armies did not stop. They crossed New Jersey, entered Pennsylvania and headed for Philadelphia. Clinton's spies tracked their movements but he failed to respond. "They may be heading for Virginia," he said, "But New York is the prize and is not to be left unguarded."

Crowds turned out to cheer and welcome the allied forces, as they passed through towns and villages along the route. Reaching Philadelphia, the generals called a halt to rest the men.

Doctor Peabody met with Washington and provided the latest intelligence on the enemy's position. "Cornwallis is at Yorktown," he said. "General Lafayette has trailed after him, but has avoided any major confrontation. We estimate there are now about 7,000 men in the British camp. The way there lies open to our armies."

"Very good, Peabody," replied the General. "You always provide reliable information. I am most grateful to you."

"Thank you, sir," the Professor said. "Also, I wonder if you might wish to meet one of our best spies, a lady."

Intrigued, Washington responded, "A female spy? I would like that very much. This afternoon at three o'clock would be a good time."

They shook hands and the headmaster left to seek out Grace. Arriving at the house, he found Jonathan also there, making a visit before leaving with the troops.

"Doctor Peabody," Grace exclaimed when she opened the door. "It is so nice to have you visit us. Please come inside."

Entering and seeing Wolfe, he said, "Hello Jonathan, I am delighted to find you at home." Then added, "Where is the little boy?"

"He is sleeping in the cradle," Grace said and pointed to it.

Peabody went there and looked at the infant. He bent, kissed the child, smiled, and said, "Soon he will be too large for his cradle." Looking at Grace, Peabody added, "I am delighted to see the Wolfe family together. But I came to speak to you about paying General Washington a visit today. He is eager to meet my best spy."

"How exciting," she replied. "But it would mean leaving Jonathan and the baby. He leaves shortly for the fighting."

"Bring everyone," replied the Professor. "I believe the General already knows your husband and would be eager to see little George. Do not refuse, our Commander wishes your compliance."

"We should go, Grace. You deserve the honor," Wolfe added.

She thought for a moment and responded, "Very well. I will go, but first we must eat, feed the baby, and permit me to change into suitable clothing. Doctor Peabody, you must have some food with us."

"With pleasure," he answered.

After feeding the infant and a hurried meal, Grace put on her best clothes. Peabody looked at his pocket watch. "It's time to leave," he said.

Arriving at the Commander's headquarters, they were told he was in conference. It shortly ended and an aide brought them to him. The General rose from behind his desk and came to greet his guests.

Wolfe saluted and it was returned. Peabody stood at attention and said, "General Washington, I would like to present Mrs. Grace Wolfe. As a spy she was Miss Lockhart, my finest intelligence agent. She succeeded in penetrating General Howe's headquarters in New York and provided information about the attack against Philadelphia. In addition, she stayed with the British and gave us intelligence regarding Howe's decision not to strike Valley Forge. When he withdrew from here, this lady obtained his route back to New York."

The General replied in a measured voice, "Mrs. Wolfe, I am honored to meet you. Our country owes a great debt to those, such as you, who have risked all to give us valuable information." He took her hand and kissed it. Then, looking at Jonathan, said, "With your permission, Major Wolfe." Saying so, he held Grace's shoulders and kissed both her cheeks.

Blushing, she curtsied and replied, "It is my honor to meet you, sir."

Washington, towering above them, continued. "If it were possible, I would give you a medal, madam. However, at present we have none for brave citizens. Nevertheless, you are one of our true heroines. While we cannot now grant you proper recognition, I would like to offer a small token of personal appreciation."

He turned to his desk on which lay a pamphlet. Taking a quill, he wrote quickly. Handing Grace the publication, he said, "This is my own copy of Tom Paine's inspiring work, *Common Sense*. I refer to it frequently and indeed know it by heart. With my compliments, it now belongs to you."

Grace took it and read what he had written. It said,

"To Grace Lockhart Wolfe, a brave and gallant lady.

With great respect,

George Washington."

"Thank you, General," she smiled. "I shall treasure it and, when he is older, read it to my son."

The Commander also smiled and said, "I have not had the pleasure of meeting your son. Please tell me his name."

"His name is George, sir," she answered.

Laughing, the General came to the baby being held by Wolfe. He took the infant, kissed it, and said, "George, I wish you a happy and healthy life. You have wonderful parents and I expect great things from you." He shook hands with Jonathan and returned the child to him. After spending several more minutes with them, he bid farewell and they left.

"What a glorious day," Grace said.

"You deserve every accolade he gave you," Jonathan responded, hugging and kissing her. "Your radiance lit the room and charmed General Washington."

"I wholeheartedly agree," Peabody added. "But he was even more charmed after learning the baby's name. As a general, he is sometimes a bit formal. But, when he heard "George," his eyes widened and he melted."

They continued speaking for a time, then parted and drove to their homes.

That evening Wolfe said, "The army goes south in four days, Grace."

“Yes, I did not ask,” she said, ”But was certain you would be leaving soon. What will be happening before then,” she asked.

“Tomorrow, the Americans parade through the city, the next day the French. Then we will rest for a day and leave. You can bring George tomorrow and watch our army. I will be in the rear with my aides. I plan to stay well back and let the dust settle before moving forward.”

The following day was September 2nd and, while they slept, Jonathan kissed his wife and child. He was gone when Grace awoke. She washed herself and George, and dressed them both. Going to the kitchen, she started a fire, placed a pot of water and oats on the swing bar and moved it over the fireplace flames. After it cooked for several minutes, she took a potholder, swung the bar back and removed the pot.

“It’s time for breakfast, George,” she said, nursed him, gave him several spoons of porridge and then ate the remainder. Afterward, she played with the baby for a short time and doused the fire. “It’s going to be a lovely day, and we will watch a parade,” Grace said, kissing him. “We should go quickly. I can clean the kitchen later, while you sleep.”

They arrived after the parade had begun. Crowds lined the roadside and cheered. Flags fluttered in a soft breeze as the Continentals and militia passed. Grace found a place and lowered the top of her coach to feel the sun. She picked up the baby, saying, “Look, George, the army is marching and daddy will soon come by.”

A handsome, mustached French captain, resplendent in his uniform and mounted on a white charger had come alongside. Seeing her holding the infant, he smiled, raised his hat, and in quite good

English said, "Good morning, madam. It is a glorious day for a parade. Today, your countrymen march. Tomorrow it will be our turn. May I ask the name of your little boy?"

"His name is George," she said and added, "We are here to watch the troops and my husband. He is a doctor with the army."

"I hope we do not provide him with much work," he smiled. Then with a wistful look, the officer said, "I have a little girl and boy at home with my wife. I confess to greatly missing them. Still, my duty lies here."

"Hopefully, the war will end soon and you can return to France and your family," Grace said. "In the meantime, we are most grateful for your presence."

"Thank you, madam," he answered. "It is kind of you to say that." Staying by her, the captain watched and said, "Your men march proudly but many are young and others are old. Many are barefoot and I hope the weather stays warm as we go south."

"Do you know where the armies are going?" she asked.

"It is no longer a secret," he answered. "We go to Yorktown to fight General Cornwallis. Together with our navy, we will trap him there. Of course, providing he is still present when we arrive."

"That would be wonderful," Grace replied.

The French captain turned to watch the marchers. Their flags held high, Rhode Island and Massachusetts units came by. "I see many Negroes are here," he remarked. "They look strong and march well. It appears nearly one out of five of those men are black."

"Yes, I noticed that," she replied. "They are free Negroes from the North."

As the parade drew to a close, the medical teams began to pass.

Grace raised the baby and waved his hand. "Jonathan Wolfe," she called out.

Mounted with his aides on their wagon and barely hearing her above the noise of the crowd, he waved and blew a kiss. The aides with him also waved as the wagon moved on.

"So," the officer smiled, "Your husband's name is Jonathan Wolfe and from his shoulders the bronze says he is a major. I am Captain Paul Le Clair with the cavalry, Madam. May I ask your given name?"

"My name is Grace," she said.

"It has been my pleasure to be with you and George today, Madam Grace Wolfe. Please come and watch us parade tomorrow." He lifted his hat again, replaced it, and saluted her. Then, the captain backed his horse away and departed.

"Good luck, Captain Le Clair," she called after him.

Grace returned with George the next day and watched with him, as the French army, marching behind their band, came forward. Jacqueline and Simon had come with Gwendolyn and placed their coach adjacent to hers.

They greeted one another and Grace asked, "How is Agnes, Simon? We heard the baby was due and you would be overseeing the birthing."

"It came last evening," he grinned. "Actually, the midwife carried out the entire procedure except for my cutting and sewing a bit. The older children had not been large and she had no difficulty when they birthed. This was a large baby girl and the tissues had stretched thin. I did what was necessary and she and the child are fine. The infant has been named Lorraine, as was Agnes' mother. Oliver was there and is delighted. He was given a short leave and will catch up with the army later. Once again, he will be in a wagon nearby Jonathan."

"You bring good news. But I believed Oliver would stay here at the hospital."

"A hospital is to be established closer to the fighting. Farnsworth insists he is now able to move well and has persuaded Agnes to permit him to go nearer the battle. I trust God will keep him and Jonathan safe." Then he said with sadness, "Having given my word, I must remain here like a coward, while they face danger."

"You are also needed in Philadelphia, Simon," Jacqueline said. She placed a hand softly on his arm, saying, "Women who are bringing forth the future generation require your assistance. They and the children are surely as valuable as the men doing the fighting. At the same time, you are also serving the husbands. We know you are not a coward!"

"Jacqueline speaks the truth, Simon," Grace added. "This is where you belong. But now let us watch and enjoy the parade."

She placed George on her shoulder. Jacqueline stood Gwendolyn on the coach's seat. "You can see better this way," she said to her.

"Daddy, put me on your shoulders," the little girl said.

Hunt laughed and did as she asked, saying, "Up you go."

The French infantry marched by in long columns. They were fully equipped and wore elegant white uniforms. Then came artillery units with horses pulling cannon and caissons filled with ammunition. At the rear came the cavalry astride powerful horses. They were boldly clad with fine tunics, trousers of yellow, and long black boots extending well into their thighs.

"Hurrah for the French cavalry," the crowd cried.

Captain Le Clair rode toward them, leading a company he commanded. "Hurrah for Captain Le Clair and the French," Grace shouted. Jacqueline and Simon took up her call. "Hurrah for brave Captain Le Clair and the French," they yelled.

Hearing their shouts and casting his eyes in their direction, he called something to his men. Facing forward, he came abreast of them, turned, saluted, and again faced forward. As they rode by, each man turned and saluted. The crowd cheered wildly and Jacqueline excitedly shouted, "Vive la France." The entire crowd began shouting, "Vive la France," as the French cavalry rode past.

The following day, Grace visited Agnes early and came to the army hospital in the afternoon. Wolfe was packing supplies, but stopped to spend time with her and George.

"How was your visit with Agnes and the new baby, and how are Oliver and the children?" he asked.

"Everyone is fine," Grace replied. "Agnes is radiant and recovering nicely. Oliver is beyond joyful. As for Randall and Sally, they are eager to hold their new sister and play with her. Simon had told me the babe will be named Lorraine and they confirmed it."

"That is a lovely name. I am overjoyed for Agnes and Oliver that a child has arrived. It adds extra happiness to their lives. Also, Randall and Sally will surely love her and treat her well. However, I heard Oliver is to be with us. I am concerned. He has not been in the field for over two years and is just beginning to walk normally. And what about Agnes and the new child?"

"Agnes said he could go. Like you, Oliver promised to stay well behind the fighting. Jonathan, he wants to be with you and the army. It is a matter of pride and comradeship. Do not try to discourage him. He will take it as an insult."

Wolfe nodded in acknowledgement. "I understand," he said.

"Now, I would like to hold our son and walk with you for a time."

They strolled in the sunshine and warmth of early September and came near a group of camp followers. Some women were busily hanging washed clothing on makeshift lines. Others were mending clothes or scrubbing pots and sauce pans.

Grace waved at them and they responded in turn.

"You know, Jonathan," she said, "If I were not still nursing George, I would leave him with Martha and Aunt Evelyn and join those women. That way I would always be near you."

"I am not sure it would be seemly for an officer's wife to be among them," Wolfe replied. "The General does not look favorably on camp followers."

"Dear husband," his wife responded, "I was not aware that, since you became an officer, my conduct would be so restricted. Please do not become one of those stuffy men I sometimes meet. As for General Washington, he should think better of these women. They appear to be rendering real service and I understand the army does not feed or provision them."

Jonathan smiled. "Tell me, what you would do if you were with them?" he asked.

"Why the first thing would be to demand food for them."

"I do not think the Commander would take kindly to any sort of demands. You would certainly be drummed out and sent home."

"And you would be terribly embarrassed. However, I very much doubt he would have me punished or sent home. When you honor one of your best spies and kiss her on both cheeks, it is rather difficult to ship her back home a week or month later."

Wolfe laughed and said, "I recall mumbling at our first meeting, you are always correct. I bow to you once again and say without equivocation, Grace, you are always right." Still holding the baby, he kissed her.

"That is much better, sir. But have no fear. I am needed at home. Still, I will think about what we discussed. Perhaps not now, but some day women will demand better treatment. It is certainly due them."

"I doubt we will be here if it happens," he grinned.

"Jonathan, you are incorrigible," Grace fumed. But then said, "Despite it, I do love you. Now, I must go home and nurse George. You should get ready to leave tomorrow."

The sun rose the next morning to find the armies already on the march. The American columns led and the French followed. News was received that de Grasse was in the Chesapeake. They hurried south, but delays occurred at the major water crossing. Days went by before the armies came together at Jamestown.

"I wonder if Cornwallis will be there when we arrive at Yorktown," Oliver said. "He may have overcome the little French general and started north."

"Possibly," Wolfe replied, "If he has, Generals Washington and Rochambeau will get the news and we will engage him. Still, it is best to contain him near the Chesapeake. Today is September 26th. We must move quickly. Word is that Admiral de Grasse will only stay through October. He wants to leave before hurricane season arrives."

"Then we surely must come to Yorktown in haste," Oliver answered.

XXXX

Cornwallis became aware of de Grasse's arrival on August 31st. "How many ships do the French have?" he asked.

"The sloop we sent out believes over twenty-five vessels, sir," his aide answered.

"My God," responded the general, "They have brought a huge fleet. He can effectively blockade and prevent reinforcements and supplies reaching us."

A council of war was called. "General," many urged. "We can defeat Lafayette, then strike north toward New York. General Clinton will send an army and meet us. We do not know what other enemy forces will come and add to our predicament."

"I will consider all options," Cornwallis declared. "This meeting is concluded."

By himself, he thought, "To attack and break through the enemy may be feasible. It means leaving the sick, the wounded and the Tories behind. We have enough provisions to hold out for months. Hurricanes may scatter their ships. An English fleet with reinforcements may arrive, defeat de Grasse, and evacuate us." Finally, he muttered, "Clinton ordered us to Yorktown. The burden is on him to extricate me."

Washington, Rochambeau and de Grasse met to plan strategy.

"A frontal attack will be costly," said the French general. "A siege is the better option."

"I agree but have no experience there," Washington replied. "You must conduct it."

"It will be my pleasure," answered the Frenchman.

The armies gathered outside the English stronghold, and French and American hospitals were constructed.

Wolfe and Farnsworth were helping set up their area and Oliver said, "Apparently, it will be a siege. If so, our casualties will not be too great."

"I agree," Jonathan relied, "But the Negroes have been digging entrenchments for the English. They have also built two formidable redoubts on our end of the battlefield and one on the French side. Direct assault may be required."

"And how did you come by all this military knowledge, sir?"

Jonathan confessed, "Captain Le Clair, one of their cavalry officers, paid a visit here yesterday. He introduced himself and mentioned meeting Grace and George at the parade. He explained the armies' plans and is quite certain of success."

"I hope he is right," Oliver said.

In October, the siege began with the digging of a parallel trench in the American sector. It would bring artillery close to Yorktown. Cannon were placed and their fiery balls fell on the town day and night. Those within it crouched in terror as buildings crumbled.

Two English sergeants, Ronald Cameron and Alfred Lehigh, crouched together in the cellar of a battered house. With them were twelve other regulars. As canon balls struck, the ceiling collapsed. Screams erupted as three men were buried under rubble.

Lehigh's left foot was crushed. Battle hardened, he still cried out in pain. Cameron dug the injured foot out. "You've got a lovely wound, Alfie," he said. "It's a hospital bed for you. No more fighting." Telling the others to remain where they were and despite the bombardment, he helped his friend to the surgeon. Returning, he resumed his position and slept fitfully as cannon balls continued to fall through the night.

In New York, Clinton failed to act. Lord Germain, Britain's American Secretary, repeatedly sent orders for him to aid Cornwallis. He remained immobile.

The digging zigzagged forward and a second parallel, closer to Yorktown, was begun. "Redoubts 9 and 10 are blocking the parallel's completion," Rochambeau said. "They must be taken. Our French will attack Number 9 and the Americans Number 10. Each group will have four hundred men."

On October 14th, the troops gathered with fixed bayonets, readied for close quarters fighting. At the other end of the line, French units launched a diversion. Then, as rockets lit the night sky, forts 9 and 10 were assaulted. Both defenders and attackers fought with bayonets, axes, knives and fists, but it was short-lived. "The redoubts have fallen," came the report.

The American and French hospitals rapidly filled with walking wounded. "Oliver, we are not needed in the wagons." said Wolfe. "It is not far to the forts. The aides can fetch the seriously wounded. We are required at the hospital."

"I agree," Farnsworth replied.

The French had attacked against a far greater number of defenders than the Americans, and sustained greater casualties. Their doctors were overwhelmed and sent some wounded to Oliver and Jonathan. Working through the night, they staunched bleeding from bayonet and sword wounds and stabilized broken arms and legs. Several men had head wounds and were unconscious, one a major fracture.

"I do not think he will recover," Wolfe said.

"I recovered," Farnsworth replied. "We must treat them as though all will recover."

"Certainly," Jonathan answered, and they continued their efforts.

With the second parallel completed, the siege cannon were close to Yorktown and firing at point blank range. Cornwallis launched an attack against the encircling lines. Sergeant Cameron and his men were among those who fought and died, but the attack failed and the bombardment continued.

On the 17th of October, Clinton stood on a ship-of-the-line in New York's harbor. Under pressure to rescue Cornwallis and ready to sail, he said to an aide, "The promised twenty-five warships finally arrived from England. We will destroy de Grasse and provide Cornwallis supplies and 7,000 men."

On the same day, Yorktown awoke to another huge bombardment. As the ground shook about him, the British Commander sat in his underground headquarters. "We are desperate," he said. "Our casualties continue to mount. I see no alternative but surrender."

A white flag was raised above the British lines. A drummer boy and officer stepped forward carrying a proposal for a meeting of truce and surrender. Officers from each side hammered out an agreement. Cornwallis signed the terms of surrender on the 19th. The Tories with him would be permitted to leave on a ship bound for New York. Forsaken by their British protectors, the Negroes would have to fend on their own and hide in the woods.

That afternoon, stunned and almost in disbelief, the English and Hessians marched from Yorktown's ruins behind muffled drums and fifes draped with black ribbons. Their soldiers passed between the French and American armies.

Wolfe and Farnsworth watched from a tall-seated wagon. In the lead of the surrendering troops, mounted on horses, were the senior officers. One carried a sword.

"That must be Cornwallis," Jonathan said.

"Not so," Oliver replied. "I heard he claimed to be ill. That must be his second in command, General O'Hara."

"He is going to the French side, looking for Rochambeau, but they are pointing to Washington," said Wolfe.

"General Washington will not accept the sword from O'Hara," laughed Farnsworth. "He has taken as an insult Cornwallis' claim of illness and his sending a lesser officer. Washington is pointing to General Lincoln and he is accepting the sword."

"That," said Jonathan, "Borders on the ridiculous. It was Lincoln who surrendered our Southern Army at Charleston. He forgot he was supposed to preserve it. His men rot on prison ships, but he is here to receive the honor of accepting Cornwallis' sword."

"War can be quite peculiar," Farnsworth replied. "It is our good fortune to be here on a propitious day for our country, watching the surrender of eight thousand of the enemy. Still, we have casualties to attend and best return to our posts."

They reached the hospital as the surrendering troops were stacking arms. A British major was shown in. He approached Wolfe, who was the senior officer. The major saluted him and said, "I am Doctor

Fielding, sir. We have many wounded and ill men. Our supplies are gone and there is no adequate shelter. May we borrow from you?"

Jonathan remembered Doctor Rush telling him how well the English surgeons treated General Mercer. He answered, "Sir, I am Doctor Wolfe. We have adequate supplies and will be happy to share them with you. We are fairly full with our own and some French wounded. Nevertheless, bring your twenty most seriously injured and we will make accommodation for them. I will see about tents for your other casualties."

"Thank you, Doctor Wolfe," he said and extended his hand.

Jonathan took it, saying, "We must remember that our first duty is as physicians."

"Yes," answered Fielding, saluted and left.

As the sun was setting, the English and Hessian wounded arrived. Using oil lamps for light, Fielding and other doctors removed shrapnel and dressed wounds. An area of putrefaction was opened and the same scalpel used on the next patient.

Watching, Jonathan said, "May I provide some clean instruments, Doctor Fielding?"

The Englishman replied, "What for, sir. These are functioning quite well."

Jonathan's face flushed. "No disrespect intended, Major," he said. "I will be happy to discuss it with you later this evening. You can stay and have dinner with us."

Fielding and another surgeon stayed. Over coffee, Wolfe explained how he had come to boil instruments between different patients.

"That is like witchcraft," Fielding's colleague exclaimed.

"But it works," he replied. "In the morning, you can examine our patients. Compare what you see with your own results. Then tell me what you think."

The following day, the English doctors accompanied Oliver and Jonathan as they changed dressings and repacked wounds. Then the American doctors trailed the English.

"Yours definitely look better than ours," Fielding said.

"I smelled vinegar," his colleague said. "Perhaps it gives you the better findings?"

"First, I boiled my instruments and that improved results. Then, Doctor Farnsworth was injured, his thigh laid open to the bone. Purulence showed and he ran a fever. I remembered people cleaning kitchens with vinegar. I used it and here he stands."

"Indeed," Oliver said, and dropped his trousers to expose the long, wide scar.

"My word," Fielding exclaimed. "You said to the bone. That is an excellent result."

That afternoon, he again spoke to Wolfe." If you are cleaning and boiling so much, you must require more instruments. That is costly."

"We spend most of our army's funds on war material, Major. Our soldiers are not always properly fed or uniformed, and many go barefoot. Still, I have managed to scurry about and obtain funds needed to buy equipment. I have even received money from the families of grateful soldiers. The additional cost is worth it, saving both lives and money. We bury fewer men, shorten hospital stays, and return them to the army or home."

"Yes, I understand," said the Englishman, "But why does it succeed?"

"The why does not really matter," answered Wolfe. "Results are the important thing. However, I have thought the same why. Did you ever look through a microscope?"

Fielding shook his head.

"Using one, a friend showed me tiny creatures swimming about and magnified almost four hundred times. Those tiny things were from my mouth and are not causing me harm. But little beasts we cannot yet see may cause harm. We know not what causes the pox or why variolation can prevent it. The future must discover the why."

Fielding looked thoughtful and said, "Doctor Wolfe, I have enjoyed being educated by you. You have made me a convert. Eventually, I will return to England. They may think me crazed but, henceforth, I will do as I have learned. If I am as successful as you, I will proselytize to the other heathens." He laughed and shook Jonathan's hand.

During the following weeks, the doctors continued to tend the wounded. A ship arrived and carried away the Tories. The Continental's free Negroes remained restricted to camp, while a great effort was made to search the woods for runaway slaves. General Washington recovered two of them from Mount Vernon. Many others were found and returned to their owners. Almost all those uncaught perished from starvation and disease, few escaped.

XXXXI

Three days after the surrender at Yorktown, Congress learned of the great victory. Word spread through the city. Church bells rang and jubilant crowds emerged. Grace was nursing George and, hearing the bells, was unsure as to their meaning.

"Finish suckling quickly, sweetheart," she said. "We must learn what is happening."

After he was satisfied, she wrapped him in a blanket and placed a shawl over her shoulders. Leaving the house, she walked down the road and came near several neighbors who were excitedly speaking.

"Grace," one of them called, "Have you heard the news? We have won at Yorktown! Cornwallis has surrendered his army. The British can no longer hope to win!"

"Thank the Lord!" Grace responded. She looked at the baby and said, "Your father will be home soon, George." The infant smiled and burped. She laughed, saying, "I see you are also happy at the news." She remained with her neighbors, as they cried with joy and hugged one another. Several had a husband or son with the army at Yorktown, anxiously awaiting news of whether they had survived unharmed or were injured or dead.

Grace felt certain that Jonathan and Oliver were both unscathed. She had prayed for the battle to end victoriously and it had.

At Yorktown, Washington pondered how George III would respond to the surrender of so large an army. "They still hold coastal cities like Savannah, Charleston, and New York," he said. "We must maintain our army until peace is signed. However, furloughs are due."

In mid-November, Wolfe and Farnsworth returned to Philadelphia. "We must all get together at the farm," Oliver said, as they shook hands and parted. Jonathan nodded his agreement and continued on his way. A chill was in the air and it was late afternoon when he arrived home. Grace ran to him as he entered. "Husband," she cried, as Wolfe opened his arms to receive her, "You have been greatly missed."

They kissed, as tears rolled down Grace's cheeks. Holding her tightly, he whispered, "My love, I believe the war is over. I am home safely, here with you and George."

Holding one another, they kissed repeatedly. "I should prepare dinner," she said. "George is asleep but you can spend time with him."

He went to the cradle, picked up the child and held him to his chest. "Your father is home, George," Jonathan said, kissing him. Then, he continued to hold and rock the baby until dinner was ready.

They sat, ate, and spoke of the battle and the future. Occasionally, Grace leaned across the table, cut his meat and potato and fed it to him. He laughed, and said, "Wife, you are again stuffing me."

"I must express my love," she laughed.

When dinner was over, Grace nursed the infant, then burped and cuddled him. Wolfe took the child, bounced him on a knee, and held George tightly. He and Grace spoke for a time and then went to their bedroom. Once in bed, they hugged and kissed, feeling the warmth of each other. Jonathan stroked her hair and back. Later, he fondled her breasts and began to lick and suck a nipple. Warm milk entered his mouth.

She pulled away and laughed. "Husband," she said, "The milk is for the baby."

"But it tastes so good," he replied. "However, I have had my fill and will desist from piggishness." He slowly massaged her abdomen and later his hand moved lower. They made love until well past midnight.

As November ended, they visited the McKenzie home. Jonathan was warmly welcomed and urged to relate the events at Yorktown. The family listened closely as he described the progress of the siege. They all cheered when he spoke of the surrender. Tears of joy were shed and many hugs and kisses exchanged. Elias and Evelyn were almost overcome, embracing Wolfe and Goode. They had survived the war, one wounded and one unscathed.

To Grace, her uncle said, "No more spying. A married woman's place is at home."

She smiled and replied, " One never knows, Uncle."

The following weekend, the Wolfes were invited to Oliver and Agnes's farmhouse. Simon, Jacqueline, and Gwendolyn were also there. All admired baby Lorraine and wished her parents well. Hunt escorted Jacqueline with great care. Her swollen abdomen indicated she was close to birthing.

Randall and Sally welcomed each child, showed their rooms and toys, and played games with them. The children ate first and hungrily consumed their food. Then, they returned to their games and the adults sat down to eat.

Adelaide and Lauren had eaten with the children. Now, they served a splendid dinner to the adults. A moderate amount of wine served to relax the gathering. They spoke about the war drawing to a close and the future of the country. A question arose as to whether George Washington would be crowned king, or would he be a first president. All agreed he would refuse a kingship. Lastly, each revealed the hopes and dreams they had for themselves and their families.

As coffee and pie were consumed, Farnsworth said, "The war's end will bring peace and harmony. Hopefully, in the interim, there will be no further casualties. My fondest wish is that we remain close friends and see one another frequently."

"Indeed," the others chimed in.

The entire gathering began singing patriotic songs, feeling a spirit of friendship and unity. Sorrow and joy were expressed, as they spoke of the difficult times they and the nation had passed through. All were convinced that bountiful years lay ahead.

It was a glorious day, unusually warm for early December. The Hunts and Wolfes began their departure. Oliver and Agnes joined them outside. Suddenly, they heard a great screeching in the air and, looking up, saw a large bird. It screeched again as it flew overhead, flapping its wings and climbing.

Seeing it rise above the setting sun, Jonathan said, "That is a Golden Eagle. Let us hope, like the bird, our country soars ever higher."

"Amen," they all responded.

Postscript

In thinking about writing this novel, I recalled an article describing the use of variolation at Morristown, how it saved the army and the revolution. Research led to Mary Montagu who brought it to England. As a physician, I became involved with colonial medicine and surgery. Benjamin Rush, a practitioner of variolation came to mind. The idea developed that a Rush apprentice would be the main protagonist. He, other young doctors, their wives and sweethearts would carry the story. Further research occurred, and the novel took form over a period of two years. The historic events described are accurate. The conversations are, of course, assumed.

Benjamin Rush was an outstanding physician, teacher, and signer of the Declaration of Independence. Calling him Doctor Dracula is well founded. While the book *Dracula* was not written until the late 19th century, the character was well known in Europe and America by the seventeen hundreds. Rush persisted in using bloodletting into the eighteen hundreds, well after its abandonment by most physicians, and was posthumously referred to as Doctor Vampire.

Edward Jenner did not stumble across cowpox, and develop it for inoculation, until 1796. Thereafter, it began to replace variolation as the method of choice in preventing smallpox.

The golden eagle has provided the title for our book. A large bird with a wingspan that can exceed seven feet, it hunts small game, and requires open fields for survival. Unlike the bald eagle, its neck has golden feathers. In addition, feathers at the back of the head gleam bight gold in the sun. At the time of the revolution, its habitat extended into New England. Civilization has reduced the bird's northeastern territory to Canada. It is still prevalent in the western United States, Europe, and Asia.